·THE CHEAT·

·THE·

·CHEAT·

PAT JORDAN

VILLARD BOOKS
New York
1984

Library of Congress Cataloging in Publication Data
Jordan, Pat.
  The cheat.
  I. Title
PS3560.07615C4   1984   813'.54   84-40058
ISBN 0-394-52421-7

Book design by Charlotte Staub

Manufactured in the United States of America
9 8 7 6 5 4 3 2
First Edition

For Susan

*The great tragedy is
that everyone in the world
has a very good reason
for doing what he does.*

—JEAN RENOIR

·THE CHEAT·

· ONE ·

Bobby Giacquinto was thirty years old when he began to cheat on his wife, but he did not take a mistress until he turned forty. She was forty-two. He had known her, or rather known of her, for over twenty years. He had first heard about her from his brother, who was, then, twenty-two years ago, the basketball coach at a local college. The star of his brother's team was a feinting, little guard, who, despite a considerable talent, played a deferential game that had grown even more deferential once he began dating Sheila Doyle. "Christ, that girl's ruining his game," his brother said one night, and ever afterward, Bobby made a point of looking for her in the stands. But she did not stand out as he would expect, and almost the entire season passed before, finally, one night, she was pointed out to him. She was seated alone, behind the visiting team's basket, high up in the bleachers, conspicuous only by her distance from the game and her obvious disinterest in it. She was reading a book resting in her lap and only occasionally, when a cheer went up from the fans, would she look up, pick out her boyfriend on the court, and follow his play through dark, furrowed brows before returning a few moments later to her book.

By the time Bobby was a senior at that same college, she had already been married to that deferential guard for four years and had borne him two children. Bobby would not have thought of her again if he had not, on a whim, enrolled in an advanced theater course in his final semester. He did so only because of the excellent reputation of the professor, an austere little man who once dismissed a student from his course for yawning in class. The professor had a Vandyke beard and porcelain skin stretched tautly over his skull, and he wore European-cut sports jackets and suede, wheat-colored, Italian loafers. He was reputed to be a homosexual, if for no other reason than, at his age —forty-five—he still lived with his aged mother. He talked often about her in class, without emotion, as if she were merely a character in a play in which he was living daily. He lectured always standing up, perfectly erect behind his desk, but one day, after telling his students that he had awakened that morning to find his mother trying to vacuum up the flowers printed on the living room carpet, he spread his hands flat on his desk for support, and sat down.

Midway through his course, he informed his students that he needed volunteers to work as stagehands at night at the school playhouse, of which he was the artistic director. Without looking up from his class book, he called out five names. Bobby's was one of them. That night, Bobby went to the playhouse to tell his professor he could not work evenings because he already had a night job that he needed in order to pay his tuition. The playhouse was dark and deserted except for the professor, who stood on the bare stage looking down at Bobby in the aisle as he pleaded his case. Bobby spoke without drawing a breath, and when he stopped, the professor just stared at him before finally saying, "All right, Mr. Giacquinto. I will excuse you. But do not tell the other volunteers." Bobby thanked him, and then, exhausted, he walked back up the aisle. Just as he was about to leave the playhouse he saw, in the darkened lobby, a poster advertising the playhouse's next production, *Cat on a Hot Tin Roof*. He went closer to it. Beneath the title was a silhouette of a woman dressed only in a slip. She was kneeling, legs spread, on a four-poster bed in such a way that, even there, alone in the darkened lobby, Bobby felt himself getting aroused. Beneath the silhouette was listed the cast of characters and Bobby saw that "Maggie, the Cat" was being played by Mrs. Sheila Hunyadi.

Bobby did not think of her again for over ten years. By then, he was married, the father of a son, and beginning a

career as a magazine writer. His wife was a soft, pale girl
who bruised easily and feared penetration. After their son
was born, she feared pregnancy, too, and so she got into
the habit of allowing their small son, who was prone to
nightmares, to sleep between them in their bed in the
house Bobby had inherited after his mother's death. In his
dreams, the son kicked against his father's side until finally, amid soft curses, Bobby woke and got out of bed. He
walked down the narrow hallway, past his own bedroom
as a child—his son's unused bedroom now—until he came
to a tiny guest room at the end of the hall where he would
spend the rest of the night. When Bobby was a child his
father always slept in that same tiny guest room after one
of his daily arguments with Bobby's mother. Those arguments, which always began the same—with his mother
nagging at his father to abandon his gambling—were
played out early in the morning in their kitchen.

His parents would savage each other back and forth
across the white linoleum floor, while Bobby, a child shiv-
ering in his pajamas, sat on the floor, wedged into the
narrow space between the gas stove and the wall. Bobby
hugged his knees to his chest and rocked back and forth,
whimpering and pleading with them to stop. But they
could not hear him above the sound of their own voices.
Bobby's father, his fist cocked low to his side as if to throw
a punch, snarled at his wife, a tiny, dark, steely-haired
woman, as if he were a rabid animal. Bobby's father cursed
that bearded bastard who deserved to be crucified. He
cursed the grave of Bobby's grandmother, who had given
his wife life. He cursed his wife's whore-soul to rot in hell.
Spittle formed around his twisted lips, as if each curse
whetted his appetite for still another. Finally, as always,
he cursed her son—*his* son—for ever having been born.

Bobby's mother, hands on hips, unafraid, cursed the day
she met her husband. She cursed the day she married him.
She cursed the day she bore him a son. And finally, as
always, she cursed his gambling. This enraged Bobby's
father anew, and he pulled back his fist and lunged at her
as if to deliver a blow. She did not flinch. Bobby screamed

out, "No, Daddy! No!" But he never hit her. She knew he would never hit her. Both his feigned attack and her mock defiance were merely the theatrical gestures of a couple who, no matter how often they played this scene, had a tacit understanding of how it would end. There would be no climax. Only a denouement. A punch never thrown. More curses. Threats to leave. More pleas from Bobby. A slammed door. And silence. Bobby's mother would not even be crying. She turned on Bobby, wedged into the corner between the stove and wall. His hysterical sobs were now deafening in the silent kitchen. She looked at him as if aware of him for the first time. "Stop behaving like a baby," she would say. "Over nothing." And then, as she began to clear the breakfast dishes from the table, she would add, "Go upstairs and wash your face with cold water!"

At night after one of those arguments Bobby could not go to sleep until he heard his father return home. He read comic books late into the night in his bedroom and then listened to the radio—"The Green Hornet," "The Shadow," "The Bickersons"—until, finally, he heard the downstairs door open and close. Bobby clicked off his light and rolled over onto his side. His father climbed the stairs and went directly to the tiny guest room next to Bobby's room. Bobby heard him undress and get into bed; then after awhile, he heard his father tossing and turning in bed. His father got out of bed and came to Bobby's bedroom door.

"Are you asleep, Bobby?" Huddled under the covers strewn with comic books, Bobby feigned sleep. His father asked again. Bobby's heart began to pound, but he did not answer. He heard his father going down the long hallway to his mother's bedroom.

"What do you want!" she said in a voice that gave Bobby chills. His father whispered something he could not hear. "What?" she said. His father whispered again. "Why should I?" she said. And then, softening, "Besides, we'll wake the kid."

His father whispered again, and then there was a moment of silence. Finally, his barely audible voice broke the silence, "Please, Maria?"

"All right!" his mother said. "But this is the last!"

Bobby heard the dresser drawer open and the sound of aluminum foil being unwrapped. His father, amid soft curses, began to struggle with the contents of the foil.

"Hurry up!" his mother said. "I want to get some sleep!"

Then Bobby heard them fumbling on the bed and, suddenly, his mother's brief, inward, gasp of pain. His father began to grunt softly, in rhythm with the creak of the bed springs. His mother began to grunt, too, but more with discomfort than with pleasure, as she did when navigating their cellar stairs with a load of wash. His father's breathing began to come faster now, and, for a brief moment, his mother's breathing seemed to be in union with his. Then, she caught herself. "Well!" she said. "Are you gonna take all night!"

His father let out a high-pitched sigh of surrender, and the springs stopped squeaking. Bobby could hear only their labored breathing, and then his mother's voice. "Get off me!" She grunted with great emphasis as his father rolled off and sat on the edge of the bed. He sat there for a long moment, catching his breath, and then Bobby heard the snap of rubber, and the springs creaked one last time.

"And don't flush it down the toilet!" his mother said as his father went into the bathroom. A few moments later, his father came back down the hall. He paused a moment at his son's bedroom door, then he got back into his bed in the tiny guest room.

Years later, when Bobby was in his early thirties, and already he had stopped sleeping with his wife, he began to use that guest room, too. It was a dark, little room fit only for a child. Often, Bobby had trouble sleeping there, and when he did, and was on the verge of getting out of bed and walking down the hallway to his mother's bedroom— his wife's bedroom, now—he would stop himself by remembering how it had been with his parents, late at night, after an argument, when he was a child.

It was not long after that that Bobby began cheating on

his wife with an assortment of women, all of whom had in common only their acquiescence. He made love to a fifty-year-old widow who lived in a mansion with her black maid and a Doberman pinscher. When they coupled on her bed the dog licked the soles of his feet. He made love to a cashier at a 7-Eleven, whom, he discovered afterward, was only a junior in high school. He made love to a woman who hadn't had sex with her husband in six months, and to another who had had sex with twelve men at a party while her husband watched. He made love to his next door neighbor while downstairs in the backyard his wife chatted with the woman's husband as he barbecued hot dogs. He made love to a stranger in his wife's bed across the room from their son's crib. He made love to a woman who screamed so loudly at orgasm that it melted his passion, and to another who climaxed with a soft whimper he mistook for a sigh. He made love to a woman who scratched his back until it bled, and to another who reached out with a languid hand to turn the dial on the radio while he labored over her. Afterward, she said brightly, "Oh, I never come." He made love to a woman who came when he entered her and to another who came only after he had exhausted himself for an hour. He made love to a homely woman who smoked cigars and kept tubes of Nair on the dresser in her motel room. He made love to an exquisite blonde in her TR6, after they had shaken her husband who had followed them everywhere in his van. Afterward, she clutched Bobby's arm and pleaded, with birdlike eyes, for him to marry her. He made love to a girl on the beach and then took her to a bar where he picked up a woman whose husband had just gone to the men's room. Days later, on the beach with that same woman, he picked up a blonde when the woman went to the ladies' room. He made love to the wife of a football coach in a weight-lifting gym at midnight while, outside, a policeman on his rounds peered in through the window at what he thought was moving gym equipment. And, finally, one warm night in Ft. Lauderdale, he took a woman in a silk dress to a peep show located in a small concrete building without windows.

They staggered in, slightly drunk, with towels draped over their arms. The woman asked the cashier for three days' worth of quarters and then they went into the darkened back room. Peep show booths lined both sides of a narrow corridor that smelled of stale sex. Lone men stood, arms folded, alongside those booths that showed only homosexual movies. Whenever a man would enter one of those booths, the man standing sentinel beside it would peel in after him. Bobby and the woman picked an unattended booth and went inside. It was dark and cramped and suffocatingly hot. Bobby put a quarter into the change slot and images flickered onto the wall. Bobby watched the images while the woman, drenched with sweat, her silk dress matted to her body, got down on her knees and made love to him.

At first, when he worked at home in an attic room, Bobby made love to his women wherever he could. In the rest room of a 747 passing over the Grand Canyon. On the infield grass of a Little League baseball diamond where he once pitched a no-hitter. In a car in a crowded church parking lot while, around him, parishioners were getting into their cars after midnight mass. On a wrought-iron bed in a barren, old motel room that looked out over the muddy Yazoo River in Greenwood, Mississippi. He made love with an Ole Miss coed with three first names who claimed she had never been in a man's apartment before. She had also never been completely naked with a man before, and so she resolutely refused to remove her half-slip. It bunched up around her waist as she writhed on the rickety old bed. Afterward, she said, with all seriousness, "I'm saving my stark nakedness for my husband."

Years later, Bobby took an office on the third floor of an old colonial building in the center of town, where he could take his women without fear of his wife discovering. He made love to them on the floor beside his desk. Often, in daylight, their cries of orgasm would still the muffled voices in the adjoining office. Once he was laboring over a woman when he heard a knock on his door. Instinctively, he put his hand over the woman's mouth and did not release it until he heard footsteps going down the stairs. "Christ!" said the woman, gasping for breath as Bobby stood up, naked, and moved to the window. He peeked out from behind the curtain and saw his wife get into her car. He waited awhile, until his wife reached home, and then he telephoned her. He asked her what she was having for supper. She answered, told him some small thing about their son. Bobby exhaled deeply, as if unburdened of a great weight. They talked some more while the woman, still naked, stood behind Bobby and massaged the back of his neck.

At night Bobby coupled with his women to the eerie light of the street lamp outside his office window, the occasional sound of a passing car, and, even less frequently, a word of endearment from him. Afterward, he dressed quickly and hurried home to his wife, always expecting, upon his arrival, recriminations that never came. The next day it was always the same. Bobby could not write. His office smelled of strange perfume and sex. If it was winter, he would go to a bar near the beach and drink shots of Calvert and draft beer with the town's working men, who ignored him. In the summer, he would go out and sit on a blanket on the beach, looking, as always, for still another woman. A college student on vacation. A housewife with a small child. A working girl eating her lunch at the picnic table. It was there, late one summer afternoon, that he saw a woman sitting on a blanket near the water. Her back was to him. He could make out only her short, black hair and the straps of her orange bikini bathing suit. She was reading a book. He watched her read, waited for her to look up, bored, but she didn't. Her face was buried in that book for what seemed like hours to Bobby, when, finally, she stood up, took her blanket, and walked off toward the street. Bobby noticed that she had brought no clothes with her. He got up and followed. She walked across the sand, swiveling on the balls of her feet as if crushing out lighted cigarettes. She had long legs and the calves of a dancer, which were almost as large as her slim thighs. Her back was broad and lightly muscled, like a swimmer's, and it tapered to a high ass whose cheeks tightened with each step she took across the sand. When she reached the street and began walking toward town, Bobby followed her on the opposite side. He was parallel to her now, but she did not look either left or right. She just walked resolutely, in that distinctive way of hers, head up, back straight, staring ahead through dark, furrowed brows. When she reached the first intersection she turned left. Bobby stopped, his heart pounding, and followed her with his eyes. She turned into the second house from the corner, passed behind a tree, and then Bobby heard a screen door slap shut. Bobby stood there, until his heart stopped pounding, and wondered, why? He recalled that silhouette of her in a slip, and the sight of her sitting alone high up in the stands, and then his brother's words, "Christ, that girl's ruining his game!" Bobby marveled at the power she must have.

Later that night, Bobby stood in a phone booth by the side of the road and called a friend of his, who, he remembered, had known her in her theater days.

"And what if it was her?" said the friend.

"Come on, Jimmy!"

His friend sighed. "Yes, it probably was. Her father lives near the beach."

"What's her story?"

"Whatever do you mean, Robert?"

"Come on, you bastard. . . ."

"Tch . . . tch . . . tch . . . musn't get testy, now."

"Well . . . ?"

"Well, she's very happily married. *Still!* And she doesn't fool around."

"Everybody fools around."

"Well, Sheila doesn't! She's a lady. And if she did, she certainly wouldn't have anything to do with a pseudo-macho, superstud Guinea like you. Ciao, Robert."

He went to the beach every day for the rest of the summer, and, although she was always there, at the same spot, reading, he never talked to her. She just read her book, and, when he walked past her, which he did a number of times, she never looked up. When she left the beach, always at the same time, he followed her. He walked parallel to her on the opposite side of the street, but she never looked left or right, never noticed him smiling at her. She just stared straight ahead through those dark, furrowed brows as if her every waking moment was spent in contemplation of some irresoluble problem.

After that summer, Bobby did not see her again for a long time, but he could not forget her, the way she walked; her slim, lightly muscled body; that burdened look on her face. When he made love to women in his office, he found himself thinking of her. He did not know why.

Four years later, Bobby went to a cocktail party at the country home his friend Jimmy shared with a roommate, Peter. Jimmy was a theater critic for a small-town newspaper, who, when drunk, liked to remind his friends that he was a Tony voter, and Peter was a set designer on Broadway, so this night their house was filled mostly with theater people Bobby knew only vaguely. A bearded playwright in overalls who smelled. A balding young actor in a Yankee baseball cap. A young actress with blonde hair and small features that would not age well. A lanky choreographer who glided, sideways, from room to room as if exiting a stage. A man in tennis whites, who owned an opera house in the country, and his wife, who wore a neck brace and a twisted grin. A director who spoke with a nasal whine and was wearing one red and one green high-top sneaker. A public relations woman who weighed three hundred pounds and was nibbling hors d'oeuvres while cutting out Simplicity Patterns in an easy chair. Bobby's former drama professor from college was there, too. He was standing by the fireplace with a white-haired man who stuttered and a woman whose back was to Bobby. The professor's mother had long since died and he had moved into a house by the beach with the white-haired man. The professor was still neat and trim after seventeen years. He had not aged much, except for his Vandyke beard, which was white, and his skin, which was now soft and loose and pink, like a baby's. Bobby could not make out the woman, except to note that she resembled most of the women who came to Jimmy's parties. She was older, in her forties, too thin, and she gestured with her cigarette when she spoke. She was wearing a frilly white dress that looked vaguely southern and hung on her body in layers, like the petals of a wilted flower. Bobby dismissed her. He had brought a woman of his own, a nineteen-year-old blonde with big eyes and pouty lips. He had picked her up that same night in the parking lot in front of Caldor's where she was leaving work, still wearing her nylon uniform. He asked her if she wanted to go to a party. She said no, and hurried to her car. He followed. She got in her car and locked the door. He tapped on the window. She lowered it just a crack.

"Come on, babe!" he said. "It's all right."

"No!"

"Why not?"

"I know what you want."

He smiled. "And what's that, babe?"

She stared straight ahead, her hands on the steering wheel. Finally, she said, "Verbal abuse."

"Huh?"

"I said, 'verbal abuse.' "

Bobby laughed. "That I can get at home."

"You know what I mean. . . . You just want cardinal knowledge of me."

Bobby stared at her, and then he smiled. She looked up at him as if he was a child. "Do I have to spell it out for you?" she said. "All right. . . . S-E-X!" Bobby, still smiling, shook his head as if in disbelief.

"Don't worry, babe. I'm not gonna hurt you. Have a good night." He turned to go.

"Wait a minute," she said. "How do I know?"

Bobby shrugged. "You don't. You'll just have to take a chance."

She looked at him again and then reached across the front seat and opened the passenger side door. Bobby walked around the car and got in beside her.

When they left his office later that night, Bobby took her to Jimmy's party.

Jimmy met them at the door. He looked at the girl in her Caldor's uniform, stepped back dramatically to take all of her in with one glance, then turned to Bobby.

"Oh, Robert! You *are* perverse!" He was a big, soft, stoop-shouldered man with a crewneck sweater tossed, like a small cape, over his back. The arms of the sweater were tied just so at his throat.

Bobby introduced the girl to Jimmy, whom he referred to as a minor league Rex Reed.

"I love his reviews," said the girl.

"That's nice, love. And what is your last name?"

She hesitated a moment and then said her name so softly that Jimmy made her repeat it. "Kowalski," she said more firmly. "Suzzane Kowalski. It's Polish."

"It is? Oh, Robert, she's priceless! Our little Polish princess. And what do you do, love?"

"I work."

"No, love. I mean, what do you do?"

"I work at Caldor's."

"No! No! I mean, What Do You Do?" Jimmy put his hands on his hips.

"It's no big deal. I'm just a check-out girl at Caldor's."

"NO! NO! NO! LOVE! WHAT DO YOU DO?"

Suzzane looked to Bobby, who was smiling, and then back to Jimmy, and then she looked down. When she raised her eyes again she looked at Jimmy and said, very softly, "What I do mostly is ball. I've probably balled half the town." She gestured with her head toward Bobby. "Presently, I'm ballin' him."

Jimmy blinked, once, as if focusing, and then said, "B-B-B-Bobby, she IS p-p-p-priceless! Come with me, p-p-p-princess. I have to show you to Peter." Suzzane looked back over her shoulder at Bobby as Jimmy led her by the elbow across the room to a slight, pale man with blue eyes and thinning blond hair. He was wearing khaki pants and penny loafers and, from a distance, looked boyish beyond his years. Jimmy introduced Suzzane to Peter, who bowed slightly as he shook the tips of her fingers. Bobby watched from the doorway. Jimmy was speaking rapidly so as not to stutter. Suzzane was looking at him with her big eyes and Peter was listening, as always, with his pained smile and a nervous nodding of his head. Jimmy said something that made them all look over at Bobby for a second, and then Bobby heard Suzzane speak up in her thin, little girl's voice that carried. "He says it's peach, but I say it's pink. I call it his Fag Shirt." Peter's smile dissolved, and then a few beats later his head stopped bobbing. He stared at Suzzane, and then at Jimmy, and then back to Suzzane with her big-eyed smile, and then Peter began to laugh, loudly, so loudly in fact that other guests who knew him turned to see what was making him roar so uncharacteristically.

Bobby moved to the bar and poured himself a drink. He drained it and poured another. He looked around at the people in the room. He smiled, as if at some private truth he saw validated every time he came to one of Jimmy's parties. He drained that drink and poured himself another. His smile faded as if that same truth that only seconds before had delighted him now wearied him. He moved away from the bar and drifted around the edges of the party. He was a big man in jeans, cowboy boots, and blue-tinted sunglasses. He had curly black hair and a full-face beard. He moved in that loose-limbed way of athletes perpetually limbering up for some as yet unspecified contest. He was built like an athlete, too, only heavier in the chest, beefier. If not for his face, which was drawn and lined beneath his beard and his glasses, he would have looked younger than thirty-eight. But not much. Bobby knew precisely how he looked. He was aware of himself, oppressively aware of himself, and that fact wearied him daily. He had always seen himself as others did, close-up, and from the outside. Over the years, however, he had begun to distance himself from what others saw, the distance growing with the years so that what he now saw was very small and dark and barely recognizable. Now, when he made love to a woman on the floor of his office, he seemed to recede from the act, farther and farther, until, finally, he saw himself as from across a vast distance—a speck writhing ludicrously in a black space. One night he laughed out loud. The woman beneath him looked up, startled. "What's the matter?" she said.

It was after midnight and the man in tennis whites and his wife were arguing. Suzzane was talking to the actor in the Yankee baseball cap. The actor leaned down and whispered something in her ear. Suzzane looked around the room, as if for Bobby, and when she did not see him she looked back at the actor and smiled. Bobby smiled, too, and then moved across the room to the sofa where the woman in the white dress was seated alongside the playwright who smelled. She did not notice Bobby. The playwright was telling her that after ten years of poverty he had finally struck it rich with a small play he had written in two weeks.

"I made two and a half million on the movie rights," he said. The woman nodded. "Dustin Hoffman's gonna direct." The woman nodded again, but her attention was partly diverted by the public relations woman who was trying to extricate her three-hundred-pound bulk from the easy chair. The fat woman pushed with both hands against the arms of the chair, rose a few inches, then fell back. The chair tottered.

"I spent almost a hundred and fifty grand on coke over the last six months," the playwright was saying. The woman in white nodded again, while, out of the corner of her eye, she watched the fat woman. The fat woman pushed again with both hands, rose a bit farther out of the chair this time, then fell back. The chair tottered again.

"I had to commit myself," said the playwright. "Another month and I woulda blown my brains out." The woman in white did not even bother to nod now. She was transfixed by the fat woman who was marshaling her energies for one last try. She was wearing an Afro wig and heavy gold jewelry and her face was made up to resemble that of a pharaoh's queen. Her low-cut dress exposed the top half of her enormous bosom. Throughout the night she had been nibbling steadily at Jimmy's hors d'oeuvres so that now the exposed half of her protruding bosom was littered with a small banquet of cracker crumbs, onion dip, and bits of deviled egg. She placed both hands firmly on the arms of her chair and pushed with a grunt. She rose slowly and was almost free when her hips were caught by the arms of the chair. She was motionless for a second, half-standing, half-sitting, wedged into the chair. The chair began to totter. The woman in white gasped. The fat woman started waving her arms in circles out from her sides as if she was trying to take flight. One of her waving hands knocked a wineglass out of the hand of the college professor who was standing with his back to her. He turned, startled, to see the fat woman wave her arms one last time before falling back into her chair, which tipped backward and hit the floor with a whoomph. All eyes turned toward the woman wedged into the upturned chair. Her stubby legs were flailing the air above her as if she was pedaling a bicycle. Her wig was lopsided on her head. She gripped it with both hands and gave it a twist. The professor and the man in tennis whites bent over and tried to right her but they couldn't budge her. The fat woman began to whimper like a small dog. The wife in the neck brace bent down stiffly to help. Her husband shooed her away. She said something to him. He cursed her. Jimmy came rushing out of the kitchen with a handful of paper towels. He knelt down on the rug and tried to sop up the spilled wine. "My Oriental! My Oriental!" he cried. "It's ruined!" He turned on Peter. "It's your fault! I told you never to serve red!"

The woman in white sat stiff-backed and motionless on the sofa as if she had turned to stone. She stared, unblinking, at the fat woman and the people bustling around her. Finally, Bobby realized, it was her. After all these years! She had straight black hair that framed her face, thick brows, clear blue eyes, and a slight overbite. She wore no makeup. She was pretty, but without distinction, like a young girl who had somehow aged beyond her years. Her face was not heavily lined but her skin had lost tone over the years, and she seemed smaller than Bobby remembered, more frail, diminished. She no longer had that earnest, furrowed look of someone forever trying to come to grips. In its place was the look of one who had finally lost control. She stared at the fat woman with the eyes of an animal caught in a hunter's sight. Bobby had seen that look often, on women he learned never to take back to his office. They clutched his arm at midnight and pleaded with him not to leave.

"It's all right, babe," he would say to them. "I'll call you in the morning." But it wasn't all right. They squeezed his arm with an inhuman strength.

"Please, Bobby! You don't understand!"

"Sure I do, babe," he'd say as he tried to disengage their fingers. Their eyes became wide and unblinking.

"Bobby! Don't leave me!" And then, in a voice even more shrill, "I love you!"

Sheila stared at the fat woman for a long moment and then she turned her head away and noticed Bobby for the first time. He had moved across the room, facing the sofa. He was leaning against a wall, his arms folded across his chest, and he was smiling at her. She stared at him, wincing, as if confused by his smile. Without taking his eyes off her, he made a little sideways gesture with his head toward the fat woman who, by now, had been helped to her feet. His smile broadened. She glanced again at the fat woman and then back to Bobby. She closed her eyes, as if suddenly very tired, and then she opened them toward Bobby. She gave him a single, barely perceptible nod of recognition. Then she got up and left the room. A few seconds later, Bobby heard a car start up, and then the crunch of tires over the gravel driveway, then the squeal of rubber on the road, and then nothing. Bobby wondered what had happened to her after all these years?

The next morning he called Jimmy.

"Oh, Bobby! Not today. I have this head."

Bobby insisted, and finally Jimmy told him everything

he knew. She was forty now, but she was thirty-six when she'd left her husband with their four children, the house, and the dog. She took only her clothes and a ten-year-old Pinto with body rot. She lived with some theater friends in a house in the country for a few weeks, with her father during the summer—Bobby had seen her at the beach— and then she moved to New York City. She worked first as an actress in commercials and soaps, then as an assistant casting director. Of course, there were the obligatory affairs. Her affairs had only two things in common. They were never with actors, and they were always brief. She moved around a lot, from one sublet to another, and, as if by design, she never left a forwarding address. She had been living in the city for three years when her mother got sick. She returned to her parents' home by the beach in Connecticut and cared for her mother until she died, at sixty, of cancer. She lived with her father for awhile, commuting to her job in the city. She met a businessman returning on the train one night, dated him for a few months, and then, when he asked her to marry him, she broke it off. Shortly thereafter, she quit her job and dropped from sight. Jimmy heard that she had taken a job teaching English at an exclusive prep school in an old Connecticut factory town in the middle of the state. It was a depressed town. Most of the factories had closed. There were no jobs. There was nothing there but the school on a hill looking down over old women in babushkas and young men in soiled Levis drinking quarts of Colt 45 in the shadow of the deserted railroad station. She seemed to like it at first, and then Jimmy began to get telephone calls from her at odd hours of the evening. She talked about nothing much, the theater, a new play, old friends; never herself, her job, her life. Always when her voice began to crack she would break off in midsentence and hang up. Jimmy did not see her again until the following summer, this summer, when she returned to her father's house to spend her vacation near the beach. She went alone each morning with her books, and talked to no one.

"I was surprised she showed up last night," said Jimmy.

"She never goes out." He made a hissing noise into the phone. "And then she doesn't even say good-night, or anything! I don't even know why she left!"

"Something she saw, maybe."

"Oh, Robert! Why are you always so fucking superior? It's a bore."

"I'm sorry, James. I lack your charm."

"Well! I'm glad you finally admit it. I've been telling you for years, Robert. You can't get by forever on that macho shit. Especially not with Sheila Doyle. That doesn't play with her."

"I'll remember that."

"You do that. Now, tell me, just what are your intentions toward that poor thing." He paused a moment, then added, "Another scalp?"

Bobby laughed. "No, I'm afraid not. One time, maybe, but not now."

"Why not?"

"She's on the brink, Jimmy. A burned-out case. She sure as hell doesn't need me."

"My goodness, Robert! Going against type at this late stage. Wonders, wonders. Well, if you change your mind, she's home for the summer. You can always ring her up at her father's."

"No chance."

After Bobby hung up, he tried to put her out of his mind once and for all. But Jimmy wouldn't let him. Now, whenever they talked, Jimmy always seemed to find an excuse to mention her name. Bobby never responded. Jimmy persisted. Finally, one hot August morning when Bobby was not working well in his office, he called Jimmy and asked him if he wanted to go to the beach.

"I'm tired of talking to myself," Bobby said. "Even you would be an improvement."

"I can't, Robert. I have this review." And then, after a pause. "Why don't you call Sheila? She goes every morning anyway." When Bobby did not say anything, Jimmy added, "What harm, Robert? You don't have to play hearts-and-flowers. Just talk. You *can* talk for goodness sake, can't you?"

"I don't know."

"Oh! You're impossible."

"All right. Give me her number."

She answered the phone at her father's house. Yes, she remembered him from the party. "You saw, too," she said. "I couldn't take it. I asked Jimmy about you the next day. He had nothing but nice things to say."

Bobby laughed.

"No, really. He did. He's always bringing up your name now. It's funny, sometimes I have this feeling that he's looking for an excuse to bring you up. Isn't that odd?"

"Yes, it is. . . . Listen, Sheila, I was wondering. It's too nice a day to work. Would you like to meet me at the beach this afternoon?"

"Of course. Where?"

"Do you know where the jetty is? Down by the private end. It's that line of rocks stretching out from shore for about a quarter mile. I'll be on the last rock from shore. Just me and the gulls."

"I'll be there."

They lay on their backs, side by side, not touching, on the last wide, flat rock of the jetty. Waves lapped around them. The hot sun was directly overhead. She raised a languid hand to shield her eyes from the sun.

"I'm sorry about the party," she said. "The way I ran off like that. It just got to me. Those people. Jimmy. That woman. A few years ago I would have laughed. It must be my age. I don't seem to have the energy or the patience to put up with some things. And then I think, why should I? It's such a waste. I've already wasted too much of my life." As she spoke she stared at the back of the hand that shaded her eyes from the sun. Bobby lay motionless beside her, his eyes closed.

"I learned you don't have to do things you don't want

to," she said. "I learned I didn't have to stay with my husband if I didn't want to, and when I left, I didn't have to take my children with me, either."

"You've reached a place I haven't," Bobby said.

"It's easy, really, when things become intolerable. You just can't care what people think, that's all. You do things for yourself finally." She turned toward him onto her side. "Do you know what I mean? It's like knowing that if you go to bed with a man you don't have to stay the night if you don't want to. You're not obligated. You can get up at three in the morning, and go back to your apartment." She rolled onto her back again, and stared up at her hand. "It's refreshing."

"Why is that?" said Bobby, his eyes still closed.

"What do you mean?"

"I mean, I *have* to go home. I have a wife and son. It would be a luxury for me to spend the night with a woman I liked."

She turned her face toward him, her hand still shading her eyes. "Then why don't you?"

"Guilt," he said. "I can't do it."

"What makes you so guilty?"

He turned his face toward her and stared at her. Then he turned back to face the sun. He closed his eyes. "Maybe I don't have the luxury of an intolerable situation," he said. "My wife is a sweet girl. She would never knowingly do anything to hurt me. Still, I want to cheat on her. It must be me, then. The way I am."

"What way is that?"

He smiled into the sun. "Guilty," he said, and threw up both hands as if to surrender.

"Oh, yes," she said, turning back to face the sun. "It's the most destructive of human emotions, you know. Guilt. It paralyzes you. I know a lot about guilt. Three years after I left my husband and children, my mother died of cancer. I was very close to her. I think I loved her more than anyone in this world. She was the only person who knew me. When I told her I was leaving, she cried. 'But why now?' she said. 'After seventeen years!' She was never the same.

She had always been such a happy woman. While she was dying, I began to read about cancer." She looked over at him, again. "It's caused by stress, you know. Emotional stress. My leaving killed her. But still, I didn't feel guilty. I didn't know, you see." She turned back to face the sun. She closed her eyes and put her hand down by her side. "The thing is, I would do it all again. Knowing what I know now, I would still do it all exactly as I have done."

Bobby sat up, squinting into the sun. The water stretched out before him. He could see sailboats in the distance, and a lighthouse, and, farther off, across the sound, the hazy shoreline of Long Island. He looked over at Sheila. She lay still, her eyes closed, as if dozing. She was wearing an old-fashioned, two-piece bathing suit that was too big for her. Her loose breasts no longer filled out the hard cups of her bra, which stood up like twin hollow peaks. The bottoms of her suit reached almost to her navel and covered up most of her faint, grayish pink stretch marks. When she turned on her side toward him, her breasts spilled down, filling only half of her bra cups, and the stretched-out skin at her stomach bunched up in tiny, curtainlike folds. Yet, her body was still beautifully proportioned and devoid of fat. Her swimmer's back and her flat stomach and her long legs were still lightly muscled. It was only her skin that was loose, stretched out, as if, with age, her hard, perfectly shaped body had somehow shrunk inside it.

"Tell me about your writing," she said, her eyes still closed. "I'm ashamed to say I haven't read anything you've written."

Bobby laughed. "You and a few hundred million others," he said. "It's no big deal."

She opened her eyes and sat up. "Why do you do that?" she said. She stared at him with her wide, blue eyes. "Why do you mock yourself like that?"

He shrugged. "A habit, I guess."

"No, really. Why do you do that?"

"Maybe it's the way I see myself."

"No, it isn't."

"Oh, it isn't?"

"No. I think it's a pose."

He laughed again. "You do, huh?"

"Yes." She smiled at him. "It's a little self-pitying, too, don't you think?"

"If you say so."

"I do." She did not say anything for a moment and then she said, "Why do you go to Jimmy's parties?"

"They're fun."

"No, they're not. They're sick."

He laughed. "Then maybe that's why I go. I fit right in."

"No, you don't. You're not like those people and you know it. That's why you go. It must make you feel very good, looking at those people from such a distance."

He looked over at her without expression. "You know everything, don't you, babe?" He stared at her but she did not look away from him. He looked down and then away from her. "Maybe you're right," he said in a barely audible voice.

"I do know things," she said. "And I know you value your writing a lot, don't you?"

"Yeah."

"Come on." She reached over with her hand and gave him a gentle nudge in the shoulder. "Well?"

Bobby looked at her for a long moment before speaking. Finally, he said, "What would you like me to say? That my writing's the only clean thing I've ever done in my life? That I've fucked up everything else, but at least I get it right on paper? Sometimes, anyway? Maybe even only once in a great while? A little bit in one piece out of twenty? But at least I get something right?" He smiled at her again. "Is that what you want to hear, babe?"

"Yes," she said. She looked away from him and stared out to sea. "I envy you," she said. "At least you have something."

"You have your teaching."

"No. That's just a place to hide for now."

"What about your acting, then?"

"Oh, I loved the theater. It saved me. I fled back to the theater when my marriage broke up."

Bobby recalled her silhouette kneeling on a bed in the lobby of that playhouse almost twenty years ago. He looked at her now, as if confused. "But you went back to it in your twenties."

She smiled. "I know," she said. "I was married seventeen years, but I knew it was over on my honeymoon. He didn't like me very much. We had had to get married and he always resented me for that. I felt guilty—like you— and so I stayed with him and had three more children and if it wasn't for the theater I would have gone out of my mind."

"You can always go back to it, can't you?"

"No. I have no interest anymore. New York killed that."

"What do you mean?"

"In New York I made commercials. The director would tell me to bat my baby blues and hold the can of coffee a bit higher. Do you see this face?" She looked at him and pointed a finger at her face. She smiled brightly and batted her eyelashes. "This is the face that launched a thousand coffee cups. Hills Brothers, to be exact."

They both laughed at that. Then Bobby said, "You think my writing's any different? You think I sit in my office eight hours a day, five days a week, fifty-two weeks a year writing *War and Peace?*" He laughed once, loudly, and went on. "Babe, I am a Knight of the Free Lance. A magazine writer. Do you know what that means? Last week I did a piece on a dyke tennis player—married no less—who shills for lace panties and women's rights. And before that there was the baseball player whose idea of heaven is two hundred hits a year, two stews sitting on his face, and a best-selling autobiography he claims he hasn't read yet."

Bobby paused dramatically, as if thinking, then brightened. "Oh, yeah, and then there was the born-again senator, a great family man, who spends his lunch hours getting head from his best friend's seventeen-year-old daughter, whom he promised a summer job in D.C. And before that . . . let me see . . . ah, yes . . . the six-foot spade chick who majored in psych at Bryn Mawr and spent her summers haunting every fag joint in Manhattan until she was finally 'discovered.' She cut an album—'Queen of the Gay Disco,' they called it—that was very big among the fist and Vaseline set on the waterfront. You know, basic stuff, shaved head, loin cloth, whips, white slaves. She whips the slaves on stage, and dry humps them from behind, too. The audience loves it. Ha! A real Zulu warrioress from the south side of Chicago."

Bobby stopped and smiled at Sheila. She was staring at him with her mouth slightly open, her eyes wide and unblinking, as they were at Jimmy's party. Bobby went on. "Sound interesting, babe? Well, the real interesting part is that I can't write any of it. Not the good stuff, anyway. The senator and the teenybopper. The ballplayer and the stews. Nope. The magazines only want to know about the dyke's backhand and the Zulu voice. Which isn't bad, really. Better than it used to be. Now, she's got . . . oh . . . I'd say . . . total mastery of three or four basic notes. . . . So what do I do? I try to find a place in each piece where I can do some small thing that keeps me going. Maybe I do the way the Zulu breast-feeds her infant son backstage before she goes on. Or maybe the sad way the baseball player's eight-year-old son sits in the dugout wearing a perfect miniature of his father's uniform. I do it at my own expense. Maybe it takes me a week, when I should only be spending a week on the whole fucking piece. So what? At least I get it right. And I do get it right, babe. Of course, I know some editor is going to cut it anyway, because maybe it doesn't fit or maybe it doesn't show the ballplayer in an 'upbeat' light. Which it sure as fuck doesn't. But I do it anyway. For me! That's my big secret, you see." Bobby leaned close to her face, looked left and right as if for eavesdroppers, then smiled at her and whispered, "Once I get it right, babe, *on* paper, then they can't ever take it away from me." He threw back his head and laughed as if at some great joke.

Sheila stared at him with her wide eyes. He continued to laugh, a forced laugh it seemed to her. When he stopped, she said, "You *are* an angry man!"

"Me?" he said with raised eyebrows.

"Yes."

"Babe, I'm the most amiable guy I know. Why should I be angry? Just because I spend my nights sleeping on a sofa in the living room and my days writing shit just to pay the grocery bills? Because sometimes I'm sitting in my office and it's like a fucking cell and pretty soon I'm staring out the window at all that quiff walking by and I start to get an itch, you know?"

"What do you mean?" she said. "Quiff?"

He laughed again, but she only looked more confused. "Didn't Jimmy mention that part?" he said. She shook her head. "What *did* he tell you about me?"

"He said you had been friends since college. Why?"

"It was no picnic being a fag in college in the fifties. Especially at a Jesuit college. I never put him down then, and he never forgot it." She nodded. Bobby said, "What else did he tell you?"

Sheila didn't respond right away.

"Well?" Bobby said.

"He said you were a good man."

Bobby turned away from her and looked out to sea. The tide was going out. They were surrounded by a sandbar that stretched halfway to the lighthouse. A man in hip boots had walked to the edge of the sandbar and was fishing. "Yeah, well, you can't trust Jimmy," Bobby said. "He's got a thing for me."

"What do you mean?"

"He fantasizes a lot. He likes to think he's every lady he sees me with."

"Is that why he was so anxious for us to get together?"

Bobby shrugged. "Could be. Could be something else, too." Bobby laughed, a breath, and shook his head. "Maybe he thinks we deserve each other."

"In what way?"

Bobby smiled at her. "I don't know, babe. Do you?"

Sheila did not respond, and then, after a long silence, she said, "Doesn't it bother you? His infatuation."

"Nope. Never. He won't let it intrude. I respect that. It must take a lot out of him to keep it down. Even when we both know it's there. Don't let Jimmy fool you, babe. He's not as shallow as he acts. God forbid anyone should discover that though. Christ, he'd be crushed. He works so hard at being a bitch."

"You're a lot alike in that way, aren't you?"

Bobby looked over at her with a broad grin. "You *are* a smart cookie, huh, babe?" He turned back. His grin vanished. "Yeah, we're a lot alike. We amuse each other."

"He was right then."

"About what?"

"You *are* a good man." Bobby said nothing. "That bothers you, doesn't it?"

"No. Should it?"

"It shouldn't . . . and yet you make me feel I should apologize." Bobby said nothing. "Should I apologize?"

"No."

She smiled at him as if he were a child. "Yes, I should. I've offended you, haven't I? Your self-pity, I mean. You're so comfortable with it."

Bobby made a sound of disgust under his breath, but Sheila was not sure whether it was meant for her or himself. She said nothing. Finally, Bobby turned toward her. "What makes you think you can talk to me this way?" His voice was light and he was squinting, as if from the sun.

"I don't know," she said. "I just know I can."

They sat there for awhile, not speaking, and then Bobby stood up into the glare of the sun. Sheila shaded her eyes to see him. "I think I'll get wet before the tide goes too far out," he said. "Want to join me?"

"No, thank you. I'll stay here."

He stepped off the rocks and began walking away from her, toward the water. He moved in that pigeon-toed, loose-limbed way of his. He was wearing a bikini bathing suit. His broad back tapered to a *V* at his waist. Like

Sheila, he was deeply tanned and well muscled, although his muscles were much larger than hers. And yet, despite his bulk, he looked softer than Sheila, less lean. There were deposits of fat at the small of his back. Sheila, shading her eyes, watched him as he walked to the end of the sandbar. He said something to the man in hip boots and then stepped into the water. The water reached only to his ankles. He bent over at the waist and rubbed water onto his legs and arms and chest until they glistened in the sunlight. Then he stood up, his back to Sheila. The sun reflected off the water in a wide, white path that led directly to him. From the rocks he appeared to Sheila now only as a small, dark figure in the distance.

Although he wanted to, he did not call her again for the rest of the summer. She disturbed him. The things she saw in him. Then, in early September, he found himself dialing her number at school.

"I've been waiting," she said. "I knew you'd call."

"You did, huh? Well, I didn't."

They talked for awhile in a strangely formal manner, as if feeling each other out after a not quite forgotten dispute. She told him she was going to teach a writing course at the private school where she worked and she wondered if he had any books that would help her with the course. He said he did. She offered to pick them up at his office. He suggested, instead, that she meet him for a drink at the bar by the beach where he usually drank.

Bobby sat on a stool at the end of the bar near the back door. He ordered a beer from the bartender and put his books on the bar. Two youths with lank, oily hair were playing a desultory game of pool beside him. He watched them for a moment, then turned his attention to the soap opera on the television set over the bar. A gaunt-looking man, obviously gay, was about to be married to a pretty young woman. The man had thinning blond hair tortured into curls. When he kissed his bride Bobby smiled and sipped his beer.

The bar was dirty and it smelled of urine and stale beer that had been spilled and left to dry overnight. Three construction workers—two young and blond, one older and dark—were seated side by side, hunched over the bar, wolfing down sandwiches. Standing beside them was an old man in a cardigan sweater buttoned to his throat. He held his shot glass with his thumb and forefinger, his pinky extended; he threw back his head like a bird and tossed off his shot. Then, with trembling hand, he sipped delicately from his beer chaser. Seated at the end of the bar, near the front door, was a man perusing the racing form. He held his head up and rigid, like a stern headmaster, while he peered down over his bifocals at the form. Behind him, seated at a table by the window, were two fat men in colorful Qiana shirts. They played cards silently and smoked long cigars. Without taking his eyes from the form, the man at the bar said, "The sixth? Who do you like?" His voice was high-pitched, and his false teeth clattered. Neither of the men at the table looked up. The man at the bar circled a horse on the form, and then said, "The seventh? Who do you like?" Just then a bent and withered old couple shuffled into the bar. The man wore a crossing guard's uniform with a bright orange sash, and the woman wore a babushka, a tattered cloth coat, and rubber boots that reached only to her ankles. Each of the men at the bar nodded hello as the couple hobbled to a table along the wall and sat down. The bartender appeared before them with a tray of shots and beers. "Good afternoon, Jim, Mary," he said as he deposited the tray before them. They said hello, too, and began to sip their drinks. The construction workers paid their bill and got up to leave. Each in turn nodded respectfully at the old couple as they passed. Bobby smiled at the deference accorded this old, immigrant couple, as if they were deposed royalty holding silent court. The two young workers went out the door, but the older one stopped to say a few words to one of the fat men playing cards. He reached into the pocket of his painter's pants and withdrew some bills crumpled in his fist. The fat man did not look up from his cards. The construction worker reached out to shake his hand, in that peculiar, backhanded way of a restaurant diner slipping a gratuity to a maître d'. The card player stuffed his fist into his pants pocket.

Without asking, the bartender refilled Bobby's glass. He was a slim, boyish-looking man with delicate features. His son, a boy of eight, was seated on a high stool alongside the cash register. He was a perfect, fine-featured miniature of his father. The son was eating a jelly doughnut, holding it in both hands and eating from left to right as if it were a slice of watermelon. He ate in silence and stared, big-eyed, overhead at the huge, stuffed marlin on the wall. The marlin, painted turquoise on its back and silver metallic on its belly, glared down at the boy through its big, round, malevolent glass eye.

"Hello!" Bobby turned to see Sheila smiling at him. She sat down beside him and ordered a drink. She looked around the bar and then said to Bobby, "One of your usual haunts?"

"Yes. Not one of yours?"

"Not really," she said. "I didn't see you when I came in so I went straight to the ladies room to gather my forces. There's some interesting graffiti on the ladies room walls."

"Really?"

"Yes. Now I know where to get a good lay if I need one. It seems that a certain young man named Jeff is the best. Who is Jeff?"

"I wish I could help you out, but I don't know him."

"My life story," she said, exhaling with great exaggeration. "Missed opportunities." The bartender brought her drink and she took a sip, after first inspecting the glass. Then, twirling the ice cubes with her finger, she said to Bobby, "I'm sorry I was so hard on you last time."

"That's all right. I'm just not used to it."

She nodded, then brightened. "Oh, you've brought my books! Thank you!" She began flipping through them with great enthusiasm. Bobby watched her. She looked younger, more refreshed. She was wearing a crewneck sweater, jeans, and more makeup than Bobby remembered her wearing.

"These will be such a help," she said. "Thank you, again. And how's your writing going?"

Bobby smiled. "Great," he said. "Really great. I just got another story rejected." Her enthusiasm dissolved and she looked at him wearily. "No, really," he said. "I'm not kidding. I wrote a nice little piece on this guy. A nobody, really, but I got him just right. The magazine sent it back with a letter." He withdrew a letter from his pants pocket. "Want to hear it?" She nodded. Bobby began to read:

"Thank you for the piece on Mr. Balise. A number of us here have read it and we all agree that the problem is with the subject, even though we did assign it to you, and not the writing. The piece is extremely well written and your observations on Mr. Balise are very astute, possibly too astute. Mr. Balise comes across as an obsessed man, which I am sure he is, but that is not the kind of man our readership would identify with. The tone of our stories is generally upbeat. Unfortunately, I'm sure you could not have written him up any other way, considering your perceptions, and he certainly does leave a strong impression with the reader."

Bobby put the letter down. He was smiling. "There's more," he said, "but I think you get the picture."

"Yes, you're right. 'Too astute.'" She raised her glass and touched it to his. "Here's to your astuteness."

"Salute!" They drained their glasses in unison and then burst into laughter. The bartender looked over at them. Bobby pointed to their empty glasses and the bartender brought another round. Then Bobby said, "How's school?"

She rolled her eyes heavenward. "Bizarre," she said. "As bizarre as ever."

"What do you mean?"

"How can I explain it . . . ? Let me see . . . well, we had a faculty meeting the other night. The administration has faculty meetings at least three times a week for no other reason than to keep us off the streets, so to speak. It's sort

of like summer camp—six A.M. swims in a freezing lake so
you won't linger in bed playing with yourself, which, God
knows, some of those women could stand a little of. The
meeting was typical. It was chaired by the dean of faculty,
who calls the meeting to order with a cowbell, and the
dean of students. The dean of faculty is a shambling, fifty-
two-year-old preppie who thinks that being pitiful is the
apogee of charm. When he hired me he told me that he'd
love to have an affair with me, but, at his age, he was afraid
he might not have the energy. I said, 'Good! Save your
strength because I'm not interested.' The dean of students,
now, is a smashing-looking woman of forty, with a foreign
accent that everyone thinks is French, but I swear it's Leb-
anese. She's not very bright but manages to hide this fact
behind her silk blouses and slit skirts and a habit, when
cornered, of putting a long, elegant finger to her jaw and
holding that pose, not speaking, until her adversary backs
off. Anyway, she *is* or *is not*—no one is quite sure—married
to a six-foot, six-inch Tunisian-Spaniard who favors
double-breasted blazers and yachting caps and claims he
is a Maoist revolutionary, which is why he can't hold a job.
He also favors young girls, it seems, because he can't keep
his hands off the female students. Every year the Parents'
Association tries to oust her because of him, the Moor in
the attic, and every year they fail because, I think, she is
having an affair with the dean of faculty. Are you following
me so far?" Bobby, smiling, nodded. "Good!" Sheila said,
and continued. "Anyway, the faculty meeting began as always, with all the women faculty members, most of whom
are unmarried and fierce, taking seats on one side of the
room, and all the male faculty members, most of whom
are married and frightened, taking seats on the other side.
. . . Is that cause and effect, do you think? Married-
Frightened? Unmarried-Fierce? Or is it just Male-
Frightened? Female-Fierce? Either way, it's certainly true
at our school. The men are so defeated that the women
won't allow them to smoke during these meetings. And the
women, well, the minute they sit down, they whip out

their knitting needles and begin clicking away in unison like an army of Madame DeFarges watching the heads fall. One of the women even brings her dog to the meetings and no one dares complain. It's a bitch, naturally, a Doberman pinscher, and she sits in the aisle between the men and the women like an avenging angel. She's a particularly vicious beast and only recently attacked the poor father of a fourth-former because the man had the effrontery to pass her mistress's house with a cigar in his hand. The woman came screaming out of her house, demanding that the man remove his ankle from her baby's jaws. Later, in defense, she claimed that baby was justified in her attack because the man was, and I quote, 'A big, dark man with a big, black thing in his hand!' " Sheila raised her eyebrows and paused dramatically, before adding, "Hmmm! A big . . . black . . . thing! I wonder? Oh, well, nothing ever came of it and the bitch has not attacked anyone else since, although she has managed to terrorize all the male faculty members, none of whom are that virile to begin with. Except one. A big, strapping football coach, who is getting a little soft around the middle. He's in his mid-forties, a bachelor, and he has been at the school for twenty-five years. The latter two facts are symptoms, I believe. Still, he *is* a humorous man, even if his sole human response is ironic understatement. You know, raised eyebrows, insouciant shrug, and a remark that is not so much spoken as it is hissed out of the corner of his mouth. The only thing that redeems him is that he's not afraid of the women or the bitch, which counts for something. The bitch, by the way, has been trained to hate men, if you can believe that. Whenever one of the male faculty members, or the dean of faculty himself, rises to speak, the bitch springs to the attack, snapping and frothing until the offending man shuts up and sits down." She stopped for a second, as if to draw a breath. Then she said, matter-of-factly, "And so, it is thusly that we, the ladies of the school, run the revolution."

Bobby looked at her for a moment. She gave him a bright-eyed, faintly lunatic grin, her head slightly tilted.

Bobby could not help but laugh at her. She began to laugh, too. Then Bobby said, "What the hell are *you* doing there?"

"Hiding," she said. "I told you. I'm not ready for the real world yet. Of course, they, the administration, think I am there as a role model for the female students, and, possibly, to warm the bed of the dean of faculty. You see, I am the only single, semiattractive woman at the school who is not a drunk, a spinster, a lesbian, a seducer of sixth-form boys, or, like the students' mothers—all of whom seem to be thin, ash blondes—neurotic as a jaybird. Which reminds me, I had to deal with such a mother recently after her daughter, a fifth-former, suffered a nervous breakdown. That breakdown was precipitated by a letter from Mumsy, which began, 'Dearest Jonna, I know you'll understand and forgive me, since you love him, too, but Skip is such a handsome boy I just couldn't help myself.' "

Bobby smiled and shook his head. "I think I know that woman."

"Possibly," she said. "Although I tend to think there might be more than a few of them around. Can I have another drink, please?"

"Sure." Bobby ordered another round. When it arrived, he raised his glass and said, "To the asylum, and the inmates who run it!"

Sheila raised her glass and touched it to his. "And to your astuteness," she said. They both took long swallows, and Bobby noticed that she had old hands. Her fingers were long and thin, and the backs of her hands were skeletal and veiny. For a brief moment, he was disturbed. They *were* old hands, but that was not what disturbed him. It disturbed him that he noticed they were old hands.

They put down their glasses and began to talk some more. They talked and laughed and drank until it got dark outside and the bar was deserted, except for a new bartender, a college student, whom they did not notice. Bobby ordered sandwiches from the kitchen and, when they arrived, they wolfed them down in the dimly lighted bar just as the construction workers had done earlier in the day. Sheila wiped mayonnaise from the corner of her mouth and then absentmindedly sucked it off her finger. They both tried to speak at once, with their mouths full, and they began to laugh.

Bobby did not see her again for a few weeks, but one day, when he was writing well in his office and wanted to share it with someone, he called her at school. She answered the phone, breathless, as always. She was thrilled he had called. He read her what he had written and she commented, favorably, on it. Then she told him about school, some new lunacy over which they both laughed. Soon, he got into the habit of calling her at odd moments, always when he was writing well. She answered the phone always in the same way, as if, somehow, she had anticipated his call. Bobby began to look forward to these calls and, in a strange way, they inspired him in his writing. He did not want to call her unless he had something solid to read to her. Then, in December, his writing began to go bad. He spent long hours staring out the window of his third-floor office. He stopped calling her. She called him a few times, but he seemed distant. Embarrassed. Then, one day, she called him and realized he had a woman in his office. She stopped calling after that.

He was at the beach bar with a girl of twenty late one afternoon when Jimmy called him there. Jimmy asked him if he wanted to go out to dinner. Bobby said he was busy, and then Jimmy said, almost as an afterthought, "Sheila will be there."

"I'll be there," Bobby said, and hung up. He told the girl, who had driven him from his office, that the call had been from his wife. "She's on the way here to pick me up," he said.

"I'd better go then," said the girl, and she left.

Bobby took a taxi to the restaurant where Jimmy and Sheila were waiting for him. It was a noisy, brightly lighted restaurant-bar across the street from the railroad station. Always, at supper time, it was filled with commuters, men and women dressed identically in double-breasted trenchcoats, who worked in New York City, lived in Connecticut, and spent their hour-long commute drinking in the bar car. By the time Bobby arrived at the restaurant, those commuters had already reached that point, which they reached nightly, when they must decide whether to continue drinking or stop and call their spouses to pick them up. Most of the commuters were drinking noisily at the bar. Only a few, remnants of a defeated army, lingered impatiently by the pay telephone near the door. Each, in turn, made their call, and then moved to the window and silently stared out toward the street.

Bobby found Sheila and Jimmy at a table in the corner. Sheila, rising silently in her chair, smiled at Bobby and squeezed his arm. "I missed you," she said.

"Me, too," he said. Jimmy, already slightly drunk, looked first to one, then the other, as if annoyed that their relationship had taken a turn he had not been apprised of.

"Well, if it isn't Mr. Superstud," Jimmy said. Bobby ignored him and sat down beside Sheila. She was wearing a plaid skirt and knee socks.

"Why haven't you called?" she said.

"I don't know," Bobby said. "I wasn't writing well and . . ."

"Not fair," she said. "I looked forward to your calls."

"I'll bet!" said Jimmy, loudly. "Robert is *such* a scintillating conversationalist. Aren't you, Robert?" Bobby smiled, but said nothing.

They ordered dinner, and while Jimmy drank, Sheila and Bobby devoted the evening to one another. They picked up the thread of their relationship without effort, as if each, in solitude over the months, had been weaving the design of that relationship in their minds and discovered, upon meeting again, that they had both been weaving from an identical pattern. They seemed physically unable to speak without touching one another. On the hand, the arm, the shoulder. At one point Sheila laughed at something Bobby said and laid her head against his shoulder. Bobby hugged her close. Jimmy stared at them through narrowing eyes.

When it came time to leave, Jimmy insisted on paying the bill. "Shall we stop for a nightcap at Mrs. Watson's?" he said.

Bobby looked at him. "No!"

"Who's Mrs. Watson?" Sheila said.

"A friend of mine," Jimmy said. And then, after a deliberate pause, he added, "And of Robert's." When Bobby did not respond, Jimmy said, "Isn't that so, Robert?"

"Yes."

"Then it's settled," Jimmy said.

"No, it's not goddamned settled," Bobby said. Sheila looked at him. Jimmy, grinning, shook his head at Bobby as if he was being a naughty child.

"Temper, Robert! My goodness. It was only a suggestion. I'll take you back to your office then."

Jimmy got into the driver's side of his Volkswagen Beetle. Bobby sat in front, beside him, and Sheila sat in back. She leaned forward and draped an arm over Bobby's shoulder. They drove in silence for awhile, past colorfully lighted gas stations and car lots and hamburger stands and a few single-story motels. Jimmy's face glistened under the passing street lamps. His eyes were tiny points of light in the darkened car. When they passed a shopping center, Jimmy turned right onto a dark, two-lane road that was bordered on either side by low-lying marshland. Sheila nuzzled her face against the back of Bobby's neck, and he shivered slightly. Jimmy turned left onto a winding road and soon they were passing huge baronial mansions with circular driveways. Bobby took Sheila's hand and kissed her palm. They came into a clearing and, suddenly, off to the right was a sandy beach and the ocean. The water was calm; under the light of the moon it looked as black as oil. The beach was only a quarter of a mile long; then there were houses again, only smaller and much closer together than the mansions they had just passed. Still, they were big, white colonials out of the revolutionary past. They all seemed to have black shutters; one big, old oak tree in the front yard; and a small white plaque with black lettering nailed alongside the front door. They passed a stone Gothic church with a spire and a few more houses; then Jimmy stopped the car alongside a white Victorian house with a widow's peak around the roof and a lot of gingerbread trim. A front porch ran the entire length of the house. There was a light over the front doors, one of which was opened so that you could see through the glass door inside.

Jimmy turned toward Bobby. "Well, Robert, the light's on?"

"I told you, we're not going," Bobby said.

"Oh, p-p-p-please, Robert! Just one drink."

Sheila whispered in Bobby's ear. "Come on. Make him happy. We'll leave after one drink." Bobby shook his head no. Sheila said, "Bobby, what harm can it do?"

"You'd be surprised," Bobby said.

"Is there something I shouldn't know?" Sheila said.

Bobby looked at her for a moment before speaking. "No, there's nothing you shouldn't know, babe. You should see everything." He got out of the car, and Jimmy and Sheila followed. Jimmy rang the bell. They could see into the house, down a long, wide hallway with parquet floors. Halfway down the hall, to the right, was a winding staircase. Jimmy rang the bell again. There was the sound of a dog barking and the scratch of claws over the hardwood floors, and then a Doberman pinscher appeared, half galloping, half sliding sideways, as if on ice, toward them. The Doberman lunged high against the glass door. Sheila screamed and grabbed Bobby's arm.

"Jesus Christ! The fucking dog!" said Bobby. The dog bared its teeth and repeatedly lunged at the door.

A voice called out, "Adele! Adele! Stop that!" A tall, thin woman in slacks appeared at the door. She held a drink in one hand, and, with the other, she began to massage the Doberman behind its ears until it backed off and sat down on its haunches. The dog made a little sideways gesture with its head and began to whimper.

"What have we here?" said the woman in a bright voice.

"Gentlemen callers," said Jimmy.

The woman raised her eyebrows in a theatrical way, and added, "And a lady."

"I'm sorry, Pat, but it was his idea," said Bobby. The woman looked at him without expression, but then smiled. She was in her early fifties with faded red hair cut close and combed back over her ears. A pair of reading glasses hung from a gold chain around her neck.

"Well, do come in before Adele gets loose and terrorizes the neighborhood," said the woman.

As she opened the door for them, Jimmy said, "This is Sheila. Sheila, this is Patricia Watson."

The woman smiled at Sheila, as she had at Bobby. Sheila said, "I'm terribly sorry, if this isn't . . ."

"Oh, poof!" said the woman with a limp wave of her hand. "No trouble, my dear. I expect you've come for booze. To the kitchen then."

They followed the woman down the hallway. She walked with the posture of a deposed monarch leading her family into exile past a jeering crowd. The dog trotted beside her. The house smelled of age. There were cobwebs on the high ceilings and the paint high up on the walls was peeling. They passed a library filled with books that ran down the ceiling-to-floor bookcases like dying ivy. Their dust jackets had faded with the years.

There was a reading stand in the shadows at the end of the hall and split open on it was a dictionary. The walls around it were covered with photographs from both the recent and the distant past. Three little girls in summer dresses stood stiffly beside a man wearing dark-rimmed eyeglasses and an Ivy League suit. In another, much older photograph, a pale, thin-lipped teenaged girl dressed in evening clothes was being led through an adoring throng by a man wearing sequined robes and a hooded mask. The girl wore a strapless gown with a hoop skirt that was too large for her young, boyish body. A silver crown rested on her faded red hair.

"Well, what shall it be?" said the woman, cheerfully, as she led them into a brightly lighted, old-fashioned kitchen. The stove, the refrigerator, and the sink were made of white enamel that was chipped black in spots. "Bourbon for you, Jimmy. And vodka for you Bobby, of course." She went to the refrigerator to get ice. "And you, dear? What is your preference?" The woman looked over her shoulder and smiled at Sheila. Sheila did not smile back.

"I'll have vodka, too," Sheila said in a flat tone.

The woman yanked at a tray of ice cubes that was frozen to the freezer. "Why don't you get the booze, Robert? You know where it's kept."

Bobby looked at Sheila. She turned away. He went to the cabinet and took down a half gallon of bourbon and a half gallon of vodka. He put the bottles on the table along with some glasses.

They all sat around the kitchen table and began to drink. The table was cluttered with *New Yorker* magazines and bills from Saks and Bonwit's and postcards with scenes of the Rocky Mountains on them. An opened checkbook lay beside a fountain pen and an ashtray filled with cigarette butts. The woman lighted a cigarette. Her hand shook. She had the ruddy complexion of someone who enjoys winter sports. The woman, exhaling smoke, raised her glass and smiled. "Cheers!" she said. Everyone raised their glasses and sipped, except Jimmy, who drained his glass and poured himself another.

"You have a lovely home," said Sheila. "I love the floors and the high ceilings."

The woman looked at Sheila through a haze of smoke and smiled. "Impoverished gentility," she said. "It's a way of life, my dear." She reached down with a languid hand and began to stroke the dog lying at her feet. The woman had a long face with tiny blue eyes and a thin, almost lipless mouth. She wore no makeup, except for a line of light green eyeshadow above her stubby lashes.

"Well, Pat, what do you think of my little match?" Jimmy said in a loud voice. The woman looked at him. "I mean Bobby and Sheila," he added. "It was all my idea, you know. I thought it would be great fun to watch. Guinea Stud meets the Irish Princess." Jimmy laughed once. Sheila looked quickly to Bobby. He shook his head wearily.

The woman did not say anything at first. She took a drag on her cigarette, tilted her head back, and blew smoke toward the ceiling. She held this pose for a moment, looking down at Jimmy through half-lidded eyes, before finally saying, "I think it's a lovely match, Jimmy. Really, I do. Very perceptive on your part."

"Oh, it was, Pat! It was! But now, goddamn it, they're like two moles. They're so fucking secretive I can't have any fun."

"Poor baby," the woman said. "But what do you expect? It has to do with breeding."

Jimmy began to laugh so loudly that he choked on his drink. Bobby slapped him hard on the back, once, twice, three times, until Jimmy had composed himself. When he did he poured himself another drink. Sheila stood up and said, "Excuse me, where's the john?"

"Down the hall and to the right, dear."

Sheila left the kitchen. In the bathroom she sat, legs crossed, on the toilet seat and smoked a cigarette. When she was returning to the kitchen she heard a strange voice. It was the woman's voice, only it was somehow different, less brittle. Sheila stopped in the shadows by the kitchen doorway. Under the harsh kitchen light, she saw Jimmy slumped motionless in his chair, his jaw resting on his chest. His eyes were slits and his moist lower lip protruded like a petulant child's. Bobby was hunched forward, staring down at his drink. The woman was leaning forward too, her elbows propped on the table. She was looking directly at Bobby.

"But you could, Bobby," she was saying. "You know you could. You could stop by for a drink one night, and maybe a bite to eat. We could talk about it." The woman took a quick drag on her cigarette, but she did not tilt her head back to exhale. Instead, without taking her eyes off Bobby, she twisted her mouth to one side and exhaled smoke. When Bobby did not respond, the woman said, "But why couldn't you, Bobby? Please!"

Jimmy lurched suddenly to his feet. His knee banged against the table, spilling his drink. The dog leaped up and began to bark and bare its teeth. The woman looked at Jimmy as if she could kill him.

"I want to go home!" Jimmy said. "I feel ill."

"Oh, sit down, Jimmy!" the woman said. "You're fine."

"I'm not fine! I'm hateful! I'm a hateful person, Patricia. You see it. Everybody sees it." Jimmy staggered away from the table and the dog began to bark more furiously.

"Shut up, Adele, for Chrissakes!" said the woman. "Now, see what you've done, Jimmy! You've started her off!"

"Even the dog knows," Jimmy said. "Hateful. I hate myself. God, Bobby, why do I hate myself so?"

Bobby stood up. "We'd better go, Pat. When he gets like this there's no stopping him."

"No, Bobby! Don't go! You know he's fine. Why do you indulge him so? It's disgusting!"

Bobby smiled at her and said, "I have to, Pat. I have no choice." He took Jimmy, muttering, by the arm and led him out of the kitchen, past Sheila, down the hallway. Sheila did not move. She was staring at the woman, half-risen in her chair. The woman slumped down in her chair and stared across the deserted kitchen table.

"I'm sorry," said Sheila. The woman turned her head toward Sheila in slow motion. She stared at and through Sheila for a brief moment; then she closed her eyes and opened them as if drawing Sheila into focus. She smiled.

"Excuse me, dear?" she said.

"I'm sorry," Sheila said again.

The woman took a drag on her cigarette, tilted her head back, and blew smoke toward the ceiling. Looking down at Sheila through half-lidded eyes, she said, as if truly puzzled, "Sorry, my dear? Sorry about what?"

Sheila left the woman at the kitchen table and went out to the car. Jimmy was half sitting, half lying in the back-seat, mumbling to himself. Bobby was in the driver's seat. Sheila stood by the door and looked over the car's roof toward the house. The woman was silhouetted in the brightly lighted doorway. A haze of smoke hovered around the woman's face and then there was darkness, and Sheila heard the doors close.

They drove back to Jimmy's house in silence. When they

got there Bobby helped Jimmy into the house; Sheila got into her car and waited for him. Bobby was gone for a few minutes. When he returned, Sheila said, "Is he all right?"

"Yes, I put him to bed."

"Why does he get like that?"

Bobby shrugged. "Fag guilt? Who knows?"

She smiled briefly, then said, "Can I give you a lift?"

"Thanks. Just back to my office." They drove the short distance to his office without speaking. Sheila stopped the car in front of the building. She kept the motor running and the headlights on. They sat there in the darkness for a long moment, staring straight ahead, not speaking. Finally, Bobby said, "I'm sorry about Mrs. Watson." Sheila nodded but said nothing. Bobby got out of the car and stood at the front door, searching through his keys. He was illuminated by the spotlight on the front grass. The collar of his navy peacoat was pulled up, obscuring his face. Sheila watched him through the rearview mirror for a moment, and then she put the car in gear and drove off.

Bobby unlocked the door and went up the three flights of stairs to his office. It was a small room filled with dark shadows and slabs of light from the spotlight below. A large L-shaped desk faced the triple windows that looked out over the town. The desk was made of thick pine that had been distressed and stained a dark mahogany, and it dominated the small room. Bobby shut the door behind him but did not bother to turn on a light. He sat in the darkness at his desk and stared out the windows. The street was deserted. A piece of paper with a few lines typed on it was rolled in his electric typewriter, which faced the windows. Bobby tried to read it, but the room was too dark. He exhaled as if blowing a toy sailboat across a pond. He leaned forward in his chair and stared down at the floor. There was a pillow under his desk. He remembered a night, not long ago, when he was easing a naked young girl down to the floor. He held one arm firmly around her waist. Just as the back of her head would have touched the floor, Bobby, as always, reached deftly for the pillow and

laid it under her head. Unlike the others, the girl had snick-
ered.

The room was filled with gifts from women Bobby had
known. A college student who had had an abortion gave
him three plants in macramé holders that hung from each
window. A woman whose husband had introduced her to
swinging, against her wishes, gave him a fat, black fountain pen with a gold nib that lay beside his typewriter. A
woman with inflamed stretch marks on her stomach sent
him a metal sculpture of a typewriter, which Bobby kept
on one corner of his desk. On another corner he kept a
Tiffany lamp from a woman whose last boyfriend used to
tie her up and beat her on the buttocks with his belt.

Along the wall, to the left of Bobby's desk, was a high-
backed wicker chair and a tall cactus plant from a homely
woman who edited a magazine Bobby occasionally wrote
for. Next to the plant was an antique storage trunk filled
with copies of magazines in which Bobby's stories had
appeared. The trunk was a gift from a young woman who
had just broken off an engagement. She had told Bobby
that when her fiancé demanded his ring back, she ripped
it off her finger and made as if throwing it into a pond. The
fiancé, cursing, waded into the pond to search for it.
The girl put the ring in her mouth and did not speak all
the way home; instead, she held a handkerchief to her
mouth and sobbed. The next day she sold the ring for
$2,500.

Along the wall behind Bobby's desk was a bookcase filled
with books, most of which were first editions of Bobby's
favorite authors, which had been given to him by Mrs.
Watson. Leaning against the bookcase was a vacuum
cleaner from Bobby's wife. Next to the vacuum cleaner
was a pair of lavender, lizard-skin cowboy boots and,
hanging on the door, an assortment of clothes—designer
jeans, silk shirts, velour jerseys, a black velvet blazer covered with cellophane—all of which had been given to
Bobby by various women whose names he could no longer
match up with the clothes.

The walls were painted white and there was nothing on them except a single orange stripe that bisected the room horizontally. The stripe terminated in an arrow that pointed to a large, orange question mark near Bobby's desk. Bobby had used contact paper to make that stripe, the arrow, and the question mark. He had done it on a lark one day because of something his brother had said to him. His brother was twelve years older than he and a renowned basketball coach at a nearby Catholic university. Jesuits dined nightly at his home. Bobby had been a constant source of disappointment to his brother. The last time they had talked, almost four years ago, his brother had told Bobby his life was a mess. At the time, his brother had only recently been released from a private sanitarium where he had been confined in a straitjacket after suffering a nervous breakdown in a light airplane returning from Albany. His brother had gone to Albany on a recruiting trip and, during his free time, had seen the movie *The Exorcist* five times. He had been so moved by the film that, somewhere over Long Island Sound, he had begun to think he was God. When he was released from the sanitarium, he immediately telephoned Bobby to tell him what was wrong with his life. "You refuse to accept life's answer," he told Bobby. Bobby said he did not even know the fucking question, and hung up. Shortly thereafter, Bobby bought the orange contact paper and completed his room.

Bobby heard someone knocking on the front door. He looked out the window and saw a car in the shadows. He could not make out the car or the person knocking. He went downstairs and opened the door. Sheila stood there for a second, looking at him, and then she stepped inside and began walking upstairs. Bobby followed her. She went into his room and turned around to face him. Before he could speak, she put her arms around him and buried her face in the crook of his neck. She whispered in his ear, "Such a gentle man. You are such a gentle man."

They undressed and lay down on the floor. Bobby lay on his back, staring at the slabs of light fanning out across the ceiling. Sheila lay on her side, facing him, tracing his body

with her eyes. Then she moved over on top of him and
began to make love to him. She made love as if for the first
time, unpracticed, in slow motion, as in a dream, and yet
so naturally, without guile, that soon Bobby was lost in
the act.

She came as if stunned, her eyes wide and unblinking,
and then she smiled. She was on her back now, and Bobby
was kneeling over her. He looked down at her through
weary eyes and shook his head. Her smile dissolved.
"What's the matter?" she said. He did not answer. She rose
up a bit on her elbows. "What's the matter?" she said
again.

Bobby's voice was barely a breath. "I love you," he said.

"What? What did you say?"

He sighed, as if with profound despair, and then he said
again, clearly, "I love you."

· TWO ·

They spent the last few weeks of winter making love on the floor of his office. When he knew she was coming after school, he could not work. He paced back and forth, from his small office to the bathroom in the hall where he could see out into the parking lot. He paced and peered and mumbled to himself, for she was always late. When, finally, he saw her car, he would go and sit at his desk, as if working, with his back to the door. She bounded up the stairs, two at a time, as he prepared her admonishment. She swept, breathlessly, into his office amid a torrent of excuses (he glanced over his shoulder as if startled) while simultaneously bolting the door behind her and beginning to take off her clothes. She tossed off each excuse with an article of clothing until, finally, she was silent, except for her labored breathing, and the room was littered with her things. Sweater. Bra. Jeans. Boots. Panties hooked on a thorn of his cactus plant by the window. She stood over him, smiling, perfectly naked now, reaching out with both hands to pull him out of his chair. She eased him down to the floor with a soft, insistent, animallike growl that came from deep in her throat. As always, she came with a start, wide-eyed, as if stunned. He came in a whimper, like a child, and buried his face in the crook of her neck. They lay together for awhile, breathing heavily, and then, having forgotten his anger, he began to tell her about his day.

Afterward, they would go to a bar where they would talk and laugh and drink before going back to his office to make love in the darkness. They made love always as if for the first time, each one a bit surprised, but for different reasons. Sheila had never known she possessed such passion, and Bobby, after so many women, never realized he had so much left.

They fell asleep to the sounds of cars passing below and woke with a start at midnight. Bobby began dressing in a daze. Sheila tried to calm him, but Bobby could not hear her for his guilt. He saw, in his mind's eye, his wife and son, sleeping alone in their house, innocent and unaware of his deception. And then, he saw himself as a child, alone in bed, forcing himself to stay awake until he heard, late at night, the sound of his father, finally, entering the house.

They drove home in their separate cars, waking as they drove. Bobby followed Sheila onto the thruway. He drove parallel to her for a few miles, glancing at her until he was sure she was awake enough to get back to school safely. Then he honked his horn, they waved, and Bobby got off the thruway, doubled back, and headed home to his wife and son.

In April, Bobby got a magazine assignment, a profile of a once-talented baseball pitcher who had become an alcoholic. It took him to a depressed factory town in the northern part of the state that was not unlike the one in which Sheila taught school. He brought her with him. They parked their car on a hill in front of a sagging, wood-frame tenement sided with asbestos. A car in the driveway was covered with a clear plastic sheet dusted with soot from the smokestacks of the factories below. The tiny front yard was paved over with cement that had been painted green. The porch was festooned with a variety of plastic plants and colorful imitation flowers in plastic pots. A woman in horn-rimmed eyeglasses met them at the door and led them to a parlor where an old woman was seated in a rocking chair by a window. The room smelled of old things. Bobby and Sheila sat down on the edge of the sofa. Filigreed lace doilies were pinned to its back and arms. The doilies, once white and delicate like snowflakes, had turned yellow with age and were as rough to the touch as burlap. They had not been removed in years for fear of crumbling. The younger woman excused herself. The old woman said nothing. She hugged her cardigan sweater to her chest and did not look at them. The walls and rugs and furniture were a miasma of floral prints, faded with the years, and there were knickknacks everywhere. Plaster figurines. Ashtrays from Niagara Falls. Bits of colored glass. Bronzed baby shoes. A glass jewel case. There were a few strands of hair inside the jewel case. They rested, like a corpse, on a faded, aqua-colored velvet cushion.

The younger woman returned with coffee in imitation china cups and saucers as light as plastic. She handed one each to Bobby and Sheila and then sat in a straight-backed chair across from her mother. Bobby and Sheila, the old woman, and the daughter now formed a perfect triangle in the parlor. Bobby took out his tape recorder and placed it on the coffee table. He flicked it on.

"What do you want to know about Stashu?" said the younger woman, looking directly at Bobby. She was cross-eyed behind her rhinestone-studded, horn-rimmed eyeglasses.

"I can answer a lot of questions," said the old woman. She had a voice like a small bird. Everyone looked toward her, and she seemed to wither in her chair.

"Oh, Ma! It's all over," said the younger woman. "Everybody knows. Stashu's an alcoholic." The old woman hugged herself more tightly and began to rock in her chair. Her daughter turned to Bobby. "People ask me. His high school coach. His friends. I tell them I don't know him anymore. I haven't seen him in fifteen years."

"He called me up once," said the old woman, staring straight ahead. "He said, 'Ma, I'm all done.'"

The room went silent for a moment, except for the sounds of the old woman's rocking. Then Bobby spoke. "Can you tell me about Stanley's childhood?" he said, looking first to the old woman and then, when she did not respond, to her daughter. The younger woman squared her shoulders almost imperceptibly and cleared her throat before speaking. She was a pale, plump-faced little woman with a pointy nose and a small, prissy mouth. Her hands were folded in the lap of her shirtwaist dress, and her tiny feet, which barely reached the floor, were crossed at the ankles. She was wearing brown tie shoes with crepe soles.

"This was a tough town," she said, "a man's town. The men worked hard and drank hard. There was a bar on every corner, and after work the men drank their way home from bar to bar. The women expected it. They expected it of their husbands and of their sons. Boys in this town always knew their future. They were gonna work in a factory and drink their way home for forty years. They never thought of leaving. They looked forward to their lot, to becoming a man. Boys in this town learned how to work and drink long before they ever learned baseball. Stashu was one of the few exceptions. We used to say he was so lucky. Gifted. We thanked God every night. But where did it get him?"

"It was the old timers who started him drinking," said the mother. "After a game they bought him shots and beers. At the White Eagle Hall over on Pulaski Street. They all wanted to slap him on the back."

"Stashu had no father," said the daughter. Her mother began to rock more rapidly. "Our father left when I was born. Stashu was only about six."

"Oh, my, it was an exciting time," said the old woman. "So exciting."

"What do you mean?" said Bobby.

The old woman would not answer. Finally, her daughter said, "When Stashu was in high school, he made this town come alive. The factories and businesses closed for two hours in the afternoon whenever Stashu pitched. The whole town would be there. Workers with their thermoses of coffee and whiskey. Businessmen. Lawyers. Young mothers with their baby carriages. Boys and girls on their bicycles leaning against the homeplate screen. It was like the Fourth of July twice a week from April to June. Everybody knew me and Ma. They always made a place for us in the stands. The workers would roughhouse and push one another until a place had been made. I was only a girl then, about eleven, but I was never afraid of those men.

They treated me and Ma like royalty. They cheered Stashu's every pitch and booed the umpire whenever he didn't
call a strike. Lots of umpires wouldn't work Stashu's
games, and those that did never failed to look over their
shoulder when they called a ball. Stashu's pitching meant
a lot to those men. I remember once in April, the day after
we had had a freak snowstorm, the umpires were gonna
call off the game. The men threatened them, and then they
went out and got snowplows and shovels and cleared the
field so the game could be played. Those men loved Stashu.
They wanted him to escape the town even if they couldn't.
They didn't mean any harm, buying him drinks. They
didn't know no better. Now they think Stashu let them
down."

"Oh, yes, they loved my boy," said the old woman. "It
was so exciting! There were seventeen big league teams in
our house the day Stashu graduated from high school. I
made a wonderful spread. Fresh ham and kielbasas and
gyuumpki and . . ."

"Yes, Ma. We know."

"Oh. . . ."

The daughter looked at Bobby and said, "What can you
write about him, anyway? He had it, and he lost it. That's
all."

"They were wonderful fellows," said the old woman.
Everyone looked at her. "Their cars were lined up all the
way down the hill. Big, beautiful cars. One of them came
with a chauffeur in a uniform and a cap. He leaned up
against the car and waited all day. They were so nice to
me, those men. 'Mrs. Muraski this' and 'Mrs. Muraski that.'
I couldn't even concentrate. And, oh, how they were
dressed! Rubies and diamonds! They were big shots. Only
Pittsburgh didn't come."

"It was very exciting," said the daughter with a sigh.
"It's all gone."

"He calls every once in awhile. From California."

"Grapevine," said the daughter. "It's near Fresno."

"With a wife. I never saw her. She must be very nice. He
tells me. I tell him, 'I think of you when I go to bed, Stashu,

and I think of you when I wake up.' We talked all the time
when he was growing up."

"You could never get too deep with Stashu," said the
daughter. "He didn't question."

"About girls and everything. . . ."

"He was a follower. Like a puppy dog. He'd follow anyone."

"And do anything they said," said the mother, nodding
to herself. "Stashu would get drunk and then somebody
would egg him on and. . . ." The old woman stopped in
midsentence and, for the first time, turned to Bobby.
"You're not gonna say anything bad about Stashu, are
you?" She had stopped rocking. "He was a good boy. He
threw the ball too hard, that's all. So hard. He was a
pitcher, you know. He pitched the ball and nobody hit it. I
told him to throw it easy. When he went away, he would
call me up, and I would tell him to throw it easy, like
Rodney. 'Fool 'em, like Rodney,' I would say."

"Rodney James," said the daughter. "You know, the
pitcher for the Stars in Hollywood. He won the Cy Young
Award. Rodney and Stashu and Tony Vincent were room-
mates in the minor leagues. They were inseparable. Like
brothers. Tony, he liked the girls, you know. He was so
handsome, with his curly black hair. Him and Rodney
stayed with us for a few days the year Stashu and them
went to spring training with the big club. In Ft. Lauderdale."

"What year was that?" said Bobby.

"I think 'sixty-eight," said the daughter. "That was the
year Stashu almost made it. But something happened.
They kept Rodney and Tony and sent Stashu to the Mexican League. Stashu never understood why. He had a better
spring than both of them. Tony, he didn't last—he drank
as bad as Stashu—but Rodney became a star. His picture
is in all the magazines . . ."

"Why didn't Stashu make it that year?" said Bobby.

The daughter did not answer at first, and then she said,
"I ask myself. They say it was his drinking, but he didn't
drink that much then. No more than Rodney and Tony.

They all drank then, you know, like ballplayers do. After a game, looking for girls, although Rodney didn't really like girls all that much. Only Stashu and Tony still drink now. They're alcoholics. Rodney stopped drinking that spring. He had a vision, he said. He became a Christian. It was in all the papers. That spring Rodney was the rookie pitcher who gave up alcohol for Christ and made the big leagues. He speaks at Billy Graham crusades now, with actors and singers and politicians. He's like a God in Hollywood. Everyone loves him. He's the president of the CCABA, the Coalition of Christian Athletes for a Better America."

"His wife is so pretty," said the old woman. "Like an actress. I see them on the television all the time. With Merv and Mike and that cute boy, Regis. She's such a good wife. She lets her husband talk. She just stares at him with love. You can see it. He talks so nice, too. In his suits with the vest. Like a politician. He leans back and hooks his thumbs in his vest and just talks and talks and talks."

"Rodney never lost touch with Stashu until a few years ago," said the daughter. "He always tried to help him, beginning that spring in 'sixty-eight when Stashu got to drinking bad. Even when Stashu left baseball, and he was picking vegetables in Stockton and Fresno and Grapevine, Rodney would always manage to find him. It was almost like he felt guilty that he made the Stars that spring and Stashu didn't. But, of course, that wasn't Rodney's fault."

"Stashu was his cross to bear," said the old woman. "Rodney always said that. 'I love your boy like a brother,' he said. 'He'll always be my cross.'"

"A few years ago Stashu was living in a wino hotel in Grapevine. In a room without windows. He hadn't left it in weeks when Rodney found him. He couldn't eat. All he could hold down was a few sips of sweet brandy. He was dying, Rodney said. He had the shakes and cold sweats. Rodney bundled him up in a blanket and drove him straight to his house in Hollywood. Stashu stunk so bad, Rodney said, that he had to keep the sunroof and all the windows of his car open on that drive."

"Power windows," said the old woman. "And an electric sunroof. Can you imagine? My boy in Hollywood."

"When Rodney got him home, he washed him like a baby in the tub and put him in his own bed. His wife wasn't too crazy about Stashu staying with them, but she's a religious girl too, so she gave in. He got Stashu sober for the first time in ten years, and then he got him a job. Stashu was sober for ninety-nine days, and everything seemed to be all right, when Rodney decided to take him to Hollywood Stadium one day before a game. Stashu sat in the dugout and Rodney introduced him to all those famous big leaguers. 'This is the fastest pitcher who ever lived,' Rodney said to each one. It embarrassed him, Stashu said. 'I ain't nuthin' but a picker,' he told Rodney. 'And a drunk.' He got up and left. That was the last time Rodney ever saw him. He wrote us a letter saying that he had done all he could for Stashu and now his fate was in God's hands. We still got the letter."

"Oh, a beautiful letter," the old woman said, as the daughter left the room. "Handwritten." The daughter returned with a scrapbook and handed it to Bobby. "Page twenty-two," she said, as she sat down.

Sheila looked over Bobby's shoulder as he turned the pages. They were filled with yellowed newspaper clippings that chronicled Stanley Muraski's baseball career in bold headlines: "Falcons Beat Red Devils, Muraski Fans Twenty." "Muraski No-Hits Indians." "Muraski Signs with Stars." "Phenom Faster than Feller." "Rookie Slated for Bigs." "Muraski Sent Down for Seasoning." "Flame-Thrower Vows Comeback." "Muraski Returns to California League." "Muraski's Last Chance." "Booze Dims Career." "Stanley Muraski Released." "Ex-Fireballer Battles Bottle." "Legend Won't Die." The headlines stopped. They were followed by small columns of which only the last few paragraphs were devoted to Stanley Muraski and his once-promising career. Those paragraphs warranted only sub-heads: "From the Diamond to D.T.'s." "Migrant Worker Once Pitched." "Ex-Pitcher Arrested for Drunkenness." "Whatever Happened To. . . ." The last column, dated April 3, 1978, was written for the *Grapevine Gazette* by a man in a fedora hat with a press pass stuck conspicuously in its band. The man's photograph appeared at the top of a column entitled "Babe's Banter." The story below was sub-headed, "Ex-Pitcher Settles Here, Seeks Rehabilitation." It began . . . "The fastest pitcher who ever lived, Stanley Muraski, recently returned to the Valley where he had had some of his greatest pitching triumphs, in Fresno and Stockton and Visalia years ago, and where now he is battling alcohol addiction. . . ."

On the next page was Rodney James's letter. It was centered on the page and covered with a glassine sheet. It was written in a young boy's practiced hand.

Dear Olga and Mrs. Muraski,

    As you know, I have been trying with all my God-given powers to save Stanley, but to no avail. There seems to be nothing Rodney James can do to stop his drinking, except to pray for him daily—which I do, on my knees, each night. I pray that Stanley will be saved, as Rodney James has been, and that he will come to know the peace and glory of a life lived solely for the edification of Jesus Christ, Our Lord and Savior, Amen.

                      Your Faithful Servant in Christ,
                        Rodney Edward James
                      Pitcher
                      Christian
                      American
                      Cy Young Award, 1974

Bobby and Sheila finished reading the letter. They looked at one another as if in silent recognition. Bobby turned to the younger woman and nodded his head. "A fine letter," he said. Sheila cleared her throat.

"There's more," said the woman. "Turn the page."

Bobby turned the page. There was a photograph of three young men in baseball uniforms with the word *Stars* scripted across their chests. They were standing side by side, their arms thrown over one another's shoulders, smiling at the camera. The shortest player, on the left, was squinting at the camera through thick-lensed, wire-rimmed eyeglasses. He had small features, scrunched together in the center of his face. His smile was faint, slightly bewildered, as if he was squinting into the sun at something he could not make out. The tallest player, on the right, had dark skin and curly black hair and the slightly flattened features of a Mexican matinee idol. His head was cocked a bit to his left, his eyebrows were raised, and his mouth was pulled back and down into his jaw in an ironic smile of disavowal. It was the self-mocking smile of a man who takes himself so lightly that he is constantly amused by what he is. The player in the middle was staring directly into the camera. He had fine blond hair, parted to one side, and the smooth, perpetually boyish handsomeness that was once so prized in the fifties of Tab Hunter and Troy Donahue. His perfect features were undistinguished either by flaws or characteristics, so that upon leaving him one was left only with the single, clear, unified impression of good looks. He had an odd smile. Both humble and smug. It was the smile of a man who saw himself as blessed, his due, in a world of the unblessed.

"That picture was taken in spring training," said the daughter. "The year Stashu got sent down. Me and Ma were there."

"Oh, my, yes," said the old woman. "It was the best spring we ever had. We sat in the bleachers with all those rich womens on vacation. When they found out I was Stashu's mother, they were so nice to us. They asked a million questions. My head was swimming." The old woman was rocking again, slowly, rhythmically, the top of her gray hair moving in and out of the sunlight slanting through the window. She was smiling, a beatific smile, at something only she could see high up on the ceiling. Without looking away from her vision, she said, "How far is Grapevine from Hollywood?"

•   •   •

The younger woman stood at the front door as Bobby and Sheila drove off. Sheila glanced back at her, standing there amid all her brightly colored plastic flowers, and smiled. The woman looked at her without expression and went inside. Bobby turned the car onto the main road and they drove toward home in silence. Sheila stared out the side window. She saw an old woman in a babushka, a cloth coat, and ankle-length rubber boots, laboriously climbing the stairs toward the towering, brass, double doors of a Byzantine church with a needlelike spire. They crossed railroad tracks and then Sheila saw a group of young boys throwing stones at a burned-out, red-brick factory whose windows were boarded up with plywood that had been spray painted with graffiti.

"It seems like such a terrible intrusion," she said, still looking out the side window.

"It is," Bobby said.

She looked at him. "Do you have to do it?"

Bobby nodded. "It's what I do," he said. "But I hate this part of it. The meddling in people's lives. You get them to open up old wounds."

"Why do they?"

Bobby shook his head. "Everybody wants to tell their story, I guess. They want to get it right at least once in their lives. . . . And then I come along." He laughed, a breath. "Father confessor. They trust me. They think I'm gonna see everything through their eyes. Which I never do. I know that, but they don't. Besides, they figure they'll never see me again, and they won't. It's not like telling their neighbor some dirty little secret when they're drunk, and then having to face them over the hedges the next morning. And the morning after that, and after that. . . . Once they get started they can't stop, and afterward they feel so relieved, and a little embarrassed, so they conveniently forget what they told me. I leave and it never happened. They don't really expect it to come out in print. . . . But it does." Bobby laughed again, barely a breath. "It always does."

Sheila looked away. "It seems like such a deceit."

"It is, babe. It is a deceit."

Sheila did not speak again for a long while. She stared out the window through her dark, furrowed brows.

The things she saw often depressed her for hours, days even. She was the kind of person who, when confronted with one of life's unpleasantries, instinctively flashed back to a similar moment in her own past. Unlike most, however, she did not merely recall that moment, she relived it. She felt its pain anew, was lost in it for hours, grew distant, moody. One night, she and Bobby had gone to a movie. It was a strange yet simple and haunting film about prehistoric cavemen's quest for fire. During that quest, one of the cavemen saved the life of a woman who was from another, more advanced tribe. She was pale and slight, but full of life, and during the course of that film she taught her savior—a plodding yet heroic caveman—not only how to make fire, but also about laughter and affection and loving sex and the pain of loss. When she slipped away from her lover one night, he woke and cried out in pain. He lay back down in the grass where they had slept and began to sniff it for her scent. He curled up into a fetal position, pulled clumps of that grass to his body, and slept.

In the darkened theater, Sheila laid her head on Bobby's shoulder and hugged his arm. "Oh, he misses her so much," she whispered in his ear. "We forget sometimes how much we can mean to men, too."

The film drew to a close with a shot of the two lovers in darkness, illuminated only by the light of a full moon. They stared up at the white moon; then the camera panned to the woman's swollen belly, as big and white as the moon itself, and then to the man's hairy, pawlike hand as it reached out to touch the woman's belly. The film ended. On the way back to Bobby's office, Sheila was unusually quiet, withdrawn, while Bobby talked about the movie. Finally, she said, "Did you ever do that?"

"What?"

"Put your hand on your wife's stomach when she was pregnant?"

Bobby looked confused.

"Did you?" Sheila's voice was sharp, insistent.

"Sure, babe." He looked at her in confusion. "It scared me a little, at first. I was afraid to press too hard. She would tell me the baby was kicking but I pressed so lightly I didn't feel it. She made me press harder and harder, until finally I felt it."

That night, they made love on the floor of his office, and, for the first time, Sheila did not come. She was moody and distant for days. Bobby was wracked with guilt. What had he done? He could think of nothing, and yet. . . . He questioned her daily, but she said it was nothing. Not to worry, she said, it has nothing to do with you. Finally, she told him. Her husband never touched her during her four pregnancies. He refused to touch her stomach or have sex with her. He was repulsed by her, she said, as if her swollen stomach was the visible manifestation of some filthy thing he had done to her, which, now, the whole world could see.

"He hated the fact that I turned him on sexually," she said. "Not only was it dirty, it was my hold on him."

"Why didn't you tell me?" Bobby said. "I thought it was something I had done."

"I told you it wasn't you."

"I know, I know, but still, I thought it *had* to be me."

Sheila looked at him in that cold way she had reserved for certain men, over dinner, in New York City, when they had presumptuously laid a hand on her hand across the table. Invariably, they withdrew their hand as if scorched. "I didn't make you feel guilty, Bobby," she said in a clipped voice. "You did that all by yourself. You are a master at it." Bobby looked away from her. "Why does it *always* have to be you, babe?" she said.

He shook his head as if dazed. "I don't know," he said. "I just feel it."

.   .   .

In many ways, they were not alike. Often the things that depressed her amused him (Rodney James's letter), which was why, at times, he accused her of being self-indulgent and she accused him of being callous. She found repugnant the words he used to describe the acts they performed on the floor of his office—"a piece of ass," he called it, or "a blow job"—and yet, she performed those acts willingly, naturally, and with such obvious relish. At times, even, her ardor confused him, made him reticent, shy, despite his wealth of sexual experience.

Unlike Sheila, Bobby saw life's harsher realities as the natural condition of man, and so he was rarely depressed by them. He went to Jimmy's parties not only because the people there amused him but also because, in a strange way, he was in sympathy with them. Like himself, they were outside of conventional life. Freaks. Fools. Cheats. When he told Sheila about the time in Florida when he had gone to that peep show with the woman in the silk dress and about those furtive men waiting beside the booths, he smiled at her reaction.

"How sad," she said.

"Why sad, babe? Everybody got what they wanted."

Such things depressed her because, longer than most, she had been able to retain at least vestiges of her innocence. Which was why she could not countenance depravity in others. Depravity was palpable to her. She would feel it so intensely that her features would instantly be contorted with disgust. What depressed Bobby, what caused him to wince from a very physical pain he found unbearable, was innocence. Its inevitable loss. The remembrance of his young son, at ten, coming to him in the night as he slept, fitfully, on the living room floor while his wife slept upstairs in bed. His son covered him with an old patchwork quilt and then bent down to kiss him on the lips. "Good-night, Dad." Bobby woke and sat up. He hugged and kissed his son, and told the boy he loved him. His son looked at him with that sad, sweet smile reserved only for Bobby. "I love you, too, Dad."

After his son had gone upstairs to bed, Bobby put his

hand in his mouth and bit down hard so as to stifle his hysterical sobs. He cried most of the night and, upon waking in the morning, was not sure whether he had cried for his son's innocence or his own guilt at knowing that he was, daily, responsible for its loss.

A few months after that night with his son, Bobby was lying as if drugged on a chaise lounge in the backyard of his parents-in-law's house. It was the summer before he met Sheila on the rocks. It was midafternoon. The air was hot and muggy and heavy with the aroma of cooking meat. Not a leaf or a blade of grass moved. The sun was merciless overhead. It bleached the sky and the trees and the grass so that, lying there, drained of strength, Bobby seemed to see everything as through a haze. His father-in-law, shimmering in the heat, hovered over a smoking charcoal grill. His mother-in-law, carrying a tray heaped with food, appeared behind the screen door that led from the kitchen. She turned her back to the screen, pushed her rear end against it, struggled sideways through the opening, protecting the tray of food as if it were an offering to the gods, and then turned again and waddled quick-legged across the lawn as the screen door slapped shut. Bobby's entire body was jolted by the noise. His mother-in-law deposited the tray of food on the picnic table in the middle of the yard. Bobby's wife, Elizabeth, seated at the table, looked across at her mother and smiled. Her mother began to talk as she arranged the food on the table. Beth listened, smiling. She wore a yellow sundress and a floppy-brimmed straw hat to protect her skin from the sun. Her mother wore a shapeless shift that reached almost to her ankles. She was a short, thick-set, immigrant-looking woman who thought it her duty to fill every silence with the sound of her voice. She talked and talked, while Beth listened. Beth liked to listen. She smiled and listened and let her mind wander to places she made privy to no one. Especially to Bobby. "What are you thinking?" he would ask. "What?" she would say. "What are you thinking?" he would repeat. "Nothing," she would say.

Bobby heard a thud, and then another, and another. He

saw, framed between Beth and her mother, but farther off, his son. He was throwing a tennis ball against the side of the garage and catching it on the rebound with the big leather baseball glove Bobby had bought him. Bobby watched, smiling. His son fielded the ball with a boy's energy and fired it back against the garage. "Thud!"

Beth, still smiling, was listening to her mother. "Thud!" Beth winced. "Thud!" Her smile began to fade and her features clouded over at this intrusion, not upon her mother's words, but upon her own serenity. "Thud!" She turned her head in slow motion toward her son. "Thud!" She called out, "Bobby! Stop that! You're giving me a headache!" Her son fired. "Thud!" She screamed, *"Bobby! This instant!"* His head jerked toward his mother as the ball skipped, untouched, through his legs and rolled into the bushes. Her cheeks were pink, her eyes bulging, and her mouth a thin, tight line. The boy's head drooped, and he shuffled after the ball in the bushes. Beth turned back to her mother, who was still talking. Slowly, her smile reappeared. A faint, detached, almost beatific smile.

Bobby, lying on the chaise lounge, closed his eyes. The heat pressed against his face. He tried to sleep, dozed for a few moments, and then was jerked awake by the sound of the screen door slapping shut. He opened his eyes. His mother-in-law was waddling across the lawn with yet another tray heaped with food. Again, she rearranged the food on the picnic table as she talked to Beth. His father-in-law was still standing over the grill, poking at the hot dogs with a long-handled fork. He never spoke. A small, stoop-shouldered man wearing thick-lensed eyeglasses, he worshiped silence as devoutly as his wife abhorred it. Bobby squeezed his eyes shut so tightly his head trembled.

"Dad! Dad! You wanna have a catch?" Bobby opened his eyes and was blinded by the sun. He squinted until he could make out the dark shadow of his son's face above him. "Do you, Dad?"

Bobby reached up a hand, with great effort, and let it fall on his son's shoulder. He could feel the thin bones beneath the boy's T-shirt. "Not now, son," he said. "The heat's wiped me out." He smiled at the shadowed face. "Maybe later."

"Okay, Dad." The shadow moved away and then Bobby could make out his son more clearly as he walked across the grass toward the garage. He was a thin, delicate boy, prone to high fevers and bad dreams. Especially when Bobby and Beth argued. When he was a baby he slept in a crib across from their bed. Their arguments, late at night, always woke him. He stood in his crib, gripping the wooden bars with his fists, and watched them without crying. Afterward, when Bobby would go down the hall to sleep in the tiny guest room, he would hear his son begin to whimper. It was the soft, sad, insistent whimpering of a bruised animal. Bobby slapped his flattened hands over his ears but still he heard that whimpering until, finally, he heard Beth get out of bed to pick up their son and take him back to her bed.

The boy stood in the grass near the garage looking up into the sky. He fired the tennis ball straight over his head, high into the air. The ball hovered a moment, a black dot shadowed by the sun. The boy circled it, dizzily, and then it descended, and he had to make a last second dive for it far to his left. He tumbled over in the grass, holding the ball in his hand in the air.

Bobby called out across the lawn. "Great catch, son!" The boy smiled at his father and got up. He dusted himself off and then he fired the ball into the air again. Bobby watched him, a boy of ten playing in the grass. Then he heard his mother-in-law's voice.

"The pot roast at the Grand Union," she was saying to Beth. "It's always so tender you could cut it with a fork. A dollar eighty-nine a pound! Melts in your mouth." Beth was nodding to her mother's advice. Bobby looked at them, mother and daughter. An old woman talking about food. And then toilet paper. Where it could be bought with a coupon for two cents off a roll. Her husband spent silent hours scouring the newspapers, cutting out each of those coupons along the dotted line with his wife's big, black sewing shears. Beth's mother never answered the front doorbell. It could be a rapist, she said. Or a burglar. She didn't live life, she defended against it. Beth always called ahead to tell her they were coming, or else they would have to stand for hours at her front door ringing the bell.

Beth listened and nodded to her mother's advice. Beth. A beautiful girl. Woman. Even now, approaching thirty. Soft. Pale. Untouched. Suddenly, Bobby caught sight of a black dot suspended, for a split-second, high in the sky directly over the table, and then, out of the corner of his eye, he glimpsed his son staring up at the dot in disbelief. The ball landed with a clatter among the dishes on the table and then bounced off onto the grass. Beth froze for a moment, then leapt to her feet. She squeezed her fists at her sides until her body began to tremble. Her eyes were wide with rage. She began to scream at her son, jabbing both fists toward the ground. She raised her clenched hands before her eyes and began to shake them as if pounding on a door. The boy looked at his mother with a look of pain beyond his years, and then he looked toward his father, but he was already gone.

Bobby sat in his car for a moment, and then he turned on the ignition. Beth appeared around the side of the house. She walked slowly toward him, composed now. She came to the window on the driver's side and looked down at her husband.

"What's the matter?" she said.

He shook his head. "I'm going for a ride."

"Why do you have to ruin everything?" she said. "It was such a beautiful cookout."

Bobby and Sheila drove the rest of the way home from the Muraski house in silence. When they reached his office Bobby stopped his car alongside hers in the parking lot. She did not get out right away. Finally, she turned to him, "Do you have to go to California?"

"Yes, babe. This could be a great piece. I've already got a feel for it."

"I'll miss you," she said, got out of the car, and hurried

to her own car. She turned around. "I don't want to, Bobby, but I will." Bobby watched her drive off.

She was depressed for days, and there was nothing Bobby could do to dispel her mood. She assured him it was nothing he had done, although she admitted it had to do with him. "When I sort it out, I'll tell you," she said. "Be patient." He was patient, at first, and then he grew angry. She avoided his calls and refused to see him. She always had an excuse. "School work," she said. Finally, Bobby stopped trying to fathom her mood. For the first time since he had made love to her, he began to contemplate other women. It surprised him that he had not thought of another woman since he had known her. Before, he could not pass an attractive woman on the street without instinctively flashing forward to certain possibilities. Now, it was such a conscious effort. He had no stomach for it. He felt like a grown man trying to conjure up a childish taste for sweets that made him sick to his stomach. He grew even more furious with her, and in his fury he could not work. He sat over his typewriter for hours and cursed her in every conceivable way.

On the night before he was to leave for California to interview Stanley Muraski, Sheila called and asked him to meet her for a drink.

"Someplace where we can talk," she said. Bobby suggested the commuter bar near the railroad station. She said fine, and then, after a pause, she blurted out in that breathless way of hers, "I have to talk to you, Bobby!" Her voice dissipated his anger. It was childlike in its urgency. Even her brooding was childlike. Consuming. Eternal. Dark, furrowed brows. And then, inexplicably, it was gone.

Of all the women he had known, she confused him the most. He could not reconcile that wide-eyed, breathless innocence that disarmed him, with that clipped voice and that cold stare that could wither a man. He called her on it more than once. They were in a bar one night, when he asked her about the men she had known since she had left her husband. She did not like to talk about them, she said, and besides, there were only a few. Bobby pressed her. She began to tell him. The first was a pale, neurotic Irishman, an actor with whom she had worked in summer stock during the last stages of her marriage. She lived with him for a week, and then fled. "He was so dependent," she said. "He wanted me to mother him, or maybe save him. I think he was gay. All I wanted was a friend." The next was a wealthy, Canadian businessman who took her to the Virgin Islands on his yacht. He speculated in gold, she said, and kept a doctor's beeper on his hip at all times so that he could be apprised of any changes in the gold market. "He was a nice guy," she said, "but absolutely amoral in business. He would do things, unconscionable things, and I would just look at him aghast. 'What's the matter?' he'd say." After the Canadian came a Jewish boy of twenty-six, an assistant television commercial producer ("Really just a gopher," she said) who defended her one day against a homosexual director who was screaming at her to bat her baby blues while holding up a can of coffee. She left the set in tears. In the dressing room she could hear the boy shouting at the director. "You can't treat her like that!" he said. "She's a lady!" That night, after dinner and some grass, she went to bed with the boy. The next morning in bed, he turned to her and said, "You know, I can have any young fluff in New York I want, and here I am with you." He sat up in bed with such enthusiasm he momentarily frightened her. "Imagine!" he said. "Me with you!" She gave him her telephone number but he never called. "I must have been his first *shiksa*," she said. Finally, there was the Wasp businessman to whom she was engaged before she broke it off after spending a weekend with him in Boston. "He attended to business and I shopped alone," she said. "I saw him for dinner and when he left in the morning." Like all Wasps, she said, he was terribly competitive. He pursued her as he would any trophy, single-mindedly, and when he thought he'd won her he placed her in a corner of his life and went on to other things.

There had been others to whom she was attracted, she said, but for one reason or another nothing sexual ever came of that initial attraction. Shortly before she met

Bobby, she had been vaguely attracted to the chairman of the Drama Department, who was responsible for her getting her present job at the prep school. He was a rumpled, gray-haired man in his early fifties with a certain weary physicality that Sheila found endearing. He walked slightly hunched over, plodding, as if the cares of the world were on his shoulders alone. Sheila saw a bumbling sweetness in the man, which she made evident to him over flirtatious lunches in the student cafeteria. Before their flirtation could be consummated, however, Sheila saw him devastate one of the school's spinster teachers who had dared to question his actions during a faculty meeting. He was so cruel to that woman, the cruelty of a bully, that Sheila realized what she had mistaken for sweetness was actually weakness. He was weak and mean, and he cultivated his shambling facade as a device for seduction.

Sheila looked at Bobby and shook her head with disgust. "And I *did* feel sorry for him," she said. "He seemed so different from the others."

"He doesn't sound it." Bobby said.

"What do you mean?"

"He sounds like all of your others. You have an affinity for weak men."

"I beg your pardon."

"I mean all those men were safe. You were on top."

She drew away from him. She was seated on a bar stool alongside of him. She arched her back and stared down at him in that threatening way of hers. Bobby grinned at her.

"You trying to scare me, babe?" he said. His voice was light, amused. "I'm not one of those pussies you're used to, you know. So don't waste that shit on me." He was still grinning.

She held her rigid pose for a long moment, staring down at him, and then her shoulders sagged and she smiled. "You're right, Bobby." She nodded her head. "You're right."

Later, she claimed her threatening look was merely a device she had acquired in New York City as a means to protect herself. It was disposable, she said, but secretly Bobby wondered whether it had become so much a part of her nature that she could never excise it.

She came directly to the bar from school, still dressed in her pleated skirt and crewneck sweater. Bobby was waiting at the bar. It was crowded with men and women in business suits who had just gotten off the 6:05 from New York. The women, legs crossed, sat sideways to the bar like painted porcelain birds while the men hovered over them in a predatory way. The men leaned down to whisper in their ears and the women threw back their heads and laughed harshly. They were heavily made-up. The men's suits were wrinkled and their ties loosened. Some had attaché cases that they had lain at their feet, propped against the bar, and every so often, no matter how engrossed in a woman they seemed to be, they would feel around the floor with one shoe as if keeping track of a small, untrustworthy dog.

Sheila brushed past the men and women on her way to Bobby. A few of the men glanced over their shoulders after her, then returned to their women.

"I'm sorry, Bobby," she said. Bobby nodded, but did not speak. She went on. "I can't go on like this. At first I just lost myself to it. I didn't think. I was so amazed by it all." She stopped for a moment, then said in a controlled voice, "Bobby, I am a greedy woman. I don't want just a romance. Do you understand? There are things I have to know."

"What things?"

"I have to know about your wife." Bobby turned toward the bar. He ordered himself another drink and one for Sheila. After the drinks arrived, he began to tell her, from the beginning.

His mother was a fierce, dark, birdlike woman with a big nose and wiry hair. In her youth she resembled an Arab street urchin. She married a man handsomer than herself, a gambler, who ran out on bad debts, and she had two sons by him. She loved Bobby and his older brother, Tom, as only an Italian mother could, with a love bordering on lust. She used to hold Bobby at arm's length—a quaking child in short pants—and scrutinize his features with her fierce black eyes. *"Quanta bella da face!"* she would say, and kiss him hard on the mouth with her painted lips. Years later, when Bobby was a man, she continued to make him kiss her in a way that never failed to embarrass him. "Here!" she would say, as he bent low to her dark face. "On the lips!"

Bobby's brother was tall and thin, with a bloodhound's face. Even as a boy, Tom had had an old man's weary face. Bobby always knew his brother was homely, because his mother told him so for as long as he could remember. Your poor brother, she would whisper, shaking her head. He is so homely. But he is good. A saint, she would say. What Bobby was, besides beautiful, she never said.

Bobby married at twenty-nine. Elizabeth. Beth. A soft, pale girl of nineteen with translucent skin. He could see through her, bluish veins and blood vessels, faint fibers in exquisite parchment. She had milky blue eyes and the face of an angel. That was what his mother used to tell her as she sat primly on the edge of the sofa, sipping tea. His wife, his girlfriend then, told his mother that she loved Bobby. "Your son is such a good man," she said. His mother nodded and said, "Yes, Tommy is a saint."

His wife bruised easily, cried often that first year when Bobby tried to enter her. Her vaginal muscles would tighten, and she would cry out in pain. Bobby feared he was not being gentle enough, but no matter how gentle he was, still she cried out. One moonlit night he was kneeling over his wife, about to try again, when he saw that his shadow had enveloped her. It was the shadow of a Stone Age savage, and he stopped trying. He settled, instead, for oral sex, which repulsed her. Even on the hottest summer nights, when he made love to her with his tongue, she pulled the sheets up to her neck. Underneath those sheets, his face buried between his wife's soft, pale thighs, Bobby could barely breathe. He worked feverishly to make her come before he passed out, and when she did, her thighs pressing tight against his ears, he would rip off the sheets and gasp for air. She, in turn, insisted that the sheets cover her head as she worked, eyes open, over him. She looked like a nun bobbing for apples. When Bobby was about to come, she would stop, look out from under the sheets, her face dripping sweat, and beg him not to come in her mouth. Bobby finished himself off with his own hand.

They lived with her parents that first year, in a bedroom off the kitchen in a ranch house in the suburbs. Bobby was going to graduate school full time and working from 6 P.M. to 2 A.M. as a waiter. Beth stayed home to clean up their bedroom and talk with her mother, who did all the cooking. When Bobby came home from work, he sat at the kitchen table doing homework while his mother-in-law— a short, stocky woman in a shift—stood over the stove preparing his supper. Beth stood by her mother's side, holding a plate, waiting for her mother to ladle the hot stew onto it, just as she had done ever since Bobby had known her. When they were going together, Bobby used to stop over Beth's house late at night, and they would lie on the sofa, watching Johnny Carson on television and, during commercials, pressing their bodies together until finally Bobby's pants would be stained with his come. Beth would get up, embarrassed, and offer to fix him something to eat. It did not matter whether he was hungry or not, he always said yes so that Beth could go into the kitchen to compose herself. She always refused his offers to help, and to punctuate that refusal she closed the door behind her. Bobby stayed in the living room, watching television, looking down at his wet pants in shame. One night, after his pants had dried, and still Beth had not returned, he opened the door to the kitchen. Beth's mother, in a nightgown, was hunched over a shank of ham, vigorously slicing off pieces, her bulbous breasts swaying as she cut, while Beth stood beside her holding a plate.

Nothing changed when they got married, except that

now Bobby sat in the kitchen with them, reading Andrew Marvell's poetry out loud to them while they waited on him. They laughed when he read, with exaggerated enunciation, "To His Coy Mistress." The louder they laughed, the more exuberant Bobby became until finally he would be standing on top of the kitchen table, the book in one hand, gesturing wildly with the other, as he read,

> . . . then worms shall try
> That long preserv'd virginity
> And your quaint honor turn to dust.
> And into ashes all my lust.

Bobby stopped reading only to eat. When he finished, and the dishes were cleared, his mother-in-law would go upstairs to bed and Bobby would go back to his reading. He read silently now. Beth sat across from him, trying desperately to stay awake so that her husband would not be alone. Always, she succumbed, laying her head on her arms on the kitchen table. Bobby looked across at her. In repose, she did have the face of an angel. Bobby marveled at her innocence. At that moment, he knew he loved her more than he would ever love her again. It was a warm spring night. Through the screen door he could smell the grass and hear the crickets. He dreamed. . . .

In the morning, he woke alone in bed. He heard whispers coming from the kitchen. He could make out only a few words whispered by his mother-in-law. "Pregnant . . . children. . . . It's been a year." He heard Beth sobbing softly. The next day they went to a gynecologist. Bobby sat in the waiting room with pregnant women and small children while Beth went in with the doctor. After what seemed like hours, the doctor summoned him through a door, down a corridor of narrow cubicles, and into the one occupied by his wife. Her clothes and her long-line bra and her flesh-colored rubber girdle lay neatly folded over a chair. Beth, dressed only in a johnny coat, lay on the examining table. Her legs were spread and her feet were hooked high into stirrups. The johnny coat was pulled back to her waist, exposing her sex. Bobby noticed for the first time, that she had sparse reddish hair and a mole. Bobby turned away and began to cry. He heard the doctor's droning voice and felt the doctor's hand on his shoulder. Bobby turned around to face his wife. She looked up at him with pleading eyes, but he could do nothing. Her sweat, mingled with her orange makeup and black mascara, ran down her cheeks. The doctor, still talking, held his hand, fingers spread, before his face. He pulled a rubber glove over his fingers with a snap, lubricated the middle finger, and bent over Bobby's wife. He began to insert the finger into Beth's vagina. Her eyes grew wide with terror. She bit her lip but did not cry out. Bobby watched as the finger slid a fraction of an inch more into his wife's vagina. Her entire body went rigid. The doctor stopped, reassured her. She forced herself to breathe deeply, and her body went limp. The doctor began to slide the finger in deeper and deeper until it was all the way inside Bobby's wife. He kept the finger there all the while he talked to them.

A few months later Beth became pregnant. Before his son was born, Bobby's mother died, and they inherited her house, since her husband, Bobby's father, had long since failed to return one night after one of their morning arguments. When Bobby's son was born, it was a painful birth. Beth remained in the hospital for almost two weeks. When she finally came home, to the house where Bobby was raised, she refused to let him touch her. She would not even lie in his arms on the floor when they watched television unless he promised not to "start anything." And when he did, when he let his hand slip onto her breast, she got up and sat on the sofa behind him. "See," she would say. "You always have to ruin it."

When they were first married, she always undressed for bed in the dark, hiding herself from him. Now, she went into the bedroom and locked the door behind her. She wore her panties and her nightgown to bed. If Bobby threw his arm over her, she shrugged it off. If he persisted, she would bolt up in bed and scream at him to stop. The sound of her voice invariably woke their son. If Bobby screamed back at her, she would grow rigid in bed, her eyes bulging, and she would lash out at him with a blind, unthinking, almost animal intensity. She grabbed clumps of her hair in both fists and yanked it. Bobby grew terrified. Soon, he learned to do anything to avoid such outbursts. He began to make love to other women. He no longer touched Beth at night, but if she realized this, she never let on. Her rages became less and less frequent. Their lives became tranquil and remained that way as long as Bobby continued to protect them all from Beth's terrible rages, which, always, the next morning, she denied having.

Bobby began to sleep in the tiny guest room where his father had slept when Bobby was a boy. Beth slept in his mother's bedroom, her bedroom now, with their infant son in a crib across the room. When the son began to have bad dreams, Beth would let him crawl into bed with her. Often, Bobby could not sleep. He would lie in bed in that tiny room for hours before finally getting up to go downstairs to the living room to watch television. When he passed his wife's bedroom, he would look in and see his wife and his small son wrapped, like innocent lovers, in one another's arms. Downstairs, he lay on the floor and watched television before finally masturbating himself to sleep.

When Bobby finished telling about his wife he saw that Sheila was crying. She cried silently, without expression, the tears sliding down her cheeks to her chin where she wiped them off with the back of her hand.

"But why did she marry you?" Sheila said.

"She loved me."

"How could she? She didn't want . . ."

"I know. I've thought about it every day for the past ten years and still I don't understand it. I just know she loved me. She still does."

"What about you? Why did you marry her?"

Bobby smiled at her. "I loved her," he said. "She was the first person I ever knew who thought I was a good man. And she was so sweet. Even now, she's almost thirty and still she looks . . . untouched." Bobby laughed, a breath. "She is untouched. Like a child. Every morning, without fail, she insists on making my coffee and driving up to the drugstore to get the newspapers. Sometimes I get up at five o'clock, and still, as soon as she hears me, she comes running down. It means nothing to me, but for some reason it's so important to her. Her day would be ruined if she came down and saw I had made the coffee or got the newspapers. We sit across the kitchen table from one another, just as we did when I was in college." Bobby laughed. "I guess we were always at our best across a kitchen table. Me, wideawake. Her, half asleep. It's pleasant. She spreads her paper flat across the table and begins to read, so seriously, her face low to the paper. It takes her a long time to read a page. Every so often she'll look up and smile. . . . It takes my breath away, and I want to cry. Sometimes she looks up with this furrowed brow and asks the simplest question. Not dumb, mind you, but simple. Obvious. How could anyone vote for Teddy Kennedy after Chappaquiddick, she'll say? And the thing is, it's not a rhetorical question. She really doesn't know."

Bobby was silent for a moment, and then he said, in a voice filled with wonder, "Do you know, babe, I have known that woman for over ten years and still I don't know her. She's unfathomable."

Sheila looked away from Bobby as if embarrassed. Without looking back at him, she said, "Do you still love her?"

Bobby did not answer right away. He drained his drink. Then he said, "Yes. Not like I love you, but, yes, I do. I always will."

"Even after what she did to you?"

"She did nothing to me. She meant no harm. She didn't know. She was just a frightened girl who thought I would protect her. But I hurt her in some way. I don't know how, but I did."

"And you, babe," she said. "What did you want?"

He shook his head, almost a twitch. "I don't know. I . . . I . . . I had other expectations, I guess. I should have known."

"How could you?" said Sheila.

Bobby looked at her and said in a voice devoid of inflection, "I should have known."

Late that night they went back to his office and made love on the floor. Afterward, they lay in one another's arms. Sheila said, "Bobby, what do you want from me?"

Without looking at her, he said, "Peace. Happiness."

Sheila waited for him to go on. When he didn't, she said, "Do you know what I want?"

"No."

"I want you to marry me."

Bobby was staring up at the ceiling. He closed his eyes. A breath escaped him. "I can't," he said.

Sheila propped herself up on one elbow and faced him. "Yes, you can."

· THREE ·

Bobby flew to Los Angeles in April. He met a woman in the coach lounge. She was tall, big-boned, in her forties, with streaked blonde hair held in place at her forehead by a leather headband. She wore a loose, gauzy blouse over pendulous breasts, and a ruffled western skirt over flaring hips. Her red suede cowboy boots were made in Tokyo. She had a wide, predatory mouth, and when she spoke, in a deep, hollow voice, her mouth pulled down into her jaw. She told Bobby she was in real estate and handed him her business card.

"Call me," she said, looking directly into his eyes. "I'll show you a piece or two."

Bobby laughed, and put the card in his wallet. Her eyes, behind smoky, gold-rimmed sunglasses, moved down from his face and began to roam, at leisure, over his body in a way that embarrassed even Bobby. She reminded him of most of the women he had met in L.A. Bold. Lascivious. Slack. A respite, actually, from the thin, tentative, tightly strung women he knew in the East. He had first gone to L.A. ten years ago to cover the Long Beach Grand Prix. It was there, in a cheap motel room in Torrance, that he had cheated on his wife for the first time. They had argued before he left. As always, it was about sex. A few nights before he left he had lain on his back in bed alongside Beth, who was curled, as always, away from him. He dared not move until he was sure she was asleep. Then he rolled toward her and pressed his body against her back and buttocks. He slipped his hand over her side. She stirred. Bobby froze, his heart pounding, just as it had

years before, on a hot summer afternoon, high up in the
balcony of a darkened movie theater.

He was fourteen. The best Babe Ruth League pitcher in
town. He pitched once a week at the park near his home.
The games were played at twilight, before a small crowd.
Mothers and fathers sat in the skeletal wooden stands
along the third-base line. The mothers, in Bermuda shorts,
chatted amongst themselves like colorful magpies, stopping on occasion only to glance down through the wooden
slats to chastise their small sons fooling around underneath the stands. The fathers, in shirt-sleeves and loosened
ties, came directly from work. They sat hunched forward,
like Indian scouts, shading their eyes with the flat of their
hands as they tried to follow the action unfolding on the
field under the harsh orange light of the sun setting behind
a line of trees in the parking lot beyond right field.

A college boy sat at a folding card table directly behind
the homeplate screen. He kept the official scorebook and
worked the record player that played only the national
anthem to begin the games and, between innings, choruses
of "They Call the Wind Maria" sung by Frankie Laine. He
was surrounded by teenaged boys and girls on bicycles.
The boys leaned against the homeplate screen, gripping
the screen with their fingers to keep their balance, heed-
less, as always, of the umpire's warning of a foul tip that
would smash their fingers. The umpires were gnarled, unshaven, ex-ballplayers of local repute who had once
starred in the Senior City League for the White Eagles or
the Naples A.C. or the Magyar Club, and who, now, in their
fifties, still liked to keep a hand in the game. They parked
their cars in the right-field lot and waited, sipping coffee,
until game time before beginning their long, heavy-bellied,
pigeon-toed walk to homeplate. They carried inflated
chest protectors under their arms. When they reached homeplate they acknowledged, with a nod, the respectful greet-
ings of those few fathers in the stands who remembered
them from their playing days.

Before the game was more than a few innings gone, a dozen girls, cheerleaders from the high school, would assemble underneath the maple tree behind the left fielder. They formed a chorus line and, led by their blonde captain in rolled-up jeans, they began practicing their cheers for the upcoming football season. They kicked their legs high, in unison, and their voices rang out with football cheers amid the sounds of the baseball game in progress.

The crowd and the noise always made Bobby nervous, which was why he never did fulfill his very real, yet fragile, talent when he went on to high school. It was also why, on days he was to pitch, he spent his afternoons downtown in a vain attempt to take his mind off that evening's game. He went first to each of the town's three stamp shops. He bought mint new issues with birds and rockets and athletes on them from Freddie Glatz, a stooped, ferretlike little man who wore thick-lensed eyeglasses and always seemed to be eating a tuna fish sandwich with too much mayonnaise on it. Freddie talked and chewed with his mouth open, the mayonnaise oozing through his teeth, dropping in tiny white spots on the stamps he was trying to sell Bobby. Freddie knew little about stamps, and Bobby always stopped at his store first in the hope that he would find a bargain. The store was sandwiched in between a pawnbroker's shop and a secondhand jewelry store across the street from the railroad tracks where winos congregated. Both stores were owned by the same man, Jacques DuPree, a Polish immigrant who sported a goatee he stained black with shoe polish and who, it was reputed, dealt in stolen goods. One day, Jacques posted a sign in the windows of both stores, "Fire Sale," and the next day both stores were burned to the ground. Only Freddie Glatz's Railroad Stamp Store—a tiny, square, one-story building—was still standing, untouched, between the two charred wrecks.

After Freddie's, Bobby would go uptown to Harold Turner's Yankee Stamp Shop on Main Street, near the bus stop, across the street from Morrow's Nut House ("Nuts from All Over the World"). Hal was a gaunt man in his forties, with thinning, close-cropped hair and a protruding Adam's apple that was underlined by a bow tie. He always greeted Bobby with a smile that seemed more a sneer, really a baring of teeth, and then tried to sell him defective old used United States stamps he had acquired from the estates of deceased Yankees whose relatives would rather be shortchanged by Hal than have to deal with either of the two Jewish dealers in town, Freddie Glatz and Shlomo Wasserman.

Bobby always saved Mr. Wasserman for last. His one-room office was on the seventh floor of a tall building occupied mostly by doctors, lawyers, and accountants. Bobby's heart began to race the second he got off the elevator and saw Mr. Wasserman's frosted glass door with the stenciled letters, "Classic Stamps." He would sit enthralled for hours in the chair by the door while Mr. Wasserman, combing his fingers through his thick shock of swept-back white hair, would lecture him on stamps and girls and sports and his native country, Austria. He was an excitable man, in his early sixties, who could not sit for long. He was always jumping up, pulling up his trousers, pacing around his tiny office, waving his arms to punctuate a point. "That fuckink Turner," he would say. "He is a fuckink anti-Semite." (Hal Turner, smiling his bared-teeth smile, referred to Mr. Wasserman simply as "The Jew.") Bobby told neither man he patronized the other, which always made him feel guilty whenever he entered one of their stamp stores. He felt most guilty with Mr. Wasserman, however, as if, somehow, those canceled old United States stamps he fingered in his pocket before he sat down were a sign of his betrayal.

Mr. Wasserman never minded that Bobby patronized Freddie Glatz's store, though, and not simply because he, like Freddie, was a Jew. Mr. Wasserman seemed to delight in knowing that what he taught Bobby about stamps one day, Bobby would use the next to outsmart Freddie. Grinning, Bobby would hold out in his palm, like an offering, his latest bargain from Freddie Glatz. "That fuckink *putz!*" Mr. Wasserman would shout with a backhand swipe at the stamps. "He's hopeless! He wipes his elbows after a shit!" Then, planting his hands on his hips, he would say to Bobby, "And I suppose you spent all your money there! Huh?" Bobby would shake his head no and produce some bills from his pocket. "Good!" Mr. Wasserman would say, going over to his old, black safe. "Now, let's see what we have for you today." He perused his stock books with great deliberation before finally withdrawing one and bringing it over to the glass counter where Bobby sat. He opened it across the counter, under which he had arranged cheap topical sets—birds, flowers, rocketships—from a host of Third World countries. The stamps under the glass were curled at the edges and yellow with age. "Rocketships!" Mr. Wasserman would say with a shake of his head. "Rocketships from a country of fuckink Zulus who can fit a watermelon, lengthwise, in their mouth, but can't read or write!" Mr. Wasserman never expected to sell those stamps. He kept them there only to amuse the mothers of his clients, boys like Bobby and younger, who studiously poured over his stock books while their mothers exclaimed over the pretty stamps under glass. Mr. Wasserman, being a widower, was not averse to flirting with those mothers, either. More than once, in Bobby's presence, he would refuse to believe that the woman ("Goirl," he would say) standing before him was old enough to be the mother of that grown-up little man hunched over a used Austrian number one. "Oh, Mr. Wasserman!" the woman would say, smiling and blushing, as she led her son out the door. As soon as she was out the door, Mr. Wasserman, eyes wide, tongue protruding, would grab his genitals with both hands and make a thrusting gesture with his hips toward the door that both delighted and embarrassed Bobby.

Mr. Wasserman took a pair of sterling silver stamp tongs from the breast pocket of his shirt and, like a surgeon making a first incision, slipped a stamp from the stock sheets and laid it on a piece of black paper. He slapped the black paper with his knuckles. "Superb!" he said with a nod. "Look at the centering!"

Bobby looked, and then took the tongs from Mr. Wasserman and turned the stamp over to examine its gum. He shook his head and said, "Hinged."

"Hinged?" Mr. Wasserman shouted. "What do you mean, hinged?" He grabbed a magnifying glass from the table, hunched low to the stamp, and examined it carefully. "A gum imperfection. From printing, that's all."

Bobby reached for the magnifying glass, but Mr. Wasserman pulled it away from him and thrust it in his shirt pocket. Bobby withdrew his own magnifying glass from his pants pocket and examined the stamp.

"Don't buy it!" Mr. Wasserman said, leaping to his feet. He shot his fingers through his swept-back hair. "Go to that *putz* friend of yours by the railroad tracks and see if he has such a stamp. At any price."

Bobby looked up at him. "It's definitely hinged," he said. The old man sat down, exhaled, his eyes drooping shut. He withdrew a soiled handkerchief from his pants and mopped his brow.

"Hinged. Shminged," he said. "Who cares? You are a collector, not an investor. I taught you."

"You taught me unhinged," Bobby said, looking at the old man, as if confused. The old man shook his head. "Well, you did!" Bobby said.

The old man threw up his hands and held them there, as if surrendering. "Take it, for Chrissakes," he said. "I'm an old man." Bobby took the tongs and began to slip the stamp, his stamp now, into a smoky glassine envelope. Mr. Wasserman pointed an ominous finger at him. "You'll kill me, yet," he said, and then, a grin slowly moving across his face, he added, "You out-Jew a Jew." Bobby smiled.

At first, Mr. Wasserman was proud of the things Bobby learned from him, even when he used them against him. But as they grew older—Mr. Wasserman suffering two heart attacks and Bobby ceasing to be a boy—the old man's feigned and gregarious outrage at his protégé's behavior took on a very real hint of bitterness. He took to goading Bobby by offering him expensive stamps at ridiculously low prices he knew Bobby could not afford. Then, after whetting Bobby's appetite, he offered him stamps he both needed and could afford at unfairly high prices. He no longer allowed Bobby to bargain with him. At first Bobby was confused by the old man's meanness. He would grow silent in his chair, while the old man, standing over him, his hands planted on the glass case for support, berated him. "How do you ever expect to build a collection if you can't even afford this stamp?" he would shout. Then he would laugh, a bitter laugh, scoop up the stamp with his tongs, and return it to his stock book. He made an even greater production of returning that stock book to his safe. Later, when Bobby left the office, he vowed to himself that he would never return. He stayed away for weeks at a time, wondering what he had done to make the old man despise him so. But he could think of nothing, so finally he would return, and it would begin again.

After one especially long absence, shortly after Bobby had turned eighteen, he returned to the old man's office with a hundred dollars in his pocket. He had never, until that time, spent more than twenty dollars in Mr. Wasserman's office. As usual, within an hour, Mr. Wasserman offered him a set of Renner Sheets for ninety-five dollars, which was almost half their real value. Bobby said nothing. The old man laughed at his inability to take advantage of such a bargain. "Ninety," the old man said. "Take it for ninety if you can." Bobby stood up, dug into the pocket of his tight jeans, and withdrew his hundred dollars. He counted it out for the old man on the glass table. When he reached one hundred, he said, "Keep the change, Mr. Wasserman," and picked up his Renner Sheets and left. All the while he was counting out those bills, and even as he left, he could not bear to look at the old man.

Bobby never returned to Mr. Wasserman's office. He got married, his son was born, and he stopped collecting stamps. Then one day he received a card in the mail. It was from Mr. Wasserman's daughter. It was the announcement of her father's death. On the back of the card she wrote that she had gone through all of her father's old ledgers, combing them for the names of his steadiest clients, who, she was sure, would want to attend her father's last rites at the Rodeph Sholom. Bobby's name had turned up most frequently.

Long before Mr. Wasserman's death, on days Bobby was to pitch in a Babe Ruth League game, he would leave the old man's office at noon and go to a movie theater. He watched double-features of Abbott and Costello, or Roy Rogers, or Tom Mix, and then a Buck Rogers serial that seemed never to be resolved, week after week, and finally a host of Looney Tune cartoons, before, finally, he staggered out of the darkened theater into the blinding midafternoon sunshine. He stood blinking into the sun, waiting for his eyes to adjust to the light, and then, examining his stamps along the way, he walked to the bus stop. When he got home he spent the rest of the afternoon putting his stamps in his album, and then he dressed into his baseball uniform and went to the park near his home. His routine never varied on days he was to pitch. He took comfort in it. One such day, however, he was standing in line at the movie theater when he noticed an older woman a few places ahead of him. She looked out of place among all those children and young teenagers. She was in her late twenties, with arched eyebrows and a mouth smeared with color. She wore a tight knit dress that made her breasts stick out like perfect cones. Bobby was mesmerized by the rhythmic heaving of her breasts. He grew light-headed with excitement. He followed the woman into the theater and sat a few rows behind her. He watched her instead of the movie. When she got up and walked past him, he feared she was going to leave. But she returned a few moments later. She walked down the aisle smoothing her skirt with her flattened palms. Bobby saw, beneath the hem of her skirt, a thin line of white lace. He looked around to see if anyone was watching him. He noticed, for the first time, that the theater was filled with couples his age huddled in the darkness. Some of them were kissing. He got up and went to the back of the theater. He waited there until a girl came by. She was short and plump, with breasts like the woman, only smaller, rounder, softer-looking. She wore an angora cardigan sweater unbuttoned at the throat and a long black skirt that fell almost to her ankles and was so tight she could manage only small steps. Bobby said hello. She smiled at him, a gape-toothed smile. He asked her if she wanted to sit with him. She thought a moment, chewing her gum, said something inaudible, and then nodded. She followed him up the stairs to the balcony. They sat high up, underneath the light from the projection room. The light fanned out over their heads, grew wider and fainter as it approached the screen far below in the darkness. There were particles of dust suspended in the light. Bobby put his arm around the back of the girl's seat. She shifted slightly toward him. He stared ahead, unseeing, at the movie, and let his hand drop onto the girl's shoulder. She glanced at his hand and then back to the screen. They stayed like this for awhile, staring straight ahead, perfectly still, Bobby's hand resting ever so lightly on the girl's shoulder. When she sank lower in her seat Bobby let his hand drop down above her breast. He held it there, suspended in midair like a claw over her rising and falling breast. She looked at him, a knowing look, but said nothing. Bobby dared not move. His heart pounded so fiercely in his breast he could not breathe. He struggled for a breath and waited. A long moment passed, and then Bobby's hand formed a perfect cup, suspended over the girl's breast. Ever so slowly, his hand began to move toward her breast. He felt, first, the angora of the girl's sweater. It tickled the palm of his hand. Then he felt her breast, firm yet soft, liquidy yet solid. His hand closed over her breast, remained there for an instant before she flung it off with the back of her hand. She leaned, sideways, toward him. Still staring at the screen, she whispered, "I told you. I'm not dirty."

Bobby remembered that moment years later, lying in bed beside his wife a few days before he was to leave for Los Angeles that first time to cover the Long Beach Grand Prix. She was curled away from him. He was pressed against her back. He slipped his hand over her side and gently cupped her breast. In a dream, she pressed her buttocks back against Bobby's groin. He began to massage her nipple with his flattened palm. Her nipple grew hard and distended. An animallike groan came from deep in her chest. Then she stiffened, and, with the back of her hand, she flung his hand away. She curled even tighter into a fetal position and moved farther away from him. Bobby lay on his back, staring at the ceiling, quaking with fear. His breathing was labored and he began to sweat.

The next morning, as always, his wife denied having done what Bobby accused her of. They argued, and for the next few days did not speak. Bobby left for L.A., in silence, early one morning before his wife had awakened. He rented a car at the airport and began to drive south toward Long Beach where he would cover the Grand Prix. The freeway was elevated above the flat, red-clay land. He could see only the roofs of houses, orange mission tile, and the tops of palm trees faded by the sun, and telephone poles with their endless web of crisscrossing wires. Bobby was dripping sweat from the heat of the car that had been sitting for hours in the hot sun at the airport parking lot. He turned on the air conditioner and then the radio. He fiddled with the dial until he got music. A long ballad about the sinking of a ship. A tanker on Lake Superior. More story than song, really. Spoken, not sung. It drew Bobby away from the heat and the strange land and the California freeway, back to a stormy winter's night on board the S.S. *Edmund Fitzgerald*. The ship began to founder. The cook served supper with an ominous warning. An SOS was sent. Too late. The ship went down. All hands were lost. Silence. Then the balladeer's voice. "Does anyone know where the love of God goes, when the waves turn the minutes to hours?" Bobby began to cry. Uncontrollable sobs. On a freeway in California.

He checked into a cheap motel off the freeway in Torrance. The teenage girl behind the desk asked him if he wanted a bucket of ice. Bobby said no and went to his room. The drapes were drawn against the sun and the room was dark. Bobby sat at the small desk-dresser near the television set and began to write his wife a letter. He wrote slowly, in the darkened room, bent low to the paper. When he finished, he signed only his name, Bobby, and then added the telephone number of the motel where he would be staying for the next ten days.

He mailed the letter that night, on his way to a cocktail party at the Long Beach home of one of the sponsors of the Grand Prix. A black maid opened the front door of an imitation Mediterranean villa. A man and a woman, wearing identical red blazers, stood at the head of a receiving line of other couples wearing identical navy blazers. First the man, then the woman, greeted Bobby with a smile and a handshake. The man was tall and trim, with silvery hair. The woman was younger, with short, black hair and the perfect tan of one who spends her days at the club playing golf and tennis. Bobby moved down the receiving line, smiling and shaking hands, until he got to the last woman, who handed him a felt-tipped pen and a blank name tag. He printed his name on the tag and slapped it onto his silk shirt. It was the color of a robin's egg. His flared pants were white, his ankle-high boots chalk-white. They had a zipper on the side.

Bobby moved among the guests, men and women in their late forties and early fifties, dressed similarly in tailored suits. They glanced curiously at him. He smiled back. They turned away. Bobby stopped to admire a painting on the wall over a sofa. It was a Picasso illuminated by a tiny overhead light. There was a painting on every wall, he noticed. Miro. Cassatt. Chagall. Bobby began to circle the room. He paused an appreciable moment before each painting, studied it with a hand to his jaw, as if comparing it to a work in his own collection, and waited, in vain, for someone to assume a similar pose beside him. He went from painting to painting to painting until, finally, he came to sliding glass doors that opened onto a patio of tropical foliage that shone, oily, in the moonlight, like a rain forest. He stepped outside, into the hum of muted conversation. The warm night air smelled of jasmine and hyacinth and orchids. Paper Japanese lanterns were strung like large, luminescent, colored beads among the foliage. The light from the lanterns bathed the men and women in yellow and red and blue. A waiter circulated among the guests with a tray of drinks held, stiff-armed, above his head. His white vest took on various hues as he moved. When the waiter passed, Bobby reached up and speared a drink. He took a sip, drifted among the foliage and the guests, barely noticed; finally, the woman in the red blazer approached him. She glanced quickly at his name tag, and then, calling him by his first name, struck up a polite conversation. She spoke without expression, standing perfectly erect before him in her red blazer and navy skirt. She was one of those women who, no matter how attractive they might be, in a Hunt Club sort of way, seem curiously without femininity. Masculine. The kind of woman who performed sex like a successful man, with gusto but without spontaneity, as if it were a contest. Suddenly, her husband was standing before them. He smiled at Bobby, a thin-lipped smile, and then, still smiling, turned to his wife. "It's just like you," he said, "to track down the most macho guy here." His smile broadened. "Cunt." His wife looked at him without expression and then turned, as if in slow motion, toward Bobby. She resumed the thread of their conversation. The husband, still smiling, excused himself with a little nod in Bobby's direction, and was gone. The woman was asking Bobby a question. She repeated it.

"The Lotus?" she said. "Are you still driving for Colin?"

Bobby shook his head. "You must have me confused with someone else," he said. "I'm not a driver. I'm a reporter."

"Oh," she said, and left.

Bobby returned to his motel room late that night. He telephoned the motel office. The girl answered sleepily.

"Sorry to wake you," he said.

"Oh, that's all right."

"Listen, I'm expecting an important call in a few days. I'd appreciate your taking the message if I'm not in."

"Sure. Is there anything else?"

"No. Thanks."

Bobby woke late the next morning and dressed quickly. He opened the drapes to the sunlight and saw the girl standing by the lip of the pool. She was scooping scum and leaves off the water with a long-handled net. He went outside and she greeted him with a smile.

"There's coffee in the office," she said. She was wearing a loose-fitting T-shirt and cut-off jeans, and she was barefoot.

"Thanks. But I have to run. See you."

He spent the day at the track, interviewing drivers and mechanics during time trials. He returned to the motel exhausted and fell asleep on his bed without taking off his clothes. The next morning, the girl was by the pool again.

"No calls," she said with a smile.

"That's all right. I didn't expect one yet. It'll be a day or two."

She nodded. "There's coffee," she said, gesturing toward the office with her head while she scooped off leaves with her net.

"Thanks, I could use some." Bobby went into the office, poured coffee into a Styrofoam cup, and went back outside. He stood by the girl, sipping his coffee as she worked. She was dressed as she had been the day before.

"An important call?" she said.

"Pretty important. My wife."

"Oh." She scooped up some leaves in her net and tapped them out onto the lip of the pool. She was a thin girl, with long arms and legs, and Bobby could see that beneath her baggy T-shirt she was not wearing a bra. She had reddish-colored hair that frizzed in the heat, and pale, freckled skin. Her eyes were a pale green. Bobby followed her around the pool as she worked. After a few moments she asked him what he was doing in Torrance. When he told her, her eyes grew wide, like a child's, with wonder.

"Oh, how exciting!" she said. "Nobody much ever stops here."

"I noticed," Bobby said, gesturing toward the deserted parking spaces in front of the motel's few rooms. "Am I your only guest?"

"Yes and no. I get mostly long-haul truckers who arrive late at night and leave before sunup."

"Do you run this place by yourself?"

"Yes. My father stops by every now and then. He really owns it. But I run it."

Bobby nodded his head as if impressed. The girl blushed at his approval and asked him where he was from. He told her.

"Is that near New York City?" she said.

"Yes."

"Oh, gee. I've always wanted to go to New York City. It sounds so exciting."

"It's all right."

"I'll bet it's something. I wanted to go to college there. Not college, really. The New York Theater Wing." She laughed, as if embarrassed. "I've always wanted to be an actress. A real actress. You know, Broadway. But then my mother and father split up, and neither of them wanted me or my brother, so I had to go to work. My father had this motel, so he let me run it with my brother. He's fifteen now. I could leave in a few years, maybe, but I guess I won't."

"Why not?"

"I don't know. This is the only home I've really known. The motel. I don't think I can leave it."

"Sure you can. You can go to L.A. It's only a few miles away. You can become an actress there."

She turned on him with fierce eyes. "No! I won't ever go to L.A.! I hate it! I hate it!" Bobby looked at her, startled. "I'm sorry," she said. "I didn't mean to snap. It's just I have this thing about L.A. I had a boyfriend once. I loved him." She turned back to the pool, as if to avoid his eyes, and continued talking. "I did anything he wanted. He took some pictures once. You know, of me. I thought they were just for him. But he sent them into *Playboy,* and then I got this letter offering me a job as a Playboy Bunny in L.A. I broke up with him over that." She exhaled deeply, her narrow shoulders sagging. "It would be so easy for me," she said. "I have to fight it every day. I know once I started using my body like that I couldn't stop." She turned and looked directly into Bobby's eyes. A woman now, no longer a girl. "Do you understand?"

"Yes, I understand."

She turned back to the pool, and after a long silence, Bobby left for the track.

When he returned to his room that night, his telephone was ringing. "It's just me," she said. "No calls. I'm sorry." Then, after a pause. "Can I bring you something? A bucket of ice?"

"No, thanks. I'm beat. But thanks for calling."

He talked to her every morning by the pool before he left for the track. When she wasn't there one day, he went to the office looking for her. A teenaged boy with freckles was behind the desk. "She went shopping," he said with a suspicious look at Bobby. "What's it to you?"

"Nothing," Bobby said, and left for the track. When he got back to the motel that night, he called the office. She answered.

"It's just me," he said.

"Hi. I'm sorry, but still no calls."

"That's all right. How was your shopping?"

"Oh, that was you! Buddy told me some suspicious-looking guy was nosing around. Wait'll I get hold of him!"

Bobby waited a moment for her to ask him if he wanted a bucket of ice. When she didn't, he just said good-night and hung up. He had trouble sleeping that night, and when he woke, late in the morning, she must have finished cleaning the pool because she was nowhere in sight. He didn't bother going to the office to look for her. It was his last night there. After the race the next morning he would fly back home.

Bobby returned to the motel at midnight. Someone was swimming in the pool. She waved to him from the water. He went over to the pool just as she was climbing out into the moonlight. Her wet hair was slicked back, glistening. Her eyes looked three-dimensional in her long, narrow, high-cheekboned face. She was wearing a bikini bathing suit. Bobby noticed, for the first time, that she was one of those thin women with inexplicably huge breasts. Her freckled breasts heaved and fell before him as she gasped for breath. She smiled at him and bent over to towel her legs dry.

"I'm sorry," she said, straightening up. "Still no call. I was here all day." Bobby nodded. She looked at him strangely, as she might have looked at her brother, when twelve, as he slept that first night in his motel room bed. "It's none of my business," she said, "but . . . is it really important?"

"It was. Yeah." They sat down in deck chairs by the pool, and she asked him about his wife. He began to tell her. Their argument. His note.

"I don't know," he said. "It must be me."

"Why?"

He shrugged. "She's a soft girl. I think I frighten her."

She looked over at him. "You don't frighten me." They didn't speak for awhile, and then Bobby got up to go to his room. She followed him. They took off their clothes in the dark room and lay down on his bed. Bobby shivered, as if from a chill, when she pressed her body against him. They began to make love. When he entered her, she gasped with pain.

"I'm sorry," he said, and stopped.

"No! No! It's all right! Don't worry." She gripped his buttocks with both hands and, with unbelievable strength, pulled him deep inside her. She wrapped her legs around the small of his back, locked them at the ankle, and began to thrust with such power that her winglike pelvic bones bruised his waist. She came with a cry, half pleasure, half pain, before he did. "Now, you," she said, smiling up at him.

"I did," he said, and spilled off her onto his back.

"You sure?"

"Yes." She rolled toward him, wrapped her thin arms and legs around him like a child, and fell asleep. Bobby lay perfectly still on his back until he was sure she was asleep. Then he disentangled himself from her and got out of bed. He went to the window and peered out between the drapes. He saw the headlights from an eighteen-wheeler swing into a parking space in front of a motel room. The lights flicked off and a dark figure in a trucker's cap leaped down from the cab and went into the room. Bobby turned away. She was still asleep, one long, thin arm thrown over the bed where Bobby had been. He went to the dresser and began to pack his suitcase. When he finished, he put it beside the door.

The next morning she woke alone in bed. Bobby was already dressed, standing by the drapes.

"What's the matter?" she said.

"Nothing, babe. I have to get to the track early. It's race day."

"Oh, I forgot. Gee, I'd love to go with you."

Bobby fixed his eyes on her shoulder, and said, "Yeah, well, I'd love to take you, babe. . . . It's just . . . you know, I'll be running all over. . . ."

"Sure," she said. "I understand."

Bobby picked up his bag and opened the door. He glanced back at her as he was about to leave the room. She was sitting up in bed, her breasts exposed, looking at him through pale green eyes he would never forget. Without taking her eyes off him, she reached down and pulled up the sheets to cover her breasts.

Bobby thought about that girl as he sat across from the real estate woman with the leather headband on his flight to L.A. in April. He always thought about her when he went to L.A. He had been back many times, but he had never seen her again. He found other women. But never like her. He had made sure of that. The first woman he made love to in L.A., after that girl, was a Danish steward-ess. She laughed at him in bed when he told her, in all seriousness, that he was married. "Who cares?" she said. After her, he made love to a beautiful model he met at a cocktail party crowded with incredibly handsome young actors in Gucci work shoes, who spent the night feeding each other grapes. "You were the only straight one there," she said, with a shrug, when Bobby asked, "Why me?" He made love to a woman he picked up at a hotel bar by complimenting her on her long eyelashes. "Thank you," she said, and then frowned. "Maybe they're too long?" She took a pair of tiny scissors from her purse and trimmed them right there at the bar, before returning with Bobby to his room. He made love to a Beverly Hills lawyer in her thirties who said to him, when he mispronounced treatise as treatsie, "And you claim to be a writer?" He made love to a six-foot, two-inch professional woman basketball player who performed in bed with the same studied seri-ousness she exhibited when taking a foul shot. He made love to a cocktail waitress who wanted to be a writer for *True Confession* magazine and whose husband, she told Bobby at the moment of orgasm, was an accountant for a Vegas businessman who was connected. He made love to an aging ex-model with lacquered yellow hair who dropped a lacy hanky at his feet while he was having breakfast in the Beverly Hills Hotel. She wore frilly under-wear, and garters, and she refused to have oral sex with him because, as she put it, "It is dirty." She also demanded he go out to a drugstore at four o'clock in the morning to purchase a condom or else she wouldn't have sex with him at all. She was adamant. When Bobby returned, he found her asleep on her stomach. He knelt over her, pried apart her ample cheeks, and entered her anally. She woke with a scream, and then came twice. On his most recent trip to L.A., almost a year ago, Bobby made love to a woman weight lifter with thick, creamy thighs, billowy breasts, and callouses on her hands. She made love the way she lifted weights, with a bloodcurdling scream and a wild toss of her tangled, jet-black hair. After Bobby had come inside

her she informed him, off-handedly, while lighting a cigarette, that she had just returned from a weekend in Ense-
nada with three bikers from the Fresno branch of the
Grateful Dead Motorcycle Club. Bobby spent the next
week examining himself with clinical thoroughness under
the bathroom light until, finally, he put his mind at rest.

Bobby got off the plane and followed the other passengers to the baggage claim area. The real estate woman was
already there, staring up the baggage chute, her hands on
her hips. Bobby smiled across at her through the crush of
passengers. She looked away. When her bags tumbled
down the chute, she grabbed them off the conveyor belt
and hurried to the turnstile exit. Bobby watched, shaking
his head slowly, as she fumbled in her purse for her claim
checks. She handed them to the attendant, a black man,
who checked them against the stubs on her bags. She
glanced at Bobby. He smiled. She turned away and looked
out the window. The attendant handed back her stubs and
she hurried outside. Bobby stared after her. A tall man in
a white tennis sweater greeted her at the curb with a hug.
The man put her bags into the trunk of a Porsche Speedster
and then held the door open for her. She got in. As he
walked around the car to the driver's side, she glanced
through the terminal window. Bobby laughed, and waved
only the tips of his fingers. The man got in the car and they
drove off.

Bobby rented a car and drove to the television studio in
Hollywood where Rodney James was going to be inter-
viewed that afternoon on a talk show. Bobby arrived just
as the interview was about to begin. Rodney James and a
thin, blonde woman were seated on a white sofa under
bright lights. They faced a battery of cameras in the shadows. Bobby tiptoed over the camera cables and wires and
found a place in the shadows against the wall. A makeup
man with a gold hoop earring was fussing over the blonde,
dabbing at her cheeks with a brush, shaping her hair with
his palms, bending over now and then to coo in her ear.

She stared straight ahead, sipping from a mug of coffee while he worked. She was pretty, in a country and western sort of way, angular, square-jawed, but too thin, gaunt almost, a gaunt, heavily made-up blonde in a pink jogging suit and white tennis sneakers with a pink stripe down each side. Rodney was wearing a three-piece suit. With a silk tie. And a matching silk handkerchief that spilled out of the breast pocket of his jacket like a waterfall. He was holding a mirror up to his face. His lips were peeled back, exposing white teeth. He turned his face slightly to the left, then to the right, looking for particles of food that might be lodged in his teeth. When the producer, in the shadows behind the cameras, called for quiet on the set, the blonde put her mug down on a glass coffee table. The cup was smudged with a perfect half-moon of lipstick. The producer began to count down, out loud, from ten. Rodney put down the mirror and smiled at the camera. It was an odd smile. Humble, yet smug. It was the same smile Bobby had seen in that photograph of Rodney and Stanley Muraski and Tony Vincent taken over fifteen years ago. Rodney had not changed much since then. He was still boyishly handsome, only not so sharply defined. At thirty-four, he had begun to blur around the edges. His fine blond hair was thinning on top.

When the producer counted down to one, he pointed a finger at the blonde and nodded with great exaggeration. She smiled instantly at the camera and began to speak:

"Hello out there in Hollywood! This is your hostess, Candy Thompson, with 'Hollywood Hot Seat,' the show that sizzles! My guest today certainly needs no introduction . . . especially to all you ladies." She smiled lasciviously at Rodney. He was smiling at the camera. She looked back at the camera and went on. "He's none other than Rodney James, superstar pitcher for the Hollywood Stars . . ." she leaned toward the camera, looked left and right, as if for eavesdroppers, then whispered, ". . . and sexy heartthrob for just about every lady in Los Angeles." She sat back, and then said in a crisp voice, "We'll be back with sexy Rodney in a moment, but first a word from our sponsor." She sat perfectly still, smiling at the camera for a long moment, and then her smile broke. She reached for her mug. Rodney, still smiling at the camera, leaned sideways toward her.

"Excuse me, Miss Thompson. But . . . uh . . . you forgot to mention my Cy Young Award. Remember? My agent discussed it with you."

"Sure, Rodney. And it's Candy, okay?"

Suddenly the blonde brightened. She began to speak to the camera in a voice that was meant to generate an enthusiasm in her audience that was out of sync with her own emotions. She welcomed the audience back, reintroduced Rodney James, and then turned to him and asked a question. Rodney shifted in his seat, stretched his neck as if the collar of his shirt was too tight, cleared his throat, looked into the camera, and began to speak in a soft, monotone that emanated from a point behind his eyes.

"Well, Miss Thompson. The Stars have a great team, as you know. They are a credit to Hollywood and to the entire state of California. Although I am certainly not putting down the other fine major league teams in our state. But the Stars are something special. I like to think they are God's team. They stand for all the basic Christian and American ideals we all cherish. As such, Rodney James can not conceive of the Stars failing to fulfill their responsibility to this city . . ."

The blonde began to speak. Rodney continued.

" . . . this state . . . and this country." He stopped and smiled at the camera.

The blonde cleared her throat. "Those certainly are beautiful sentiments, Rodney. Aren't they, folks?" She smiled quickly at the camera and then turned toward Rodney. He was still smiling at the camera. The blonde put her arm over the back of the sofa so that her hand rested behind Rodney's neck. Unseen by the audience, she gripped his neck between thumb and forefinger and squeezed. Rodney's eyes opened wide. She twisted his neck until he was looking at her, not the camera. She smiled at him and said, "Still, Rodney, we all know the Stars had an off-season last year and you yourself were only a .500 pitcher. Could it be age catching up to the great Rodney James?"

The blonde released her grip. Rodney turned back to the camera. He cleared his throat. "Well, Miss Thompson, I don't think last season had anything to do with age." He smiled. "Rodney James has a lot of good years left in his trusty limb."

"I'll bet you do, Rodney." He glanced at her with furrowed brows, and then turned back to the camera.

"Actually, I had a sore arm last year, but I kept on pitching for the good of the team. They needed Rodney James on the mound every fifth day. You know, Miss Thompson, Rodney James hasn't missed a start in ten years." He smiled and nodded into the camera.

"That's some kind of record, isn't it, Rodney?"

Rodney lowered his head a bit, and then, looking up through his eyebrows, said, "Yes, it is. I'm very proud of it."

"And well you should be, Rodney. But enough of this jock talk. Let's have your fans get to know the real Rodney James." She looked at the camera and nodded vigorously. "Isn't that right, folks?" The blonde pulled up her legs and sat cross-legged on the sofa, like a child. She gripped her ankles with both hands and said, breathlessly, "Tell us, Rodney, how did you become such a sex symbol? You know, we ladies think you throw quite a bit of heat off the diamond, too."

"Well, I really don't think of myself that way, Miss Thompson. I think of myself more as a family man and a Christian than a sex symbol. Sex is okay, I mean. I'm not putting it down or anything. You know I have a child. A boy. He's got big hands. He's going to make a fine third baseman some day."

"I'll bet he will."

"Thank you, Miss Thompson."

"Oh, Rodney, you can call me Candy. Everyone does." She looked at him with her lascivious smile. "Do you know what Reggie Jackson and I have in common?" Rodney shook his head. "Well . . . they were going to name a candy bar after me, too. Yep! They were going to call it 'Candy's Candy—Sweet to Eat!' " She laid her hand on his thigh. He looked at it. "You do like candy, don't you, Rodney?"

"Well . . . ah . . . actually, Miss Thomp . . . I mean, Candy. I don't eat much candy. It's bad for the teeth." He smiled.

"Oh, that's a shame," she giggled. "Well, enough of this talk or we'll get thrown right off the air. Now, tell me, is it true that the great Rodney James has political ambitions once he leaves baseball?"

Rodney cleared his throat again and looked directly into the camera. "Well, not really political, Candy. I'd like to think Rodney James is above politics. I have so many fans in both parties I'd hate to alienate any of them by running for office on one ticket or the other. As you know," he leaned back in his seat and hooked both thumbs into his vest pockets, "I'm a born-again Christian. It happened during spring training of 'sixty-eight. I was a rookie, and like most rookies I used to raise a little heck now and then." He smiled at the camera. "I was in a bar one night with Stanley Muraski and Tony Vincent, two other rookie pitchers less fortunate than I, when I heard over the television that Goose Whitlaw, the pitching preacher for the old Brooklyn Eagles in 1938, had just died. Do you remember Goose, Miss Thompson?"

"It's Candy, Rodney," she said with a quick smile that vanished. "And I'm afraid Goose was a little before my time."

"Oh, sure. Yes, of course. Well, anyway, Goose was the only Christian preacher ever to pitch in the major leagues. He won a Cy Young Award in 1938. It came to me right then and there in that bar that it was my duty to fill the void left by his passing. From that moment on I dedicated my life to Christ and shortly thereafter I formed the Coalition of Christian Athletes for a Better America. It's not strictly a religious organization or a political organization, as you well know. It's just a group of concerned athletes, like myself—I'm the president of the CCABA—who want to foster good Christian ideals throughout this country. And it works, you know. The CCABA has turned around the lives of many people, not only athletes. Why, Rodney James was nothing until he accepted Christ, and now look what he's become. A star for the greatest baseball team in the world in the most glamorous city and state in the world, and . . ." He lowered his head a bit, fluttered his eyelashes, and said even more softly, "the 1974 Cy Young Award winner."

The blonde was staring at him. Her mouth was open. She blinked and closed her mouth. It took her a long second before she could speak. Then she said, "You *are* to be congratulated, Rodney. The CCABA is certainly an exemplary organization, although I myself am really not too sure just what the CCABA's *specific* goals are. Could you elaborate?"

"I'd rather not, Miss Thompson, other than to say that the CCABA is simply a force for Christian good. Our specific goals have not been firmed up yet."

"Firmed up! Oh, you rascal, Rod! May I call you Rod, Rod?" She grinned at him. He nodded. She unfolded her legs and sat back in her seat. "Well," she said in a bright voice, "we'll have more of Rodney James, superstar pitcher and all-around sexy guy, in a few moments. But first, a word from our sponsor." She held her smile for a long moment, and then it vanished.

Rodney smiled at her. "I thought it went pretty well, didn't you, Candy?"

"Yeah. Listen, Raaahd!" She drew out his name as if to punctuate a point. "Cut the Christian shit, okay. Who the fuck do you think pays my salary?"

When the interview was over, the blonde left the set and went to her dressing room. Rodney stood under the bright lights, smiling. The producer thanked him and led him behind the cameras to meet the stagehands. They asked for his autograph. He signed bits of paper and photographs of himself. Bobby went over to Rodney and introduced himself. Rodney smiled and pumped Bobby's hand.

"It's a great magazine," Rodney said when Bobby presented his credentials. "I'd be glad to grant you an interview."

Bobby thanked him.

"Will it be a cover story?" Rodney said, smiling.

"Well, it isn't actually just about you," Bobby said. "It's more a story about Stanley Muraski.

Rodney's smile faded a bit, and then reappeared. Still smiling, he shook his head as if in despair. "Poor Stashu," he said. "God bless him. I loved him like a brother. We were tight, you know. But his drinking. . . . I couldn't help. Not even the CCABA could turn him around. It's a sad story."

"Yes, I know. I'm not looking forward to it."

"Have you found him?"

Bobby looked at him, as if confused. "Yes. I thought you knew. He's a migrant worker in Grapevine."

Rodney smiled at him. "No, I'm afraid not. I lost track of Stashu long ago."

Bobby did not answer for a moment, then said, "I'm going to see him in a few days. After I talk with you. If you have some time?"

"Of course, of course, I do. Why don't you come out to the house tomorrow night for dinner? We can talk then." Bobby nodded. Rodney looked down at the floor. His eyes, unseeing, were looking inward. He laughed without a sound. "Stashu," he said under his breath, and shook his head slowly. Suddenly, he looked up and smiled. "Welp, it's settled then. Tomorrow night at seven." He shook Bobby's hand and walked off.

Bobby watched him go. A boyish-looking man moving stiffly in a five-hundred-dollar suit. He held his arms away from his body as if to keep his underarms dry. Bobby had seen that same precise self-conscious walk on television whenever Rodney pitched for the Stars. He would step out of the dugout in his cream-colored uniform with the blazing orange star on the chest, pause a second, give his arms a little shake away from his body until his uniform fell just so, and then begin his long, agonizingly meticulous walk to the mound. He moved like a man forever maneuvering over strange terrain, an astronaut on the moon, fearful that at any moment his arms and legs and head might explode away from his torso and go spinning endlessly into outer space. Rodney held himself together by an act of will. Unbending. Unthinking. When he reached the mound he toed the rubber, adjusted the peak of his cap with one tug of his thumb and forefinger, and began his first warm-up pitch. In midmotion he glanced down at himself, with obvious satisfaction, as he successfully navigated each stage of his delivery. Pump, just so. Kick, just so. Follow through, just so. He had the classic delivery of the textbook, self-taught, studied, without grace. His motion was a series of distinct parts, each one perfect, that never seemed to come together into one smoothly flowing piece. Rodney grunted each pitch up to the plate. Bobby liked to watch him pitch, admired him even, his discipline, his effort. He was so predictable. Fastball, up and in. Curveball, low and away. It did not matter who the batter was, his strength, his weakness. Rodney pitched everyone the same way. Fastball, up and in. Curveball, low and away. Fastball, up and in. Curveball, low and away. He was a machine. Relentless. Nothing disturbed his single-focus concentration. An error by his shortstop. A heartbreaking home run in the ninth inning of a tied game. Rodney just took the new ball from the umpire, tugged his cap, and began again. Fastball, up and in. Curveball, low and away. In this way, year after year, with only a modest natural talent, Rodney James fashioned a record of consistency that was sure to earn him a place in the Baseball Hall of Fame.

It was late afternoon when Bobby reached the Hotel California, a pink-stucco building surrounded by tropical foliage on a residential street of Beverly Hills mansions. The pink hotel was set far back from the street, on top of a hill

layered like a wedding cake. Bobby parked his car underneath a pink-and-green-striped canopy and gave his keys
to the attendant. The lobby was hushed. A fire was blazing
in the whitewashed corner fireplace. An actor, renowned
for his personal elegance and flawless tan, was sitting, legs
crossed, on a Louis XVI sofa, next to a beautiful younger
woman. A rock singer stopped before them to say hello. He
wore a black T-shirt and soiled sneakers. His white arms
were as thin as sticks. Bobby gave the desk clerk his American Express card, got his room key, and went to his room.
It was decorated in pinks and greens in the style of Louis
XVI. Love seat. Sofa. Writing desk. Armchair. Thick brocade curtains. Bobby did not bother to unpack his bags.
He lay down on the bed and tried to fall asleep. He thought
of calling his wife. Then he thought of calling Sheila. He
took the real estate woman's card from his wallet and
looked at it. Her office was in Beverly Hills. He put the
card down on the end table and closed his eyes. The
woman had big breasts and wide hips. Beth was small and
soft. Sheila was thin and hard. She had no hips. She was
built like a teenaged boy. The woman was slack and lascivious. Beth was frightened and removed. Sheila was
moody and demanding. "I want you to marry me," she
had said on the night before he left for L.A. Bobby lay there
for a long while, unable to sleep. Then he reached for the
telephone and dialed room service. He ordered a sandwich
and a diet soda.

In the darkened room, Bobby woke with a start to an
insistent knocking on the door. He jumped up and opened
the door in a daze. An Oriental youth in a waiter's jacket
was grinning at him. He had glossy, shoulder-length, black
hair, and he was wearing black slippers. He entered the
room and deposited the tray of food on the desk. Bobby
signed the check while the waiter grinned and nodded at
him. "You no need diet cola," said the waiter. "You have
wunnaful figer." He left the room and closed the door behind him. Bobby lay back down on the bed and within
minutes fell fast asleep again.

Bobby woke early the next morning and went to breakfast in the glass enclosed patio called "The Greenhouse." As he sat down at a wrought-iron table he heard a man's voice behind him. "Will *this* do, madam?" the voice said. There was a momentary silence, and then Bobby heard a woman's voice. "Well, I just don't care! I won't be seated near the service area."

The waiter returned with coffee, and Bobby ordered breakfast. The room was filled now, at seven o'clock in the morning, with voices and the clatter of silverware against glass and porcelain. Seated alone, an old man in a shimmering aqua-colored suit was watching a waiter sprinkle powdered sugar over a cut-glass bowl of strawberries that were the size of plums. The waiter tapped the tiny silver spoon against the bowl, the old man nodded, and then the waiter poured thick cream over the strawberries. A woman in a turban, seated across from a man, was talking into a telephone. The man leaned over the table and said something to her. The woman turned her head away from the man, put a finger in her ear, and continued talking. There was a telephone at every table, Bobby noticed. They were green, hospital green, and their wires were a faded pink. Everything in the patio seemed to be done in green or pink. Plants (green). Wrought-iron tables and chairs (pink). Table cloths (pink). Napkins (green). Carnations (pink). Stems (green). Bobby saw a small comic-actor, who had a reputation as a lover of statuesque women, seated across from a broad-shouldered blonde in jeans and boots. The blonde was leaning toward him, brushing the tips of her fingers along his forearm. The actor was sitting sideways to the table, one arm draped casually over the back of his chair. His eyes flitted left and right around the room, and when he caught Bobby staring at him, he smiled.

As Bobby was leaving the patio, he saw the maître d' go over to the woman whose voice Bobby had heard behind him. The maître d' apologized to the woman for not having recognized her earlier. He was ashamed of himself, he said. Why, he had seen her latest movie. She forgave him with a smile, and then brushed his cheek with hers, her lips puckered into a kiss that caressed the air.

Bobby spent the rest of the morning sitting by the pool. It was a hazy, overcast day and there were only a few people. Two producers were playing cards at a table while talking into telephones. They paused in their business conversation only to acknowledge each other's play of cards with a nod and a flourish of their long cigars. They were in their sixties, distinguished-looking men in that typically Southern California manner. Tanned. White-haired. Mustachioed. Vigorous-looking, with the faint muscle tone of older men who train daily with chromium-plated weights. They had taken off their suit coats and silk shirts against the morning heat. They were wearing gold medallions on chains around their necks, the medallions partially obscured by the white hair on their chests.

The pool boy circled the pool, laying pink towels over the arm of each deck chair. A woman was swimming laps. She swam from one end to the other and back again, alternating her stroke only to lift her head from the water for a breath, before plunging on. The pool boy was oblivious to the woman in the pool. He wore white tennis shorts and moved with a ponderous, thick-legged slowness. He was blond, but no longer youthful, and his body had not aged well as it had taken on flesh. He stopped to hand a towel to an actress reclining on a chaise lounge, reading a script. She was wearing dark glasses and a string bikini bathing suit. She accepted the towel with a languidly raised hand without taking her eyes from the script. She resembled Sheila, only younger, fleshier, without passion. It was, above all else, Sheila's passion that drew Bobby to her. He had been so long without it. When he had returned from that first trip to L.A., years ago, his wife was standing at the kitchen sink. He stood in the doorway with his bags. She glanced at him. "Hello," she said. She wiped a drop of sweat from her brow with the back of her forearm and plunged her hands back into the soapy dishwater. She never mentioned the letter Bobby had sent her. "How could she do that?" Sheila said. "She made a special dinner for me that night," Bobby said. "So?" Sheila said. "That was her way of showing all was forgiven," Bobby said. Sheila shook her head with disgust . . . Sheila . . . who never walked, but always ran to him, smiling, as if he had been gone for months. She loved him more passionately than anyone ever had or would. Bobby knew that. It was Sheila or no one. Sheila, who felt *everything* so intensely, who could not feel an emotion without expressing it. She showed disgust, anger, despair, all with the same passion with which she showed Bobby love. She could not detach herself, as Bobby did, from base emotions. They consumed her as completely as her love for him did. Always the extremes, never the middle ground. She could not countenance lesser emotions—amusement, chagrin; she seemed to have banished them from her nature as if they were a sign of weakness. Bobby knew that if he wanted her passionate love he had also to accept an unwanted gift, her passionate despair. At times, he was not sure he was up to it. Even more than her passion in his life, he wanted peace. A respite from the pressure. "Marry me!" she said. How could he? With a wife. And a child. And no money. And his fear.

A few chairs away from the actress who resembled Sheila there was a group of men in shorts. They were seated around a table, under an umbrella, finishing their breakfast. Bobby recognized one of them as the son of one of the wealthiest men in the world. A few years ago the son had been kidnapped and held for ransom in Italy, and after he had been released there was talk that he had engineered his own abduction to bilk his father out of millions of dollars. Every so often, one of the men would glance over at the actress. Finally, the youngest-looking man, red-haired and freckle-faced, with part of an ear missing, leaned forward and whispered to one of his friends. The friend got up and went over to the actress. He was wearing Bermuda shorts and white, patent-leather loafers without socks. He hovered over the actress for a long moment, waiting for her to acknowledge him. She did so, only after she had finished a page of her script. He smiled at her and said something. She took off her dark glasses, looked at him closed her eyes as if to erase him from her sight, and, without speaking, went back to her script. The man stood there a moment, uttered a curse, and went back to his friends. The actress did not look up from her script again for a long while, and when she finally did the men had gone. Only remnants of their breakfast remained. Two hummingbirds hovered over the plates, pecking at morsels of food.

The uniformed guard at the entrance to Pasadena Estates, Luxury Condominiums, had curly orange hair, a ruddy complexion, and a tattoo on his forearm. Jill, in a heart. He checked his pass list and then motioned Bobby through the gate. Bobby drove slowly past identical redwood-fronted condominiums. He tried to steer with one hand, while leaning across the seat, looking out the passenger-side window. He narrowed his eyes against the twilight sun that flashed in between each building. Suddenly, Bobby jammed on the brakes. He pressed his eyes shut, as if to erase a blinding mirage. Then he opened them again. It was still there. A six-foot-high cross over the front door. The cross was outlined with small light bulbs, like an actress's mirror. Without checking the address on the piece of paper in his pocket, Bobby parked the car and went up to the front door. Rodney James greeted him with a smile.

"Welcome to the Lord's house," he said. Bobby, smiling, nodded. Rodney led him through the living room, decorated in an Oriental motif, to the kitchen, where his wife was cooking dinner. He introduced Bobby to his wife, Claire. She smiled, a harried smile, and went back to her steaming pots and pans. She removed a cover and stirred vigorously with a long-handled wooden spoon. Then she took a long sip from a glass of wine. She put the glass of wine on the counter and grabbed a pot holder. She opened the oven door, bent over, and peered inside at a pot roast. She stabbed it with a fork and nibbled her lower lip.

"Smells delicious," Bobby said. She gave him a quick smile without looking at him, and took another sip of wine. Then she poured milk and a stick of butter into a pot of boiled potatoes, and began to mash them. The flesh under her thick arms shook as she mashed the potatoes. She was a handsome woman, big-boned, with a broad-featured, Slavic face. She was wearing a brown sweater and tan slacks with an elastic waistband. Hanging from a piece of string around her neck was a wooden cross. It was the size of a soup spoon. When she bent over the oven the cross dangled between her huge breasts.

Rodney led Bobby through sliding glass doors to an outside deck. There was a child's swing set in the backyard. Beyond the yard was a line of tall trees. Dusty shafts of sunlight filtered through the trees at a sharp angle. Beyond the trees was the fairway of a golf course. Men in brightly colored slacks sat on golf carts that putted, with agonizing slowness, up the fairway.

"The eighteenth fairway," Rodney said, smiling. "My number." When Bobby did not respond, Rodney added. "With the Stars?"

"Oh, yeah. Sure."

"Do you play?"

Bobby looked at him. "You mean golf? Oh, no, Rodney, I'm afraid not."

"Too bad. It's a wonderful game. Reflective, you know. It gives me a chance to think and pray. I feel close to the Lord when I'm walking those fairways." Bobby looked at him. Rodney was staring off toward the fairway, with its brightly dressed golfers putting by in their carts, as if he was looking into the Sistine Chapel. He raised an arm, like Moses, and pointed down the fairway. Bobby saw, far in the distance, a white building with a portico and columns. "The Pasadena Country Club," Rodney said. His face grew even more beatific. After a moment he said, softly, drawing out the first word, "Old money. . . ." Then he woke, as if from a trance, and turned, grinning, toward Bobby. "Welp, let's eat!"

Rodney James, Cy Young Award winner, husband, father, Christian, sat at one end of a long dining room table heaped with bowls of food while Bobby Giacquinto, writer,

husband, father, cheat, sat at the other end. Claire James
hovered over each, in turn, pouring white wine into crystal
glasses. Her dangling cross made a sound like chimes
against the bottle of wine. She put the bottle on the table
and sat between the two men. She folded her hands and
surveyed her table with a smile. Steam rose from the bowls
of hot food. Bobby reached for the mashed potatoes just as
Claire and Rodney James lowered their heads. Rodney
began to say grace. Bobby pulled back his hands and lowered his head. Rodney James thanked the Lord for the next
ten minutes, and then raised his glass of wine, cupped in
both hands, and blessed it. He took a sip and passed it to
his wife. She held it in both hands, too, and sipped, and
then passed it to Bobby. Bobby sipped, too, and handed
the glass back to Claire, who returned it to Rodney. Rodney put down the glass, looked up, smiling, speared a thick
piece of pot roast and dropped it onto his plate.

"Are you a Christian, Bobby?" Rodney said as he heaped
his plate with food.

"Yes, I guess so," Bobby said. "I'm a Catholic."

"Oh," Rodney nodded solemnly. Claire was heaping her
plate with food, now. Her fork flashed over the table so
swiftly Bobby saw it only as a blur. She speared a piece of
bread, lathered it thick with butter, and began to eat, her
head low to the plate. Bobby complimented her on the
meal. She nodded, without speaking, her mouth filled with
food. Still chewing, she reached for her glass of wine and
drained it. Then she poured another.

"It's the only way to go," said Rodney, in between bites.

"Excuse me?" Bobby said.

"A Christian," Rodney said. "It's the only way to go. I
mean, it really works. Rodney James's whole life was
turned around when he accepted Christ. He made things
happen."

Bobby looked up from his food. "Who?"

Rodney stopped chewing and looked at Bobby. "Who
what?"

"Who made things happen?"

"Oh! Christ, of course. He's the source of it all. Fame. Success. Money. Boy, it just pours in. Like a rainbow. Isn't that right, Claire?"

Claire James looked up, startled, from her plate, as if she had been caught napping in church. Her eyes darted first to Bobby, then to her husband, and then she saw that the wine bottle was empty. "Certainly, dear. More wine?" She jumped up and went into the kitchen. Rodney grinned across the table at Bobby. He held the grin for a long moment and then it faded. Claire returned with a bottle of wine. She poured wine into Bobby's glass, then some into Rodney's glass, and then she sat down. When the men resumed their conversation, she poured more wine into her own glass.

"That's why I founded the CCABA," Rodney was saying. "Rodney James wanted to give something back to Christ. He wants to turn others around, too." Bobby looked at him again. Rodney added, quickly, "Rodney James. I mean me. *I* want to turn others around."

Bobby nodded. "You mean, like by running for political office?"

Rodney smiled at him, that same humble yet smug smile of his that seemed reserved for a child. "Sort of, Bobby. But I'd like to think I'm not that shortsighted. I'd like to affect more than just politics, or the media, or the family. Rodney James would like to have a profound Christian influence over every facet of American life. He owes it to himself, and to every American who hasn't been as fortunate as he. When Rodney James leaves baseball in a few years, he will put all his energies into that end."

"How do you plan to do that?"

Rodney smiled. "Well, let's just say I plan to, Bobby, and leave it at that."

They ate in silence for awhile. Every so often, Claire James would look up from her plate and her eyes would dart over the table. Then she would jump up with an empty bowl, leave the room, and return with it filled. She drank steadily from her glass of wine. Every so often Rodney would look at her as she raised the glass to her lips, but she pretended not to notice him. Finally, Bobby asked about Stanley Muraski. Claire James sucked in air and looked to her husband. Rodney was shaking his head.

"Poor Stashu," he said, then sighed. "Him, I could do nothing for. I found him a few years ago in a wino hotel in Grapevine. He was dying. Hadn't eaten for days. His teeth were rotted. His skin was covered with sores. I made him get down on his knees with me and pray, right there, for Christ's help. He started to cry, like a baby. I'm not ashamed to admit I did, too. I took him home with me, to Pasadena. He smelled so bad I had to open all the windows and the sunroof in my car. I washed him in our bathtub and put him to bed. He lived with us for almost three months. I got his teeth fixed, and his skin, and then I got him into a Christian detoxification program. When he sobered up, I got him a job. As a school crossing guard. The kids loved him. One day I even took him to the stadium and they let him come into the Stars locker room. I got him an autographed ball, from all the guys. He was moved, I think. Then a few days later, Claire found an empty wine bottle in the garbage can. I confronted Stashu, but he denied it. And then Claire found another, and another, and one day Stashu was gone. I guess he returned to Grapevine but I haven't seen him since, God bless his soul."

"What do you think started his drinking?" Bobby said. "His mother thinks it had something to do with what happened that spring you were both rookies with the Stars."

" 'Sixty-eight," Rodney said. "Yes, I guess it did. We used to run together, Stashu, me, and Tony Vincent. Do you remember him?" Bobby nodded. Rodney smiled and shook his head. "That Tony, he loved the . . . he was very popular with the female fans. Anyway, I admit, I was a little wild then myself. I'm not proud of it. Nor ashamed of it. It's just a fact. The world knows. After I accepted Christ, I gave witness to my past sins many times. Once on the 'John Davidson Show.' After my rookie year. It was my first prime time appearance on a network show. Since then, of course . . . well . . . you know. I've been on all the shows." He stopped speaking and looked at Bobby as if he no longer recognized him. "Where was I?" he said. "Oh, yes. Stashu. 'Sixty-eight. Well, the Stars were only going to take two of us back to Hollywood that year. It was a toss-up, really, between me, Tony, and Stashu. We all pitched well that spring. Since Tony had matinee idol looks, the front office felt he would bring in fans, so it really all came down to either me or Stashu. Then one night, Stashu got drunk and couldn't pitch the next day. The front office decided he was too much of a headache, so they sent him back to the minors. It was a terrible blow. Poor Stashu never got over it. He just drank more and more heavily each year, until, well.... Tony only lasted a few years with the Stars ... the ladies, you know. And I, well, I became a star and won the Cy Young Award in 1974. It was all Christ's will, you know, although still I feel somehow responsible for Stashu's life. If only I could have helped him that spring. I had found Christ by then, you see, and so I didn't go drinking with Stashu that night. If I had, I might have been able to get him back to the hotel before he had gotten too drunk, and maybe everything would have been different."

Rodney closed his eyes and shook his head slowly, as if in great sorrow. Then he opened his eyes and looked at Bobby. He held his hands, palms up, in a gesture of helplessness. Bobby nodded and looked down at his plate. Claire James let out a sigh, as of relief, and got up to get more wine. Just then, there was the sound of a small child crying out for its mother. Rodney looked up. "My son," he said. "He must have had a nightmare. Excuse me, Bobby, I'll be right back."

Rodney James left the room just as his wife was returning with another bottle of wine. She leaned, unsteadily, over Bobby's shoulder, and began to pour wine into his glass. She swayed, lightly, as if with a breeze, and Bobby could feel her breasts against his shoulder. She tottered against him, spilling wine in his lap.

"Oh! I'm sorry!" She dabbed at the spilled wine with the hem of her sweater. Her face turned a pale rose color.

"That's all right, Mrs. James. It's nothing." She sat down, poured herself more wine, and took a long drink. She averted her eyes from Bobby and picked at the few bits of food left on her plate. Bobby smiled at her and said, "How many children do you have, Mrs. James?"

"Two," she said. "Two sons."

"You mean one son, dear." Rodney James was standing in the doorway, grinning at his wife. Bobby looked at him, and then back to Mrs. James.

"Oh. yes. We *had* two sons," she said staring at her plate as she spoke. "One of them died. He was only three months old. Rodney, Junior."

"Oh, Jeez! I'm sorry. I didn't know," Bobby said, but she seemed not to hear him.

"He got this terrible fever late one afternoon. Rodney said it was nothing, just something babies got all the time. He said it would be all right to take the baby to the hospital after I drove him to the ballpark. He was supposed to pitch that night. It was a very important game. Against the Reds or the Giants or . . . I don't recall, just now. By the time I got my baby to the hospital he was sleeping, I thought. I had to sit in an office answering questions for the nurse. When she found out I was Mrs. Rodney James she got so excited. She called in some other nurses and they asked me a million questions, you know, about Rodney. What was he like at home? Was he really as handsome as he looked on television? I had to tell them—I was his wife—so I began to talk. I was holding my baby in my arms—he felt so hot—but for some reason I couldn't stop talking about Rodney. Then I felt his body go limp and I looked down and there was a speck of blood in the corner of his mouth, no bigger, really, than a teardrop, but still, I couldn't stop talking about Rodney."

Finally, she did stop talking. No one spoke for a long while. Bobby could not look away from her. She looked up at him and smiled, a beatific smile. The smile of one who has already found heaven. "I'm sorry," she said. "I talk too much. Rodney told me you were a writer and there were things I shouldn't tell you."

•   •   •

It was dark when Bobby left the house. Rodney James stood in the doorway, a dark silhouette framed by light, and waved. Then he turned his back on Bobby, went inside, and closed the door. Bobby drove a few yards and then pulled the car over to the curb. He took out a notebook and began to write. He wrote quickly in the dark, and when he was finished he put the car in gear and began to drive off. He looked into the rearview mirror and saw the cross over Rodney James's front door. The cross was outlined with red lights. The lights were blinking on and off, like a beacon.

· FOUR ·

"He's dead," the old man said. Babe Henry stood in the doorway of his trailer in the late morning sun, a stooped, old man with dark glasses and slicked-back yellowed hair that had once been white. He wore a soiled, white, dress shirt buttoned at the throat and wrists.

"I didn't know," Bobby said standing outside in the dust. "I'm sorry."

The old man nodded. "Died at the Detox. Vitaminosis."

Bobby was standing inside a low picket fence that circled the old man's aluminum Airstream trailer at the far end of the Grapevine Trailer Park. The other trailers were modern rectangular boxes whose once bright colors had faded and chipped with neglect. The park was barren of trees and shrubs and grass and, instead, had been landscaped with wheelless old cars propped on cinder blocks and deflated black tires and crankshafts and short blocks and cylinder heads that had turned orange in the dust. A small child in soiled underwear sat playing in the dust. A grinning blond-haired boy with wide, unblinking eyes had assumed a fencer's pose in the middle of the lot and was slashing the air with an automobile antenna. A mongrel dog yapped at his heels.

"I talked to him a month ago," Bobby said. "I wanted to write a story about him. I came all the way from the East."

"He told me you was comin'," the old man said. "I didn't believe it. You know them winos." He tapped the side of his head with his forefinger. "Wet brain. Like mush. He couldn't tell the truth 'cause he didn't know it. Except when it come to baseball. He couldn't lie about that, and he couldn't forget it." The old man laughed to himself.

"Baseball players is funny drunks, you know. They can't remember to tie their shoelaces in the morning, but, Lord, you ask them about a game twenty years ago, and they can tell you how the shadows fell across homeplate in the third inning of a twilight game in August, and how they hung a slider to this big, dumb rookie who fouled it off behind the first-base boxes where this pretty blonde was sittin' with her legs spread just so." The old man grinned and shook his head. "They can remember the smell, too, if you know what I mean. All the way from the pitcher's mound."

Bobby smiled at the old man and said, "Old sportswriters are supposed to have pretty good memories, too, I hear."

"That's what they say. We just don't have much to remember, that's all."

"You remember Stashu, don't you? You knew him better than anyone." The old man nodded. "That's why I'm here," Bobby said.

"All right, then. Come on inside." The old man turned and disappeared inside. Bobby followed him. The trailer was dark. Shades were drawn against the sunlight. Bobby smelled cat urine and stale food and sweet cough medicine. When his eyes adjusted to the darkness he saw a sink filled with dirty dishes. A cat lay sleeping on the counter. Stacks of yellowed newspapers filled the room, ran from floor to ceiling, spilled onto the sofa, the floor. Some of the papers had been spread over the linoleum floor and were soiled with cat droppings. Another cat was eating from a bowl on the floor. The old man gestured with a toss of his hand toward the sofa. Bobby shooed away still another cat and sat down. He took out his notebook and a pen.

"Better than fish," the old man said as he sat in a rocking chair.

"Excuse me?"

"The newspapers. Some people wrap their old newspapers around dead fish. Me, I use my old columns to soak up cat piss." The old man laughed, and then began to cough. Without looking, he reached a hand toward the end table alongside his chair. His fingers, stained with nicotine, crawled over the table until they felt a bottle of cough medicine. They wrapped around the bottle. The old man threw back his head and drained the sweet syrup in a gulp. He wiped his lips with the back of his hand.

"A tickle in my throat," he said. "Had it twenty years. Cheracol is the only cure." Again his fingers crawled over the table until, this time, they felt an ashtray. The fingers sifted through the cigarette butts in the ashtray, feeling each one until they found the largest butt. He raised the butt to his lips, his fingertips now coated with gray ash, and turned his face toward Bobby. "Do you mind? A light."

"Oh, sure." Bobby lighted the butt. The flame from the match illuminated the old man's face. Bobby saw, behind the dark glasses, that the old man's eyes were pink-rimmed and moist.

"Cataracts," the old man said. "Had three operations in three years and still can't see worth a shit." He shook his head. "Too many goddamned years pounding a typewriter in some press box after they turned out all the lights. I had to light a match after every sentence to see what I'd written." He laughed. "One night at Hollywood Stadium, I was in such a rush to make a deadline I dropped a lighted match into my typewriter. The whole last page of my column went up in flames. Jesus H. Christ! I thought I was gonna burn down the ballpark. It was a good lesson though."

"What do you mean?"

The old man looked at him, grinning. "I phoned in the column without the last page. Nobody knew the difference. A humbling experience, I tell you." He leaned back in his rocking chair and took a long drag on his cigarette butt. "Now, let me see . . . Stanley Muraski . . . Nickname: Stashu . . . Born: December 7, 1946, in Bristol, Connecticut . . . Number: forty-eight . . . Position: pitcher . . . Bats: left . . . Throws: left . . . Height: five foot ten . . . Weight: one fifty-five . . . Major league experience: none . . . Minor league experience: nine years . . . Acquired: signed as free agent out of high school in 1963 by Floyd 'Pappy' Wright

... Background: led all high school pitchers in the nation in strikeouts and bases-on-balls in senior year ... Minor league: won twenty-eight games and lost fifty-six games in first five professional seasons despite setting strikeout records in every league he pitched in. Also set bases-on-balls and hit-batsmen records each year. Found control in summer of sixty-seven and fashioned a ten-ten record in the Three-I League,with a league-leading 2.01 ERA.Considered one of the Stars's three top rookie pitching prospects in spring training of 'sixty-eight, along with Tony Vincent and Rodney James ... Major leagues: pitched fifteen innings in 'sixty-eight spring training for the Stars. Fanned twenty-one batters, walked five, hit one, surrendered seven hits and two earned runs. Returned to the Stars minor league training complex for further seasoning ... Personal: Stashu Muraski never did fulfill his promise of the spring of 'sixty-eight. Played five more seasons of minor league baseball with only modest success before retiring from professional baseball in 1972. Last known address: Grapevine, California. Occupation: unknown. ..."

The old man closed his eyes and laid his head on the back of the rocking chair. Facing the ceiling, he began to rock slowly. Bobby's pen was poised over his notebook. The old man said, "I first saw Stanley in the spring of 'sixty-eight. My column, 'Babe's Banter,' was in the Hollywood papers then, so I used to follow the Stars every spring at Ft. Lauderdale. I saw him pitch by accident. A B-squad game at 10:00 A.M. You know. A lot of rookies with no chance. Some veterans hanging on. A few front-liners working their way into shape because they reported late. It didn't mean nuthin'. Just a good sweat, you know. A quiet game under a hot sun. Lord, it was hot! Every sound was muffled by the heat. Every color blurred. The ball all soft-edged like a clump of cotton. It moved kinda lazylike over the grass and it seemed to hang in the sky like it didn't weigh nuthin'. Weren't hardly anybody in the stands. Just me, lookin' for a column. You know, something different. I was sittin' along the first-base line, behind some wives. Rookie wives, you know. Cheering their husbands on. Ha!

Like it made any difference. Maybe it did. The difference between a summer in Portland or Odessa. In between innings, they took turns going high up to the shaded part of the bleachers so they could change their babies' diapers. There were a few old-timers, too. Retired folk with nuthin' to do but spend their mornings trying to pick out a rookie who'd become a star someday. Just so they could say, 'I told you so,' to their neighbor. The funny thing is, they'd all be dead before they ever knew if their predictions came true.

"Stanley was the middle man. He came on in the fourth. A little guy with these thick-lensed eyeglasses and a short-arm motion. He just sorta flipped the ball from the side of his body. He didn't look like nuthin'. Just another scared rookie blinkin' too much when he took the sign. His first pitch rose four feet over the batter's head and rattled the homeplate screen. The opposing dugout, I think it was the Braves, started laughin' and wavin' white towels. You know, surrendering. Then he started to throw strikes. They swung right through everything. Like they couldn't see the ball. He struck out the side that inning, so the next I went behind the homeplate screen to see what he had. You wouldn't believe it. The ball left his hand nuthin' more than a white dot, and then it disappeared, and then all of a sudden it reappeared the size of the moon. I mean, it exploded! Batters dove away from pitches right down the cock. Sometimes they just swung in self-defense to get outta there. They weren't laughing when they walked back to the dugout. Their faces was white. I never seen such fear in batters' eyes before.

"I don't remember how many he struck out that day, but it don't make any difference. Everybody took notice. I wrote a column about him, and then pretty soon everybody was writing about him. He filled those stands when he pitched after that. People you wouldn't believe. I mean, old-time baseball people. People who don't think there's been a pitcher since Walter Johnson. They was fallin' all over themselves predicting Stanley Muraski would win the Cy Young Award in 1968. And he ain't even made the club, yet! Oh, he had his drawbacks. But they didn't seem like nuthin' then. He was kinda dumb, you know. Too trusting. He believed everything the last person told him. But for a baseball player that ain't fatal. And he didn't believe how good he was. Maybe because he didn't earn it. He was just blessed. Who knows why? I mean, why him and not Rodney James? Rodney deserved it more. He worked his ass off every day, and he didn't have shit compared to Stanley. I seen Rodney get ripped one day. Five runs the first inning. *His* infielders shoulda been wavin' white towels. But he come back out the next inning, and the next, and the next, and before you know it he hung up eight goose-eggs and won the game, six-five. Stanley couldn't do that. But why should you expect him to? He was just this simple, dumb kid with a gift that was inhuman. People asked him if they could just touch his arm, you know. I saw it one day. I couldn't believe it. Stanley had this funny look on his face when this grown man asks if he can just touch his arm. 'I wanna be able to tell my kids someday,' the guy says. So Stanley just sort of hangs his arm out in the air, and both he and the guy look at it as if it's suspended there by itself, like it ain't really attached to anyone. And the guy touches it, real light, with the tip of his finger, and then he smiles.

"Now, I mean, that's too much to expect from anyone. How do you live with a blessing? Especially when you're just a Polack kid from Bristol who likes his booze. You could see it on the mound. He threw easylike, without effort, and yet he was always sweating bullets. A boozer's sweat. The front office was aware of it, but they weren't overly worried. It wasn't bad, mind you. His drinking. Just like ballplayers do. After a game they hit the pizza, the beer, and the broads. What else is there to do at midnight in Modesto? Stanley usta run with Tony Vincent and Rodney James, and then Rodney got religion that spring and dropped out. It was a smart move. The Stars were only gonna take two rookie pitchers back to Hollywood, and Rodney knew he was on the short end of the stick. He needed any edge he could get. Being a born-again was an edge. Runnin' with Stanley and Tony wasn't. I always respected Rodney's talent, if you know what I mean. On the mound, that is. Off it, he didn't appeal to me. Not my type. Too shifty, you know. The kinda guy who offers too much. You wonder why.

"Tony, now, he wasn't that bright, either, but he thought he was. He thought being slick was being smart. That's where Rodney had him. Tony's problem was his cock. Most of us carry it around with us. But Tony, his cock pulled him around. He had a nice talent, though, on the mound, I mean, but you knew the women were gonna ruin it. You could see it even then. He almost ruined Stanley, but I don't think he did. A lot of people think Tony was the one who got Stanley so drunk that night he couldn't pitch the next day. Which was why the front office sent him down. To teach him a lesson. You know, scare him a little, so's he'd snap to. They was gonna call him up real quick. They didn't know it was gonna ruin him. But it did.

"He took a train from Ft. Lauderdale to the minor league camp in Jacksonville. Maybe a five-hour ride. Took Stanley two weeks. He got off at every stop, drank himself blind, got into a few fights, and then got on the next train. When he finally got to Jacksonville, he was a sight. Black and blue. Bruises. His clothes filthy and ripped. He drank his way through that camp, and for the next five years in the minors before they finally released him. 'Seventy-two, I think. He still threw good, though. Not like he usta, but good enough. Good enough for a mortal, but not Stanley Muraski, the Fastest Pitcher Who Ever Lived. That's how the Stars billed him in the minors. They trotted him out every fourth day, drunk or sober, and made money off him. He always filled the park. It was sad, though. He was always unshaven, with the shakes, his face all blotchy, his uniform a mess, but still he could bring it. Even then, they say, those poor kids' faces was white when they stepped into the batter's box. More than one kid shit in his pants when Stanley Muraski squinted down at him through those thick glasses. By then, the Stars had given up all hope he'd ever make it back. They just wanted to get what

they could outta him. But it wasn't worth it. He was a bad
influence on the young kids. The front office couldn't hide
him anymore. They made him room alone to protect their
kids, but that only made Stanley drink worse. They even
told him he didn't have to come out to the park on days he
wasn't pitchin'. But that just gave him more time to drink.
Finally, they chucked in the towel.

"He drifted around a bit, trying to hook on, but none of
the teams would take a chance. He ended up in South
America, pitchin' in Venezuela, the Dominican, Mexico,
and then he disappeared for awhile. There was rumors,
you know. He was a Hell's Angel in Oakland. He was with
Ché Guevara in Chile. He was a fugitive from the FBI. They
was all the same. Bigger than life. Like his talent. But
Stanley wasn't his talent, that's why he never made it. His
talent was never a part of him. It didn't even belong to
him, you know. Not like Rodney's. Anyway, what Stanley
was doin' all them years was pickin' fruits and vegetables
in the California Valley. Visalia. Fresno. Stockton. He liked
the work. It was simple. He picked all day in the fields
with a lot of Mexy families—you know, wetbacks—and
then drank cheap wine with them at night. He liked the
Mexys. They always treated him right when he pitched
there after he left the States. He used to say, 'The Mexys
and me, we the same people. We ain't got nuthin'. We work
hard to make a day. That's all the field is.' He was the only
white boy in the fields and they was amazed—the Mexys.
I mean—at how fast he worked. He usta make a game out
of it. He'd pick faster 'n' faster 'n' faster until he got ahead
of all the Mexys, then he'd sit down at the end of a row and
drink wine until they caught up. Then he'd start all over
again.

"Finally, he settled in Grapevine. He met this woman in
the fields, I think. A white girl. An Oakie. They took up.
She didn't drink or nuthin'. She just worked her ass off
with him in the fields. Boy, she could pick. They say she
was even faster 'n him with potatoes. She'd been in the
fields since she was a kid. Her first husband usta sleep in
the car, while she picked with her kids. Stanley was a

prince for her. And she, well, she was the only person who could get him sober. When he got to drinkin' too bad, she'd threaten to leave. He'd get so scared he'd sign himself right into Detox. He'd sober up for a few weeks, she'd take him back, and then it'd start up all over. He musta signed himself into Detox ten or twelve times for that old girl. Ruth was her name. I don't know much about women. I been a bachelor all these years. But I got an idea that old girl was a saint. She loved him to death. Know what I mean? She's still in the fields. Every day 'cept Sunday. You can find her at four o'clock in the morning, standing under the Cuerveca sign at the Cal-Mex Liquor Store over on Espinosa, waitin' for the pickup to take her out to the fields.

"Funny, thing is, much as they loved each other, they never talked. Ruth usta write him letters in her diary, but she never showed him. And Stanley, when he was sober he didn't say nuthin'. He never told her about his baseball. She didn't find out until I wrote a column about him one day, and she read it. She showed him the column and he said, 'Shoot, girl, that ain't me.' That night he got drunk and come stormin' out to my trailer. First time I seen him since 'sixty-eight. He told me to leave him alone. He didn't want no one to find him and start bringin' up that baseball shit again. That's why I didn't believe him when he told me you was comin' out. Only thing I can figure is he knew he was dying and he wanted to set the record straight. Now that I recall, the last month or so before he died he started comin' out to my trailer pretty regular. He'd sit there, right where you are now, drinking his wine and telling me stories about his baseball. It was like he was refreshin' his memory for a test, you know. Lord, he told me some stories. One year at Brownsville, him and Tony and Rodney got arrested so many times for tearin' up bars that their manager, an old-timer named McDuff, got a heart attack in midseason. Seems McDuff had been away from the game for years and, like most of 'em, never adjusted. He got bored tendin' some orange tree in St. Petersburg so he thought that maybe, if he got back into the game—you know, just an easy job, managing in some Class B league someplace—it might make him young again. Well, they let him manage Brownsville, and then gave him Stanley, Rodney, and Tony. The poor old bastard couldn't sleep at night. He'd get the shakes in bed waitin' for the police to call him with news his three best pitchers was in the drunk tank again. Tony put the capper on it. He called the old boy himself one night at two o'clock. 'This is the coroner,' he said. 'I got three dead bodies down here in the morgue, and they's all wearin' Brownsville Stars uniforms. You wanna come identify 'em?' McDuff had his seizure right there in bed alongside his old lady.

"That Tony, he had a sick sense of humor, you know. Stanley told me one night in Yakima he was on first base when the inning ended. He walked direct to the mound and waited for someone to bring his glove, you know, the way they do, so's he could warm up. Tony come trottin' real quick outta the dugout, stops a few yards from Stanley, and tosses his glove. Before Stanley could put it on, he sees smoke coming from it. He lets out this scream and tosses it into the air. It exploded. All the fingers flew apart like petals from a flower. Tony was laughin' so hard tears was streamin' down his face.

"Another time, in Ft. Walton Beach, the police broke down Stanley's door at midnight—shoot, musta been the only time ever he was in bed by then—and hauled him off to the lock-up for rape. Seems this little girl, she weren't fourteen yet, told her mama she was bangin' this here Stars' pitcher pretty regular. She gave her mama the address and the old girl pressed charges. The police hauled in the only guy they found there. Just Stanley's luck. Everybody knew it weren't him. It weren't his style. More like Tony's. He'd fuck a snake if somebody'd hold it. As it turned out, the charge was dropped. Seems like that bitty girl been bangin' half the town, including the policeman who dragged Stanley in. It wasn't till later they found out it was Rodney all the time. Imagine! Rodney James! Stanley was always taking the rap for him, even then. Stupid loyalty. He trusted Rodney. Shoot, he trusted everybody. Remember that night Stanley got drunk in spring training? 'Sixty-eight. It was Rodney he was drinking with.''

Bobby looked up from his notebook. "What? What did you say?"

"I said, 'It was Rodney he was drinking with.' ''

"Are you sure?"

"Yep."

Bobby sat forward in his chair. "Rodney told me he wasn't with Stashu that night."

The old man cackled, and shook his head. "That Rodney's a fox. And him a born-again. He ought to be ashamed."

"How do you know he was with Stashu that night?"

"Stanley told me so. Right there. Where you're sitting. He didn't remember nuthin' else that night 'cept it was Rodney who suggested they go out drinking. I don't know what happened that night, but I think Tony Vincent does. I asked him once. He just looked down, you know, the way he does with those bushy black eyebrows of his, and said, 'What difference does it make? Everything's gonna catch up to everybody sooner or later.' You go find Tony Vincent, he'll tell you. Last I hear, he was living out in Reno. You know, one of them legal cat houses where you can't get arrested but you sure as hell can get the clap."

The old man laughed. Then he began to cough. His fingers reached for the bottle of Cheracol.

It was four o'clock in the morning at the corner of Espinosa and Grand and the fog was so thick it obscured the railroad tracks and the wino park and the Tampico Cantina and the occasional passing car that could be heard but not seen until its green-tinted headlights cut through the fog only a few feet from where Bobby was parked. The cars passed slowly while he sat hunched down in his seat, sipping coffee from a Styrofoam cup. Across the street, the Cal-Mex store was illuminated in a haze, like a grainy photograph, by the neon Cuerveca sign over the front door. The plate glass window was protected by an iron gate.

Bobby opened his window. The fog made him shiver. He held the cup with both hands for warmth. Across the street, he could make out three shadowy figures standing under the neon sign. Their heads were bowed and their shoulders were hunched up around their necks against the morning chill. They swayed rhythmically, left and right, on the balls of their feet. One of the figures lighted a cigarette. He cupped his hands around the match and held it close to his face. Another figure raised a paper bag to his mouth and threw back his head. The third figure stood a little apart, its arms folded at the chest, its hands flattened under its arm pits. Bobby heard, behind him, the sound of hard-soled shoes on the sidewalk. Another figure appeared out of the fog and took its place under the Cuerveca sign. None of the figures spoke. They just looked down, swaying left and right, blowing warmth into their cupped hands.

Bobby got out of the car and crossed the street. He approached one of the figures and asked if he knew Mrs. Stanley Muraski. The figure raised its head and looked at Bobby. He had thick black hair and dark skin and sideburns that followed the line of his jaw like a scimitar. The features of his broad face were flattened like those of a cartoon character who had walked into a wall. *"No comprendo,"* he said, and looked away. None of the other figures bothered to look at Bobby.

"I'm Stanley's woman," said a voice. It came from the figure standing apart from the others. Bobby went over to her. She wore a kerchief, like a nun's habit, that shadowed her face, and a man's nylon windbreaker that was too big for her. The windbreaker was elasticized at the wrists and had a drawstring at the hips, like those worn by baseball pitchers when they reach first base.

Bobby introduced himself, and then said, "I'm sorry . . . about Stanley . . . if I'd known, I wouldn't. . . ." She turned her face away and held up a hand, palm out, as if to fend off light. Bobby fell silent.

Finally, she said, "That's all right. We knew you'd come. We talked about it. Sooner or later someone would be findin' him."

Bobby told her what he wanted from her. "It's an intrusion, I know. If it's too painful . . . so soon, I mean . . . I'll understand. It's just . . . I've come a long way. I thought, maybe. . . ." He stopped talking and shook his head.

She nodded. "We can talk," she said. "But I've got to work now. I'll be in the fields all day. Today is potatoes, I think. But you come by my place tonight. We'll talk some then."

While she was giving him directions to her apartment, a flatbed truck clambered over the railroad tracks, emerged from the fog, and parked alongside the liquor store. A squat woman, in a kerchief and a cloth coat that reached almost to her ankles, climbed down from the cab and went around to the rear of the truck. She unhooked the tailgate and let it down. The figures underneath the Cuerveca sign drifted over to her. Each, in turn, spoke a few words in Spanish to her, and then climbed up onto the flatbed. They sat down on the bed on either side, facing each other. Ruth Muraski was the last one onto the bed. The woman pushed up the tailgate, fastened it, got back into the cab, and drove off. Bobby followed behind in his car. His headlights illuminated the shadowy figures sitting on the bed of the truck. The truck moved slowly down Espinosa, turned left onto a dirt road, bounced noisily past wooden shacks, and then came to a stop in the dirt parking lot of a small, darkened bar. The woman got out, went around to the back door of the bar, and returned a few minutes later with a large paper bag. She went to the back of the truck, withdrew small bottles from the bag, and tossed them up to each of the figures on the bed, except for Ruth Muraski. When the truck moved off again, Bobby could make out the figures in back putting the bottles to their mouths and tossing back their heads.

After awhile the truck turned onto a two-lane blacktop. The fog grew thicker. Bobby pulled his car up closer to the truck. The figures loomed in his headlights. They stared, unseeing, across at one another. The fog was so thick Bobby could see only a few yards in any direction. The road was bordered on either side by a dirt embankment. A few feet below the embankments, on either side of the road, were the beginnings of row after row of vines that vanished, after a few feet, into the fog. Suddenly the truck pulled over and stopped by the side of the road. Bobby stopped a few yards behind. One of the figures jumped down from the bed. Caught in Bobby's headlights, he raised a forearm across his eyes. He was carrying a sack. He tossed it over the embankment and then stepped down, half-walking, half-sliding in the moist dirt. He braked himself with the palms of his hands until he reached bottom. As he bent over to pick up his sack, the truck pulled off. A few hundred yards later, the truck stopped again by the side of the road and another figure jumped down.

Ruth Muraski was the last figure off the truck. Bobby parked his car a few yards back and turned off his headlights. He saw her through the haze as a gray figure, all soft-edged and blurred. She climbed down the embankment, moved toward a row of vines, got down on her hands and knees, and began rooting in the dirt with her hands. She dragged her sack behind as she crawled, like a crab, from plant to plant. She, too, disappeared into the fog. Bobby laid his head back on the seat and closed his eyes. He woke, hours later, when a trailer truck roared by almost blowing his car off the road in its wake. It was daylight, a morning seen through a gauze curtain. The road went straight as far as the eye could see until the two lanes came together at a point on the horizon. On either side of the road were flat, irrigated fields lined, like huge sheets of paper, with endless rows of vines that vanished, far off, on the horizon. The monotony of the fields was broken, here and there, by towering oil derricks that looked like the upright skeletons of dinosaurs.

Bobby sat up and looked around. He could not spot her. Then he saw, far off to his right, at the edge of the horizon, a speck, inching forward between two rows.

It was early evening, twilight, when Bobby turned his car into the narrow dirt driveway of Ruth Muraski's apartment complex. His way was blocked by two pickup trucks that were parked facing each other at such an angle that neither could pass. Their front bumpers were only inches apart and both of their driver's-side doors were open. Two men, shirtless, grappled in the dirt. Two women, flanking them, shrieked exhortations. The men rolled over in the dirt, first toward one woman, then back toward the other. The women, leaning toward the action, shrieked and back-pedaled like defensive backs when the men rolled toward them. When the men rolled away, they quick-stepped forward and shrieked even louder. Men and women watched in silence from apartment windows. Children played on jungle gyms and swings.

Bobby backed his car out of the driveway and parked it on the street. He walked around the screaming women and the grappling men toward the back of the plain, red-brick building that had only recently been built. He passed empty cans of paint and putty and chunks of Sheetrock strewn across the sparse, new grass. He heard a siren in the distance. The siren grew louder as he pushed the buzzer to Ruth Muraski's door.

"I see you found it," she said.

Bobby nodded. "Good directions." The siren was almost deafening now. Ruth Muraski pursed her lips and shook her head.

"Always trouble," she said. "Fightin'. Drinkin'. No regard for the childrens." She motioned him inside. "I was makin' some coffee," she said. "Sit down over there." Bobby sat on the sofa in the living room while she busied herself at the kitchenette. The apartment was sparsely furnished with a few nondescript Danish-modern pieces that looked as if they had been purchased, on time, as a set— sofa, coffee table, easy chair, end table—off a Sears, Roebuck showroom floor. The furniture looked neither new nor old, merely unused. Its drab colors—olive, brown, rust —had either faded with time or else had already been drab when purchased. The apartment was timeless, without a past. There were no photographs, knickknacks, mementoes; nothing that could in any way distinguish its inhabitant from that perfect, unseen, All-American family who lived on the showroom floor of Sears, Roebuck.

"Milk and sugar?" she said looking back over her shoulder. She had a weathered, sharp-featured face with skin the color of red clay. Her small eyes were a soft brown.

"Fine," he said. She turned back to the coffee. Her reddish brown hair, tinged with gray, was pinned into a bun at the nape of her neck. She was wearing a gray sweatshirt and hip-hugger, bell-bottom jeans that had been tie-dyed, as was the fashion during the sixties. The jeans were worn thin and the flared bottoms had shrunk above the ankles. She wore no socks, just old-fashioned tennis sneakers. She was a rangy-looking woman—except for her well-rounded behind—with a hard, unpampered physicality particular to women in their forties who have spent their lives waiting tables, driving trucks, picking in the fields, fighting in darkened parking lots alongside their men, all without any loss of femininity. She was unlike those soft, pampered older women who are attractive precisely because they do not look their age. Ruth Muraski, in her hardness, was attractive precisely because she looked her age, forty-nine.

She brought him his coffee and then sat across from him in the easy chair. He sat forward, on the edge of the sofa, and sipped his coffee.

"I suppose I should start from the beginning," she said in a hard, flat voice. She sat back in the chair and crossed her legs. "It musta been about eight years ago. I was workin' in a hotel on Espinosa. Night clerk. He come in from Stockton with a buncha pickers. Just another drunk, I thought. He didn't hardly speak. He'd just go to work in the darkness and come back in the darkness, with his wine and his chili dog. He never left his room. It didn't have no windows. Just a rickety ol' bed and a chair. I started takin' notice after awhile. He wasn't like the others. Blacks. Mexicans. He was the only white boy in the fields them days. I wondered why. I tried to talk to him but he didn't hardly answer. He'd just put his head down and shuffle his feet and nod. Like a little boy. He seemed so sweet. Weak maybe. We womens is suckers for weak men, ain't we?

Sometimes I think we don't really want a man. Just a little boy. After awhile I wanted to mother him so bad. Hell, I was ten years older.

"He usta leave his key over the door. I started leavin' him notes under the key. Little ones at first. Then longer ones. Love letters, I guess you'd call 'em. He didn't even know where them notes was comin' from at first. He'd come down in the morning readin' my note, shakin' his head as he went out the door. When he realized who it was, he got even more shy. Couldn't hardly look at me. He wouldn't mention them. Finally, I just went up to him and told him I was gonna do his laundry. Man, his T-shirts and shorts was so dirty. Black. I had to soak 'em in Purex. I'd just take so many pains with them clothes, you know. Fold 'em. Take 'em up to his room. He'd be layin' there on his bed, eatin' his chili dog, drinkin' his wine, lookin' so tired. He worked so hard, you know. He worked his ass off in them fields. He usta put a bottle of wine at the beginnin' and end of each row and then just pick his way, like a machine, from bottle to bottle.

"Finally, he got up the nerve to ask me out. We went dancin'. It was just like I thought it'd be. . . ." She averted her eyes from Bobby, as if embarrassed. Then she said, "It weren't long after that we took up. I quit my job so's I could work in the fields with him. It was like heaven. I was with him every minute. Even waitin' in the fog at the Cal-Mex was heaven. I'd hook my arm in his, you know, so proud. . . . Workin' in the fields wasn't new to me. I'd been pickin' since I was a girl back in Oklahoma. And then in Grapevine for years before I got the job at the hotel. But I'd been away from the fields a bit when I started pickin' with Stanley. Lord, it likta kill me the first day! It was grapes, I think. I ain't no good at grapes. Grapes is nasty. It's hot under them vines. And gnats! Lord, them gnats! You pull grapes off like you was milkin' a cow. Enda the day you all blue from them grapes. I worked as hard as I could, you know, to show him. I wanted him to be so proud of me. But he worked so fast I could hardly stay up. I remember he said to me, 'Hell, girl, you just sittin' around,

ain't hardly workin'.' He was just kiddin', but I cried. I just
worked harder. Then the next day it was oranges and the
same ol' thing. He was the fastest I ever seen with oranges.
You supposta use a clipper to nip 'em off the tree, but he
just used his hand. One twist and they was off. He said it
was from his baseball. 'Same motion as throwin' a curveball,' he said. I didn't know what he was talkin' about. I
never knew about his baseball for months. Anyway, on the
third day we picked potatoes and I was faster'n him. I got
way ahead and looked back to see him sweatin' and puffin',
his face all red. I likta cry again, so's I just slowed down,
you know, let him catch up. Finally, he passed me, and I
made believe I could hardly stay with him. He said, 'Hell,
girl, can't you work?' I didn't cry that time.

"I don't know why he loved it, so. It was a game with
him. Made him so happy. He didn't know no better. I did.
He could do better'n that. After awhile I couldn't stand to
see him work so hard. Now, I think it was all because of
his baseball. When he was playin' baseball he had to live a
higher life than he wanted. He liked it lower. He couldn't
handle that high-class life. Couldn't be himself . . . until he
got out. He felt comfortable pickin'. Those were his peoples, he said. Don't matter whether I think it was true or
not. He did.

"It weren't long before his drinkin' got worse. I thought
maybe if we got an apartment, you know, settled down.
. . . He ain't had a real home since he left Connecticut. Just
hotels and rooming houses. So we took this place. But it
didn't help. His drinkin' just got worse and worse. Whenever I asked him why, all he would say was, 'It makes me
happy.' He got up every morning at three o'clock, put a
chew of tobacco in his mouth, and got dressed. He was
funny like that. Soon's he hit the floor he had to get dressed
just so. Hat and all. He usta wear this funny little sailor
hat with pictures of Budweiser beer cans on it. He pulled
the brim down over his forehead so all you could see was
his eyeglasses. Then he went into the living room and put
on the T.V. He never hardly noticed it, he just liked the
sound for company, I think. I could hear him pacin' back

and forth, back and forth. He had these keys hooked onto his belt, and they jingled, you know. He walked so delicate, Stanley. On the balls of his feet. Like he didn't want to leave no marks on the carpet. I could hear the 'ping' when he spit his tobacco juice into an empty coffee can. After awhile, he'd start to get sick, so he'd go to the bathroom where he kept the wine. On the back of the toilet. He'd take a sip or two, and then start to talk to our hamster. We had a hamster in a cage, and a cat, too. The cat was always lookin' at the hamster like it was a meal. Drove that hamster crazy. He raced around and around his cage while Stanley tried to calm him down. By the time I was ready to go to the fields with him, Stanley was feelin' pretty good. He'd be talkin' a blue streak in the living room. Sometimes to me. Sometimes to the television. Sometimes just to himself. He didn't make no sense. Just talk. Every once in awhile, if he was *really* feelin' good, he'd try to pitch again. Right there in the livin' room. He'd begin his motion, and sort of totter backward like he was gonna fall over. 'Damn, girl,' he'd say, 'I almost had it. One a these days I'm gonna get it right.' Then he'd begin again, real serious, with that stupid ol' hat pulled down over his ears. He'd do real good, too, least it seemed to me, till he got to where he was standin' on one leg, you know, like one a them Florida birds with the pink feathers. Then he'd start to totter backward again, and he'd have to stop. I'd be sittin' in this very chair, drinkin' my coffee, watchin', tryin' not to laugh. But then, after he tried five or six times, I got to feelin' bad for him, you know. He was tryin' so hard to get it right. I watched him more times than I care to remember and, still, I don't know why he kept on. What was he tryin' to get right? I asked him once. 'Nuthin',' he said. 'I ain't tryin' to get nuthin' right.' "

She shook her head and said, "Stubborn! That man was stubborn! 'Specially when it come to his baseball. He wouldn't tell me nuthin'. 'Cept sooner or later someone would be findin' him. I had to find out on my own how good he usta be." She stopped talking and leaned toward Bobby with a wincing look on her face. Her head was slightly tilted. Finally, she spoke in a small, light voice. "What I can't understand. . . . I read all them clippings. Stanley was so good. Everybody said so. Then why did it happen that way? Why didn't he become famous? I asked him once, when he was sober. He looks at me with this little, smart-ass grin, like I just asked him the stupidest question in the whole world. 'I had it,' he says, 'and I lost it. That's all, girl.' "

She sat back in her chair and crossed her legs again. Her face was blank now, without emotion, except for her eyes. They gave off light, like diamonds. Bobby was transfixed. It was the same look he had seen in Sheila's eyes when she told him about her mother's death from cancer. They were so different, he thought, Sheila and Ruth, from different worlds really, and yet, in a way, they were alike. Fierce women. Too much for most men.

"Not that I care, mind you," Ruth said in that hard, flat voice of hers. "I'm glad what happened to him, his baseball. I never woulda met him if he became famous. Ain't that selfish? Just like a woman. But I don't care. I don't care maybe he wouldn't a died if he became famous. I only care that I had him for a little bit at least."

She stared across at Bobby and through him for a long moment, and then she shook her head as if to break a spell. She forced a smile. "Here, let me get you some more coffee," she said.

"No, thanks. That's all right."

"Well, let me get you sumthin'," she said, standing up. "I sure ain't very hospitable, talkin' your ear off."

"No, really. You've been great. I don't want to impose any more than I have."

She laughed. "Impose! Shoot, boy, I hardly talked to anyone since Stanley died."

She went to the kitchenette and opened the refrigerator. Bobby watched as she bent over, her backside to him, and looked inside. He sat back on the sofa, curiously sapped of strength. But not unpleasantly so. Rather, strangely comforted, at ease, unburdened of a great weight. She had called him "boy." He smiled. Ruth Muraski would make

any man feel like a boy. A nice feeling, at times. She was a
maternal woman, fiercely so, like an animal. Like Sheila.
It scared most men. Only the very smart or the very innocent could handle it. Others turned on it, which was why
Sheila fought it so, her instinct to please. It made her vulnerable. He remembered the time he had met her in a bar.
She smelled of perfume.

"For me?" he had said with a smile.

"No!" she said, so quickly it stunned him. "I had a faculty meeting. I always give myself a little spray just before."

"Oh" he nodded, grinning. "Sure, babe."

Later that night, after they had made love on the floor of
his office, she sat up, cross-legged, and said, "I *did* do it for
you! The perfume, Bobby! I want so much to please you!"
He raised himself on one elbow and looked at her. "I didn't
want you to know," she said.

"But why?"

"I don't know."

From the kitchenette of Ruth Muraski's apartment,
Bobby heard her say, "I searched everywhere. No liquor.
No beers, Nuthin' but a bottle of Stanley's wine."

"I'll have a taste of that," Bobby said. "I should try it, at
least, huh?"

"Suit yourself." She brought him the bottle and sat
down across from him. A hard woman. Yet vulnerable, too.
Without pride. Or memory. It was how she differed from
Sheila. Sheila never forgot. And always, the next man paid.

Bobby unscrewed the cap from the small green bottle
and sniffed. It smelled of sugar and chemicals.

"That wine never seen a grape," she said. "Sooner or
later every drunk becomes a wino, and every wino drinks
White Port."

"Why's that?"

"It's cheap. Less than a dollar a bottle. And it gets you
high fast. Keeps you there, too. Longer than beer or liquor.
It's got ether in it. You know, like laughing gas. Why, I
seen rich peoples come across town in taxis so's nobody
would recognize them, just so's they could buy some White

Port at the Cal-Mex. Stanley, he never went nowheres without his bottle tucked into his belt at the hip."

"But why White Port and not red?"

"Because when a wino starts throwin' up, he wants to see if there's blood. Then he knows he's hurtin'."

Bobby nodded, then raised the bottle to his lips and sipped. He gagged on the syrupy sweet liquid that tasted like medicine.

"Killer, ain't it?" she said with a grin and a shake of her head. "Turns your brains to mush. Most winos go insane. If they're lucky they die of vitaminosis. No vitamins. Winos never eat. Stanley, before he died, he didn't eat for a week. I couldn't force food into him. Finally, I threatened to leave him. It was the only way I could get him into Detox. I never woulda left that man for nuthin', though, I knew what I was gettin' when I hooked up with him. I just threatened him a lot. Once I even did throw him out. He went back to the hotel where we met, over on Espinosa and Grand." She laughed, silently, and shook her head. Bobby sipped from the wine. "Likta fix me good," she said. "I waited a few days, you know, to scare him good. All the while I could hardly stand it, the worry, so finally I go to get him. He was gone. I was sick to my stomach right there in his room. I went crazy, lookin' all over town for him. Other hotels. The wino park. Everywhere. Then I get this call from a guy, his name was Rodney James, he said he usta play baseball with Stanley years ago. He was a star out in Hollywood. I swear, that's what he said. Then I remembered I seen his name once or twice in them stories about Stanley I read in newspapers. Do you know him?"

"Yes, I know him," Bobby said. He sipped again from the wine. He felt a strange buzzing in his head. It was a new sensation, different from the high, light-headed buzz he was used to. This one was a heavy droning at the temples, very loud, insistent, one that would not be gone by morning.

"Well, it seems this Rodney fella been lookin' for Stanley for years. I don't know why, but he was. So he takes him back to his house near Hollywood, cleans him up and all, gets him sober, and pretty soon Stanley's callin' me every day. Stone sober, mind ya. I'd pick up the phone and there he'd be. He wouldn't say nuthin'. He never talked when he was sober. He stayed there . . . I don't know . . . a coupla months . . . all the time me wantin' him back so bad, but I never said nuthin'. Then one day he calls up drunk again. 'Damn, girl!' he says. 'I can't take any more of this boolshit!' I says, 'What boolshit?' And he says, 'This religious boolshit! The man ain't my people anymore. He makes me get down on my knees every night and pray to the Lord before I go to bed. Me and him, side by side. Two grown men. It ain't right. I think I rather be drunk. I be comin' home.' "

She looked again at Bobby with that blank face, and then she said, "I was glad. I rather have him with me drunk than not with me at all. I know that ain't right, but that's me." Her voice seemed to be receding, to be coming from some place behind her. It passed through a tunnel. Bobby forced himself to concentrate, to bring it into focus without the echo. He heard her voice. "You feelin' all right? You lookin' kinda funny."

Then he heard his voice, too, coming from somewhere else. "No, I'm fine. Go on." He took another sip of sweet wine and waited for her to speak. His features began to arrange themselves into a smile. He tried to stop them but he couldn't. He tried hard, and harder until, finally, what seemed a long while later, his smile dissolved.

"That was about a year ago," he heard her voice say. "Stanley been drinkin' bad ever since, until he ended up in Detox this last time. I could tell sumthin' was wrong 'cause when I threatened to leave him if he didn't sign himself in, he agreed right away. His eyes was scared, like sumthin' was happenin' inside him he didn't know. Sumthin' new. I asked him if he was feelin' pain. 'Worse,' he says. 'I ain't feelin' nuthin'. Not even sick.' Soon's they took him off the wine he got a seizure. Almost swallowed his tongue. They had to strap him down. I think he broke sumthin' inside. When I visited him a few days later, he didn't look right. Like always before, after a few days off the wine, he'd be up and about. Soon's I'd come through the front door I'd spot him, wearin' that silly johnny coat with his skinny legs hangin' out. And them backless slippers they always give him. He'd be shufflin' up and down that narrow hallway, you know, them slippers makin' that slappin' sound you always hear in Detox. They had a brass handrail, like dancers use, on either side of the hallway. There was always a line of winos holdin' on to that rail for dear life as they shuffled so slow up to the front door, and then back down on the other side to the wall. Them tile floors was as smooth and shiny as glass. They never had to wax 'em. Anyway, like I said, always before I could pick out Stanley, no matter how dark that hallway was, or how many winos was there. He was so proud, you know, he would make sure I never caught him holdin' on to that rail. It was like he was showin' me he weren't as far gone as them others. But this last time when I come, he was holdin' on. Not only that. He weren't movin'. Just holdin' on to that brass rail with two hands, like he was on a wavy boat, with this look in his eyes, like a little boy who done sumthin' so bad nobody will ever forgive him."

The voice stopped. Bobby tried to focus on her face, her soft brown eyes, but it began to soften at the edges, to melt like hot wax. His eyelids grew heavy, closed, then opened again. The room was spinning. Slowly at first, then faster and faster, like a ride at an amusement park, and he was pinned, by the centrifugal force, against the back of the sofa. He opened his eyes very wide, kept them from blinking until the room began to slow down just enough for him to hear her voice, now coming from a very great distance away. "He died the next day. They called me. . . . I'll never understand why that man threw his life away like that. He thought it was a big joke. Like it weren't really happenin' to him. I mean, even when it did happen to him it was like he didn't feel it. Like he was outside, lookin' in. Laughin' at what he saw. That's the way he was. Until the end. He weren't laughin' then. He was scared. Awful scared. He knew it was happenin' to him then. . . ."

Bobby, in a dream, is lying sideways on cool sheets, his naked body pressed tight against Sheila's naked backside. His cock grows hard and painful against her buttocks. His face, nuzzling the nape of her neck, is tickled by her sweet-smelling hair. He feels, in the palm of his hand, a breast. Soft, malleable, floating loose inside her stretched-out skin. He slides his flattened hand down over her ribcage into the scooped out hollow of her stomach. He feels each ridgelike muscle beneath skin as light as tissue. The skin bunches up under his hand until it reaches her hard, half-moon, baby-scarred belly. He pauses, caresses the belly with small circles. She stirs. His hand moves down into her hair. Black garnish around tenderest slices of sex. His hooked finger slips, without effort, up into her moist, warm sex. She shudders, hooked, and begins to undulate backward like an eel. . . . They sleep. . . .

Bobby heard a voice. "You was passed out." He opened his eyes wide to see where the voice was coming from. He saw a shadow bathed in morning light standing over him. He tried to sit up but the pain over his eyes forced him back down onto the bed. He pressed his eyes shut against the pain and the light, and then opened them. She was standing by the bed, dressed in a worn bathrobe. "Boy, you was heavy," she said, smiling. "I had to put you to bed myself." She hugged herself and looked away. "I slept on the sofa."

Bobby tried to sit up again, but the pain was unbearable. "Jesus!" he said. "My fucking head!" His mouth tasted of sweet medicine.

"You be all right," she said, smiling again. "I got you some aspirin and some coffee in the kitchen. Your clothes is over there." She left the bedroom. Bobby lay on his back, under cool sheets, and tried to focus his eyes on the ceiling. Slowly, his vision cleared. The pain subsided slightly. He reached for the sheets and pulled them off. He was naked.

•　　•　　•

Driving toward the airport, Bobby pulled the car off the freeway and stopped beside a pay telephone. He dialed long distance and billed it to his office. He heard Sheila's voice amid the roar of passing traffic.

"It's me," he said.

"What? Who is this?"

He shouted over the noise from passing cars and trucks. "It's me! Bobby!"

"Oh, Bobby! Thank God! I've been so worried!" She was silent for a moment, and then her voice became distant. "Why didn't you call?"

"I couldn't. I was working and . . ."

"Not even to say hello?"

Bobby did not answer. Then he said, "Listen, babe, I love you. Isn't that enough?"

"I don't know."

He stood there by the side of the road. He was silent for a long while.

"Babe, I have to go to Reno for a few days. Nevada. Can you meet me there?" She did not answer. "Can you?"

Finally she spoke in a small voice that he could barely make out. "Yes," she said. "I'll be there."

· FIVE ·

In Reno, they made love in a bed for the first time. Sheila, kneeling, straddled Bobby, lying on his back. She leaned over him, her hands planted into the bed for support, and ground her hips into his. Her stomach undulated like a snake. It sucked in so deeply that it looked hollowed out, as if it had no insides. The slack skin at her stomach hung down in folds. Bobby reached down and laid the flat of his hand against the soft, dead skin. He could feel no fat underneath the skin, only muscle, undulating like a snake shedding.

She straightened up and glared down at him with fierce, unblinking, blue eyes. He reached up with both hands and grasped her loose breasts. She closed her eyes and threw back her head. He squeezed her breasts. She moaned, arched her back, and planted her hands behind her on the bed. The skin at her curved belly was taut now, and the muscles underneath seemed about to burst through. With one final thrust of her hips, she came. Her body went limp, her breasts and stomach sagging, and then she slumped forward on top of Bobby. With a thrust of his hips, he spilled her off him. She lay, breathing heavily, on her stomach. Her legs were spread in a V. Bobby knelt between her legs. Her face was buried, sideways, in the pillow; her black hair spread across the sheets. With his eyes, Bobby traced the curve of her back down to the valley of her spine and then up sharply to the rise of her high, taut, perfectly shaped ass. He leaned over and ran his tongue between the crack. She shivered. He grasped her hips with both hands and pulled her up onto her knees. Her hips and the cheeks of her ass flared out. Her face was still buried in the pillow.

She reached out on either side of her and dug her fingers into the sheets. Still gripping her hips, Bobby entered her. The muscles in her back bunched up. He began to thrust, slowly at first. She raised her ass higher and pushed it toward him. The curve of her spine became even more pronounced. Sheila began to grunt in unison with each thrust. The two, small, knotlike muscles on either side of her spine where it met her ass began to twitch as he buried himself into her. Bobby spread her legs wider with his knees and began to thrust faster and deeper. His belly slapped against the cheeks of her ass, which quivered. He squeezed her hips until the flesh turned white. The muscles high up on her back turned bright pink and bunched up toward her neck. Sheila was grunting loudly now, with each thrust. Her knuckles were white. Her body began to shudder and then she cried out. Bobby buried himself deep inside her. He held himself there without moving until her shuddering stopped and her body went limp. He withdrew from her and rolled her onto her back with both hands. Her face was splotchy and she was breathing heavily through her open mouth. Still kneeling between her legs, Bobby gripped both of her ankles in his hands and raised her legs into the air and back toward her head so that her ass was elevated a few inches off the bed. Her sex was split open. Bobby looked at it for a moment, and then lowered his face to it. Sheila began to moan. Bobby's face, buried in her sex, moved up and down as she moaned. She reached down with both hands and grabbed his hair. Suddenly, her body stiffened, and she forced his face tight against her. She held him there, by his hair, until her body relaxed and then she let go. Bobby raised his face, gasping for air. He knelt between her legs, still holding her ankles above her. When his breathing subsided, he entered her again, and began to thrust. Trapped in his grip, unable to move, she could only raise her head a bit and look down at him. She watched in wonder as he entered and withdrew from her body. He began to thrust faster and deeper. She closed her eyes and her head fell back on the pillow. She reached behind her with both hands and gripped the headboard of the bed. Her head was twisting left and right on the pillow as Bobby thrust faster and faster. "Fuck me, Bobby!" She said. "Fuck me! Fuck me! Fuck me!"

They came together, with a cry, and Bobby, drenched with sweat, released her legs and slumped forward on top of her. She winced with pain as she brought her cramped legs slowly back down to the bed. Bobby's face was buried in the crook of her neck, his labored breathing in her ear. "Shhh, babe," she said. "Shhh." She stroked the back of his head until his breathing was steady and then she reached down with her hands and gripped the cheeks of his ass and pressed him tightly to her. Soon, he was asleep. She lay there, awake, bearing his weight for as long as she could, and then, without waking him, she eased out from under. He curled up on his side, away from her. She pressed her hot body against his, and threw her arm over him. Soon, she fell asleep, too. When she turned away from him during the night, Bobby instinctively rolled toward her and pressed his body against her backside. He cupped one breast in his hand and swung a leg over her, as if to prevent her from fleeing. In this way, they slept through the night, rolling back and forth against one another as if drawn on a string.

She woke at 4:00 A.M., and went to the bathroom. Bobby reached behind him with his hand and searched the bed. He woke. Through the open bathroom door he heard her peeing. He got up and went into the bathroom. She was seated on the toilet under the bright flourescent light that cast shadows under her eyes and her neck. She was rocking back and forth, hugging herself, her legs pressed together at the knees, her face scrunched up like a child's. "Got to go sooo bad," she said. Bobby laughed. It was the first time he had seen her in the bathroom. Always before, she locked the door. Even when putting on makeup. A habit from her marriage, she said. Once, at his office, Bobby pounded on the bathroom door. "For Chrissakes, babe!" he said. "I gotta go, too!" She refused to open the door until she was finished. "Jesus Fucking Christ!" Bobby said. "What are you hiding? I've seen it all!"

Now in Reno, she was sitting before him on the toilet seat, peeing. A woman's weak trickle. So different from a man's powerful stream. When she finished, she half-rose from the seat, poised as if to sprint, wiped herself, and flushed the toilet. She went to the bathtub and turned on the shower. Bobby stepped in front of the toilet and spread his legs. He leaned forward, bracing himself with a flattened hand against the wall and holding himself with his other hand, peed. She stood up and watched, hands on hips.

"I always wondered," she said. "Who teaches a boy to pee? It looks so much more complicated than for a girl."

"It is. You gotta have brains to be a guy." He grinned at her, and as he did he peed on the wall. Sheila burst into laughter.

"Yes, I see what you mean. And dexterity, too." Sheila stepped into the tub and drew the curtain. Bobby followed her. They soaked themselves under the hot shower, and then Bobby got down on his knees in front of her. He soaped up his hands and began to wash her feet. The shower spray flattened the hair on his head into the shape of a poinsettia. He soaped each of her toes, and the rough bottoms of her feet, and her ankles, and then he began on her legs. He ran both hands up and down her legs as if he was cooling off a racehorse. He soaped his hands again and washed between her legs, both front and back. She closed her eyes and seemed about to totter backward. She braced herself with one hand against the wall. Bobby soaped her pubic hair and her belly, and then he stood up. He washed under her arms, and across her upper chest, hard and bony, and then, more delicately, always a little bit in awe, he began to wash her breasts. Light, shriveled, liquidy sacks, they seemed somehow as if they should belong to an older woman, certainly not to a woman with a body like Sheila's. She had a young athlete's body—leanly muscled, big-shouldered, small-hipped, long-legged—except for her breasts and the stretched-out skin at her belly. Reminders of her children.

When he finished, she rinsed herself off under the

shower. "Now, you," she said, getting down on her knees in front of him. She began to wash his toes, his ankles, his legs, the force of the shower sweeping back her hair so that her slightly protuberant eyes looked three-dimensional, like a doe's. When she soaped between his legs, his sex began to grow. She stopped and watched. It continued to grow. "Amazing!" she said, with a smile. "It's a wonder, Bobby!" She waited until the shower rinsed off the soap, and then, gently cradling his balls in one hand, as if an offering, she took him in her mouth. Her head moved up and down underneath the spray of water. Bobby's body began to shudder from the legs up. He grabbed the shower curtain; it ripped off in his hand. She buried his sex in her mouth and held it there until his shuddering stopped.

As they dressed, both in jeans and cowboy boots, they heard men's voices through the thin walls of the old hotel. "A poker game," Bobby said. "Jesus, I wonder what they heard in here?"

"Whatever, it doesn't seem to have disturbed their game much," Sheila said.

"I guess not," Bobby said, and they went downstairs to the casino. It was almost deserted at 5:00 A.M. A few old ladies off the early Sunday morning bus from Bakersfield were working the nickel slots. They were lined up in a row, some in wheelchairs, others in walkers, all of them facing their slots as they chatted back and forth, inserted their coins, pulled the handles, scooped up their winnings in coffee cans, inserted their coins again, all without missing a beat. Over by the reception desk, a woman in a business suit was checking into the hotel. She put her attaché case on the counter and opened it toward her. Sheila elbowed Bobby in the ribs. Inside the attaché case were fresh decks of cards, boxes of dice, colored chips, and stacks of dollar bills. Bobby smiled, then gestured with his head toward a cowboy wearing a stiff Stetson hat made of straw who was shooting craps. The cowboy had an airplane ticket sticking up out of the breast pocket of his snap-button shirt. Every time he leaned over to toss the dice, he tapped the ticket with the hand that held the dice.

Bobby and Sheila, arm in arm, began to drift through the room, past the green felt tables and red brocade curtains fastened with sashes of gilt. They stopped to admire an oil painting on the wall—a plump, pale nude reclining on satin sheets—and then some sepia photographs—sheriffs and gunfighters with handlebar mustaches and blank, startled eyes—and then some photographs of the hotel as it was when it had been first built—a log cabin by the side of a dirt road—and then later—a white, Victorian house with a wraparound porch on whose railing sat three dark, homely women in dresses with bustles—and, finally, as it was now—a nondescript, red-brick building with a blinking neon sign on Virginia Street in Reno, Nevada.

They stopped beside a kidney-shaped blackjack table where five women dealers, dressed identically in black vests and pants, were seated together, jabbering like housewives over laundry. They were plain-looking women of indeterminate age. They sipped coffee, black, from Styrofoam cups and smoked thin cheroots. One was knitting, another painting her fingernails, a third reading a paperback book about love's fiery passion, a fourth counting her tips, the fifth writing a verse poem with a lilac-colored felt-tip pen. Sheila leaned over the woman's shoulder and asked if she could read her poem.

"Why, sure, hon," the woman said, and handed it to her. Bobby and Sheila, their heads close, read together. The poem was about sweet little old ladies with hope in their hearts, and sweet little old ladies who press their bets when the dealer isn't looking. It was about dishwashers who break the bank at keno and blow it all in three days, and about husbands who lose their paychecks at craps and then beat their heads against a telephone pole on their way home so they can convince their wives they were robbed. It was about a woman blackjack dealer who was given a box of asparagus as a tip by a grower from Salinas, and about spinsterish dealers who run off with hardware salesmen after dealing them nothing but winning hands, and how, now, their photographs are plastered on the walls of all the catwalks above all the casinos on Virginia Street.

And finally, it was about the men in the lives of the women who deal blackjack in Reno. When young, these women tended to gravitate toward gamblers and drinkers, and then, in their thirties, to bartenders and crap dealers, and, finally, after too many years of living out the lyrics to a Tammy Wynette tune, they pinned their hopes and dreams on a marriage to a pit boss.

The poem went on, lyrically, about just such a pit boss. He was a stern-looking man in his fifties who first came to Reno in the forties, after he left the army. He took a job as a bartender, and then a crap dealer, and, finally, in the fifties, he became a pit boss. He told stories about the casino when it was frequented by the Lemon Drop Kid, an oily little tout with a goatee; and later, during the fifties, when Jimmy Durante and Sophie Tucker used to perform here for wealthy Jewish people, and how it was not uncommon to see high-class hookers, dressed to the nines, stroll over to a piano player to request "Love for Sale." But then in the sixties Vegas came on strong, and now the hotel is just a frumpy old lady whose faded dreams have turned to smoldering embers.

When they finished reading the poem, Sheila and Bobby looked at one another for a moment. Then Sheila handed the poem back to the woman. "It's wonderful," Sheila said, with a smile.

The woman smiled, too. "Thanks, hon," she said, and turned back to her writing.

Sheila and Bobby drifted off. Sheila put her arm around Bobby's waist and rested her head on his shoulder. He asked if she wanted breakfast. "Hmmm," she said. "Nice." Suddenly her grip tightened around Bobby's waist. "Look!" she whispered. "Over there." Bobby looked toward a blackjack table where a lone Indian was seated, perfectly erect, like a chastised child. The Indian was gaunt, long-necked, with silvery hair worn in a ponytail down his back. His wife was standing in back of him. She was a heavy woman in a wrinkled man's shirt worn outside her pants.

The dealer, a modestly attractive woman in her forties,

was standing in front of the Indian. Standing behind her, his arms folded across his beefy chest, was the pit boss. He watched her through thick-lensed eyeglasses. The dealer placed a slim hand, fingers spread, on the green felt table and waited. She had beautiful hands. Each finger was adorned with a gold ring. The Indian hesitated a moment and then slid a silver dollar forward. He folded his hands in his lap and sat as motionless as a deer caught in a hunter's sight. The dealer began to hum, her hips swaying, as her slim fingers tossed cards high into the air. The cards hovered for a moment, then descended as if on a falling cloud in front of the Indian.

Bobby and Sheila went into the coffee shop and sat at a table. A waitress, in her seventies, dressed like a cowgirl, took their order and left.

"Jesus," Bobby said. "A tough old bird."

From the next table, they heard loud voices. A man was telling three other men about his first wife.

"A schoolteacher," he said. "I was the first for her, so after we got married I sent her out to the Mustang for seasoning. While she was gone I ate nothing but oysters and olives." He shrugged. "Hell, it didn't do no good. She musta really took to the Mustang because she never came back." His friends laughed loudly at this, and one of them slapped him on the back. Another elbowed him hard in the ribs and gestured with his head toward a keno runner, a tall, beautifully built Indian girl with black, braided hair. She moved languidly through the coffee shop, calling out in a lilting voice, "Keno. Keno." She slid sideways between tables, stopped a moment to collect a keno card from a couple, then moved on in that floating, sensual way of hers. "Keno. Keno."

One of the men grabbed her arm as she passed by their table. "Come on over here, sweetie," he said. The other men grinned. The girl looked down at his hand on her arm as if it was a speck of dirt. His face reddened and he took his hand away. He was in his fifties, vigorous-looking, white-haired, a rancher in lizard-skin boots. He reached up and tugged on the leather thongs tied to the end of her braids.

"Don't do that," she said in her dreamy voice. "People been pullin' on those things all night long and I'm soooo tired of it."

"Where'd you get those things, sweetie? On the reservation?"

"No," she said. "Over at the leather store on Virginia Street."

The man smiled at his friends, then said, "Virginia Street? What's a squaw like you doin' shoppin' for leather on Virginia Street?"

She smiled down at the man. "I may be an Indian, honey . . . but I ain't no squaw." And then, with a deft, sideways step, she eluded the man's grasping hand and moved off, languidly, calling out in her lilting voice, "Keno. Keno."

"Bastards!" Sheila spoke loud enough for the men to hear if they had not been laughing loudly again.

Bobby shrugged.

"Well, they are," she said. "She should have . . ."

"What, babe? Should have what?"

"I don't know. Something."

"Maybe she needs the job." Bobby grinned across the table at her. "Maybe she can't afford your pride, babe."

Sheila looked at him, in that New York way of hers, meant to wither a man. "It's not pride," she said. "It's self-respect."

"Doesn't your self-respect get tiresome at times?"

"No."

"Never?"

"Never." Her look softened for a moment and she said, "What about you, babe? Don't you have any self-respect?"

Bobby gestured with his head toward the Indian girl. "I'm like her. It's a luxury I can't afford. I've got too many people other than myself to consider."

"I'm one of those people," she said. "When are you going to consider me?"

A long moment passed and then the old waitress brought

their food and they ate in silence, their heads down. Bobby was suddenly very tired. When they finished, he suggested they go back to the room and sleep for awhile.

"If you want," she said.

They undressed and got into bed. They lay on their backs, not touching, and, after awhile, Bobby fell asleep. Sheila looked over at him and got out of bed. She lighted a cigarette and sat, naked, in a chair by the window. She crossed her legs and leaned slightly forward, her elbow on her knee, the cigarette close to her face. Through wisps of smoke, she watched Bobby sleep. He filled the bed. A big, dark man with curly black hair and a full beard. Even sleep did not soften his face, the lines around the eyes, the look of brooding, barely controlled anger that seemed always on the verge of erupting. But never did. He would not allow it to. Except in a glance. A smile. A clipped tone in his voice. Enough to frighten Sheila. Instinctively, she would marshal her forces. And yet. . . . She was not afraid of him. Of that, she was positive. Then what?

Bobby muttered in his sleep, his dark brows furrowed, and then rolled over on his side toward the edge of the bed. He reached a hand behind, feeling, in a dream, the empty space where she had been. She got up and went to the bed. She eased herself down under Bobby's groping hand. His hand found the cheek of her ass and pulled her tight against his backside. She lay there, her face against the back of his neck, not daring to move, breathing his smell, feeling his warmth, his very real and solid flesh, and then, after a long while, she, too, fell asleep.

Sheila woke at noon. Bobby, dressed only in his bathing suit, was standing by the bed. "It's a beautiful day," he said. "Want to get some sun?"

"Mmmm, yes. Give me a minute." While she lay in bed stretching herself awake, Bobby put on a T-shirt and cut-off jeans over his bathing suit. Suddenly, Sheila bounded out of bed. She stretched her arms over her head and grimaced; then she went over to her suitcase and rummaged around for the old two-piece bathing suit she had worn that first time with Bobby on the rocks.

"Wait a minute," he said. "Try this." He tossed her a black, string bikini. "I got it in L.A.," he said. "On my way back from Grapevine."

Delicately, with a thumb and forefinger of each hand, she held up both pieces of the suit before her eyes. "Bobby! There's nothing there! It's a scandal!"

He smiled. "You're a scandal, babe. Or did you forget? You're a mistress. That's a mistress's bathing suit."

"Yes," she said. "It is." She held the panties in front of her crotch and looked down. "I've got to shave first." She went into the bathroom. Bobby heard the water running in the sink. He followed her.

"Let me do that," he said. He took the razor from her. She raised one leg and planted her foot on the toilet seat. Bobby leaned over and began to shave her pubic hair. When it was a perfect, small, triangular patch, he straightened up and examined his work.

"Not bad," he said. "I guess there's a little bit of the barber in every Guinea."

Sheila bent over double and examined herself. Her legs were spread in a comical, bowlegged way. Bobby laughed at her. "Perfect," she said, straightening up. "Now, let's see." Bobby followed her into the bedroom. Sheila stepped into the bottom half of her bikini and then held the top half against her breasts. Bobby stood behind her and tied the string at her neck. Sheila bent forward, hunching her shoulders, so that her breasts fell just so into each triangle and then she straightened up. She held her hands, fingers spread, over her breasts and waited while Bobby tied the string at her back. She turned around and struck a pose, one leg forward, hands on hips.

"Well?" she said, smiling. Bobby narrowed his eyes and studied her. He hiked up the strings of her bikini bottom and hooked them over her pelvic bones so that the hollows between her thighs and her hips were clearly exposed.

Bobby studied her again.

"Well?" she said, frowning.

Finally, he smiled. "Fucking dynamite!" He shook his head slowly.

She threw her arms around his neck and hugged him. "Thank you, babe," she whispered in his ear.

Sheila put on a white blouse and a pair of loose-fitting khaki shorts over her bathing suit, and then she and Bobby drove out to the edge of town where the desert began. The desert looked a pale rose under the brilliant sun, except for patches here and there of sagebrush and pinion and juniper. They could see, far off in the distance, the Sierra Nevada Mountains, an unbroken line of peaks the color of mustard and pale green olives and, where a shadow fell, the color of purple grapes. A few miles into the desert they came upon a towering skyscraper of glass and chrome. It cast a shadow, like a sundial, across the road into the desert. The sunlight and the desert landscape, the pinion and juniper and sagebrush, were reflected off the skyscraper's windows like a mural so that, even wearing sunglasses, Bobby and Sheila had to shade their eyes. Bobby turned the car into the parking lot. The desert images on the skyscraper's windows came alive, began to shift in shape and size, grew distorted like images in a house of mirrors. They got out of the car and walked across the asphalt, shimmering in the heat, toward the red-and-white-striped canopy over the front entrance. The glass doors opened without a touch into a cool cavernous casino filled with men in polyester suits and white patent-leather belts and loafers, and women with upswept, lacquered hair and chiffon dresses of every pastel hue. Bobby and Sheila, looking conspicuously out of place in their shorts, walked through the casino, underneath row after row of cut-glass chandeliers, past blackjack and roulette and crap tables, all of whose dealers seemed to be female college students who were being watched over by pit bosses dressed like young, midwestern lawyers. One or two of the pit bosses were women, dressed in severe business suits. Bobby and Sheila followed a sign to the side door and outside to the pool. The pool was surrounded by a high white fence meant to protect its sunbathers from gawkers in the parking lot beyond and from the constantly blowing desert wind. They walked around the kidney-shaped pool, past older women with leathery skin, and younger women, pregnant, in skirted bathing suits, and a few men, mostly older, wearing boxer trunks that reached almost to their knees and loafers without socks. When they found two unoccupied lounge chairs, they undressed and lay down in the sun. One side of the pool area was close to the hotel, which was still under construction. A skeleton of steel beams and girders, extending from the completed part of the hotel, rose halfway to the top floor. Construction workers in hard hats and jeans worked jackhammers and pneumatic drills that made an almost deafening noise. A tall woman with bleached hair walked past the workers toward the outdoor bar. She wore clear-plastic, spiked-heeled shoes and a silver lamé bikini that reflected the sun like aluminum foil. Her breasts, implanted with silicone, were perfect orbs. The workers glanced down at her. Their noise was momentarily stilled. Bobby and Sheila looked up. One of the workers whistled. Another hooted and waved his hat. The woman looked straight ahead. She wore a gauzy, white shawl, like a negligée, that billowed behind her. Her skin was like alabaster, except for the bluish dimples at the back of her thighs. The dimples quivered and puckered as she walked the length of the pool with her prim-quick-little-girl steps.

"Jesus!" Bobby said shaking his head. "A painted-up Pleasure Boat. My kind of lady."

"I'll bet," Sheila said. "What the hell are you doing with me?"

Bobby grinned at her. "Dispensing a blessing. An older broad like you, who would have you?"

"Yes, I'm so grateful, Bobby. Imagine . . . an aging Irish convent girl lucking out in her twilight years." She looked over at him.

Bobby laughed out loud. "I'm glad you understand, babe. But still, it's not a one-way street. You're good for me, too."

"Really!" Sheila said, her eyes wide open. "And how's that?"

Bobby assumed an expression of deep thought. "Well . . .

to be honest, babe . . . you make me feel . . . ah . . . deep.
Yep. That's it. Deep. All those years I was banging quiff I
thought I was shallow. Now I'm banging you and I know
I've got to be deep." He smiled at her. "You are not exactly
an effortless piece of ass."

Sheila did not smile back at him. She lay down on her
back, facing the sun, and closed her eyes. "You're right,
you know. I don't know what it is, but there's something
in me that makes men furious. The closer they get, the
more they resent me. My husband . . . he could have killed
me. I drove him nuts. It wasn't his fault, really. He was
just a simple guy who wanted to watch the Knicks on
television in bed. I wanted to read, talk, make love, anything but watch those goddamned Knicks. He'd get out of
bed with this hang-dog look and I'd say, 'Let's at least talk
about it, hon.' He'd turn his head away and throw up both
hands, palms out, as if to catch a pass without looking. He
was good at that, you know, on the basketball court, looking the other way. Jesus, I was nothing more than an er-
rant pass he was always trying to deflect. That's funny,
isn't it, babe." She laughed, soundlessly. "Poor bastard,
All he wanted was a dutiful wife and he got me. He never
talked, he never asked why. Jesus, all I ever did was ask
why. Drove him nuts. God, he began to resent me. He be-
littled me in front of the kids. I spent too much money. I
couldn't cook. I couldn't clean. I was always talking. Like
a jerk, I fell for it. I was like a dervish in that house. I
cooked and cleaned and bit my tongue, and one day I
found myself vacuuming the shag rug in the family room
so that all the shag would fall in the same direction. You
know, like a freshly mowed lawn. I caught myself in the
mirror, smiling at the rug, and that's when I knew I had to
get out. After we got the divorce, he cried all the time. Not
because of me, but because he thought he was a lapsed
Catholic now. He was afraid if he left the house he'd get
hit by a car and go straight to hell. Finally, I agreed to get
an annulment from the church, just to give him some
peace of mind. It was easy then, the mid-seventies, not like
today. It took a few months but, then, there we were, after

seventeen years and four children we had never been married in the eyes of the church."

Sheila sat up and faced Bobby. He was still lying on his back, his eyes closed to the sun. "Christ, Bobby, you won't believe it! The priest who married us, who baptized all our kids, was the same one who helped get us the annulment." She began to laugh out loud. Bobby opened his eyes and sat up, facing her.

"You all right, babe?" he said.

She was smiling, shaking her head, and there were tears in her eyes. "He seemed so eager to help me get that annulment," she said. "The priest. He didn't even try to talk me out of it. When I signed the papers in his rectory, I began to cry. He came from behind his desk and put his arms around me. I was crying so loudly I almost didn't hear what he was saying. He said what I needed now was a lot of love. I looked up at him but before I could say anything he kissed me. On the lips." Sheila's features contorted into a look of disgust, as if, even now, by a pool in Reno, she could feel the priest's mouth on hers.

"Do you know what made me sick to my stomach?" she said. "Literally sick." She laughed soundlessly again. "He was so smooth at it, Bobby, so practiced with his tongue that I forgot he was a priest. I mean, for a split second I started to enjoy it. Really. When I realized what was happening I pushed him away. I started to laugh, hysterically. I couldn't stop. He got nervous and tried to calm me down. Finally, when I stopped laughing, I asked him how many times he had done that with some woman like me. His face got red. I thought he was gonna explode. 'You cunt!' he said. Isn't that funny, Bobby? My priest called me a cunt. That's when I threw up on his rug."

Sheila closed her eyes and shook her head as if she was suddenly very tired. "Oh, Bobby," she said with a sigh. "He wasn't the last either, by any means. It's always ended like that for me with men. I'd be with some man in a restaurant, you know, and he'd do something over dinner, a little romantic gesture, like brushing the backs of his fingertips along my cheek, and it would strike me as so false, so calculated, that I couldn't stop myself from laughing out loud. God, the looks! They could have killed me right there, before dessert." Sheila laughed once, and then she reached out and grabbed Bobby's hands in hers. She held them tightly and stared into his eyes. "That's why, Bobby, that first day on the rocks with you, I couldn't believe it. I was so hard on you and yet . . . I said to myself, 'This man's not afraid of me.' But then, after awhile, I started to get scared. I thought, maybe I'll push him too far someday. . . . There's something in me . . . I don't know what . . . I'm not soft like other women." Sheila looked down, away from Bobby's eyes. She spoke so softly he could barely hear her. "I don't know what I'd do if you grew to resent me, Bobby."

He said nothing for a moment, and then he said, "That will never happen."

She looked up at him with wide, frightened eyes. "It will! It will! I know it will!"

"No, it won't, babe. I promise."

"How do you know?"

Bobby looked away from her, toward the construction workers walking, as if on a tightrope, high up on the steel girders. "Because I love you, Sheila," he said. "I love you. I don't know why. I don't even think about it. I just know I do. I know I don't ever want to fuck another woman but you for the rest of my life." He laughed, a breath. "An odd declaration, huh? The best I can do." He turned and looked at her. "Fucking you keeps me clean. Without you, Sheila, I lose my soul."

"I know," she said. "You're it for me, too, Bobby. My last chance." She leaned over and kissed him on the cheek. He looked down.

"I don't know if I'll ever leave Beth," he said. "I'm afraid for her. And for my son. Those rages. She can't control them. If she ever found out about us, I don't know what she would do. I never pushed her far enough to find out. I'm afraid, babe. I'm afraid."

"Shhh, babe! Shhhh! Not to worry. I'll never leave you. I want to be your wife more than anything in my life, but if I have to be your mistress, I will." She smiled at him, and stood up. "Look," she said, striking a pose in her black, string bikini. "It fits, huh? It was made for me." He smiled up at her, and then followed her with his eyes as she walked in that distinctive way of hers, head up, back straight, swiveling on the balls of her feet, toward the pool.

It had rained late in the afternoon, a brief shower, and now the sun was setting near a mustard-colored mountain in the west, and there was a rainbow over Gamblers Stadium, Home of the Reno Gamblers of the Class A Cal-Neva League. Bobby and Sheila were standing behind the home-plate screen, looking out at the deserted playing field. There were puddles everywhere on the dirt infield.

"Jeez, they'll never play tonight," Bobby said.

"Wanna bet?" said a voice behind them. They turned around to see an old man in bib overalls seated in a box seat. "It's Cap Night," the old man said. "No way Herman would cancel a promo night. Not even if one a them god-damned nu-clear bombs the gummint got planted all over the goddamned desert went off during the national anthem." The old man turned his head and spit tobacco juice onto the seat next to him. Some of the juice dribbled down his chin. He didn't bother to wipe it off. "Herman, he'd just play right through the fall-out," the old man said, grinning.

"You mean, Herman Tapcz?" Bobby said. The old man nodded. "Do you know where I can find him?" The old man nodded again. Bobby smiled. "Where?"

"The ticket booth," said the old man, and he jerked his thumb over his shoulder.

"Thanks," Bobby said. He and Sheila walked around the homeplate stands and up a long ramp that led to the ticket booth, a wood structure the size of a Port-o-John, which faced out toward the dirt parking lot. The back door of the booth was open, revealing the backside of a squat, dishev-eled, little man who was hemmed in on three sides by dozens of cardboard boxes rising almost to the ceiling of the booth. The man was wearing a yellow-and-brown base-ball cap that was too small for him. It was propped precariously on top of his head.

"Excuse me," Bobby said. "Herman Tapcz?"

The man turned with a start, his elbow knocking a box to the floor, spilling its contents of yellow-and-brown caps. The man glared at the caps and cursed. Then he hitched up his pants and glared at Bobby. His cap was tilted at an odd angle now, the peak over one ear.

"I'm sorry," Bobby said, "but I . . ."

"Not now! Not now! Can't you see I'm busy?" The man turned back to the small window and said in a gravelly voice, "Awright! Who's next?"

The top half of a small boy's head became visible at the window. "I wanna small," a voice said. A hand reached up, clutching some crumpled dollar bills. The man snatched the bills from the hand, fumbled through the hats on the floor, and thrust one through the window.

"This is a medium" the voice said. "I wanna small."

"We only got one size," the man said. "Next!" The head did not move. A hand reached up to return the hat. The man pulled his hand away as if refusing a summons.

"I said, 'That's all I got!' " the man said. He hitched up his pants "Don't worry. It'll fit. Next!" Still, the head did not move. The hand withdrew the hat and placed it on its head. The man leaned out the window and looked down at the boy. "See! Fits beautiful," the man said. "Now, beat it!"

Bobby tried to get the man's attention again. He introduced himself and Sheila, told him he was a writer for a national sports magazine, and that he . . .

"For Chrissakes!" the man said. "Can't you see I got a fucking disaster here. All these little bastards want caps! Listen, go down to my office and wait!" The man leaned out of the booth and pointed toward the back of the home-plate stands. Next to the concession stand was a door with a sign over it that read, "Herman Tapcz, Bus. Manager."

"Right there. I'll be down when I can." He popped back into the booth, and as Bobby and Sheila walked down the

runway toward his office, they heard his gruff voice say
again, "Awright! Next!"

There was a line of fans at the concession stand an hour
before game time. A bearded man behind the counter was
selling popcorn, hot dogs, bowls of chili with onion, wine
coolers, and 48-ounce cups of Olympia beer. The bearded
man, who resembled a yachtsman without his cap, seemed
flustered by all this business shortly after a heavy shower
that should have caused this game to be postponed.

Bobby and Sheila went inside Herman's office, which
was underneath the slanting homeplate stands. The ceiling, which was the underside of the stands, slanted down
from a height of about six feet to the floor like a slanting
side of a right-angled triangle. It was possible for Bobby
and Sheila to stand without hunching over only at the
room's highest point near the wall. The small room was
dark and cramped and it smelled of stale sweat and anal-
gesic balm.

"Jesus! This is a fucking pit!" Bobby said. He switched
on a conical light over a card table. The concrete floor was
stained with tobacco juice and littered with burnt
matches, cigarette butts, and bits of adhesive tape soiled
with dried blood. There was a half-opened, black physi-
cian's bag up against the wall, a few boxes of new baseballs,
a canvas bag filled with scuffed baseballs, a grocery cart
filled with baseball bats, a steerage trunk, stacks of old
Reno Gamblers' programs, and an unopened fifty-pound
burlap sack filled with unshelled peanuts from the Han-
cock Peanut Company of Sweetbriar, Virginia.

"Bobby, do we have to wait here?" Sheila said.

Bobby shook his head. "Let's wait outside." They went
to the open area between the homeplate stands to their
right and the third-base bleachers to their left. Most of the
fans were sitting on the skeletal third-base bleachers behind the Gamblers' dugout because they were protected
by a corrugated tin roof. The concrete homeplate stands
were exposed to the elements, and only a few old men and
women in work clothes sat bolt upright in their accus-
tomed seats behind homeplate.

The sun had still not set completely and the rainbow was still curving over Gamblers Stadium. It terminated on a mountain peak far beyond the right-field fence. The mountain was a perfect pyramid bisected by sunlight and shadow. The sunlighted part was a bright ochre now, and the shadowed part was the color of green olives. Jet planes, painted red and yellow and orange, swooped down past the mountain. The planes were alternately illuminated by sunlight and shadow before they disappeared beyond the horizon and landed at Reno Airport.

The playing field was deserted except for a few Gamblers players in their cream-colored uniforms with brown piping. They milled around their dugout, talking to the small boys and girls who had wandered onto the field. One of the players was holding a baby in his arms, another was petting a small boy's mongrel dog, and still another, a pale, blond youth, was flirting with a teenaged girl in a silver lamé blouse. The girl was sucking a lollipop. Across the field, the San Jose Devils were sprawled along the exposed first-base bleachers looked bored. Their Trailways bus was parked behind the bleachers.

Three young umpires in navy blue uniforms walked onto the playing field amid a chorus of boos from the third-base bleachers. They stood around homeplate, their hands clasped behind their backs, shaking their heads. The infield dirt was still covered with puddles and the batters' boxes and pitcher's mound were swamps. The umpires, who had spent too many free nights in Bakersfield, Fresno, Visalia, and Salinas, would have liked nothing better than to call off this game so they could go into Reno and gamble. But they had no jurisdiction over the game until it had begun. Until then, the game was Herman Tapcz's province.

From behind them, Bobby and Sheila heard Herman Tapcz's voice. They returned to his office and found him seated behind the card table, screaming into a telephone. "For Chrissakes!" he was saying. "I got five hundred people in this park for a double-header and the field is one big fucking puddle! *I Need That Helicopter!*" He motioned Bobby and Sheila to sit down across from him.

"I know! I know!" he said. "But it's only *one* helicopter! Who'll miss it?" Herman Tapcz wiped his brow. He nodded as the United States Air Force colonel on the other end of the receiver tried to explain to him, in reasoned tones, that it was not the Air Force's function to land jet-powered helicopters behind second base of a minor league baseball park just so its whirling blades could dry off a drenched field and save the team's business manager that night's paid gate.

"Well then, what the hell *do* I pay taxes for?" Herman said, and slammed down the receiver. He put his head in his hands and began to moan softly.

"Mr. Tapcz," Bobby said, "I . . ." Herman Tapcz jumped up.

"No time! No time!" He bolted out of his office, Bobby and Sheila close behind, and scurried over to the concession stand. A mob of fans was screaming out their orders to the bearded man behind the counter.

"Jesus, Herman! When is the game gonna start?" the bearded man said. "I'm goin' nuts!"

"Soon. Soon."

"It better. Some kid just stole a bag of peanuts when I wasn't lookin', and then the little bastard had the nerve to bring 'em back and demand a refund." Herman waved the back of his hand at the bearded man as if he could not be bothered with such trivialities, and scurried off in that duck-waddling, stomach-thrusting walk of his. As he rounded a corner leading to the field, he almost collided with a man carrying three boxes of popcorn. The man juggled the boxes, tried to steady them, lurched after them, almost had them, then finally lost them all. Popcorn littered the ground. The man kicked the boxes, sending a spray of popcorn into the air, like snow swirling up in a wind. The man glared over his shoulder at Herman Tapcz, oblivious, and cursed.

Herman Tapcz stood between the homeplate stands and

the third-base bleachers and counted the house. His lips moved as he conducted his survey. He started to smile, and then he caught sight of the three umpires standing at homeplate. "Bastards!" he said out loud. "Not tonight you don't." He hitched up his pants and waddled onto the playing field toward the umpires. The fans behind the Gamblers' dugout began to applaud. Someone shouted, "Atta boy, Herman. It's about time."

While Herman Tapcz conferred with the umpires, Bobby and Sheila went up into the third-base bleachers and sat down. The fans were strangely quiet, now, mesmerized by the sight of short, dumpy Herman Tapcz gesticulating wildly with his arms to the three young umpires. The fans just sat there, eating their popcorn and drinking their beer, as if what was unfolding on the field was sufficient to entertain them. Herman with the umpires. The players milling about. The rainbow.

The fans stared at the field as if transfixed. A farmer with a straw hat. A gas station attendant in a soiled chino shirt and pants. A mother in a nondescript cloth coat. A slatternly high school girl with too much makeup. A small boy with a dirty face and a new Gamblers' cap that was too big for him. A lone Oriental man in a navy windbreaker. A Mexican farm worker with Inca cheekbones and a droopy mustache. An old couple, one of many, sitting on cushions to protect their bony behinds. The old man had white stubble on his knobby chin and the collar of his shirt was too large for his skinny neck. His wife was wearing a kerchief over her head. Their son, a handsome man of about thirty, was sitting beside them. He had a large head. His hands were folded in his lap, and his knees were pressed together. He stared straight ahead with unblinking, birdlike eyes. Farther down the bleachers was a girl dressed entirely in red—jersey, polyester pants that were too short, socks, shoes. She had watery eyes and a halo of golden curls. She was hugging herself and rocking back and forth as she sucked on a hot dog. She withdrew the hot dog, uneaten from her mouth, and caressed her check with it. She talked to herself, listened, her head cocked sideways to voices only she could hear.

It was dark now. The mountain beyond right field was the color of a purple plum. The lights were on at Gamblers Stadium. And Herman Tapcz was illuminated, scurrying around the infield, splashing kerosene from a ten-gallon drum over all the puddles. His players, their hands stuffed into their back pockets, watched from a few feet back of the third-base line. The umpires behind homeplate were still shaking their heads. The fans stared, mouths open. When Herman reached homeplate, he tossed aside his drum and stood there a moment surveying his work. He withdrew a match book from his pants pocket. A fan gasped. Bullfight music exploded over the loudspeaker. Herman lighted the match, dropped it at homeplate, and stepped back onto the infield grass. Flames sprang up, scurried down the first-base line, rounded the bag, and headed for second. The fans began to applaud and cheer as the flames crossed over second, headed for third, rounded the bag, and scurried home. The bullfight music built to a crescendo as the flames reached homeplate. The entire dirt infield was enveloped in flames. Herman Tapcz, smiling, was standing on the pitcher's mound with his hands on his hips. He was surrounded by flames, a sacrificial offering, and then black smoke, and, finally, he disappeared from sight. A fan cried out, "Herman'll burn himself up!" Another said, "Naw! Herman's awright."

When the fire died down Herman Tapcz reappeared, to applause, out of the black smoke. The puddles were gone and only a little of the infield grass had been singed black.

Standing in the darkness alongside the homeplate stands, Herman Tapcz smiled to himself as the first Gambler batter stepped up to the plate. Sheila and Bobby stood beside him. There was a smattering of applause from the fans, who were now spread out around the stadium. The box seats behind homeplate were occupied by the players' wives and girlfriends. They were young, mostly blonde, heavily made-up women dressed in cowboy hats and designer jeans. They chatted like magpies amongst themselves, stopping only occasionally to glance over their shoulders to catch one of the Gamblers' fans staring at them.

"If it had got outta hand," Herman Tapcz was saying, "so what? I always wanted a new stadium." He chuckled. "Besides, I gotta get the games in. The fans would be brokenhearted if I called it. It's all they got. See that old couple behind homeplate? They celebrated their fiftieth wedding anniversary right here. We let 'em throw out the first ball." Herman smiled at Bobby and Sheila. "Class, eh?" He winked. "All the fans are loyal to the Gamblers. I remember one night—Free Beer Night—the opposing team never showed. Bus broke down in Modesto. Shit, I got all these people drinking forty-eight-ounce Olympia beers and no ball game. They didn't care. Hell, they just sat around gettin' stoned and cheerin' battin' practice for three hours." Herman shook his head and chuckled again.

Bobby told Herman Tapcz that he was trying to locate Tony Vincent. "The pitcher," he said. "He played here a few years back, didn't he?"

Herman Tapcz laughed out loud. "I guess. Played more off the field than on. He was on his way down when he got here. He'd played a few years in the bigs and then he went sour." Herman Tapcz shook his head. "Sonuvabitch loved the ladies. I remember the first day he got here. He pitched that night. It was a big deal, you know, an ex-major leaguer with the Hollywood Stars down here in Reno. They televised the game. A local station. They only had one camera. They put it behind first base. Sonuvagun if Tony didn't walk the first batter on four pitches every inning. Then he'd hold him on, you know, with a long, soulful stare over his shoulder, right into the camera. Ha! One time he stared so long into that camera, I think he hypnotized himself.

The runner stole second without a throw. Tony didn't give a shit. He knew what he was doing. The next night every damn lady from the chorus line at the MGM was sitting in the third-base bleachers. He was a handsome sonuvabitch, I'll tell you. Even then, after all that booze and them ladies. Anyway, Tony spent that second game signing autographs for those ladies, and slippin' them through the wire mesh fence." Herman Tapcz shook his head and smiled. "It was quite a sight. All these ladies in shiny capri pants billin' and cooin' over Tony Vincent in the middle of all them dumbfounded farmers."

"I'll bet it was," Bobby said. "I was told he moved back to Reno a few years later, after he left the game."

"Yep, he did."

"Do you know where he is now?"

"Well, Tony's a tough man to keep track of, you know. He moves around a lot. Mostly from ranch to ranch."

Bobby looked at him. "You mean, he's a cowboy?"

Herman Tapcz laughed. "Not that kind a ranch. No brandin' or ropin'. But plenty of cows. Tony's a bouncer at one of our legal houses of prostitution. The last I heard, he was out at the Mustang. Past the MGM off the interstate. I tried to get him out to the ballpark for one of my promotions a while back. I was gonna bill it 'Fallen Star Returns to Reno.' Not everybody would remember him. Maybe just a few of his former ladies from the chorus line. Housewives, now, I suspect. Running to fat. Still, Tony had had a loyal following. I sent word out to the ranch where he was working but I never heard from him, so I forgot about it. I figured, maybe he'd soured on the game the way most of them do. Anyway, about a month later I get this postcard addressed to me personally." Herman looked at Sheila and said, "If you'll excuse me, miss." Sheila smiled at him and nodded.

"Of course," she said.

"I knew it was Tony's hand," Herman Tapcz said, "because I'd seen him sign so many autographs. There were only three words on that postcard. 'Fuck the Game!' "

Just then, a small boy came running up to Herman

Tapcz. "Herman, there's a ruckus at the concession! Edgar says he's gonna quit!"

"Oh, shit!" Herman Tapcz hitched up his pants. "You'll have to excuse me folks." He waddled off in that stomach-thrusting way of his with the small boy skipping and running alongside him.

The following morning Bobby and Sheila drove out to the desert. They passed the MGM casino, casting its shadow across the road in the sunlight, and headed straight for the line of mountains in the distance. They drove for a long while toward the mountains, but they never seemed to draw closer. There was nothing on either side of the road but the desert and, farther off, the horizon. Finally, they saw a sign, hand-painted on a rock. "Mustang Ranch." Bobby turned the car off the interstate onto a winding dirt road. The road was strewn with rocks and Bobby had to struggle to control the car. After a few hundred yards they saw another rock, painted with an arrow, and then another, and another, and another, until they came to a dilapidated covered bridge that spanned a wide, dry riverbed. Bobby stopped the car. The bridge was a long, dark tunnel through which they could see, at the other end, a patch of blue sky.

"What do you think, babe?" Bobby said.

"I don't know. We've come this far."

Bobby put the car in gear and eased it onto the bridge. The bridge groaned under the car's weight. Bobby hunched over the steering wheel. Sheila grabbed his arm. The car lurched forward, clattering over loose planks. They were in darkness, except for slivers of light here and there, where the boards had separated, and the patch of blue sky at the end of the tunnel. The patch of sky grew larger as they clattered over the planks, and then suddenly it leaped at them as the car banged down hard off the bridge onto the ground. They were in a clearing, a dirt parking lot, surrounded on either side by a few Ford Rancheros, pickup trucks, a white Lincoln Continental, and a taxi with its motor running. A cowboy was weaving unsteadily toward the taxi. A girl stood behind a seven-foot-high chain fence waving at him.

"You be careful, now, sugar!" she called out as he got into the taxi.

Behind the fence and the girl was a long mobile home propped on cinder blocks. There was a circular turret, like a widow's walk, on top of the mobile home. A man wearing dark glasses that reflected silver in the sunlight was standing on the turret with a machine gun resting on his shoulder. Bobby turned the car into a parking space and shut off the engine.

"I'm not too crazy about this, babe," he said.

"Neither am I."

They sat there for awhile looking into the rearview mirror at the man on the turret. He was staring at them through sunglasses that sent off shooting stars of light. The girl behind the fence was watching them, too.

Sheila opened her door but did not step out. She looked at Bobby. "You've got to talk to him, right?" Bobby nodded. "Well! Let's go." They both got out and walked toward the girl at the fence. The man on the turret watched them all the way. They heard the fence crackle with electricity as they got closer. There was a sign on its gate. "Notice: No more admittance to Iranian students until the hostages are released—The Owner." The girl at the gate narrowed her eyes as they approached. She was a plain-looking girl, without makeup, and she wore her long, straight, sandy-colored hair parted in the middle as was the style in the sixties.

"What can I do fer ya?" she said.

"We'd like to go inside," Bobby said.

"Both 'a ya?"

Bobby nodded.

"She gonna take a girl?" the girl said, gesturing with her head toward Sheila.

"What do you mean?" Sheila said.

"You lookin' fer a date with a girl, that's what I mean."

"No, I don't think so," Sheila said, glancing at Bobby.

"Then only him," the girl said. "We ain't got no men. Only girls."

"I don't want a man," Sheila said. "I'm with him."

The girl put her hands on her hips and gave Bobby an exasperated look. "Listen, honey. This is a cat house. A man don't bring his own here just like he don't bring his own steak to a restaurant. If he wants to come in, fine, but you got to wait in the car."

Sheila looked at Bobby. "Don't worry, honey," the girl said. "It's safer out here than it is on Virginia Street in Reno."

"You go in, babe," Sheila said. "I'll be all right."

"Are you sure?"

Sheila nodded. "Positive."

Bobby exhaled a breath. "All right." Sheila kissed him on the cheek and walked back to the car. "Lock the door!" Bobby yelled as she got in. She waved at him through the rear window.

The girl smiled at Bobby. "Okay, sugar. You're in." She opened the gate and Bobby walked through, up the stairs, to the front door. He tried the door but it was locked. Then he heard a loud buzzing sound. He tried the door again and it opened. He stepped inside.

A line-up of girls in bathing suits was smiling at him. Each one had struck a similar pose, hands on hips, one leg pointed forward. They began to call out their names, one by one.

"Dora."

"Allison."

"Bobette."

"Candy."

"Denise."

"Rachel."

"Sadie."

A husky, woman's voice called out to him. "All right, sugar. Pick a lady." Bobby saw, behind a small bar, a fat, black woman dressed entirely in yellow. She was eating a fried egg sandwich with onions. "Come on, sugar," she said. "The ladies can't stand there all morning."

The girls were still smiling at him as they tried to maintain their pose. Their legs began to wobble.

"I think I'd like a beer first," Bobby said, smiling, to the black woman.

The black woman made a noise that sounded like, "Harrumph!" Then she said, "Another big spender." She waved her fried egg sandwich at the girls. "All right, ladies." All the girls' smiles broke at once. Their bodies sagged and they returned to their various states of sprawl around the room. Some of the girls lounged on a sofa near the window, alternately combing one another's hair. Another sat in an easy chair flipping through a magazine. Bobby noticed, for the first time, that they were all wearing high-heeled shoes and pantyhose underneath their one-piece bathing suits. All but one of the girls were white. They were in their late twenties and early thirties, heavily made-up, with fleshy thighs.

Bobby sat on a stool at the bar and ordered a beer from the black woman. She banged the can down in front of him and made another "Harrumph!" sound. She was wearing bifocals fastened around her neck with a gold chain. The room was hot, unair-conditioned, except for a small, whirring fan at one end of the bar. A girl was seated next to the fan, one foot up on the stool beside her, painting her toenails with complete self-absorption. Every so often she would pause in her task, pull her head back to examine her work, and then lean her face close to the fan and close her eyes while the fan dried the beads of perspiration on her brow. With a shake of her lank hair, she returned to her task.

Another girl was watching "American Bandstand" on the television set at the end of the bar. Still another was sipping coffee from a conical paper cup in a plastic holder while staring dreamily at a picture of Elvis Presley tacked up on the wall behind the black woman. The picture was signed by Elvis, "To All the Fillies at the Mustang."

Seated at the other end of the bar, one arm thrown around the shoulders of a man hunched over a beer, was another girl. Unlike the others, she was slim, scrubbed-looking, with short, layered hair. If she had not been wearing an orange day-glo bikini and silver spike-heeled shoes, she could have passed for a college student.

"A cougar skin is expensive," the man said. The girl did not respond. "I can git five hundred dollars for it in town." He was rugged-looking, unshaven, with soiled clothes.

"I'll swap you for it, sugar," said the girl in the orange bikini.

"What for?"

"Skin for skin."

The man said nothing. He drained his beer and then he said, "Another, Willie." The black woman brought him another beer.

"What do you say, sugar?" the girl said.

The man looked her up and down. She arched her back and thrust out her chest. He turned back to his beer.

"Okay," he said. "Fifty sessions."

The girl's mouth dropped open. "Ten dollars a session!" she said.

The man nodded, but before the girl could speak again, Willie let out another loud, "Harrumph!" She looked down through her bifocals at the man and said, "Listen, sugar. For ten dollars you can just march yourself right into that john over there, unzip your pants, and look at it."

Only the girl, the man, and Bobby laughed at this as Willie shook her head in disgust. Suddenly there was a loud buzzing sound. Bobby turned around on his stool. All the girls got up and formed a line facing the door. They assumed a pose. Dusty shafts of sunlight streamed through the windows behind the sofa. The girls' flesh, caught in the hazy sunlight, took on a pale gray cast, and the bright colors of their bathing suits looked faded. A man in work clothes and a teenaged boy entered the room and stopped in front of the girls. The girls smiled and called out their names, one by one. Willie called out in her deep voice, "All right, gentlemen, pick your ladies." The man whispered something to the boy, then half-led him, half-pushed him toward a big girl with pale skin and strawberry-colored hair. She had huge, billowy breasts and big hips, and

Bobby could make out the elastic waistline of her panty-hose underneath her mint green bathing suit. She smiled lasciviously at the boy, revealing bad teeth, then slipped her arm through the boy's arm and led him out of the room. The man followed with another girl. The remaining girls returned to their lounging in a room that was filled with handed-down furniture. Floral-printed sofa. Two easy chairs. A wine-colored throw rug. All of the furniture, even the gold fringes at either end of the throw rug, took on a grayish tint in the dusty morning light. Bobby turned back to his beer.

"What about you, sugar?" said Willie. "You gonna drink that beer all morning or what?"

Bobby grinned at her and shrugged.

Willie made a disgusted sound with her mouth. "You a real sport, ain't you?"

"Actually, I'm looking for someone," Bobby said.

"Well, we got lots of someones here, sugar. Take your pick."

"I'm looking for Tony Vincent."

Willie finished her sandwich and wiped her mouth with a paper napkin. "Nobody here by that name," she said as she began to wash a glass in the sink.

"I was told he works here." Willie dried off the glass with a towel. "Tell him I'm a friend of Rodney James and Stanley Muraski."

"Stanley *what?*"

"Just tell him Stashu." Willie put the glass upside down on the bar and left the room. She returned, alone, a few minutes later and began washing another glass. Bobby sipped from his beer and waited. A few more minutes passed before Tony Vincent entered the room. He was wearing a sleeveless undershirt; tight, black pants; and bedroom slippers. He sat down next to Bobby.

"Some Wheaties, Willie," he said. Willie filled a glass with ice cubes and vodka and put it down in front of him. Tony sipped from the glass. Without looking at Bobby, he said, "So, you're the writer."

"How'd you know?" Bobby said.

Tony Vincent smiled. It was the same smile Bobby had seen in that photograph of Rodney James, Stanley Muraski, and Tony Vincent at Mrs. Muraski's home. It was an ironic smile of disavowal. Self-mocking. Distrustful. The smile of a man who holds everything he sees, himself included, in such slight regard that he cannot keep from smiling even at the things he has to say.

"Because I know everything," he said. He sipped from his drink and then looked at Bobby. "Because that fucking apple, Rodney James, called me to tell me you'd be sniffing around. You're scaring the shit out of him, you know."

"Why?"

"Stashu." Tony Vincent smiled. With his fingertips, he absentmindedly displaced a lock of hair from his forehead. It was an exquisite, almost delicate gesture done in slow motion. His black hair was long and shaggy rather than slicked back and gleaming as it had been years ago. Its blackness, coupled with his dark skin and slightly flattened features, gave him the look of a man of Mexican descent. He was still a handsome man, despite the lines at the corners of his eyes and mouth and the dark stubble of beard on his chin.

"What can you tell me about Stashu?" Bobby said.

"He's dead."

"What else?"

"What else is there?"

"You tell me."

Tony Vincent drained his drink and shook the ice cubes in the glass. "More Wheaties, Willie." She refilled his glass and returned it to him. He took another sip and then said, "He was a dumb fucking Polack."

"Is that all?"

"Isn't that enough?"

"You were tight, weren't you? You, Stashu, and Rodney."

"Sure. We were tight. Tight as a whore's asshole. Isn't that right, Chickie?" He looked toward the girl in the orange bikini, who was still talking to the man with the cougar skin. She looked at Tony Vincent and smiled.

"Sure, Tony," she said. "Whatever you say." Tony Vincent smiled and shook his head from side to side.

"Yes, sir," Tony Vincent said. "There's nothing tighter than three minor league pitchers trying to make the same big league club in spring training." He looked at Bobby and raised his eyebrows. "And only two spots open. Makes you real close. Tight. Like you said. It gets down to crunch, though, and you find yourself looking over your shoulder a lot. I was watching Rodney and he was watching me and we both were watching Stashu."

Tony Vincent began to laugh, a series of short breaths. "Stashu, now, he wasn't watching nobody. Too fucking stupid. And trusting. That asshole trusted everybody." Tony Vincent averted his eyes from Bobby. "He trusted me." He closed his eyes as if to erase an unpleasant memory and then he opened them again. "He trusted that fucking apple, too, who wouldn't pull dead rats off his own mother." He took a sip from his glass and put it down on the bar. "Stashu deserved what he got. We all did." He turned toward Bobby again, smiled, and made a sweeping gesture with his arm to encompass the room. "We all got what we deserved."

"What do you mean?"

"What the fuck's with all the questions? I told you enough."

"You haven't told me anything."

"I haven't, eh? I told you all there is to know. Rodney James is a fucking apple. I'm a pimp. Stashu is dead. End of report." He banged his empty glass on the bar. "Willie!"

The girl in the orange bikini got up from her bar stool and walked behind Tony Vincent. She laid a languid hand upon his shoulder and brushed it across his back as she passed. He seemed not to notice.

"Tell me one thing and I'll go," Bobby said. "What happened that spring?"

Willie put a full glass down in front of Tony Vincent. He threw back his head and drained the glass in one swallow. He rested his elbows on the bar and hunched forward, staring with unseeing eyes at his glass. He did not speak for a long while and then he began to talk in a hollow voice, without inflection, that seemed to be coming from a great distance. "Stashu had the club made. It was between me and the apple for the second spot. We both looked for an edge. Me, I just watched and waited. Rodney, he hit on that born-again shit. He got a little ink, you know. The rookie who pitched for Christ. People may laugh in New York, but out there that kind of shit goes over. The Stars were God's team, for Chrissakes. They had a tight little squad of those apples, and they wielded some power. I know for a fact they got one manager fired because he didn't lead a Christian life. Which means he crossed those bastards in some way. Anyway, Rodney not only becomes a born-again but he goes and founds his own organization, whatever the fuck it was. He made himself president. Isn't that a trip? I asked him on the sly once, could I be treasurer? The stupid fuck says, 'Certainly, Tony, if you accept Christ.' I said, 'Rodney, that's not the question. Will the bearded bastard accept me?' He didn't see the humor in that, but still he knew he wasn't smart enough to fuck with me so he went to work on Stashu. Got him drinking heavy every night. Which wasn't hard to do. One night I come into a bar and there was Stashu, half in the bag, and Rodney, sober as a nun, telling him it was still early, have another. The next morning in the clubhouse Stashu was too sick to pitch, but he was afraid to tell the manager. Rodney told him not to worry, he'd take care of it. My locker was right next to the manager's office. I heard it all. That fucking apple told the manager Stashu was a drunk. He wasn't good for a Christian team like the Stars until he changed his ways. The manager was a chicken-shit little bastard and he couldn't ship Stashu out fast enough." He took a deep breath and exhaled. "The rest is history."

Bobby did not say anything for awhile and then he said, "Why didn't you say something?"

Tony Vincent turned toward him. "Fuck you! I had my own ass to worry about. I was in on a pass."

"Why didn't you say something later, then, after you left the game?"

"Why should I? It was over."

"Then why are you telling me now?"

"Because I heard a cock crow, what do you think?" He smiled at Bobby. "Why not? You're here. I'm here. Stashu's dead. The apple's in L.A." He stopped smiling and stared at Bobby. Then he said in a level voice, "Don't flatter yourself. I might not have told you anything if that fucking apple hadn't called to warn me about you. I wasn't gonna be his fucking beard a second time."

Tony Vincent stood up and smiled again. "So, there," he said. "You got your story. You gonna write it?" He threw back his head and laughed out loud. Then he moved off, lightly, his body shifting delicately from side to side, his weight slightly forward on the balls of his feet. Still laughing, he said, "Go ahead and write that."

When Bobby got back to the car Sheila was waiting for him.

"What happened?" she said. "What was it like in there?" As Bobby began to tell her, she interrupted him. "Tell me everything," she said.

Driving back toward Reno, Bobby told her about the room and the whores and Willie. He told her about the girl in the orange bikini ("Like yours," he said, "the first time I ever saw you.") and the hunter with the cougar skin, and, just as they got to the MGM casino, he told her about the father and his young son.

"How sad," she said as Bobby turned the car into the parking lot. They got out and went to the pool. They had worn their bathing suits underneath their clothes, so they undressed and lay down in the sun. It was midafternoon. The construction workers were gone and there were only a few people around the pool. The public address microphone near the pool blared out a woman's voice: "Paging Mr. Weinstock! Paging Mr. Joel Weinstock!"

"What about Tony Vincent?" Sheila said, lying beside Bobby, facing the sun. "Did you see him? Did you talk to him?"

"Yes."

"Well . . . what was he like?"

Bobby exhaled through puffed-up cheeks as if trying to keep a leaf afloat above him. "You won't believe it," he said. "You won't fucking believe it." And then, for the next two hours, he told her about Tony Vincent and what he had told him, and then he told her about Rodney James and his wife, and Stanley Muraski and his wife, and how this story was the most explosive story he had ever come upon.

"Rodney James is an idol in baseball," Bobby said. "People worship him." He sat up and stared straight ahead. "Nobody's gonna believe it!"

Sheila sat up, too, and put her hand on Bobby's arm. "What are you going to do?"

Bobby looked at her. "What do you think?"

"You've got to write it. You've got to!"

Bobby laughed. "That's what he said."

"Who?"

"Tony Vincent. After he told me everything, he laughed and said, 'Go ahead and write that.' "

"He doesn't think you will, does he?"

"I don't know. He's such a perverse bastard. I don't know what he thinks. I only know I believe him. Every word."

They dressed and left the pool at sundown. Their mouths were parched and their skin was dusted white with the salt the desert sun brought out of their bodies. They went into the casino to get something to quench their thirst. On the lower level they found an enclosed shopping mall filled with tourists. Sheila and Bobby walked arm in arm among them—past a men's clothing store with windows filled with patent-leather loafers of every pastel hue; a women's furrier that had a mink bikini displayed in its window; a French ice cream shop whose items, listed on a menu in the window, included a glass of water priced at five cents; a photographer's studio where people could rent Bonnie and Clyde costumes in which to pose; a health spa run by a blonde girl dressed in an Indian serape of the Sikh

Dhrma sect; and a wedding chapel done in a Mediterranean style whose minister was named "Chickie Vantage."
They came to an art gallery that was serving browsers
California champagne in plastic, hollow-stemmed, tulip-
shaped glasses as light as air. They went inside and drank
champagne as they wandered around the gallery examining the oil paintings on the walls.

"Motel room art," Bobby said, and Sheila laughed.
There were paintings of big-eyed, no-name children and
tigers on black velvet and World War II fighter planes and
flowers whose paint had been applied so thickly, like a
fresco, that they looked three-dimensional. By the time
they came to the portraits of clowns done by a famous
comedian, they were already slightly drunk. They made a
great production of stepping back and examining the
paintings with an expert's narrowed eye.

"Nice," Bobby said, nodding solemnly. "Reminds me of
Beth's best work when she was pregnant. Paint by numbers. She only got as far as three when the baby was born."

Sheila moved closer to the wall and bent over so she
could read the printed biography of the famous comedian,
which was tacked next to the clowns. "He sells his works
for upward of forty thousand dollars," she said, straightening up. "In his spare time, before breakfast every morning,
he—and I quote—'Pens a love poem to his fourth wife,
Bernice, who is thirty years his junior.'" Sheila looked at
Bobby as if exasperated. "You don't 'pen' a love poem to
me every morning."

"No, sweet pea, I don't. But you are not 'thirty years my
junior.'"

"Beast!"

"In point of fact, you are my senior by a few years and
as such you should be penning love poems to me each
morning."

They laughed, and drank more champagne, and then left
the gallery and walked, unsteadily, toward the double
glass doors that led outside. At the end of the mall they
came upon a drugged lion chained by his ankle to a stake
on an elevated red felt pedestal. The lion's trainer, a red-

faced man with thin eyes and slicked-back yellow hair, was standing near him talking to the small crowd that had gathered. Bobby and Sheila stopped behind the crowd and, swaying gently, watched in disbelief. The lion was lounging, his eyes glassy and half-lidded. His paws were declawed. He lifted his tail, as if to flick off imaginary flies, but the effort seemed to exhaust him and his tail collapsed to the felt. The small crowd of humans watched him from behind a roped-off area. The lion, through glazed eyes, perceived them merely as shadows, a patch of tall grass swaying in a warm breeze. His master came closer with fresh meat on the end of a stick. The lion tried to raise his head and open his mouth, but he couldn't. His master forced open his mouth with the stick and pushed in the meat. The lion chewed lethargically. The meat revived him, his eyes opened wide, his tongue darted out to lick the rest of the meat off the stick. The lion raised a paw and took a playful swipe at his master as he moved away. The humans gasped and moved back. The lion turned his majestic, thick-maned head and glared, imperiously, down at the humans now more clearly perceived. His master led one of the smaller humans out of the pack. As they approached, the small human pulled back a bit before, finally, stepping up to take its place beside the lion. The lion turned his head toward the small, golden-haired human standing stiffly beside him and staring, big-eyed, straight ahead. There was a blinding flash and the lion clenched his eyes shut, shook his head. When he opened his eyes again he saw the blur of the small human running toward two large humans who were laughing. His master handed the humans something. They looked at it and smiled. The lion began to feel drowsy again. He arched his head backward as if to relieve a crimp in his neck. His pupils receded into his eyelids so that only the whites were showing. He was grinning—a white-eyed, idiot's grin. Exhausted now, the lion let his huge head fall down to rest on his crossed paws.

•   •   •

Later that night, after dinner and more wine, Bobby and Sheila joined the crowd of people walking up and down Virginia Street, past casino after casino, with their blinking neon signs that bathed everyone in an eerie colored light. The casino's sliding glass doors opened on to the sidewalk so that gamblers working the nickel slots seemed to be in the midst of couples strolling by. Bobby and Sheila let the flow of the crowd carry them up the street, under the arched sign that spanned Virginia Street, proclaiming Reno, Nevada, the biggest little city in the world. When they came to the end of the strip of casinos, they found themselves suddenly dispelled from the crowd and the lights behind them. Laughing, they stumbled over a set of railroad tracks. Bobby grabbed Sheila by the waist as she was about to lurch forward. They stood, weaving unsteadily, alone on a dark and deserted street.

"Let's go back," Sheila said, resting her head against Bobby's chest.

"Look over there," Bobby said. Set back from the street in the darkness was a small mobile home with a blinking red neon sign on its roof. "Wedding Chapel."

"Come on," Bobby said. He held Sheila firmly by the waist as they staggered over the stones and rocks of the gravel parking lot. The building was dark. They looked in the front window but could see nothing. They went around back and Bobby banged his knee against a garbage can.

"Shhhh!" Sheila said with a finger to her lips. The garbage can had a white cross painted on it.

"Oh, Jesus!" Bobby said pointing at the cross. "Look at that!"

"Garbage for God," Sheila said. "Isn't that nice?" She began to giggle. Bobby put his hand over her mouth. She bit his finger and he screamed. "Shhh!" Sheila said.

They saw a light through a window and went over to peer inside. They had to get up on their toes and hold on to the windowsill with their fingertips before they could see anything.

A young couple was getting married in a small chapel.

They were facing each other. The preacher was between them, facing Bobby and Sheila, although he did not see them. He was a small, worried-looking man with wire-rimmed spectacles. He stood at a lectern and read from a book. Standing beside him was a short, fat woman in a shapeless wrapper. She was wearing backless slippers and curlers in her hair, which was covered by a net. She held a plastic cup in her hand and every so often raised it to her lips and sipped.

The bride and groom, their eyes glazed, stared at one another and grinned like the lion Bobby and Sheila had seen earlier in the shopping mall at the MGM casino. They were both teenagers, with bad skin and long, straight hair that had not been washed in days. The bride wore a halter top that exposed her navel, a pair of faded jeans that were patched at the knees and seat with bright-colored fabric, and a pair of sandals. The groom was barefoot. His jeans were too long for him, and they had become frayed and dirty at the bottom where he stepped on them as they brushed the ground. He wore a T-shirt, and had a package of cigarettes rolled into one sleeve, exposing a long, skinny arm. The arm was tattooed with a dagger made by the ink from a fountain pen.

The preacher continued to read while the woman beside him sipped from her plastic cup and the bride and groom stared at each other with glazed grins. Suddenly, the groom began to reel. He fell forward as if passing out. The bride caught him with both hands, pushed him back upright, and held him there. The groom began to laugh.

Bobby and Sheila turned away from the window and walked back to their hotel in silence.

· SIX ·

During her summer vacation from school, Sheila lived near the beach with her father, an old man still mourning the death of his wife, three years before, from cancer. He kept the house a shrine to her memory. Everything was as she had left it. The drapes were drawn against the sunlight that, the old man feared, might fade the colors in the blue chintz sofa and so fade the memory of his wife. The house was musty and dark and the old man drifted from room to room as in a dream. He stopped before the armchair near the fireplace. He bent over and straightened it so that the curved legs fit perfectly in the deep indentations that had been made in the thick carpet over twenty years. He watched from the kitchen doorway while Sheila read the newspaper, and when she got up he went over to the sofa and plumped up the pillows where she had been sitting.

They had all their meals in the kitchen, at the Formica table, rather than in the dining room, at the mahogany table with the cut-glass bowl of paper flowers in the center. They ate off powder blue plastic plates and drank from frosted plastic glasses, the kind found in truckers' diners, that the old man had bought at a discount store, shortly after his wife died. All of her silverware, china, and crystal had been wrapped in tissue paper, put in boxes sealed with masking tape, and stored in the attic. The old man had labeled each box in his perfect, slanting, draftsman's hand, all the letters printed in capitals. "MARY'S WATERFORD, TWENTY-FIFTH WEDDING ANNIVERSARY, 8/18/63." Late at night in her bed, Sheila could hear the muffled sound of her father's slippers overhead.

Their relationship had always been strained, and now was even more so since Sheila had told her father she was the mistress of a married man. He went to mass every weekday afternoon at four, and at six on Sunday mornings, and, like most religious people who were not bright, he was without compassion for sins that did not appeal to him. He had been married to the same woman for thirty-five years, and he had never had the desire to be unfaithful to her, which was why he could not countenance, much less fathom, the adultery of his daughter. She had always wearied him, as if by spite. She was the first member of his family ever to get divorced, and then, to make matters even worse, she left her children with her husband. As a teenager, she was bold and defiant to him. He was the first man on whom she had leveled that cold stare of hers. It had shaken him so badly that he took to his room.

Yet, she was so sweetly acquiescent with her mother. She confused him. He had always resented her. She was his first child, and it had come as a shock to him when he discovered that his wife's attentions, which had been almost solely ministered to him before the birth, were now divided between himself and his infant daughter. He began to resent her for distracting his wife from his needs. Then the other children came, and he got used to it, although he would always see it all as somehow beginning with Sheila's birth. He was too moral a man to blame an infant for his loss, too selfish a man not to be annoyed by it, and too dumb a man to be able to come to grips with it. So, he merely repressed it and treated his daughter civilly, as he would any guest in his house. They sat across from one another now—an old man with pink, blotchy skin and a middle-aged woman with tanned skin—and sipped their coffee in the mornings while making polite conversation. In the evening, before dinner, they had drinks in the living room. She always sat on the chintz sofa, as if to annoy him, he thought, and he sat on the armchair near the fireplace. They chatted about the events of their respective days, and sometimes, when she grew especially animated, a look would drift across his features like a cloud and he would get up and leave the room. At first, Sheila was stunned, she thought he did this to hurt her feelings. Then she realized that his distaste for her, his own daughter, was not so conscious. She thought maybe it was just that he was a selfish old man who had lost interest in what she was saying. Finally, she realized it was not that what she was saying bored him, but that it confused him. And since he did not like to be confronted by things that confused him, he simply got up and left the room while Sheila was in midsentence.

If her mother had not died so unexpectedly, Sheila might never have seen her father again. But when she saw how he was becoming, without his wife, she forced herself to call him every weekend and to visit him once in awhile. Yet that was only part of the reason she was staying with him this summer. She also wanted to be closer to Bobby while he worked on his story about Stanley Muraski. They had arranged their days around a little routine. Bobby came by early in the morning, at daybreak, and waited in his car until she noticed him through the bay window in the living room. Bobby never honked his horn or rang the doorbell. He just sat there, hunched down in the seat, drinking coffee from a Styrofoam cup and reading the newspaper while waiting for her to wake and notice him through the window. He had never entered her father's house, and only once had he come to the front door. She was still asleep.

Bobby rang the bell and peered in through the screen door into the shadowy living room. An old man in a bathrobe and slippers was coming toward him. He was bald, with a friar's tuft of hair, like a halo, around his head. He had long, thin arms and legs, like Sheila, and his bathrobe was tied very high at the waist. As he moved toward Bobby he squinted into the sunlight streaming in from behind Bobby's head. Bobby smiled, called out through the screen, "Hello, Mr. Doyle. I'm Bobby Giacquinto." The old man was only a few steps from the door. Without breaking stride, he turned around and began to leave the room. Bobby stared at the back of his bathrobe until the old man was gone.

After that, Bobby waited in the car. As soon as Sheila saw him she dressed in her shorts and T-shirt and ran to the car with her sandals in her hand. They drove down the street, along the beach, to the beach bar where they had had their first drink together last summer. The bar was not open for business so early in the morning, except for a lone figure in the back room who was smoking a cigar and drinking his shot and beer in silence before walking to his job as a digger of ditches for a construction company. He wore a spotless, short-sleeved Hawaiian-print shirt outside a pair of brown polyester pants pressed to a knifelike crease, and a pair of polished, black, hard-soled shoes he had bought from an advertisement in the back pages of the Sunday magazine supplement of the local newspaper. Years ago, he had been a professional boxer, a heavyweight who was too light for his class. He had once been knocked out in the first round by Rocky Marciano, who told sportswriters afterward that "that man hit me harder than any man I ever fought." The man in the Hawaiian shirt never spoke. He just smoked his cigar, the wisps of smoke curling around his eyes, and drank from first one glass and then the other. He had a pencil-thin mustache and the handsome, fine-featured face of an aging silent film star.

The owner of the bar always had coffee waiting for Bobby and Sheila. They drank it outside on the sidewalk, sitting around a circular metal lawn table shaded from the morning sun by a Cinzano umbrella. The owner was a little man in his early fifties with a broken nose and poorly fitted false teeth. He sat at the table with them, reading the *Daily Racing Form* through bifocals that rested low on his nose. He sat stiffly upright, his head back, his half-lidded eyes fluttering as he looked down his nose at the paper he was holding at arm's length. A car passed. He glanced toward the street. A red Chevy. He closed his eyes and exhaled a breath before returning to his paper.

"Who do ya like in the sixth?" he said to Sheila in a high-pitched voice.

Sheila made a great production of looking at the paper. Her eyebrows drew together. She brightened and pointed at a name. "Bobby's Dream," she said.

The owner looked at the odds. "Fifty-to-one," he said, shaking his head. "Bobby's Bad Dream, you mean."

"Blue Dream," Bobby said looking at Sheila, and they all laughed.

Precisely at eight o'clock, a black Cadillac pulled up to the curb beside the table. The driver was as huge as a circus fat man. He waited with the motor running while the owner hurried into the bar and then returned with a brown envelope. He handed the envelope to the fat man and waited by the car window while the fat man thumbed its contents. The fat man gave the owner a little sideways glance and then drove off without a word.

The owner wiped imaginary sweat from his forehead with great exaggeration. "Whew!" he said when he returned to his chair by the table. "Fat Freddie always makes me sweat." He smiled to himself, as if at a private memory. Then he curled back his lips and pointed to his false teeth. "A gift from Freddie. Almost twenty years ago." He shook his head. "I was some smart-assed kid. I owed him ten, maybe fifteen grand. A lota money in them days." He shrugged. "I avoided Fat Freddie for almost a week before he finally caught up to me. Right here. My old man owned this joint then." He laughed to himself. "Poor old bastard. God rest his soul. I musta lost this place three, four times on him. Each time to Fat Freddie. My old man usta walk to the joint early in the morning and the first thing he'd see through the window is Fat Freddie counting the register behind the bar. When he went inside, Freddie would just look at him real pitiful and then he'd shake his head and hand Pop my note. I always wrote the same thing. 'Dear Pop. Did it again. Sorry. Love, Sonny Boy.' I was long gone to Miami by the time he read that note. But Pop always took me back after he bought the joint back from Freddie. You know, the old man never stopped trying to get me to quit gambling. One time we went to the track and I headed straight for the hundred-dollar window. He grabs me by the arm. 'Whoa!' he says. 'Why dontcha start off over there?' He points to the two-dollar window. I says, 'Aw, Pop. You know I can't place a two-dollar bet. It's against my principles. It's no fun if you're not afraid to lose.' He wouldn't take no for an answer, so I go to the two-dollar window and get in line behind all them nickel-and-dime old ladies. When I get to the clerk I make sure Pop's not lookin' before I tell this guy to punch me out five hundred times on number three in the first. The guy looks at me like I'm crazy. 'Listen, buddy,' he says, 'there's a long line here. Why dontcha go to the hundred-dollar window?' I says, 'Shuddup and start punchin'.' " He laughed again, and shook his head. "My pockets was stuffed with all these two-dollar tickets, but Pop don't know nuthin'. He's grinning from ear to ear when I show him one two-dollar ticket. 'Now, that wasn't so hard, was it?' he says. I says, 'No, Pop.' And, can you believe it? The horse comes in. Five lengths. My old man turns to me, still smiling, and says, 'See, sonny, I told ya. Dontcha feel just as good?' I says, 'Sure, Pop. You were right.' "

"What about Fat Freddie?" Sheila said. "Your teeth?"

"Oh, yeah. Well, when Freddy finally caught up to me here, he motions me over to his car. A black Caddy, even then, only older. He always liked black Caddys. 'Image,' he usta say. 'It fits my image.' He was ahead of his time, I guess. Anyway, he asks me for the dough and I tell him I don't have it. Maybe he don't like the tone in my voice. I don't know. But he crooks his finger for me to lean down to the window. He's smiling, so I do it. He points to a stack of baseball bats in the backseat. He was the Babe Ruth of Shylocks. He'd come at you with three bats over his shoulder like Babe Ruth leavin' the on-deck circle." He laughed out loud. "Babe Ruth in a shimmering aqua-colored suit with three Louisville sluggers over his padded shoulders. He was something, Freddie. But so was I then. I tell him those bats don't scare me one bit. He was still smiling when he grabbed me around the throat and pulled my head through the window. He shoves this snub-nosed gun in my mouth and starts rattling it around like he was tryin' to clean out a hole. My teeth was flying all around like bloody Chiclets. Two days later, I paid him."

"How'd you get the money?" Bobby said.

The owner looked at him as if he were a child. "How else? I hit a number. Ten Gs. Helluva score. I was a little shy of the money I owed Freddie so I bought a dozen color television sets on credit and sold 'em to a fence for thirty cents on the dollar and gave it all to Freddie. I was living with my old man at the time. I never told him what I done, but within a month every appliance store in the city is calling our house demanding my old man fork over the first payment on a color television set. 'But we don't even have a black-and-white!' he tells them."

The bar door opened and the man with the pencil-thin mustache stepped outside. He stood there a moment, weaving back and forth, the cigar stub clenched between his teeth. Bobby, Sheila, and the owner looked at him. He gave them an almost imperceptible nod, and then he staggered across the street. The owner of the bar shook his head and smiled. The man with the mustache walked unsteadily up the street alongside the beach. After a few yards he thrust his hands into his pants pockets and picked up his pace. His stride grew stronger and steadier as he walked until finally, a few hundred yards down the road, he was walking as briskly as a fighter warming up for his morning run.

The owner checked his watch. "Benny's as regular as clockwork," he said. "Time to clean up." He excused himself and went inside. He switched on the neon Budweiser sign over the bar, and then he began to sweep out the bar with a push broom. He opened the door and pushed the debris—broken beer bottles, cigarette and cigar stubs, lottery tickets, scraps of paper with numbers on them—across the sidewalk and into the street. Bobby and Sheila finished their coffee and said good-bye to the owner. He nodded and went back inside. As they were leaving they saw him taking down all the bar stools that were upturned on top of the bar.

They walked between two beach cottages until they came to the jetty of rocks that led out from the beach in a straight line to the sea. They walked over the rocks to the end of the jetty, about a quarter of a mile from shore. They sat on the last rock, facing out to sea, their feet dangling off the rock just inches from the water below. Bobby put his arm around Sheila's shoulders and she laid her head against him. They talked for awhile, kissing every now and then, hugging one another as the waves lapped against the rocks below their feet. After awhile Sheila asked Bobby how the Muraski story was coming.

"I didn't start writing yet," he said. "I'm still reading my notes. I want to take my time with this one, babe." He shook his head in wonder, staring out to sea. "This could be the big one. I've waited a whole fucking career for a story like this and I'm not gonna rush it. Jesus, sometimes I get as high as a kite just thinking about it. It's a great feeling." He looked at her, as if what he was saying surprised even him. "It's so pure." He shook his head again and looked back out to sea. "I've got to control it, though. I've got to force myself to calm down or it'll get away from me." Sheila smiled at him. He seemed to be talking to the sea. When he spoke like this he seemed, somehow, to recapture an innocence he had lost long ago. Sheila loved to see him like this. She was glad he had his writing. And her. They fit, she thought. His writing and her. The two things he valued most.

Bobby took his arm from around Sheila. He made a fist with one hand and smacked it into the palm of the other. "Jesus, babe, I know I've got it knocked!" he said. "I can see the whole damned piece as clear . . . as clear . . . as clear as that fucking water!" He jabbed his finger at the sea. "It never happened like this before. Not a whole piece. It seems so easy it's scary." He turned quickly and stared at her. "Do you know what I mean, babe? Do you?" Sheila, stunned, did not answer. He threw up his hands in disgust. "Ah, shit! How can I explain it?" He looked back to the sea again, wincing into the sun. Then he said, "It's like when they asked Michelangelo how he could do the *David* from a block of marble. Ha! Those bastards couldn't even *conceive* of the *David*, much less *do* it!" He began to laugh. "So you know what the little Guinea said to them?" Bobby grinned. "He said, 'Boys, I didn't do shit. The *David* was already there inside the marble all this time. All I did was chip away the excess stone so he could be free.' " Bobby exhaled through puffed-out cheeks and shook his head. "That's the way I feel, babe. All I've got to do is free Muraski. He's right there. I mean, I can see that poor bastard! I see him! *Damn*, but I see him! And his wife! And his mother! And his sister! And . . . and . . ."

"And Rodney James," Sheila said.

Bobby turned and looked at her. He looked at her and through her as if he did not see her, as if he saw, instead, someone he hated. "Cocksucker!" he said. "I see him, too! I know his fucking act. I've seen guys like him all my life. They get away with murder. They're knee-deep in shit and they always find a way to shovel it off onto someone else. Like Muraski. And me. They see me in some bar with you and they shake their heads and cluck their tongues and go home and tell their old ladies and their friends and they all feel so good about themselves and so sorry for poor, sweet, Beth Giacquinto. Fuck 'em! I protected Beth long enough. I don't mind taking the heat now. I don't mind being the bad guy. If I'm gonna play, I'm gonna pay. That's the fucking rule of the game. Those bastards don't play by rules. They fuck nigger whores on business trips and when they start picking lice off their balls they swear to God they'll never do it again if their old ladies don't find out. And when she doesn't . . . you guessed it. Those bastards think they're golden. They don't think they'll ever have to pay. Like James. But he isn't gonna escape forever. What did Tony Vincent say? 'Everything's gonna catch up to everybody sooner or later.' Well, I'm gonna see it catches up to Rodney James right now. I am gonna present that cocksucker with an overdue bill. For services rendered to Stanley Muraski. I'm gonna slip it under his door so he won't even notice it at first. I'm not even gonna give him the satisfaction of seeing himself in the piece. Except for a line or two. I'm gonna make it so subtle—it'll be beautiful, babe—he won't even be able to point a finger and say, 'There! Right there! That's where he did it to me!' " Bobby began to laugh. "It'll be fucking beautiful, babe!" His laughter grew more and more shrill until Sheila began to grow afraid for him. Bobby stood up to go. His shadow enveloped her. He was still laughing, less shrilly now, and shaking his head. "Fucking beautiful," he said. "Fucking beautiful." He bent down and kissed her on the cheek. His eyes were wide and glassy. "I gotta go, babe. I gotta go. See you later." He walked back across the rocks toward shore and then in between the cottages without looking back.

Sheila stared after him—even after he had disappeared —for a long while, and then she took off the clothes she was wearing over her bathing suit and spread them underneath her and lay down in the sun. She closed her eyes and tried to sleep, but she couldn't. She sat up and stared out to sea. His anger, she thought. His terrible anger. She tried not to think about it. It was a clear day and far in the distance she could see the outline of Long Island. It was almost a year since she had met Bobby here on the rocks for the first time. She tried to recall that day, now. How much of a surprise it had been, his call, her eager response. She hardly knew the man. And yet, they had talked that day in a way she had never talked to any man. It had seemed so natural to reveal herself to him. She sensed, even then, that he would never hurt her. That was it! He could hurt no one. Only himself. He valued everyone but himself. Always that self-mocking smile. He thought himself a fool. And worse. Not a good man. His fear. It debilitated him. Which was why he always seemed so removed from others—at times, even, from her. He deliberately removed himself because he could not bear to hurt people. Nor could he bear to be a witness to their stupidity. Which was why he took such false delight in his own stupidity. He *had* to be the bad guy. Or else, who would be?

The ones he loved? He could never admit to that. So, in this way he protected those he loved. Sheila had tried so hard to make him see himself as he really was. As she saw him. She wondered if he ever would. Why not? His wife. He saw her as innocent, and he saw himself as hurting her. Sheila marveled at the damage the unaware can do to the aware. She resented that child-woman so deeply that she never spoke of her to Bobby. The thought of her, even now, infuriated Sheila. She tried to put her out of her mind. She lay down again and closed her eyes to the sun. She saw a soft, pale woman with clear blue eyes. Would he ever leave her? How long can I go on, Sheila wondered?

Bobby would work at his office until midafternoon and then he would return to the rocks to sit with her. He talked about his work. When it was going well he had the enthusiasm of a child. And when it wasn't, he was cold, remote, silent. It consumed him. Stanley Muraski. Rodney James. "Settling an old account," he would say with a grin that frightened Sheila. She had to work hard to get his mind off the story when he was with her. But when she did, he became himself again. Smiling, laughing, loving. At dusk, they would go to the bar for a drink. It was noisy and crowded with workingmen—carpenters, masons, laborers—drinking shots and beers. Sheila and Bobby, looking out of place in their shorts and sandals, sat at the far end of the bar near the back door. They talked softly for awhile and then they left the bar, amid backward glances from the men, and went back to Bobby's office. They made love on the floor and then Bobby drove Sheila to her father's house, where she would have dinner, and he returned to his own house where he had dinner with his wife and son. In this way, they passed the summer.

The story came slowly. Bobby pored over his notes for hours, day after day, reading and rereading them until, finally, after four weeks, he had memorized them. Then he began to make outlines in longhand, outline after outline on long, yellow, legal-size sheets of paper. He explored every possible direction the story might take, discarding each possibility that might result in a dead end, until, after two more weeks, he sat staring at an outline on a single sheet of paper, which, when fleshed out, would yield the truth, as he had seen it. He walked the streets of town for days, scribbling notes in drugstores and coffee shops, on napkins and matchbook covers, waiting for that first sentence to come to him.

He was huddled in the doorway of a lawyer's office one rainy afternoon when the lawyer stepped out. The lawyer was wearing a double-breasted trenchcoat with the collar pulled up around his neck. He glanced at Bobby as if he was a vagrant loitering in his doorway, and then he looked again. Bobby was hunched over, oblivious, writing with a felt-tip pen on the palm of his hand. The lawyer shook his head and walked down the street. Bobby buried his hand, a fist, deep into his pants pocket and half-walked, half-ran back to his office where he typed out the first sentence of the Stanley Muraski story. His heart was beating so rapidly he thought it might burst. He stared at the sentence for a long moment. Then he took a deep breath and forced himself to rewrite it. He spent the rest of the day rewriting that sentence from every conceivable direction until he had proved to himself that his first sentence could not be improved upon.

On the next day, he wrote the second sentence, and the third, and the fourth, and on and on; each sentence flowing so naturally from the previous one that Bobby began to perceive himself as a magician pulling a succession of brightly colored silk handkerchiefs from the sleeve of his shirt. He forced himself to slow down so he would not lose his objectivity. He took great pains with each sentence, as he had the first, rewriting them until he was sure. He quit work, always when he was going good, so that he would have something to look forward to with anticipation the next day. The pages began to pile up, slowly at first, barely a page a day, and then, after a few weeks, more rapidly, a page and a half, and then two. Never more than two, though. He refused to let himself work more quickly than that, and always the next day he reread what he had done the day before to make sure his euphoria had not deluded him. One day, in his excitement, he brought a page to the beach and read it to Sheila on the rocks.

"It's good, babe," she said. "Very good. . . . But why did you use *miasma* there?"

Bobby explained.

"But that's not exactly what the word means," Sheila said.

"I know. But it sounds like it should. I want the reader to get a feeling from the word that goes beyond its definition."

Sheila pursed her lips and shook her head. "But the definition of the word . . ."

Bobby interrupted her. "Listen, babe. You're the teacher. You deal with denotations. I'm a writer. I deal in connotations."

"But, Bobby. . . ." She broke off when she saw the look on his face. He had never looked at her in that way before. It must be how she looked at a man who was threatening her in some way. Only different, somehow. Not cold, like her look, but white hot. Barely contained fury. His breathing was labored, yet controlled. His eyes were blank. He frightened her. She couldn't speak. They sat there in silence for a long moment. Finally, his breathing began to subside and his features softened.

He smiled and said, "I'm sorry, babe. I'm touchy about my work. Especially this. I'm finally getting it right." He put his hand on her forearm and held it tightly. "Do you understand? After all these years?" He shook his head in wonder. "It's all right there, and I've got it. I know it."

Bobby finished the story in August and sent it in to the magazine. For the first time in weeks he relaxed, as if unburdened of a great weight. A few days later the editor called him at his office.

"Bobby, it's dynamite!" he said. "Is it true?"

"Of course, it's fucking true! I wrote it, didn't I?"

"Sure, Bobby. Sure. It's just so hard to believe. Rodney James, a goddamned back-stabber! Jesus!"

"Yeah, well, there's no tooth fairy either."

"What? Oh! Ha! Ha! Listen, it's too late in the season to run it now. Hell, he's having another mediocre year. What is he . . . seven and eight, or something?"

"Who?"

"James! Jesus, Bobby! Rodney James! Who the hell are we talking about? We gotta run it at the beginning of spring training. Late February. Everybody will be following the bastard then. His last year and all, before he hangs it up. He'll be getting a lot of ink. 'Twilight Years of a Superstar.' All that crap. He'll be using the exposure to push that born-again shit, too. That's when we'll zap him. Right where it hurts. The word from the coast is he's got ambitions. The fucking guy wants to be the first United States pope, for Chrissakes! Can you believe it?"

"Yeah, well, the story isn't about Rodney James. He's just a walk-on. It's about that poor fucking Polack. He's a tragedy."

"Sure, Bobby, I know. It says something about America today. Some of that stuff about his wife, the Oakie, it's beautiful. Your best work. Tell me, did you fuck her?"

Bobby slammed down the receiver. The phone rang quickly. He waited for almost ten rings before he picked it up again. "It's me. We musta been cut off. The goddamned switchboard or something. Listen, can we count on that cunt-hound?"

"Huh?"

"The cunt-hound! Vincent. Will he hold up if we get any shit from James?"

"I don't know."

"You don't know!"

"That's what I said. He told me the truth when I was there, but that doesn't mean he'll take heat for it later."

"Fuck him, then. We won't worry about it. We'll go with your word."

"Thanks."

"Listen, I want you to come in to the city for lunch. I owe you one. How about Wednesday?"

"I don't know. I'm . . ."

"Come on, for Chrissakes! A big steak at the Kansas City Steakhouse. You're a fucking writer. No writer ever turns down a free steak."

"Yeah, well, I'm turning down this one."

There was a momentary pause at the other end of the phone and then the editor said, "Actually, Bobby, there are just a few things we have to tie up."

"About what?"

"The story."

"What *about* the story?"

"Jesus! Relax! It's nothing. Just details. We'll talk about it Wednesday, okay? See you at noon." The editor hung up before Bobby could reply. He stared at the phone for a long while, and then he dialed Sheila at her father's house. He told her what had happened.

"Do you have to go?" she said.

"I don't trust the bastard with my story. I've got to go or else he'll fuck it up behind my back. Will you come with me?"

"Oh, Bobby! You know I hate the city. All those years I lived there. It depresses me out of my mind."

"I need you, babe. You'll keep me calm. I'm afraid I'll . . ."

"Of course, I'll go with you, Bobby. Anything you want. Only one thing."

"What's that?"

"Can we take the car? I hate that goddamned train with all those corporate types."

Bobby laughed out loud. "Sure, babe. We'll take the car."

The restaurant was all dark, heavy wood and brass fixtures, and the walls were covered with photographs of athletes and sports headlines from the back page of the *Daily News*.

"Dan Rosen's table," Bobby said to the waiter, a thin, pale man with receding blond hair. He wore a white shirt with the sleeves rolled up past his elbows. He glanced quickly at Sheila and then more appraisingly at Bobby, who was wearing a T-shirt, jeans, and sneakers.

"This way, sir," he said with a smile. He led them through the crowded restaurant, past tables occupied mostly by middle-aged men in business suits.

Sheila whispered in Bobby's ear, "Fag actor." Bobby nodded. "He likes you," she added. The men eating glanced up from their food as they passed. They looked briefly at Bobby, and then more approvingly at Sheila, who was wearing a raspberry-colored silk blouse and tight, white pants.

"Corporate jocks," Bobby said out of the side of his mouth. "They love you, sweets."

Sheila made a sound, as if clearing phlegm from her throat. "My curse," she said.

The waiter led them to a booth near the back wall where a man in a safari jacket and turtleneck sweater was sitting by himself. The man had frizzy hair, like a Brillo pad, and a droopy mustache that terminated at his jawline. He wore a pair of wire-rimmed spectacles that were shaped like almonds. The man, smiling, half-rose from his seat and greeted Bobby. His smile faded when he noticed Sheila.

"Dan Rosen. Sheila Doyle," Bobby said. Rosen shook her hand and looked at Bobby. "Don't worry," Bobby said. "She's all right. She's helped me with the piece." The man nodded and smiled again. He was in his late twenties. Bobby and Sheila slid into the booth across from him and ordered drinks.

"And how do you know Bobby?" the man said to Sheila.

"A mutual friend. We met on the beach one day."

"Oh, I see. And you and he are, um . . . uh . . ."

Sheila smiled brightly at him. "I'm his mistress." The man's mouth opened as if to blow smoke rings, and his head began to bob up and down, like the head of one of those toy dogs found so often in the back window of hot-rod cars. Bobby and Sheila were smiling brightly at him.

He smiled back, still nodding. The waiter returned with their drinks. Rosen raised his glass over the table.

"Here's to the 'Stanley Muraski Story,' " he said. "The best goddamned piece I ever worked on." They all touched their glasses over the table and sipped from their drinks. The waiter handed each of them large, wooden paddles with the menu hand-painted on them in colonial script that substituted an f for an s. There were no prices.

"If you'll let me," said the man, smiling first at Sheila, then Bobby. They both nodded. "T-bones all around," the man said. "Medium-rare, right?" He looked again at Sheila, then Bobby. They both nodded again. "Fine." The waiter left.

"Tell me," Bobby said, "what are these little loose ends you want me to tie up?"

The man cleared his throat and leaned forward over the table. He folded his hands on the table and looked at them as he talked. "It's just a minor thing," he said. "A slight shift of emphasis is all. The story's absolutely beautiful the way you've approached it. We just thought . . . well . . . since that stuff about James is so powerful. . . ." He looked up at Bobby. "Maybe you could shift the focus of the piece away from Muraski and more toward James? You know, he's so much more prominent a figure than . . ."

"No."

". . . Muraski."

"No."

" Our readers will be able to identify with James more, his betrayal, I mean. They'll eat it up. For Chrissakes, Bobby, this phony bastard's been preaching God, family, and country all these years and now we find out . . ."

"No. The story is about Stanley Muraski. He deserves it, even if he is dead. That fucking James stole from that poor Polack once, and I'm not gonna let him do it again."

"Jesus, Bobby, it's no big thing? Muraski will have his say. We just want you to cut him a little bit and flesh out James more. I mean that stuff about picking in the fields is fine, great, really. *Grapes of Wrath* stuff. But it's so fucking depressing. Who wants to read it? Our readers . . ."

"I said no." Bobby's breathing was labored, yet controlled. He was looking at the man across from him with unblinking eyes. Sheila reached out a hand and laid it on his arm. The waiter appeared, smiling, with three platters overflowing with T-bone steaks, each platter balanced, one after another, on his outstretched arm.

"Be reasonable, Bobby! We're gonna pay you good money for that piece. All we're asking is . . ."

"No."

The man did not speak for a long while, and when he did his voice had changed. "Listen. We were pretty goddamned generous with expenses. We know you double-billed us in Reno so you could fly her out there." He flicked his head toward Sheila without taking his eyes from Bobby. The waiter, still smiling, leaned over the table with the three platters. "We didn't say shit about that and now you won't . . ."

Bobby's arm swung out over the table as if to hit a backhand with a tennis racket. His forearm caught the waiter's arm and lifted it up and toward the editor. The three platters began to totter and slide off as the waiter tried desperately to balance them. Sheila gasped out loud when the hot steaks fell onto the editor's lap. He screamed out in pain, banging his knee against the table and sending glasses, dishes, and silverware clattering to the floor. He stabbed at the hot steaks with his fingertips, flinging each one off his lap and across the room with the same backhand motion as Bobby's. One of the steaks landed in the branches of a ficus tree and hung there; another slid across the floor like a misshapen hockey puck; the third landed with a smack against the back of a man at the adjoining table. The steak stuck there for a split second and then dropped to the floor. The man turned around slowly, a look of great annoyance on his face, as if an acquaintance had tapped him too forcefully on the back. He looked up. There was no one there, except Bobby's waiter, who was backpedaling toward him, away from Bobby's table, with his arms outstretched and palms out as if to fend off attack.

• • •

Driving back to Connecticut, Sheila and Bobby were silent for a long while. Then she looked over at him. He looked at her and they both began to laugh out loud.

"God, but that was a funny scene," she said. "The poor waiter. I thought his eyes were going to bug out of their sockets."

"That fucking Rosen deserved it," Bobby said.

"I know, Bobby, but he really got burned badly. That hot grease." She shook her head as if in sympathy with the editor and then she began to laugh again. When she stopped laughing she said, "What's going to happen to the story, now?"

"Nothing. They'll run it the way I want or I don't sell it to them. I've got them by the nuts and they know it. They want it badly, even if I don't rewrite it. I've just got to watch the bastards to make sure they don't fuck it up behind my back."

· SEVEN ·

Bobby and Sheila were lying, naked, on the floor of his office late one night in September when he felt the lump in her right breast. It was the size of a small pea that had turned to stone and rooted to her chest muscles inside the liquidy sack of her breast. He sat up.

"What's the matter?" she said.

"Nothing, babe." He got up and went into the bathroom. He locked the door behind him and sat on the toilet seat in the darkness. He looked out the window into the parking lot. It was deserted except for her old Pinto. The bottom panel of the door on the driver's side was eaten away with rust. "Every time I slam the door," Sheila had said, "a little piece falls off. Pretty soon I'll be riding on a frame." She laughed. They took the car to a body shop to see if there was any way to repair it. "Nope," said the body man, looking at the rot and shaking his head. "It's cancer. Hereditary with these damned Pintos. Everyone I seen got it."

Bobby left the bathroom and returned to his office. Sheila was sitting up on the floor. He stood over her for a moment, looking down at her face in the darkness. She was smiling at him. The faint, sweet, pained smile of a mother.

"I know, babe," she said. "I felt it myself a while ago. I didn't want to worry you. I've already gone to my gynecologist. He doesn't think it's anything, but just to be safe, he wants me to go to a specialist in New Haven. Will you come with me?" He didn't say anything. She patted the floor beside her with the flat of her hand. "Come. Sit with me," she said. He sat down beside her as if without will.

She put an arm around his shoulders and held him.
"There, there, babe," she said, stroking his cheek with the
back of her hand. "Not to worry. I'll never leave you." He
was staring straight ahead through unseeing eyes. He felt
light, empty, hollowed out. If she let go he would float
away.

The doctor's reception room was deserted, except for an
old couple sitting, without emotion, against the far wall,
and a receptionist sitting behind a sliding glass partition
that was closed to the room. Bobby sat in a chair against
the wall and waited while Sheila went over to the receptionist. Her high-heeled shoes clattered against the linoleum floor. She was wearing nylons and a tweed suit. He
had watched her dress this morning. Panties. Bra. Garter
belt. Nylons. Slip. She had taken such care with her
clothes, her makeup, her hair. He had never seen her in a
bra or slip before. She became, before his eyes, a different
woman. Older. Severe. A middle-aged woman preparing to
go on a long journey, alone. This new woman was not like
any of the other women she could be. In jeans. In shorts.
In a bikini. Naked. He had felt, in her, he had everything
he ever wanted. Now this. It confused him.

Sheila tapped on the receptionist's window. The receptionist looked up, annoyed. She had upswept, bleached-
blonde hair that had been lacquered stiff, like hard, ribbon
candy. She slid open her window a few inches and Sheila
bent down to talk to her. She spoke in whispers in a barren
room. A plant. A few pamphlets in a rack. An oil painting
of a sailboat. An assortment of magazines, months old,
dog-eared, their covers missing. The magazines were scattered around the room on the seats of the chairs that lined
three walls. The chairs had hollow aluminum arms and
legs, and plastic seats and backs that were the color and
grainy texture of an orange. Bobby picked up a copy of
People magazine and began to leaf through it. Rock stars.
Actresses. Plastic surgeons. Teenaged millionaires. Mongrel dogs who starred on Broadway. He heard the clatter

of Sheila's heels again and looked up. She was coming toward him from across the room. She passed through the old couple's field of vision. They stared through her and beyond, as if she was invisible. She smiled, weakly, at Bobby and sat down beside him. She put her arm inside his arm and hugged it, tight, to her chest. He stiffened, feeling the soft sack against his arm.

"What are you reading?" she said. He pointed to a picture of the mongrel dog sitting in a Jacuzzi. "Oh, Jesus!" she said, shaking her head. Bobby began to turn the pages. They booth looked, without speaking, at the magazine. When Bobby turned a page too quickly, she put her finger on the page and leaned closer for a better look. After a few more seconds she took her finger off the page and nodded. Bobby turned the page. A nurse came through a door at the end of the room and stopped. Bobby and Sheila looked up. The nurse called out Sheila's name. Sheila stood up quickly, smoothed the front of her skirt with the flat of her hands, bent over and kissed Bobby on the cheek. She walked across the room toward the nurse with hurried little steps. The nurse was smiling at her. Again, the old couple did not see her. The nurse went back through the door and Sheila was about to follow her when she stopped suddenly. She turned around and looked at Bobby. The features of her face seemed to melt and sag before his eyes. Bobby stood up. Sheila forced a smile, gave him a quick shake of her head, and disappeared through the door.

Bobby looked around. The old couple didn't see him standing there. The receptionist was reading a magazine. He sat down and waited. His hands rested, one on top of the other, on the magazine spread out on his lap. He stared straight ahead. He felt light again, empty, drained of strength. A long time passed. Bobby was conscious of the room filling up with people, but he could not focus on them. They passed before his eyes only as a presence he could not make out. He tried hard to focus his eyes, but sight eluded him. He surrendered to it and just sat there. More time passed, and then, suddenly, the door at the far end of the room opened and Bobby could see again. A tall, thin man in a white coat swept into the room and went straight to the receptionist. He talked to her in a loud voice with a Scandinavian accent. He was in his seventies, but looked younger, an ascetic-looking man with skin stretched tight over his gaunt features. He turned around and headed back toward the door when he caught a glimpse of Bobby. A flicker of recognition passed over his flat, gray-blue eyes. His thin lips pursed as if in anger or disgust; then he disappeared through the door. A short while later, Sheila burst through the door and walked quickly toward Bobby.

"Hurry!" she said. "Let's get out of here!" Her face was pink and blotchy and her eyes were moist. Bobby stood up. She was already to the door. He hurried after her.

It was a day without color or light, warmth or cold. They got into his car, left the parking lot, turned onto the thruway, and headed toward the school where she lived. She did not speak for a few moments, and then, without looking at Bobby, she said, "I've got to go in for a biopsy in ten days. It's standard procedure, he said. He told me not to worry." She took a deep breath, her eyelids fluttering shut, and went on. "I know I've got it."

"How can you tell?"

"He was feeling my breast, talking to me, you know, trying to keep my mind off it. God, he had cold hands. He felt a couple of soft lumps. Cysts, he said, not uncommon, nothing to worry about, and then he felt something where you did. I have to hand it to him. He didn't skip a beat, just kept on talking. But I saw a look in his eyes. Absolute hatred. Not for me. For an instant, he had forgotten I was there. It was just him and the thing he had felt. He's been fighting it most of his life, I guess, like an exorcist. He tried to reassure me again, but I knew. He left the room for a few minutes and, when he came back, he asked me if he could do a biopsy right there. If it was positive, he said, he'd book me into a room today and operate tomorrow morning. I panicked. I had this fear that I'd never see you again, that something would go wrong. I told him. I wanted time to be with you. He asked me if you were the bearded man in the reception room. I said yes. He asked if you were my husband. I said no." She turned toward Bobby and looked at him with her dark, knitted brows. "And this is what I don't understand, babe. For the first time since I went in there, he looked at me with pity. Why?"

Bobby smiled. "He thinks he knows me. . . . The kind of man I am."

Sheila went into the hospital at the end of the month. Bobby was there in the hallway when three nurses wheeled her out of an elevator, up from the recovery room. He walked alongside the stretcher as they wheeled her down a long, narrow corridor toward her room. She was enveloped in the stench of chemicals, as if in a cocoon. Her eyes, rimmed with dried pus, were closed; her skin was a pale, grayish green; her black hair was matted to her cheeks and stuck to the pillow from sweat. He touched her face with the back of his hand and it was cold. Her eyes fluttered open. They were glassy, misted over. They kept rolling back into her eyelids. She saw him only as a shuddering shadow.

She forced her eyes open wide, like an old-time blackfaced comedian feigning surprise. "Babe, is that you?"

"Yes," he said. He was smiling.

"Are you all right?"

"Yes, babe. I'm all right." She let her eyes roll back under her eyelids and closed them. He leaned down and whispered in her ear. "I love you." A barely perceptible smile appeared on her cold, pale, purplish lips, and then was gone.

Bobby waited outside her room while the nurses transferred her from the gurney to her bed. They drew curtains around her bed so that he could not see. He heard only their voices, bright, cheerful, loud, as they spoke to her. She did not respond. When they pulled back the curtains she was lying on the bed, her black hair spread out evenly on either side of the pillow. Her head and shoulders were elevated.

"You can go in now," one of the nurses said, and they left the room.

Bobby sat down in a chair alongside the bed. An intravenous tube was stuck in Sheila's arm. It led to a bottle of clear liquid held high atop an aluminum pole. Her chest was swathed in so many layers of bandages that it looked massive, like a weight lifter's. Her eyes were closed. Bobby held her cold hand. She tried to open her eyes but they kept rolling back under her eyelids.

"Don't," he said into her ear. "Go to sleep. I'll be here when you wake." She let her eyes close and drifted off. Bobby looked around the room. It was blurred, swimming before his eyes as if seen through a rain-splattered window. He wiped the tears from his eyes with the back of his hand and tried to focus on the room. There were three other beds, two of them occupied. A withered old woman with white, mottled skin lay motionless on one. Her face was turned toward the window and the sky. The other bed was occupied by a middle-aged woman with her hair like straw that had been dyed jet-black. She wore a frilly, pink dressing gown with puffy sleeves, and she was chewing gum while sitting up in bed, painting her fingernails. Her eyebrows had been plucked bare and then penciled in black in the shape of boomerangs. Even lounging, she looked surprised. She blew gently on her fingernails and glanced up at the soap opera on the television set suspended from the ceiling in the middle of the room. She smiled over at Bobby. "'As the World Turns,'" she said chewing her words with her gum. "I just love that little Betsy. She's such a scamp."

"I don't know," Bobby said. "I don't watch. . . ."

"Oh, of course not," she said, flapping a wrist at him. Then she looked at Sheila and back to Bobby. "Now, don't you worry, hon. She'll be just fine." She held up a deck of cards, careful not to smudge her nails. "Canasta, hon?"

Bobby smiled and shook his head no.

The woman shrugged. "Suit yourself, hon. She'll be

under a long time." She finished her nails, and then, holding her hands, limp-wristed, before her, like a begging puppy, she watched the soap opera with the utmost concentration, smacking her gum.

The doctor came into the room. Bobby stood up. The doctor looked at him, then picked up Sheila's chart at the end of the bed and began to study it. Without looking at Bobby, he said, "Everything went fine. I performed a modified radical mastectomy. She only lost the breast and lymph nodes. I saved the muscles in her chest. She has a ninety-eight percent chance of complete recovery. I think we got it all."

"Thank you, doctor. I can't . . . she means. . . ." Bobby could not finish his sentence.

The doctor looked at him, as if down from a great height. He had spent his entire adult life looking down at supplicants, and, now, he could no longer differentiate between those who sought his help and those who merely passed before his eyes. He narrowed his flat, gray-blue eyes at Bobby, as if he, Bobby, were a distasteful supplicant.

"She is a very lucky girl," the doctor said in his precise accent. "Another few months and it might have been too late." He folded his long arms across his chest. He was very tall and thin, with a long neck and a tiny skeletal head that gave him the look of a praying mantis. "You know, Mr. Giacquinto, Miss Doyle told me of your . . . delicate situation. It has been a great strain on her. I would like you to know that. Despite what you may think, despite the history of cancer in her family—I am speaking of her mother, of course—it is often not heredity that activates this disease, but rather extreme emotional stress. Your situation has caused her great stress, Mr. Giacquinto. You should know that." Before Bobby could speak, the doctor turned his back on him and left the room.

Bobby got a name tag at the reception desk, which identified him as Mr. Doyle, so that he could visit Sheila every morning before breakfast and in the evening before dinner.

She recovered quickly. "She has a great will to live," the doctor said to them both one morning. Sheila was sitting up in bed, her hair washed and combed, her face lightly brushed with makeup.

"It's Bobby," she said smiling at him. "Without him, I don't know what I'd do."

"Yes," the doctor said. "Certainly."

Sheila was released from the hospital only ten days after she had arrived. Bobby was there to drive her back to school. He drove slowly on the thruway, careful to avoid any potholes or sudden turns that might jar her and cause her pain. He hunched over the steering wheel, his face only inches from the windshield, like a cautious old man driving on the thruway for the first time. Soon his neck and shoulders and lower back were stiff from tension. Sheila was sitting beside him, staring straight ahead, holding herself delicately as if she might break. She was wearing a loose-fitting, blue sweater over a few layers of gauze bandages wrapped around her chest. She looked down at herself, her chin tucked into her neck like a fat person trying to see over his belly. Her eyebrows rose.

"I can't see much difference," she said. "Maybe with the bandages off." She looked over at Bobby. "Poor thing! It was bad enough before, but now. You'll be so deprived."

"I know. I know. Don't remind me." He kept his eyes on the road. "A tit man all my life, and now look. Jesus Christ!" He glanced briefly heavenward, and then said, "What a fucking sense of humor He has." They both began to laugh, but Sheila had to stop because of the pain.

"No more!" she said. "Please!"

She lived in a sprawling, modern, white-brick dormitory building on top of a barren hill that overlooked the rest of the campus. Soccer field. Football field. Futuristic arts center. Old colonial dining hall. An even older, white-spired church. The church was framed by two towering pine trees. Ivy grew up the walls of all the old buildings and sunlight was reflected just so off the glass front of the sharply angled arts center. It was a cool, clear, sunny day. Students were walking to and from classes and the football team was practicing in gray uniforms. The thud of shoulder pads against shoulder pads echoed in the air. A whistle blew, splitting the air like the call of an exotic bird.

Bobby carried Sheila's bags into the apartment and put them down in the living room off the kitchenette. She followed behind. The living room was bathed in slabs of light slanting through windows along one wall that looked out onto the parking lot. Faint particles of dust were suspended in the smoky light. Plants hung from the ceiling in front of the windows. Their leaves were a pale, yellowish green in the light. The rug below them was littered with dried, curled-up leaves.

The living room was sparsely furnished with bargains Sheila had picked up in a junk shop and refinished, and with heirlooms handed down from her mother. A plain, old rocking chair with a calico cushion to hide its plywood seat. A dry sink whose top was painted white to simulate the marble that had been stripped off it long ago. A grandfather clock. A mahogany rolltop desk on which stood a number of photos of her mother and father and children, and a little glass case in which lay, on a faded velvet cushion, a few strands of dried hair that had belonged to Sheila as a baby. There were two, grainy sepia photographs on the wall, portraits of her great-grandparents. A homely woman in a bonnet and a sour-faced man with a high, starched collar. Over the sofa hung a big black-and-white, Alvin Ailey print, the stylized silhouette of a dancer leaping, arms outstretched, across a white field.

Sheila went into the bedroom and sat down on the bed, her hands limp in her lap. "Can you help me take this sweater off?" she said. "It itches terribly." She looked strangely small and frail sitting there, like a sad, young girl. Bobby helped her slip her arms out of the sleeves and then pulled the sweater over her head. The gauze was crisscrossed over each shoulder and down across her chest like a bandolier. The place where her right breast had been was less prominent than where her left breast still was.

"I want to see," Bobby said.

"Are you sure, babe? It's not pretty."

"I've got to see sometime, don't I?" Sheila nodded once. Bobby began to unravel the gauze with the same delicacy a woman would use to unravel green tissue from a bouquet of roses. When he was finished he looked at her. Sheila twisted her head away from his gaze as if to look over her left shoulder. A thin, dark-purple scar ran down the front of her right shoulder, passed through the center of where her breast and nipple had been, and stopped at the bottom of her rib cage. The scar was rimmed, on either side, with dried blood and inflamed skin, and it was laced, from top to bottom, with fine, black stitches that stuck up out of her skin like hairs.

Bobby got down on his knees so that his face was level with her chest. He looked more closely. There were tiny, vertical folds of skin, like a drawn curtain, where her breast had been. He brushed the folds of skin, and then the scar itself with his lips. Tears ran down Sheila's cheeks.

"Lie down," Bobby said. "Let me help you." He put his arm around her back and eased her down onto the bed. He took off her shoes, then hiked up her skirt and peeled down her panties and pantyhose together. He unbuttoned her skirt on the side, unzipped it, then slid it out from under her. He was kneeling between her legs. She lay naked on the bed, her arms at her side, her face turned away on the pillow. He moved farther down on the bed so that his knees were on the floor and his upper body was lying on the bed, his face close to her sex. He spread her legs gently with his hands and lowered his face to her sex. She stiffened. Then, after a few seconds, relaxed. She began to moan. Without stopping, Bobby looked up at her, over the dark mound of hair, the flat, faintly lined stomach, the prominent rib cage, the one breast. It spilled loosely to her side. Where her other breast had been, there was nothing, nothing but that long, dark scar that ran, like a dried riverbed, up to her shoulder.

She came softly, with a whimper. Bobby unzipped his pants and moved up over her. His body was above hers now, and parallel to it, but not touching. His hands were planted into the bed on either side of her, and his arms were fully extended so that he looked like a man about to perform a push-up. He entered her, and then, slowly, carefully, he lowered himself until his body was only inches from hers. He paused a moment, and waited for her to turn her face toward his. When she did, finally, he kissed her. Then he raised himself again until his arms were fully extended. He began rhythmically, over and over, to lower and raise himself until sweat broke out on his brow and ran down his jawline onto her scar, and his arms and chest ached with the strain. But he kept on, never touching her chest, and soon her hips began to thrust slightly to meet his, and she came with a look of pain on her face. Bobby came immediately afterward, and then held himself, stiff-armed, above her.

"You all right, babe?" he said.

"I love you. I love you. I love you." Tears were streaming down her face.

It was the first time Bobby had ever made love to Sheila in her apartment. He did not like to go there. It bothered him to distance himself from his wife and child when he was with Sheila. When he had sex with Sheila in his office, a few miles from his home, it did not bother him as much, nor did it bother him when he was out of town on business with Sheila, since he was working to support his family. It bothered him most, on those rare occasions, when he drove an hour on the thruway to her apartment. Those drives unnerved him. He always feared an accident, a broken car, an excuse to be fabricated when his wife would ask, bewildered, what he was doing driving so far upstate without telling her beforehand. He tried to explain this to Sheila once. She said she understood. But he was never sure she did.

Sheila healed quickly. Within weeks she was back teaching. She had bought a prosthesis, a liquidy sack filled with silicone and covered with silk, which she inserted into her bra each morning before going to class. It felt almost as natural as her real breast, Bobby told her one day in his office. He was standing behind her, his arms wrapped around her, his hands cupping both breasts. "Except a bit too firm," he said, squeezing her prosthesis. "Not the kind of boob a man expects to come with a forty-two-year-old broad who's had four kids."

At first, when Bobby was in the room, Sheila would go into the bathroom and lock the door before inserting the prosthesis into her bra. But, finally, at his insistence, she began to perform that task in front of him. She would turn her back to him, hunch over, rounding her shoulders, and drop the prosthesis into her bra. After awhile, she no longer bothered even to turn her back. She adjusted the sack with one hand while talking to Bobby as he dressed.

"There," she would say. "Is it straight?"

Bobby would glance up with the same disinterest he evidenced when she asked him to check her makeup. "Sure, babe. It's fine."

Teaching in class, Sheila had difficulty raising her right arm. It was still stiff and sore, so she forced herself to exercise it by writing often on the blackboard. She was able to raise her right hand, unaided, only as high as her chest, so she would place her left hand under her right elbow, and then, with the utmost nonchalance, the way women do when smoking a cigarette at a cocktail party, she would force her right arm upward, until her hand was at eye level and she could write on the blackboard. Her back was always to her students, so they could not see the look of pain on her face as she wrote. After she finished, she would turn around to face them, still propping up her right arm as if holding a cigarette. She would be smiling now, asking them questions, while slowly, steadily, lowering her right arm until it was at her side.

Soon, she was driving regularly to Bobby's office an hour away. She drove with her left hand on the steering wheel, and when she had to shift, she cradled the steering wheel between her knees, and reached across her body to shift with her left hand.

In February, Bobby's editor called and told him he had to go to Ft. Lauderdale, where the Stars still trained, to verify some quotes he had attributed to Rodney James.

"Think of it as a vacation in the sun," Dan Rosen had said, when Bobby hesitated. "We'll pay all expenses for a month . . . and you can bring your girl, too. On us. Bobby."

"I don't know," Bobby said. "Sheila hasn't been well the last few months."

"Well, then it'll be a good rest for her, sitting in the sun all day. You won't have to do much, just meet with James once or twice to check some quotes. Hell, Bobby, this piece is gonna make a big splash and we want to cover our asses, you know what I mean?"

Later that evening, when Bobby told Sheila about Rosen's call, she was delighted.

"Oh, it'll be wonderful, Bobby. It falls just on my vacation."

"I don't know. I don't trust the bastard. It seems too easy. After what I did to him. He acts like it never happened. I think he just wants me out of town while he's editing the piece."

"Then we won't go. That's all there is to it."

Bobby looked at her. Then he smiled. "Fuck it," he said. "I'll make him read it to me over the phone before he can run it. We'll go."

"Are you sure? Don't go on my account."

"I want to go," he said. "I want to get away for awhile. What can he do to the piece?"

· EIGHT ·

They stayed at a small hotel only a block from the beach in a quiet, residential section of Ft. Lauderdale that was noted for its family-run motels that were nothing more than long, narrow, single-story, stucco buildings consisting of a few efficiency apartments, one of which was, invariably, lived in by the owner and his family. Their motel, The Beacon Light, was L-shaped, with only four apartments. Three of the apartments, the stem of the L, faced sideways across a narrow strip of grass dotted with a few potted plants, a circular lawn table with umbrella and chairs, and an occasional scampering chameleon. The owner's apartment, much larger than the others, formed the base of the L at the back, facing the street.

When Bobby and Sheila arrived late in the afternoon, a man and a woman were just finishing cleaning the last apartment near the larger one. They greeted Bobby and Sheila with English accents, the man's accent decidedly more cockney than the woman's. They showed them through the three-room efficiency. A living room with bright green-and-white furniture and a piece of driftwood hanging on the wall. A tiny kitchenette with mismatched plates and glasses in the cabinets over the sink. A large bedroom with twin beds and a bathroom with brightly painted plastic fish on the walls.

Outside again, the man extended his hand to Bobby and wished them a good stay. "Everything's shipshape," he said in a cheery voice. He was smiling, a handsome man with fine, straight features; silvery hair; and the small, bright, blue eyes of a child. He looked at them with his fixed grin and his child's eyes, a man in his fifties who had always been so much more handsome than he was bright. "Dot 'n I spiffed it up real proper. Inat right, Dot?"

"Yes, we did, Ted," the woman said. "Everything's nice and tidy." She was small and dark, a plain, almost homely woman with big, wearied, brown eyes. "We'd appreciate it if you left it the way you found it. Sometimes, people away from home . . . you know."

Bobby and Sheila assured the couple they would leave the place spotless and then, after more handshakes, the couple went into their apartment and Bobby and Sheila entered theirs. Sheila went directly to the bedroom. "This will never do," she said, dropping her bags. She began to push the twin beds together with Bobby's help. When they finished, Bobby suggested they go to the beach.

"We'll unpack later," he said. Sheila hesitated a moment, and then agreed. She went into the bathroom while Bobby searched through his bags for his bathing suit. He put it on in the bedroom. When Sheila came out she was wearing the two-piece bathing suit with wire supports in the bra that she had worn that first time with Bobby on the rocks.

Bobby looked at her. "Where's the black bikini I bought you in L.A.?"

"I forgot it."

"What do you mean?"

"Oh, Bobby! Please!"

"What do you mean, you forgot it?"

"I just did."

"Goddamn it! Then you'll get another one."

"I can't, Bobby!"

"Yes, you can. You're not going to wear that fucking old-lady's bathing suit on the beach. Not with me, you won't." Her eyes grew red-rimmed and she fought back tears. "Come on," he said and grabbed her hand. They went down the street to a small shopping area and found a women's boutique. While Sheila stood behind him, Bobby flipped through a rack of bathing suits, every so often yanking one off the rack, holding it up in front of his eyes, then thrusting it back to the rack.

"Can I be of help?" said a voice from behind them.

Bobby glanced over his shoulder at a woman in her fifties, heavily made-up, with a puff of teased white hair under a lime green turban. The woman was smiling at him. There was lipstick on her teeth.

"No, that's all right," Bobby said. "We're just looking."

"We have some very with-it bikinis," the woman said as Bobby flipped through the racks. She looked at Sheila with an appraising eye. "Now, let me see. You must be a six, dear. You're so thin. Oh, I could just die for a figure like yours. You must . . ."

Bobby held up another bikini and examined it at arm's length. The woman said, "That's a very now suit, you know, and it comes in all kinds of beautiful multicolors." Bobby put the suit back on the rack while the woman continued to talk in her falsely girlish way. Her hands fluttered before her as she spoke and her face assumed a variety of expressions—frowns, smiles, contemplations—as if she had spent her entire life obliviously emoting to a dozing audience.

"Try this one," Bobby said, holding up a bikini in front of Sheila.

"Bobby, do I have to?"

"Why, of course, dear," the woman said. "It's a lovely choice. It's so . . . so . . ."

"Where's the dressing room?" Bobby said.

The woman, still talking, pointed to a stall with a drawn curtain. Sheila exhaled through puffed-up cheeks, took the suit, and went to the stall, closing the curtain behind her. The woman continued to talk while Bobby hovered outside the dressing room. After a few minutes, Sheila's small voice could be heard.

"It's no good, Bobby. It doesn't work."

"Let me see." Bobby slipped inside the curtains. Sheila was naked from the waist up. Her scar had healed considerably and now was merely a cross-hatched white line rimmed with pink running from the front of her shoulder to the bottom of her rib cage. "Try it on again," Bobby said. As Sheila slipped into the bikini top once again, the woman's shrill voice called through the curtains.

"Excuse me, sir, but you can't stay in there. It's only for ladies. What if someone should . . . I mean, I keep a respectable shop. My clientele is the very crème de la crème of . . ."

Bobby adjusted the sides of the bikini bra so that they covered the scar. Then he helped Sheila insert her prosthesis. He tugged on the bra a bit until it covered the prosthesis completely. "There," he said. "It looks fine. No one will ever tell." Sheila turned and looked at herself in the dressing room mirror. She smiled.

"You're right. It does look pretty good."

"Fucking dynamite, you mean." Standing behind her, he put his arms around her and cupped both of her breasts. "Feels good, too." He kissed the back of her neck and whispered in her ear, "I love you, babe."

They woke in darkness, before daybreak, and made love as in a dream while the wind from the sea rustled the leaves of the palm trees and rattled the screen in their window and billowed out their drawn curtain like the sail of an exotic ship. They dressed in T-shirts and shorts, by rote, still in a sleepy daze, redolent of sex, and went outside. They walked up the darkened street glistening wet from the evening's rain. They walked in silence along the deserted street amid the sounds only of the wind and their sandals slapping against the pavement. Sheila shivered against the cold and clung to Bobby for warmth. The cold began to wake them as they approached the beach. They sat on a bench facing the sea. Purple waves were being whipped by the wind into a towering, arching line of grayish froth that resembled, in the eerie darkness, an advancing army of gigantic, hooded cobras. The waves swelled and roared before striking angrily at the beach and then receding slowly, as if in shame, back into the sea. Soon, other people, singly and in pairs, joined Bobby and Sheila on the benches that faced the sea. No one spoke. They sat as in a trance, facing out to sea, watching as a thin, bluish gray line appeared on the horizon. The line grew paler and

paler, and then began to turn color, a faint vermilion, and
began to rise on the horizon as a slight curve, the curve
growing more pronounced and larger, shooting off rays of
vermilion light that fanned over the purplish sea turning
it a dark, forest green until finally the curve became a huge
vermilion ball balanced precariously on the horizon and
someone on the bench began to clap, and then another,
and another, until everyone on the benches facing the sea
was applauding the risen sun. The applause died. People
began to drift off now, talking in soft murmurs.

In sunlight, they walked along the beach. They held
hands as they walked on the wet sand close to the water.
The waves erased their footprints behind them. An oil
tanker moved slowly across the horizon. A line of sea gulls
was perched on a retaining wall in front of a motel. An old
man combed the sand with a metal detector. Bobby spoke
into Sheila's ear. She looked at the old man and shook her
head. Bobby slipped his arm around her bare waist. She
was wearing a white bikini. Every so often she would look
down at herself and adjust the bra that held her prosthesis.
They passed a woman lying on the sand close to the water.
They cast a shadow over the woman. She sat up and followed them with her eyes as they moved down the beach.
The woman's eyes narrowed as they grew smaller and
darker and closer together until they were indistinguish-
able, one from the other. They fit, joined at the hip, like
two silhouettes cut from the same paper.
    They reached a crowded area of the beach, turned, and
walked across the hot sand. They stepped between sunbathers smelling of coconut oil and climbed a set of
wooden stairs that led to an open bar alongside a pool. The
smell of coconut oil mixed with sweat was thick at the bar.
Bobby ordered drinks. They stood under the hot sunlight
and sipped their drinks. The bar and the pool area and the
beach below were packed with people. The men and
women on the beach were beautifully tanned. They lay
glistening on deck chairs, talking to one another without

turning their faces from the sun. Some of the men were playing backgammon. They were slim, with slight paunches over their bikini bathing suits, and they were adorned with chains and charms and bracelets and wrist-watches, all of gold that shot off sparks of white light in the sun. The women were dressed in bikinis of every pastel hue. They, too, were blindingly adorned with gold, and heavily made-up. Whenever one of the women got up to go to the bar, she would first check her makeup, and then put on dark, gold-rimmed sunglasses and high-heeled shoes. The people lying around the pool stared at the women from the beach, who did not seem to notice them. The people at the pool were mostly married couples, not yet pink from the sun, their faces coated with white cream. The men wore boxer shorts and the women two-piece bathing suits like Sheila's old one. A pool boy with a wispy mustache circulated amongst them, selling suntan oil. He furrowed his brow and nodded as he talked to the couples, and later, when he talked to their teenaged daughters, he smiled and fluttered his eyelashes.

When Sheila finished her drink she went over to a chaise lounge. Bobby stayed at the bar and ordered another drink. Sheila began to rub oil on her body. Bobby watched her. She adjusted her bra, held one hand over her pros-thesis, and lay down on her back. She closed her eyes. One leg was slightly raised and bent. Bobby stared at her as if she was a stranger he was noticing for the first time. Her long legs. The hollow at her stomach. Her rib cage. Her small breasts, only one of which spilled to the side. Her skin, already faintly tanned, shone in the sunlight. Bobby smiled to himself and turned back to the bar. He stood there, watching people come and go, talking to no one. A blonde girl at the end of the bar smiled at him. He smiled back, shrugged, and gestured with his head toward Sheila. The girl turned her head away and began talking to a man with a parrot perched on his shoulder. The man and the girl were facing sideways to Bobby at the end of the bar. The girl leaned toward the man, puckered her lips, and kissed the parrot on the beak. From under the parrot's tail white feces dribbled down the man's back. Bobby smiled and shook his head. He turned around to stare at Sheila, dozing in the sun. A man was standing over her, looking down. He wore a sports jacket and gray slacks. He was tall, rawboned in a western sort of way, with faintly freckled pink skin and sandy-colored hair cut short and standing straight up like sparse, spring grass. He had big ears and narrow, pale blue eyes. He squatted down, like a football coach, and spoke to Sheila. She woke with a start, raised herself on her elbows, one hand held over her prosthesis. The man was smiling at her. Sheila looked over at Bobby, her eyes wide. He nodded and she looked back at the man who was talking to her. After a few minutes Bobby went over to them. The man stood up and introduced himself.

"Jack Keane," he said, grinning at Bobby. He reached a hand over Sheila and shook Bobby's hand. "I was just admirin' your wife here." He shook his head and winked. "She's some handsome woman."

"I know," Bobby said.

"You're a very lucky man."

"I know that, too."

"Can I buy you all a drink?" the man said. Sheila looked at Bobby.

"Sure," Bobby said. "Why not?" The man went over to the bar.

"Bobby! Jeez, he scares me!" Sheila said.

"Relax, babe. He's just being friendly."

The man returned with their drinks and they talked for awhile. He told them that he was a cattle rancher out beyond Deerfield. He seldom came to Ft. Lauderdale. Ft. Lollipop, he called it. It was too crowded for him. "Nothin' but dope runners and pimps," he said. "And sluts. You're lucky to have a woman like her." He smiled at Bobby without looking at Sheila, as if he was talking about someone who was not there. "She's got the best figure on the beach," he said. "And she's a lady, too. I can tell. I been

lookin' for one like her ever since I got out of the marines
ten years ago." He gave Bobby that thin-lipped smile of
his and said, "Maybe you heard of me? Colonel Jack
Keane? Black Jack Keane they called me in Nam."

Bobby looked at Sheila and then back to the man. "No,
I don't believe so," he said.

"It was in all the papers. The My Lai thing? Calley
weren't the only one. He was just the stupidest one. He got
caught." Bobby and Sheila looked at one another and then
back at the man. He was still grinning. "You know, you
got a pretty good figure yourself," he said to Bobby. "I can
see that. You're a big guy."

"Thanks," Bobby said.

"But I can take you."

"Excuse me?"

"If I had to, I could take you out right now. Right here.
In front of all these people. Then she'd be mine, wouldn't
she?" Sheila grabbed Bobby's hand and squeezed it. The
man laughed softly. "But that wouldn't be right, would it?
You seem like a pretty nice fella."

Sheila stood up. "Well, I think we should be going now,"
she said. She smiled at the man. "Thank you so much for
the drinks." She pulled Bobby with her as she headed for
the stairs.

The man called after them. "Maybe I'll see you folks
again sometime?"

They returned to the motel at dusk. Dot was sitting alone
under the umbrella, reading a paperback novel. She said
hello and smiled. The distant smile of one who is forever
turning over and over in her mind an irresolvable problem
she cannot escape. Sheila and Bobby talked to her for a
few minutes before they entered their apartment.

"That poor woman," Sheila said to Bobby when they
were inside. "It's him. Ted. I know it. I've seen that smile
before."

"Where?"

Sheila smiled at Bobby. It was the same smile he had

just seen on Dot. "In the mirror," Sheila said. "When I knew I had to leave my husband."

They showered together, washing off the oil and sand from each other's bodies, and then they put on shorts and T-shirts and prepared dinner together. After dinner, when it was dark, they brought their coffee outside and sat under the umbrella. Dot was gone. The light was on in her apartment and they could smell fish frying through the screen door. They heard Ted's cheerful voice, but not Dot's. They sat and talked for a long while in the darkness, and when a breeze came and it began to get cold, Sheila went inside to put on her sweatsuit. She came back out and sat beside Bobby again, and they talked late into the night until they heard, coming from the first apartment near the street, the sound of an organ and then a man's voice singing in a thick, French accent.

Ted appeared at the screen door. "Sorry about that," he said, with his big smile. "That's André. He's courtin' Dot's mum. I hope it don't bother you none."

Sheila smiled. "Oh, no. It's beautiful. A lovely touch."

"Yeah, init? Mum's a sketch. We bought her a subscription to the *National Enquirer* a bit back, and now she swears by it. All those Hollywood romances. She believes it's gospel. Inat right, Dot?" From inside the apartment they heard the murmur of Dot's voice. "Well, night, now," he said in that childlike, cheerful voice of his and closed the door.

Sheila and Bobby spent the rest of the week as they had that first day. They saw the sun rise each morning, walked along the beach, stopped for a drink at the pool bar, dozed in the sun, their bodies growing browner each day, and then returned at dusk to their motel. Sometimes Dot would be sitting at the round picnic table, reading, when they returned, and sometimes Ted would be sitting there, shirtless, his feet propped up on the table, his eyes shut, smiling into the sun, but never both together. Sheila said Ted's was the smile of a man who had ceased to struggle, who lived daily in a twilight land of heaven on earth. "I don't know what happened to him," she said. "Something so tragic he's just tuned out."

Ted always gave them a hearty hello and asked them to join him by the table. He told them funny stories in that excitable way of his, blue eyes opened wide, one hand scissoring his white hair from his brow while the other tapped Bobby repeatedly on the forearm. "Inat right, Robert?" he would say with quick, little nods and a wide-eyed, opened-mouth. "Init?"

Sheila and Bobby laughed out loud at his stories, most of which had to do with his part-time job as a bellman at a small hotel that catered to little old ladies with blue hair and Pekingese dogs whose toenails were painted with frosted mauve polish.

"It ain't a bad livin'," Ted said. "A few quid for walkin' a pup down Las Olas." He made a gesture as if thrusting money in his pants pocket.

Later that night in their room, Sheila said to Bobby, "No wonder she's so tormented. She's baby-sitting for a child."

"But he's a sweet guy," Bobby said.

"Sweet's not enough," she said, looking directly at Bobby. "Not enough to live with someone, anyway. You should know that."

One day they returned to the motel just as Mum was leaving with her gentleman friend, who looked to be twenty years younger than her. Mum was thin and brown, with slack, leathery skin that fit her like a dancer's unitard two sizes too large. She wore a bouffant blonde wig and a peach-colored tube top with matching shorts. Bobby whispered to Sheila, "Not bad for an old broad, is she?"

Sheila nodded. "She must be seventy."

Bobby threw his arm around Sheila's shoulders and pulled her to him. "Some day you're gonna look like that, babe."

"I wouldn't mind."

"In about five years." Bobby laughed and Sheila laughed with him.

•   •   •

Sheila sat under a hot, morning sun on a splintered wooden plank in the right-field bleachers at Stars Stadium in Ft. Lauderdale while Bobby went into the locker room to talk to Rodney James. She was wearing navy satin running shorts and a matching T-shirt top. Her long legs were brown from the sun and dusted with golden hairs. She lay back, resting against the plank behind her, and watched the Stars' rookies take batting practice. There were only a few fans scattered behind the homeplate screen. Old men in walking shorts and straw hats. Teenaged girls in tube tops. Middle-aged men with young boys wearing Stars' caps and baseball gloves. Sitting behind the Stars's dugout along the first-base line were four blonde women with small children. They sat on the edge of their seats, applauding when their husbands were at bat while simultaneously trying to keep track of their children playing around them. One of the women took a baby high into the first-base stands, laid the child on a seat, and changed its diaper. She returned a few moments later when her husband came to bat.

Two of the children, small, blonde girls, were squabbling while their mothers tried to concentrate on the practice. One little girl pushed the other, then snatched her Raggedy Ann doll. The pushed girl began to cry. Her mother said something to her without taking her eyes from the field. Her daughter was pushed again and began to cry so loudly Sheila could hear her all the way to the bleachers.

The mother of the girl who was doing the pushing said something to her daughter and then turned her attention back to the field. Both little girls began pushing and tugging each other while their mothers watched the field. One girl fell backward and the sound of her head hitting the back of a seat rang hollow through the stadium just as her mother leaped to her feet to applaud her husband, who had just hit a baseball over the centerfield fence near a palm tree.

• • •

Bobby wandered, unnoticed, through the Stars' club-house, looking for Rodney James. It was crowded with sportswriters and coaches and veteran players in various states of undress. The sportswriters looked up with rapt attention at the players they were interviewing. Their fingers scurried across their notebooks, stopping only now and then to push up the eyeglasses that had slid down the bridges of their noses. The coaches were big-bellied men in long johns, who sat, cross-legged, at their lockers, reading the newspaper and spitting chewing tobacco juice into Styrofoam cups. The players milled about, reading their mail, sipping coffee, swapping stories, munching raw carrot slices and hard-boiled eggs from the lunch table set up in the center of the room. A black player wearing tinted sunglasses was waving a carrot slice in the face of a white player with muttonchop sideburns while lecturing him on annuities and liquid investments. A white player with curly black hair and a mustache held his genitals in one hand while saying to a teammate, "The sonuvabitch died on me last night!" He looked down. "I can't understand it!" Another black player, over 250 pounds, was kneeling, measuring a white player's foot for a pair of cowboy boots, which he sold during the off-season. A tall, lanky pitcher was telling another pitcher about his attack of prostatitis. "It scared the shit outta me!" he was saying. "I thought I had the clap! The doc says the only cure is to ball my old lady four times a day. I says, 'Jeezes, doc! I gotta pitch, too!'" A silver-haired coach, thick-waisted and stolid-looking, was telling a younger, leaner coach about the woman he had in his room last night. "What a fucking dog?" he said as the younger coach adjusted his Prince Valiant toupee. "And to top it off, she's got the rag on!" The silver-haired coach grinned, exposing white teeth flecked with dried blood, while the younger coach gripped his toupee with both hands and gave it a twist until it was firmly in place.

A female television reporter was interviewing the Stars'

home-run hitter, a light-skinned black man. The woman
was wearing a pink silk blouse that was unbuttoned to her
waist. She stood in front of the black man, who was seated
on a stool by his locker, and held her microphone close to
his mouth. She had to bend over so that his eyes were
looking directly down her blouse. He spoke with a delicate
flutter of his eyelids: "However, you have to ascertain
whether or not there are extenuating circumstances." The
woman nodded at each word, while her camerman hovered behind her, his camera propped on his shoulder and
aimed directly at the black man's face. The cameraman
was careful to capture only the black man's face because
he was completely naked on the stool, and, with one hand,
he was fondling his genitals. He was a powerfully built
black man, with thick arms and a broad chest, and, inexplicably, his genitals were the size of Michelangelo's *David*.
After the interview was over the woman thanked him. "My
pleasure," the black man said, and then, after she was
gone, he turned to a black teammate beside him and
added, "I like to give dat mofin-bitch a piecea my interview awright."

Suddenly the room fell silent. All eyes turned toward a
skinny little man, the manager, standing in the doorway
of his office. He slouched like a seven-footer with a height
complex and his eyes flitted in their sockets, alighting nowhere, as if by design. "Fifteen minutes to BP," he said,
and disappeared. He had a thin, black, villain's mustache
and he was wearing, with his Stars' uniform, a black cowboy hat and black, pointy-toed, snake-skin boots.

"A mouse studying to be a rat," whispered a voice in
Bobby's ear. Bobby looked over his shoulder and down to
see a sports columnist he knew who was standing on his
tiptoes. Bobby turned around. "The little prick hates me,
Bobby," the columnist said with a smile. He was in his
thirties, with the small-featured, hairless face of a boy who
had yet to grow pubic hair. He was wearing a shirt with
an alligator on it, and khaki-colored Bermuda shorts with
a notebook stuffed into the back pocket like a slingshot.
"Did you read my column yesterday?" Bobby shook his

head. "I ripped the little cocksucker good." The man's face beamed. "He threatened to punch my lights out if he ever caught me in the Stars' clubhouse again. Which is why I'm hiding behind you."

"Yeah. Well, you're welcome. Now you can do me a favor: where the fuck is James?"

"The 'Big Rod'? You doing a piece on the Almighty? For who?"

"Whom," Bobby said. "And it's none of your business."

"You know something I don't? Come on, Bobby, tell me. He's fucking a broad in Cleveland? He's fucking a snake? His wife? Anything? Rodney James fucks? You found out? How? How does he do it?" Bobby began to laugh. "With his clothes on? No, with his uniform on, I'll bet? And his metal cup, too? I'll bet he's found a way, hasn't he? Rodney James fucks in his uniform without taking it out of his cup!"

"Just tell me where he is, will you? God, you're a pain in the ass! No wonder Santini wants to punch you out."

"He does, doesn't he?" The little man smiled. "Makes my fucking day. It's a Sunday, you know. Did you go to mass today, Bobby?" Bobby exhaled as if weary, and shook his head. "Shame, shame." The little man held up an index finger and rubbed it with the index finger of his other hand. "You don't think the 'Big Rod' would miss chapel on Sunday, do you?" He gestured with his head toward the trainer's room. "Where the fuck do you think he is? His Rodness is holding chapel for all the born-agains. The rookies, the veterans, the disabled, and the lame. All the fucking losers looking for an edge for one more season." The little man began to giggle. He put his fingertips over his mouth as if to stifle his giggling. His little shoulders rocked with glee. "See you, big Robert. Got to go to work." The little man scurried over to a crowd of writers surrounding the black home-run hitter. He stood at the back of the pack, rising up and down on his tiptoes in a vain attempt to see over the crowd.

Bobby went to the trainer's room at the rear of the clubhouse. The door was halfway open. He could see only a few players seated on the linoleum floor, hugging their knees, looking up at Rodney James in his uniform. James was sitting on the trainer's table in the white-walled room, talking in that uninflected voice of his. "Why do you think God put this star on Rodney James's uniform?" he said. "To do His will, that's why? You, too, like Rodney James, must realize that you are set apart from all those others." He made a backhanded sweeping gesture with his arm. "From the Pirates and the Indians and the Yankees. Yes, and even the Dodgers, who, in God's infinite wisdom, were allowed to win the World Series last year. He has a plan, of that you can be sure. The Dodgers won and not the Stars for a reason. What that reason is, not even Rodney James knows, but he accepts it, and it will inspire him to work even harder this year to bring a World Championship to our loyal Stars fans."

Bobby waited by the door while Rodney James spoke. Every so often Bobby could hear the light, tentative voice of a young player ask James a question. James answered always with the patience of a parent toward a child. Then Bobby heard a voice that was young but not so tentative. "Why is it so easy for you to accept the will of God?" the voice said. Seated on the floor, cross-legged, his back to Bobby, he looked like all the others. Bobby could see that his hair was cut so short in back that his neck looked long and skinny and his ears stuck out from beneath his cap.

Rodney James smiled down at the young pitcher. "Because I have the gift of faith," he said.

"Gosh!" the voice said. "What if we don't have it? I mean, I want to have it. I'd give anything. I mean, look what it's done for you all these years. But sometimes . . . I don't know. I just don't feel it. You must know how it is. Like, remember when you gave up those two home runs, a triple, and two doubles in one inning against the Red Sox last week?" The player shook his head from left to right.

"One double," James said, still smiling. "It was a single and a fielder's choice."

"I just don't know," the young pitcher said, "how *I'd* feel if I ever got hit *that* hard."

James fluttered his eyelashes and said, "Everybody has a bad game now and then. That's God's plan. That's when you need faith most of all. That's why we are here right now, praying for God to give us all the gift of faith someday."

"Someday?" the young pitcher said. "You mean, when I get older . . ."

James began to nod his head.

" . . . like you?"

James's head stopped nodding and his smile began to fade, slowly, steadily, like the fading of light when a shadow lengthens.

The young pitcher said, "Does this faith always stay with you?"

James looked at him through narrowed eyes, as if searching for a clue. Unable to find one, he said, "Yes."

"Even when you leave baseball?"

James hesitated a moment, then said, "I'm sure it will."

"It must be very comforting to you . . ."

James nodded, unsmiling. "It is. It is."

" . . . to know that even though that day is coming you're not afraid." Again, James stopped nodding. "I mean, gosh, I can't even conceive of that day. I mean, I'm only twenty-three, not thirty-six like you, but still I hear lots of older players whispering about it in the clubhouse. You always know who they're whispering about because they make a little sideways gesture with their head toward the person without ever looking at him. It must be awful to be that person. It must be like having cancer, and everybody knows, but nobody will mention it. Admit it, I mean. And here you are, Rodney James, not afraid of it all. I mean, you have your faith and that is an inspiration to us all, and I just hope someday when I get old, too, I won't be scared either when I can't cut it anymore."

Rodney James's head jerked and he blinked once as if cuffed on the ear. He looked at the young pitcher, and then his smile began to reappear, slowly, steadily, as if the shadow had passed. He fixed his smile on the young pitcher and stood up. Then he looked out over the heads of the players seated below him. "Now, let us get down on our knees and pray," he said. The white room was filled with the clatter of cleats on linoleum as the players rearranged themselves on their knees. Their heads were bowed. Rodney James stood over them, his hands clasped at his belt. "Let us pray for faith," he said. "And that God will grant some of us a *long* enough career to allow us the time to acquire that faith." The young pitcher looked up. James fixed him with his smile. "A faith that will sustain us through those bad games and the good ones. Through those lean years and the full ones—the Cy Young Award years, which God, in His wisdom, grants to so few of us before that final season comes, as it must, to us all, when we can no longer . . . *cut it.*"

When the prayers were finished, the players filtered out of the room. One player stood behind to ask James a question. His brow furrowed as he thought. He brightened, spoke to the player. The player nodded and left the room. James was alone now. Bobby went up to him. Rodney James smiled and reached out his hand.

"I wasn't sure you'd remember me," Bobby said as he took James's hand.

"Rodney James never forgets a writer," he said. "If you'll just refresh my memory a bit."

"I talked to you last spring. Remember? About Stanley Muraski?" Rodney James's smile vanished and he disengaged his hand from Bobby's.

"Oh, yes. Now I remember." His smile reappeared. "I heard you talked to Tony Vincent, too." Bobby nodded. Rodney James shook his head and made a tch-tch sound with his tongue. "Poor Tony. The booze. It's gotten to his mind, I'm afraid. I hope he was able to help you."

Bobby looked, without expression, directly into James's eyes. "He did. Quite a lot."

James's smile expanded. "I'm glad. Truly, I am. Now, what can I do for you?"

Bobby pulled a notebook and a pen from his hip pocket. "The story's finished. It'll run in a week or two. But I just need to verify a few quotes from you."

"It is! That's terrific. I'd love to read it."

"I'm sure the magazine will send you a copy," Bobby said.

"No. I mean now. Before it's printed. I'm sure I could help you tidy it up if there are any . . . eh . . . errors, you know. Dates or facts."

"Oh, Jeez, I'm afraid it's too late for that. The story's already at the printer's. At this late stage, I can only change a sentence or two myself. Which is why I'm here." Bobby poised his pen on his notebook.

Rodney James reached out a hand and took Bobby's pen. "A fountain pen!" he said. "Well, I'll be! Not many writers use these old-fashioned things anymore, do they?"

Bobby looked at him for a moment before answering. "No. They don't."

"Most of them just use those felt-tip pens, don't they? Disposable." He pursed his lips and shook his head. "A sign of the times, eh?" He fingered the pen as if it were a rare objet d'art.

"Yeah, well a lot of things are disposable these days," Bobby said. "You learn that in my business."

"Really? Like what?"

Bobby looked at Rodney James for a moment before speaking. "Like people," he said. "And reputations. They're just like felt-tip pens."

"How's that?"

"They look substantial enough. But lots of times they're cheaply made, you know. They don't hold up. They fall apart when you look at them real close."

Rodney James nodded his head with great exaggeration. "Well, I'll be. That's something to remember." He handed the pen back to Bobby. "It sure has been interesting talking to you," he said. "Anytime I can help, you just ask."

"You can help me right now," Bobby said. "It'll just take a minute."

"Oh, gosh, I'd love to. But I've got to warm up now. I'm pitching batting practice in a few minutes."

"When can I . . . ?"

Rodney James fluttered his eyelashes, still smiling, and grabbed Bobby's hand. He shook it vigorously, "Anytime," he said, "anytime," and left the room.

Bobby joined Sheila in the right-field bleachers and told her what had happened.

"Do you need him?" She said.

"No. Fuck him. I know I got the quotes right. I was really careful with this one, babe. I'll just tell Rosen he verified the quotes and let it go at that."

"Good." Sheila draped her arm over Bobby's shoulder and hugged him to her just as Rodney James appeared out of the dugout to a smattering of applause from the fans. He tipped his cap and began walking toward the warm-up mound directly in front of Bobby and Sheila. He moved stiffly, unbending, with his arms held away from his body so as not to wrinkle his uniform shirt. A small boy appeared in front of Bobby and Sheila. He leaned over the railing and pleaded with Rodney James for his autograph. James stopped, smiled, signed the boy's scorecard, and then looked up at Bobby.

"Hello, there," he said. Sheila withdrew her arm from around Bobby's shoulders. "Is this the Missus?"

"This is Sheila Doyle," Bobby said.

Rodney James smiled at Sheila and, with a slight dip of his head, touched the bill of his cap with thumb and forefinger. Sheila smiled back.

"Your assistant?" James said. "On the story, I mean."

"No," Bobby said. "Just a friend." Sheila stopped smiling.

"Of course," James said, still smiling at Sheila. Sheila averted her eyes. "A traveling companion, you might say."

"A friend," Bobby said.

Rodney James looked at Bobby, his smile gone now. He looked directly into Bobby's eyes for a long moment, and then his smile reappeared. He dipped his head slightly, again, touched his cap once more, turned his back, and walked away.

•   •   •

A week later, walking home from the beach, Bobby and Sheila stopped at a newstand to pick up the *New York Times*. Sheila was paying for the papers when she heard, from behind, Bobby curse. "Fucking bastard!" She turned around. Bobby held up a copy of the magazine with Rodney James's picture on the front cover. He was smiling at the reader. Rodney could not see the caption alongside of his photograph. It read: "The Elmer Gantry of the Diamond."

"Fucking little Jew!" Bobby said. "I knew he'd fuck with it if I wasn't around to watch him!"

"Calm down, babe. Maybe it isn't so bad." Sheila paid for the magazine while Bobby wandered outside, flipping through the pages until he came, not to the "Stanley Muraski Story," but to the "Rodney James Story." He began to read as they walked back to the motel. At an intersection Sheila had to stop him from walking into traffic. When they reached the motel, he flung the magazine across the room.

"He cut half of my stuff on Muraski! The good stuff. The fields. His wife. His mother. Everything. He kept just enough to make it a hatchet job on Rodney James. Not that I give a rat's ass. He deserves it. But that's not what I wrote. It was Muraski's story, goddamn it! And I got it right! Fucking right on the button!" Bobby stood in the middle of the living room, breathing heavily. His face was red and drenched with sweat. Sheila did not go near him. "He couldn't let it be! Couldn't leave it alone! I've gotta call that cocksucker right now."

Bobby went outside to the pay telephone near the street. Sheila could hear his shouts all the way to the room. Then he was quiet. When he returned to the room he was shaking his head. He looked suddenly very tired, exhausted, as if he had run a great distance for nothing.

"What did he say?" Sheila said.

"What?"

"Rosen. You called him, didn't you?"

"Yes."

"What did he say?"

"He said Rodney James is suing me for twenty-two million dollars."

"You're kidding?"

Bobby laughed. "No, I'm not. Twenty-two million. I said, why not fifty-eight million, or maybe one hundred and seven million or two hundred and fifty million?" Bobby looked at her. "You know what he said?" Sheila shook her head. "He said, 'Bobby, this is no joke. You better get your ass back here.'"

· NINE ·

When they returned from Florida, Sheila went back to school and Bobby went straight to the Princeton Club in New York City where he was to meet with the magazine's lawyers. He left his bags in the foyer. The old man at the reception desk was wearing a black suit, a white shirt with a starched collar, and a narrow black tie. He looked down at Bobby's blue jeans and cowboy boots and closed his eyes. When he reopened them he directed Bobby to the club's library where attorney S. William MacIntyre was expecting him. Bobby's high-heeled boots clattered over the lobby's marble floor. The old man at the desk shook his head.

Bobby stood in the archway opening onto the high-ceilinged library and looked for someone who might be attorney S. William MacIntyre. The room was dark, even in the middle of the sunny afternoon, and it smelled of worn leather and tobacco smoke and the body odor of men in business suits. Along one wall were stained-glass cathedral windows that kept out the sunlight. High up on the other walls were painted portraits in heavy, gilt frames. The portraits all seemed to be of dour-looking men with elaborate mustaches and muttonchop sideburns and high, starched collars. Below the portraits, and running to the floor, were bookshelves filled with leather-bound volumes with gilt-edged pages that looked as if they had never been cracked. A few men in gray suits were sitting in the leather armchairs and sofas scattered around the room. They were reading newspapers under the narrow cones of light emitted by small, Tiffany lamps. Everything in the room was muted and soft-edged, all the colors blending one into another like a chiaroscuro painting.

Bobby saw a woman in a business suit sitting, primly, on the edge of a sofa, a briefcase on her lap, talking to a man whose back was to Bobby. Bobby went over to them. The man stood up, smiling, and shook Bobby's hand. He was wearing a jogging suit and sneakers, and he had a towel wrapped around his neck.

"I'd have recognized you in a minute," the man said. He did not let go of Bobby's hand. "Dan said you were a big, mean-looking SOB with a beard." He slapped Bobby playfully on the back with his other hand. "You don't look so mean, though." The man gestured with a hand toward the woman. "This is Deborah Sanchez, the magazine's house counsel. I'm Bill MacIntyre." Bobby smiled at the woman but she did not smile back. She had a dark, strong-featured, thick-browed face, like an Indian's, and her shining black hair was pulled back tight into a bun at the nape of her neck. The man was in his early fifties, very tall and thin, with long bony arms and legs. He had long, grayish blond hair that curled over his ears and was parted to the side of a windburned face that was as flat and angular as a hatchet. He had a wide, slitlike mouth with small, yellowed teeth, and the pale, gray-green, up-slanting eyes of a serpent.

"Have a seat, big guy," he said, gesturing to the sofa. Bobby sat down alongside the woman and the man sat back in his easy chair and crossed his legs. "Sorry about my outfit," he said, gripping both ends of the towel with his hands. "I had a late run today and I didn't have time to change."

Bobby looked down at his jeans and boots and then left and right at his surroundings. "I'm not exactly dressed for the Princeton Club either," Bobby said. The man grinned, his mouth and eyes slanting upward.

"It is a bit of a crock, isn't it?" the man said. "That's why we're meeting here and not in my room." He smiled through yellowed teeth at the woman. "They still don't

allow dames in a gentleman's room. But, I kinda like that
type of thing, don't you?" Bobby smiled, but said nothing.
"Of course, those aren't exactly Deborah's sentiments, are
they?" She gave him a small smile, but still said nothing.
"Well, let's get down to business, huh?" His smile faded
and he leaned forward, his elbows on his knees, and looked
directly into Bobby's eyes. "Would you like to hear the
good news first, guy, or the bad?"

"Hit me with the bad."

"Maybe we'd better start with the good news," the man
said. "First of all, the magazine will pay all your legal fees,
so, in effect, I'm your mouthpiece, too." He smiled. "Sec-
ondly, the magazine will indemnify you against any judg-
ments that might be awarded against you."

"What does that mean?"

"It means, if we lose, which we sure as hell ain't gonna,
the magazine will pay the whole freight. Its own tab and
yours." He sat back and crossed his legs. "So you see, big
guy, you've got nothing to worry about."

"I've got nothing to worry about anyway," Bobby said.

"How's that?"

"What I wrote was the truth."

"Yeah. Well, yes and no. The truth as you saw it, maybe.
But there are lots of truths, stud." He put up his hands,
palms out, as if to ward off the look in Bobby's eyes.
"Whoa, now, don't get me wrong! I think it's one hella-
cious story. Sensitive and beautifully written. Except for a
few minor details, I'd consider this case a lock. No way we
could lose on the mat."

"What 'minor details'?"

The man cleared his throat, and when he spoke again his
voice had lost its tone of boyish camaraderie. "I don't want
to scare you, stud, but . . ."

"You won't scare me," Bobby said.

". . . but their case is not without merit for a number of
reasons that have nothing to do with the story as written.
First of all, the man you claim was destroyed by Rodney
James is dead. He ain't gonna help us in the box, then, is
he?"

"What about Tony Vincent? He's not dead."

"Yeah, well, Mr. Vincent is something of a problem, guy." The lawyer put his hand on his jaw and began massaging it with thumb and forefinger as if trying to whittle it into an even sharper point that it already was. "Let me put it this way." He leaned toward Bobby again and combed his hair off his eyes. "Tony Vincent sounds like a helluva guy to have a few pops with, but for our purposes he's nothing but a drunk living in a cat house." He smiled toward the woman and fluttered his eyelashes. She nodded once. He looked back at Bobby. "The point is, it's the credibility of a drunken pimp versus the credibility of Rodney James, God's sweetheart. Now, who do you think a Southern California jury—made up primarily, I'll assure you, of a bunch of Orange County housewives moonlighting at Knott's Berry Farm—is gonna believe?" He sat back in his chair and crossed his legs.

"The guy who's telling the truth."

The man laughed, once, and grinned at Bobby as if he were a child. "That would be nice to believe, wouldn't it, stud? But that ain't the case in a jury trial. Juries don't know from true or false. That's too complicated for them. They can only understand what they see or hear. You can't see truth. Or hear it. It's a concept. It's perceived by the mind, not the senses. Juries can't perceive shit, guy. They're simple folk. They believe their eyes and ears and they distrust anything that goes on in the mind. Shoot, to reach them you've got to give truth some form. Make them see it, hear it. It doesn't even matter if what they see and hear is true or not. It's got to *appear* to be true." He leaned forward again, his hair falling across his eyes, and began gesturing with the flat of one hand into the palm of the other, as if slicing carrots. "You starting to get the picture? We're dealing with appearances, not reality; words, not thoughts. Words are powerful stuff. Certain words, anyway. Code words, I call 'em. People isolate them in a sentence, focus in on them, give them more weight than they deserve. Words are easier to grasp when they stand alone. Shoot, guy, your average jurist don't want to tramp through a thicket of words until he gets, all bloody and sweaty, to a thought. You should know that, guy, you're a writer. Some words make people feel good and some words make them feel bad, and they don't much like a guy who uses words that make them feel bad. Which brings us to Mr. Vincent. I am telling you there ain't no jury in this world that's gonna fall in love with him once he opens his yap." The man shook his head from left to right. "No, siree. Tony Vincent's 'truth' will go right down the toilet, and you and me with it. Now, God's sweetheart! Shoot, he is a master!. I truly do appreciate his talent. It doesn't matter that when you add his words up into a sentence there isn't even a glimmer of a thought there. Just words. But real nice words. And they'll make any jury in this land feel all warm and toasty. Do you get my drift?" The man stared at Bobby through narrowed eyes for a long moment, as if looking for something. Then, without smiling, he said, "Let me put it another way, stud. Rodney James may be a snake, but he looks like a duck, he walks like a duck, and he talks like a duck. He's smart enough to know that if you use words like 'dignity' often enough people are gonna assume you've got it, and if you use words like 'motherfucker' often enough they'll assume you are one." He sat back in his chair, crossed his legs, and smiled broadly at Bobby. "So, you see our difficulty with Mr. Vincent. It would behoove us, so to speak, not to hang out hat on his testimony. In fact, it would really behoove us if Mr. Vincent vanished from the face of the earth."

Bobby looked at the man, without expression, and said, "So what do we hang our hat on . . . big guy?" A faint smile appeared on the lawyer's lips. "You," he said. "You are our whole case. I know a lot about you, stud. You've been writing for over ten years and you've never been sued before. Which is a plus for the good guys. Beyond that, you have a reputation in the writing game for being unsparingly honest." He raised his eyebrows. "A tad too honest, some would say. Too honest for your own good. You are a hard SOB when it comes to putting words on paper." He grinned. "You like that, don't you, stud?" His smile faded.

"Well, a jury won't. Juries don't much like prophets. They'd prefer a saint any day. Like God's sweetheart. You try going *mano-a-mano* against him, stud, and he'll cream you with a jury."

"So what the fuck do we do, then?"

The man smiled. "That's just what I mean, stud. You are some red-assed Guinea, aren't you? Well, you're lucky you don't write like you talk. I've read your stuff, I see the anger, but it's cold, not red-hot, and most juries won't pick it up. As long as I can keep them from seeing that anger, they'll believe what you've written is true. That's our ace. Your integrity as a writer. I'll match the integrity of your work with any of that pious crap about him that his lawyers will dish out. . . . Which brings us to our final obstacle."

"What's that?"

"You notice, stud, I said 'the integrity of your work.' "

"So?"

"So, let me ask you a question?" The man spread the fingers of both hands, brought them together, fingertips touching, until they formed a triangle before his eyes. He looked at the triangle for a moment and then he looked at Bobby. "Who is Sheila Doyle?" A look crossed over Bobby's face. "I thought so. Does your wife know about her?" Bobby shook his head no. "I know about her, stud. And so does Rodney James, and his lawyers, and so will everybody in this country who reads the newspaper. Including your wife. That's their case."

"I don't understand. What does Sheila have to do with this?"

"Simple. She's proof that you are a man without integrity. You are a cheat, stud. If you can't be faithful to your wife then how's a jury gonna believe you have written faithfully about a man you probably don't even like. Worse than that. A man whose very life-style is a refutation of your own. Rodney James is what Bobby Giacquinto will never be, and that fact galls you, doesn't it, stud, so you decided to get even."

"That's bullshit! And you know it!"

The man smiled and raised his eyebrows. "Yep. I do. And so do they. His lawyers, I mean. But so what? It makes for a very convincing scenario to a jury. I told you before, guy, we're not dealing with truth here, but the appearance of truth." Bobby looked down at the floor and closed his eyes. "Sorry, but that's the way it is."

"She can't go through this."

"Your wife?"

"Sheila."

"I'm afraid she might have to."

"She can't. The stress would be too much for her." Bobby looked at the man. "She's had cancer. Her doctor said that any kind of extreme emotional stress could cause a relapse."

The man lowered his eyes and shook his head. "I'm sorry, guy. I feel for you. I really do. But it's not up to me. I'll do everything I can to keep her off the stand. That's my job. But I know they're gonna try to drag her into this."

"How?"

"They say she was your assistant in Florida when you talked to James."

"But she wasn't."

"She was there, wasn't she? She met James, didn't she? Maybe she even carried your notebooks or made a single comment about him, or maybe she just handed you a pen when you had to write something down. That's enough for a lot of judges to declare her a party to all this. And once that happens, guy, it's gonna get down and dirty, I'm telling you." The man shook his head once.

"That was a stupid thing to do!"

Bobby and the lawyer turned toward the woman and stared.

"It was!" she said. She was sitting on the edge of the sofa, her back stiff, and her dark, impassive face glaring at Bobby. "You should have known better than to put the magazine in jeopardy like that."

Bobby smiled faintly at her. "I really wasn't thinking of the magazine when I brought Sheila with me," he said.

"Well, you should have been," she said.

The lawyer smiled at her. "Really, Deborah, that's hind-sight, now, isn't it?" He spoke in a soothing voice and he held his smile and looked directly into her eyes. She looked at him, but said nothing.

"Yeah, well, as long as we're on the subject of stupidity, I think there's something you ought to know," Bobby said.

The lawyer looked at him. "What's that?"

"The story that was published wasn't the same story I wrote."

"What?"

"The story I wrote was about Stanley Muraski. James was only a bit character. Rosen cut most of my Muraski stuff and added a shitload of stuff on James that shifted the emphasis to him."

"Jesus Christ! Does anybody know this?"

"Just Sheila."

"Damn! Now, I've *got* to keep her off the stand! Listen, guy, don't breathe a word of this to anyone else, hear?"

"Why?"

The man smiled at him and spoke again in that soothing voice. "I don't think it's the kind of thing that's going to help our case. In a libel case like this, all the bad guy's got to do is prove malicious intent. It's tough with a public personality like James, but if they can prove Rosen delib-erately stacked the deck against him, that might sound malicious to a jury."

Bobby smiled at him. "That would get *me* off the hook, then, wouldn't it?"

The man turned his head sideways to Bobby and raised a hand, palm out, as if to fend off a blinding light. "Hey, guy, I don't think we want that. You see, that would divide you and the magazine and it would force me to make a very hard decision."

"What's that?"

"If it comes down to crunch, guy, between you and the magazine, I'm afraid . . . I don't think you could afford me. I'm the best damned libel lawyer in the country, and I get paid accordingly." He smiled. "One of the perks of the profession."

Bobby laughed, a breath, and shook his head slowly. "That's a pretty nice perk," he said. "You know . . . I'm the best at what I do, too. But I don't get paid 'accordingly.' In fact, for all this fucking aggravation I got paid exactly three thousand dollars. Is that about what your fee might be?"

The man stopped smiling and looked directly into Bobby's eyes. "For a day's work," he said in a level voice. "If it was an easy day."

"You getting paid for this right now?"

"You mean this little chat? Yep, I am." The man smiled.

"I'm not getting paid," Bobby said. "I'm not getting paid a fucking cent. I'm supposed to give depositions every day this week and I'm not getting paid for that either."

"In the long run, you will," the man said. "This little splash might just make your career. You're gonna be a hot item after this, guy."

"Yeah. There's a lot of magazines dying to hire some hack who might cost them three thousands dollar a day in legal fees, not to mention a possible twenty-two-million-dollar libel judgment."

S. William MacIntyre waved a limp-wristed hand at Bobby. "That's not going to happen. This isn't anything but sound and fury. It'll all go away and nobody will even remember. Trust me. I know. This case won't even come to trial."

"Yeah, well, I hope it does. I'm counting on it. I want my fucking perk, too." Bobby jabbed the index finger of one hand, repeatedly, into his own chest. "I wrote a great story before Rosen fucked it up, and I want people to know it. If it takes a trial, fuck it. That's the only perk I've got."

The man nodded, and said, "I know how you feel, guy. I feel the same way. About your work and mine. I take pride in what I do, too, even if I do get paid a ton for it. I love the law. The law is a beautiful thing, guy. It's so . . . so . . . so *fluid!*" He held up both hands, cupped, in front of his eyes as if to catch flowing water. He looked up, as if at a vision, at that point above Bobby where the water was flowing from. "You see, guy, every lawyer knows there's no

such thing as 'truth.' There are just opposing sides to every
issue, and they both have merit. A good lawyer doesn't lose
sight of that. Now, a great lawyer, he finds a way to feel
comfortable on either side." He put his hands down and
smiled at Bobby. His smile broadened and he raised his
eyebrows. "Sometimes both."

Bobby carried his bags across town to the hotel where
the magazine had reserved a room for him for the week.
The doorman took Bobby's bags and held open the heavy
glass door with the heel of his shoe. He had a florid, Irish
face and bad teeth. He followed Bobby inside. The small
lobby was all white marble and glass and chrome and leafy
green plants. Men and women sat cross-legged on white
sofas and imitation Louis XVI chairs, sipping drinks being
served by waiters in red vests. The men wore silvery gray
suits and the women wore slit skirts and nylons. The murmur of voices speaking a variety of foreign languages filled
the room. At the reception desk, Bobby checked in with a
woman who had a British accent and then went up to his
room. He sat on the edge of his bed for a long while, then
he reached for the telephone and dialed Sheila's number.

"I was worried about you," she said. "How'd it go?"

"Not so hot."

"What do you mean?" Bobby told her everything that
had transpired between himself and the two lawyers.
When he finished, Sheila was silent for a moment, and
then she said, "What do you think?"

"I think I'm not too crazy about putting my future in the
hands of S. William MacIntyre, that's what I think. Or his
dyke assistant. He thinks he's God and she could kill me
because I've got a cock and she doesn't."

"That's not what I meant." Sheila's voice was small. "I
meant about your wife. She'll have to know." Bobby did
not answer. "Babe?"

"I know," he said. "It's about time, don't you think?" He
was silent for a moment. Then he said, "I could never hurt
Beth. Or my son. I never told you this, I didn't know it

myself, but I know it now. If it was up to me I could never do it."

"But why, Bobby?"

Sheila heard a sharp intake of breath through the receiver. "I don't know," he said. "It's something in me. A weakness. I don't know. But don't worry. It's out of my hands now. I don't have a choice. It frees me. Either I tell Beth or she reads about it in the newspapers . . . or worse —she turns on the tube one night and sees that fuck, James, blabbing it all out on Candy Thompson's 'Hollywood Hot Seat.' "

"I'm glad, Bobby. I know it sounds callous, but *I am glad.* I've waited long enough. I was so afraid. I thought you'd never act. I want a free man, and if it has to be this way, then it just does. You know we should be together. It's right between us."

"We will, babe. It's just a matter of time. There's only one thing."

"What's that?"

"They might try to call you as a witness. Could you handle that?"

"Of course."

"No, I mean . . . it will be a terrible strain. They're gonna run us through the mud."

"No, they can't. We haven't done anything we're ashamed of, and they can't make us feel that way."

"They're gonna try. I was thinking about your doctor . . . what he said about emotional stress. . . . Remember?"

"Oh, babe, it won't be any stress. It will be a blessed relief. God, I can't wait!"

Later that night Bobby went downstairs to the lobby. It was deserted now, except for a lone waiter standing against one wall. Bobby sat down on a white sofa that faced the heavy glass doors that led to the street. He sank deep into the plush sofa. It enveloped him as if he were a small boy. The waiter came over to him and he ordered a drink. Bobby sat there alone, sipping his drink, watching people breeze in from the street. They entered the lobby in that hurried, preoccupied way people do when they're used to meeting friends and dining in expensive hotels. They looked left and right, without seeing Bobby, and then hurried to the restaurant at the end of the lobby. Bobby sat there for hours, drinking, watching people come and go, and then, finally, he got up to have dinner. He had trouble pushing himself up out of the sofa. He stood a moment, swaying slightly, his vision swirling, and then he walked toward the restaurant.

The maître d' led him through the dining room toward a small table near the kitchen. They passed elegantly dressed men and women leaning toward one another over the tables as they spoke. They held their knives and forks in the European manner, upright in either hand alongside their plates. Bobby sat down and ordered a bottle of wine. He had drunk almost the entire bottle by the time his waiters appeared with his dinner. There were three of them. They wheeled in his food on carts. One of the waiters lighted a fire of blue flames under a frying pan and began to cook thin slices of veal. The second waiter cracked an egg into a salad bowl and began to toss a Caesar salad. The third waiter hovered at Bobby's shoulder with a new bottle of wine. He waited for Bobby to finish the last drop in his crystal glass before pouring from the new bottle. He screwed the bottle into a bucket of crushed ice and left. The other two waiters served Bobby's food and then they left, too. Bobby drank his wine and ate his dinner alone in a darkened room, at a small table lighted by a single candle alongside a cut-glass vase that held a long-stemmed, red rose.

After dinner he staggered up to his room and fell asleep, fully clothed, across his bed. He dreamed of a house with empty rooms. The windows and the fireplaces were boarded up and the rugs had been stripped off the hardwood floors. The sound of someone pounding on the door echoed in his head. He woke, groaning, and the house vanished. But still the pounding persisted. He lurched toward the door.

"Aren't you ready, yet?" said Deborah Sanchez. Bobby closed his eyes but the pounding at his temples persisted.

"You've only got twenty minutes until your deposition." He turned his back on her and went into the bathroom. She closed the outside door behind her. Bobby splashed cold water on his face. He looked at himself in the mirror. Water glistened on his black beard, dribbled down his neck. There were dark rings under his eyes. He smiled. He looked like a hunted raccoon. Through the open bathroom door he heard her voice. "You look terrible," she said. "I don't think you appreciate the importance of all this. You've put the magazine in a very precarious position and we're doing everything we can to bail you out." She was quiet for a moment while he dried his face. "Did you have to get drunk last night?" she said. "The day before your deposition?"

They walked down Madison Avenue, with its rushing, early morning crowd, toward the law offices of S. William MacIntyre. "You should have at least considered us," Deborah Sanchez said. She was walking beside him, looking straight ahead. "The expense we're going through for you. The legal fees. Hotel room. Food. Who do you think is paying for all this?"

"I'm really sorry," Bobby said. "I feel so bad about your poor magazine."

"You should! You got us into this!"

Bobby stopped abruptly on the sidewalk. The flow of people brushed past him. Someone cursed. She stopped a few feet in front of him and turned around. "What's the matter?"

"Listen, you've had a hard-on for me from the first moment you saw me. What's your problem?"

"I don't have any problem."

"I'm not moving until you tell me."

She stepped toward him out of the sunlight into the shadow of a tall building. Her dark face was almost black in the shadows. She lowered her voice as if to avoid eavesdroppers. "I checked that story before we ran it," she said. "I told the editors it wasn't libelous. And it wasn't. If you hadn't brought that . . . that woman to Florida with you they wouldn't even have a case."

"So?"

"So, if we lose, it's my job. How many women in this city do you think get to be the legal counsel for a major magazine? I'll tell you. One. Me. Women like me don't get this kind of job. I didn't go to the right schools like Mac-Intyre. I had to work my ass off to get where I am. Here! Not Tuback, Arizona! Not some wretched Indian reservation! Do you know what it's like to be a squaw? In a white man's world? White men like you! And that pompous ass, MacIntyre! I'm not going to let you blow it all for me, do you hear?" She turned around and started walking up Madison Avenue. Bobby stood there a moment, wincing into the sun. His head was suddenly clear now. He began walking after her.

The law offices were on the twentieth floor of a glass skyscraper. The receptionist sat behind an antique Sheridan desk inlaid with a forest green leather writing surface bordered with gilt scrollwork. She was dressed and made-up like a hostess in a small, but very chic, French restaurant at lunchtime. The sitting room behind her looked out over the city. There was an Oriental rug on the floor. A Queen Anne chair. A Louis XVI love seat. An Italian Renaissance writing desk. A Greek vase. Porcelains. Objets d'art. A Miro and a Picasso on the walls.

Without smiling, Deborah Sanchez introduced Bobby to the receptionist. She smiled and offered him a seat behind her. Bobby sat in the Queen Anne chair and looked out over the city. Deborah Sanchez went down a narrow corridor and, a few minutes later, returned with S. William MacIntyre. He greeted Bobby with a smile, a handshake, and a slap on the back. They all went down the corridor past offices where people were working. They looked up from their desks and greeted MacIntyre: "Hey, Bill!" He waved. Young men and women, clutching sheafs of papers, hurried up and down the corridors. MacIntyre smiled at them, and they smiled back. He stopped beside a pair of dark, wood double doors on which was a brass plate that read "Conference Room Y." An older man, walking briskly down the corridor, stopped to talk to MacIntyre. The man was completely bald, with a bullet-shaped head and a nose like an eagle's beak. He looked like a Roman senator except that, instead of wearing a toga and sandals, he was wearing a dark suit with a vest, a bow tie, and wing-tip, cordovan shoes. Deborah Sanchez and Bobby stood silently while the two men talked about another case MacIntyre was working on. When the older man left, MacIntyre ushered them into Conference Room Y. The walls were paneled with cherry wood. There was a thick green carpet on the floor. A long, oval, cherry conference table in the center of the room. Yellow legal pads and pencils sharpened to a needlelike point in front of all twelve chairs. A pewter pitcher with water and glasses in the center of the table. Ashtrays from the Princeton Club.

Two men sitting at one end of the table stood up. MacIntyre introduced them to Bobby as Rodney James's attorneys. "From Los Angeles," he added with a grin. "L.A. lawyers, Bobby. Watch out for them." The two men smiled, as if embarrassed, and each, in turn, shook his hand without looking up at him. The younger man had muttonchop sideburns and a droopy mustache. He wore a polyester suit. The older man, in his mid-forties, wore a navy blazer with a rep tie, gray slacks, and black Gucci loafers. He was short, soft, and boyish-looking, with shining black hair parted neatly to one side and an impeccable tan. He looked like the kind of man who had never played sports as a teenager because he was late to grow pubic hair and this embarrassed him in the boys' shower room, but now, successful, he had taken up tennis with a Yugoslavian professional. He would wear Fina tennis whites and a matching headband, and he would try, always, without success, not to sweat under the hot California sun.

MacIntyre, Bobby, and Deborah Sanchez sat across the table from the two men. MacIntyre made small talk with them while they waited for the court stenographer. Bobby and Deborah Sanchez were silent. The stenographer entered, pushing his stenographic machine on a cart. He sat at the head of the table, a bald, nondescript man with glasses, and nodded to each side of the table. His fingers were poised over the keys. MacIntyre held up a hand, palm out, toward him.

"Before we begin," he said, "I'd like to make a suggestion. It's going to be a long day, guys, and I think we'd be more comfortable without these jackets." He smiled toward Deborah Sanchez. "If the lady has no objections." She nodded. MacIntyre took off his jacket, arranged it around his chair, and rolled up his shirt-sleeves. Neither of the other two lawyers did the same. The older one craned his neck and shot his French cuffs. Diamond studs sparkled on each cuff. "Suit yourself, guys," MacIntyre said, and nodded to the stenographer.

The lawyer in the blazer, whose name was Barry Feingold, began by asking Bobby his name. Bobby answered. The stenographer's fingers seemed to wiggle over the keys, which made a clicking sound. Then Feingold asked for Bobby's birthdate. His place of residence. And so on and so on, one seemingly meaningless and innocuous question after another for what seemed like hours. The lawyer spoke in a tentative, droning monotone, as if in reverence of his surroundings. The machine clicked musically for hours. Feingold's assistant stared at Bobby as if to unnerve him. He scribbled notes he pushed toward Feingold, but did not speak. Neither did Deborah Sanchez. Only Feingold and Bobby spoke, facing each other, staring into each other's eyes as if looking for a sign. MacIntyre fidgeted and sprawled in his chair. He leaned back, balancing his chair on two legs, and clasped his hands behind his head. Then, moments later, for no apparent reason, he shot forward, planted his elbows on the table, and cradled his jaw in both hands like a bored child. Before Bobby answered each question he would look at MacIntyre for a sign, but he gave none, other than an occasional smile, a wink, or what he took to be a humorous aside. "Go, ahead, guy. Don't keep the attorneys from L.A. waiting. Every second of their time is costing Mr. James a lot of money." The other lawyers smiled nervously. MacIntyre added, "Of course, Mr. James can afford it." Feingold cleared his throat and asked Bobby another question.

Sweat broke out under Bobby's armpits, dribbled down
the sides of his chest underneath his shirt and sports coat.
He forced himself to ignore the tickling sensation and concentrate on Feingold's questions no matter how innocuous
they seemed. Finally, he, too, took off his jacket and arranged it around his chair. He rolled up his shirt-sleeves
and leaned back. Feingold said, "Who is Sheila Doyle?"
Bobby came forward, glanced at MacIntyre. He nodded
without smiling. Bobby looked at Feingold.

"She's the woman I love," Bobby said.

Feingold's boyish face was without expression. He said,
"Does your wife know about her?"

Bobby looked directly into his eyes. "No." He waited,
expectantly, but the lawyer's next question had nothing to
do with his wife or Sheila. Again, for another hour, the
lawyer asked Bobby more meaningless questions. Bobby
did not lean back in his chair. He leaned forward, toward
Feingold, and stared into his eyes before answering each
question after a split-second's pause. He no longer bothered to glance toward MacIntyre before answering.

"Are you a religious man?" Feingold asked.

"In my own way."

"And what way is that?"

"I believe in God, and sin . . . and retribution."

"Do you make it a habit of ridiculing other people's beliefs?"

"No."

"Then why did you ridicule Mr. James's religious beliefs
in that libelous sto . . . ?"

"Whoa, guy!" MacIntyre held up his hand as if to stop
traffic. "*That* is up to the courts to decide." He smiled at
Feingold, who did not smile back.

"And we're extremely confident they will decide," Feingold said, "in our favor."

MacIntyre threw up his hands and shrugged. "You know
more than I do, guy."

Feingold glared at MacIntyre. "I'm sure my learned op-
ponent is being facetious," he said. "We all know of his
deserved reputation for defending libelous authors."

"Not quite true," MacIntyre said, smiling. "My reputation, be that as it may, rests on the fact that after I get through defending authors they are *not* judged to be libelous."

"In most cases," said Feingold. "We'll see about this one." MacIntyre shrugged again. "If I may be permitted. I'd like to repeat my question."

"Certainly," MacIntyre said.

"Again, Mr. Giacquinto. Why did you ridicule Mr. James's religious beliefs in that . . . story of yours?"

"I didn't," Bobby said.

"You didn't try to make Mr. James's beliefs look foolish?"

"Nope."

"Then how do you explain your venomous description of the cross Mr. James has placed in front of his home. Wasn't that an attempt to make his beliefs look foolish?"

"No. I thought the cross was foolish, not Mr. James's beliefs."

"But the cross is a symbol of his beliefs, isn't it?"

"Listen, I told you I believed in God. I know it, and God knows it. I don't have to advertise it to the world."

Feingold was silent for a moment. He looked down at his notes, shuffled them around, then looked up and said in a voice much sharper than his previous monotone: "How do you reconcile this 'belief' in God with your breaking of your marriage vows?"

"I don't."

"Didn't you break your contract with your wife?"

"Yes."

"Are you in the habit of deceiving people . . . behind their backs?"

"No."

"In person?"

"No."

"On paper?"

"No. Never on paper."

· · ·

The first day's deposition ended late in the day. The stenographer packed up his machine and left. James's lawyers scooped up their papers and stuffed them into
briefcases. MacIntyre threw his arm around Bobby's
shoulder. He smelled of body odor. "You did fine, guy," he
said with a wink. "Deborah will walk you back to the hotel.
Have a good dinner and I'll see you tomorrow, same time."
Bobby waited a moment for Deborah Sanchez to collect
her things and then they left Conference Room Y. Mac-
Intyre remained behind with the other lawyers. Bobby
heard his voice. "What'll it be, guys? Dinner at my club?"

Deborah Sanchez stopped outside the heavy glass doors
leading to Bobby's hotel. "I'll pick you up tomorrow morning," she said. "Try not to get drunk again tonight."

"I'm too tired," Bobby said. "I don't think I'd have the
energy to drink tonight." A faint smile appeared on her
lips. Bobby looked at her. "Listen, I'm just gonna have a
bite to eat and then to bed. Do you have any dinner plans?"

"No. But I have to get home. Thank you anyway." She
smiled at him. "You did fine, today," she said, and then
she walked into the crowd on Madison Avenue and disappeared.

Bobby stopped at the newsstand in the lobby and bought
all the New York and Los Angeles newspapers he could
find. He thumbed through one after another on the way up
to his room in the elevator. He found no mention of his
libel case until he came to the sports section of one of the
Los Angeles papers. On page three there was a full-page
paid advertisement that was headlined: "Rodney James
Defends His Dignity and His Honor with a Reaffirmation
of His Love to All His Fans." Bobby's mouth dropped open
and his eyes ceased to blink. "Oh, Jesus!" he said out loud.
The elevator stopped at his floor and the door slid open.
Bobby stared at the advertisement. After a few seconds the
door closed and the elevator began to descend. Underneath
the headline was a photograph of Rodney James in a Hollywood Stars' uniform. He was standing at homeplate, facing the unseen homeplate stands that must have been
filled with fans. He was smiling, that same, smug, self-

congratulatory smile Bobby had seen in that photograph of James and Tony Vincent and Stanley Muraski taken years ago. The smile never changed from year to year. In one hand, Rodney James held a small American flag he seemed to be waving in little circles, and in the crook of his other arm he held his small child. Standing beside him, unsmiling, dressed in a dark pants suit, was his wife. A large wooden cross, on a chain around her neck, was nestled between her large breasts. The elevator stopped at the lobby and the doors opened. People got in around Bobby and the door closed agian. The elevator began to ascend. Bobby read the copy alongside the photograph. It read:

> By now, all of Rodney James's many fans must be aware of the scurrilous attack made upon his pride and dignity in a recent New York City magazine article. In the face of this immoral piece of yellow journalism, Rodney James wishes to reaffirm to his loyal fans that he will continue to pursue the cherished goals he has set for himself with the same sincere dedication and dignity and Christian purpose as befits the simple, dedicated, dignified, compassionate, and humble man the whole world knows Rodney James to be.

The elevator returned again to the lobby. People got out. More people got on. The door closed and the elevator ascended again.

> Therefore, Rodney James's response to this base article, which he found so repulsive a pack of lies that he could not bear to read it (although his lawyers did), is to sue the magazine and its author for twenty-two million dollars. The money is unimportant to Rodney James since he is the highest paid player in the history of this great American game and has all the money he will ever need. Rodney James's only purpose in pursuing this suit is to verify his honor and principles and dignity all the way to the Supreme Court, if necessary, and higher.

The copy was signed:

Your Faithful Servant in Christ,
Rodney Edward James
Pitcher
Christian
American
Cy Young Award 1974

Bobby crushed the paper in his hands and shook his head. "Holy shit!" he said. A woman beside him stepped back. Bobby began jabbing his finger into the button leading to his floor. "Christ, hurry up!" The woman took another step backward and looked around. There was no one else in the elevator. When the doors finally opened, Bobby hurried down the hallway to his room. He telephoned Sheila and read her the letter.

"Do you fucking believe it?" he said. "What an asshole!"

"You're kidding me," she said. "He didn't do that."

"I got it right here, for Chrissakes! Do you think I could make up something like that?"

"Babe, he must be crazy," Sheila said. "And dangerous."

"This whole thing is a fucking joke," Bobby said, and then he told her about his deposition. "Nobody gives a shit," he said. "Nobody believes in anything they're doing. MacIntyre. Feingold. None of them. This is just playacting. None of it's real."

"Calm down, babe. It'll be over in a few days."

"You don't understand, babe! My whole fucking reputation is on the line, my work, my life, and to everybody else it's a joke! I'm the only one who's taking this seriously! Christ, they've got me doubting everything I believe! They ask me my fucking name, for Chrissakes, and I've got to think before I answer! And then they look at me as if I'm lying! My name, for Chrissakes!"

"Babe! Come on, now. Relax. Only four more days and it'll be over. I'll take the first train into the city on Friday after school to be with you."

"Fucking insanity reigns, babe!"

"We'll have dinner at the hotel, and then we'll go up to the room and have a great fuck."

Bobby laughed. "Jesus, babe! You, too? What happened to the Irish nun I first met?"

"You turned her into a Guinea's slut, that's what. Thank God!"

The depositions concluded late Friday afternoon. Feingold shook Bobby's hand and told him it had been a pleasure to meet him. Then he said, "Off the record, Bobby, I loved the piece." Bobby stared at him and his assistant as they left Conference Room Y. MacIntyre, again, threw his arm, like an eagle's wing, over Bobby's shoulders.

"You did a helluva job, guy. A helluva job." He winked her serpent's eye. "Let's have dinner tonight at my club. I've got some good news for you."

"What is it?" Bobby said.

"I'll save it for dinner. About eight?"

Bobby told him that he had already made plans to have dinner with Sheila at his hotel. "You're welcome to join us," he said.

"I'd love to, guy. I've been dying to meet that lady of yours. She must be something special."

Bobby and Sheila were laughing and sipping wine across from one another at their table when MacIntyre arrived for dinner. He was wearing a dark suit with a white carnation in his jacket lapel. Bobby introduced him to Sheila. He bent over, smiling his thin-lipped, up-slanting smile, and shook her hand. He sat down between them. A waiter brought another glass and filled it with wine.

"A toast," MacIntyre said, raising his glass.

"To what?" Bobby said.

"Just a toast," MacIntyre said. "I'll tell you in a minute." Their crystal glasses tinkled as they touched them over the table and then sipped. "I feel I already know you," MacIntyre said, smiling, to Sheila.

Sheila looked at him without smiling. "I know what you mean," she said.

They talked for awhile. MacIntyre directed most of his conversation to Sheila. He asked her questions about herself, her job, her background. She answered briefly, almost rudely, but he seemed not to notice. He was too intent upon being charming in that boyish, faintly condescending, prep school sort of way that was utterly without charm. When she told him she was born in Queens, he raised an eyebrow.

"Really! Me, too." He mentioned an old neighborhood. She remembered it, too. "It was heavy Mick in my day," he said. He shook his head. "Now, it's mostly black and Hispanic." He smiled. "It would be a rough place today for a Sean William MacIntyre, I'll tell you that."

"Sean?" Bobby said.

MacIntyre smiled at him. "The 'S,' guy. I never use it, though. It doesn't go down too well at the firm. Or the Princeton Club, either. Not many Seans there, Especially ones who went to P.S. 109 and CCNY Law School."

Bobby began to laugh. "I'll be a sonuvabitch. A fucking Mick from Queens!"

MacIntyre looked at him with a sheepish grin. "Looks like we've got you surrounded, guy. Sean and Sheila."

"Oh, I'm not Irish anymore," Sheila said, brightly. "I've lost it. It must be like virginity."

"Really?" said MacIntyre. "Then what do you consider yourself?"

"Italian," she said. "I feel very Italian."

"By injection," Bobby said.

MacIntyre smiled at Bobby like a man who has just heard a joke in a strange language. Bobby grinned at him.

The waiter appeared and they began to order dinner. MacIntyre made suggestions to Sheila from the menu. Without her asking, he translated for her from the French. She thanked him, and ordered something else. He seemed not to notice, because now he was translating for Bobby. When the waiter left, MacIntyre clasped his hands on the table, furrowed his brows, and began to speak.

"Now, for the good news," he said. He paused. Then he grinned. "Rodney James is willing to drop the suit."

"What?" Bobby said.

"It's all because of you, guy. His lawyers told him you'd be a tough nut to crack on a witness stand and they suggested he drop the suit. Of course, I don't think they ever intended to pursue it to trial in the first place. James doesn't want that kind of publicity. He just figured it was enough to make a big production of suing you to save face with his fans. You know how people are, guy. In their minds just instituting a suit is the same thing as winning it."

Bobby looked at him. "You mean that even if James drops the suit they'll think he's won it and I've lost it?"

MacIntyre frowned. "I wouldn't put it quite that way."

"I would." There was a prolonged silence at the table. MacIntyre looked down at his clasped hands. Bobby spoke. "Suppose I do agree to drop the suit . . ."

"Bobby! You wouldn't!" Sheila's eyes were opened wide.

"Suppose I do," Bobby said to MacIntyre. "What do I get out of it?"

MacIntyre fluttered his eyelashes and looked at Bobby with a faint smile. "That's not exactly the point, guy. You see, you don't have a choice. The magazine wants the suit dropped, too. It's a no-win for everyone concerned."

"Except me. I win if I go to trial."

"How's that, guy?"

"I get it known that I got that story right before Rosen fucked it up."

"Yeah, well, that's nice, stud, but what about your wife?"

Bobby was silent for a moment. He looked down at his plate and then he said, "That's out of my hands."

"You've got it all figured out, don't you, stud?"

"Yeah."

"Except for one thing."

Bobby looked at him. "What's that?"

MacIntyre smiled at him. "You're not going to go to trial. The magazine won't pay for your defense if you don't go along with them."

"They won't, huh?" Bobby's eyes narrowed and he

began to breathe heavily. Sheila reached a hand across the table and laid it on his wrist. He flung it off, leaned closer to MacIntyre. "Tell me, Sean? How do you think the magazine's gonna look when I call a news conference to tell the *New York Times* and "Sixty Minutes" and *Time* magazine that your fucking pillar of journalistic integrity is dumping me down the shitter?"

MacIntyre blinked, once, and then a smile spread slowly over his face. "I got you all wrong, guy. You are not a prophet. You are a snake, and I truly mean that as a compliment." He shook his head in admiration. Then his smile vanished. He leaned toward Bobby and looked directly into his eyes with his own grayish yellow, up-slanting, snake's eyes. "All right, hard guy, I'll tell you what you're gonna do." His voice was flat, without inflection now. "You drop the suit, and we'll reprint your story exactly as you wrote it. No cuts this time. No shifts of emphasis." MacIntyre waited for Bobby to respond. When he didn't, he said, "And an apology from the editors for fucking up your piece."

"What about James?" Bobby said.

"He'll go along. Your story was a helluva lot more sympathetic to him than the one Rosen edited. This way, everybody wins."

"Can I get it in writing?"

"Bobby!" Again Sheila's hand reached across the table and grabbed Bobby's wrist. "Wait a minute, babe!" She squeezed his wrist, but he did not seem to feel her grip. He was staring at MacIntyre. MacIntyre sat back in his chair.

"In writing," MacIntyre said.

Sheila tried to control her voice. "Babe," she said. "Don't you think we ought to talk about this?" She was trying to smile at him but her smile kept breaking down. "The things we talked about? Beth? Us? Remember?"

Bobby did not seem to hear her. He was still looking at MacIntyre. And then Bobby began to smile. The smile spread slowly across his face. Sheila had never before seen such a smile on Bobby's face. She cried out, "Babe! Please!" But still he did not hear her. She was staring, wide-eyed, leaning toward him across the table, her fingers grasping his wrist. Her face was drained of color, as it had been that day when she was wheeled up from the operating room. And then a breath escaped her. Her eyes closed, and then, after a long moment, they opened again, half-lidded now, dreamy, dazed. Her fingers released their grip from Bobby's wrist, and, as she straightened in her chair, her hand slid back across the table. She watched it. When it reached the edge, it fell off. She looked down. Her hands lay side by side, palms down, on her lap. Gray and shriveled skin. Distended veins. Skeletal bones. Old hands. She raised her face and looked at Bobby. He was still smiling at MacIntyre. Sheila saw him, now, through eyes that were as flat and pale as a hazy summer sky.

"It's settled then," MacIntyre said. "Ah, the food!"

Late that night, in bed with Sheila, Bobby dreamed of an empty house. The rooms echoed with receding footsteps. A door closed. Its echo diminished into silence. Sheila stirred beside him. The bed lightened.

"Babe," he called out in a dream.

"Sssshh. Go back to sleep. I'm just going to the bathroom." He heard a door close and he drifted off. A shadow lengthened through the empty house. It stretched over the hardwood floor, climbed at a sharp right angle up one wall to the ceiling. It loomed above him now. He heard the rustle of cloth and silk, and then, close up, the sound of breathing, or an insistent breeze. The sound was steady for a long while, and then it drew very close to him, and he felt it brush his cheek, a warm breeze, and then it began to move away. Again, he heard a door closing, a door closing, a *door closing*, the echo growing louder, growing louder, *growing louder*.

Bobby bolted up in his bed. He cried, "Babe!"

ABOUT THE AUTHOR

PAT JORDAN is 43 years-old. He has written a number of magazine articles and seven books, among them *A False Spring*. *The Cheat* is his first novel.